LOVE IN THE
AGE OF
DRAGONS

LOVE IN THE AGE OF DRAGONS

A NOVEL

FATIMA R. HENSON

SPARKPRESS

Published by SparkPress, a BookSparks imprint,
A division of SparkPoint Studio, LLC
Phoenix, Arizona, USA, 85007
www.gosparkpress.com

Published 2022
Printed in the United States of America

Print ISBN: 978-1-68463-163-6
E-ISBN: 978-1-68463-164-3
Library of Congress Control Number: 2022910124

Formatting by Katherine Lloyd, The DESK

To my family and friends,
whose love, support, and belief
made this book possible.

CHAPTER **1**

Ayanna's eyes popped open. She heard a clatter, then a thud, followed by a cry of pain.

She pushed away a torn, thin sheet from her legs and reached over the side of her small, canvas cot. Her hand touched the cool concrete floor of the closet where she slept, and she fumbled in the dark for her boots. It would be stupid to go without them.

With a small stretch and a little tug, her fingers arrived at tough leather. She hoped these were the black ones. They were sturdier than the brown pair. The brown ones had a hole in the toe—useless. She had planned to throw them out, but Maya, being a dutiful best friend, had reminded her that the militia might need the leather to patch their uniforms. Maya had always been more prudent than Ayanna.

She shoved her foot into her boot with a painful nudge. These might not fare any better than the brown ones by the time the summer was over, but they would do for now.

Ayanna's pulse beat faster. She was scared. She knew what the crashing sound meant. The same thing had happened two weeks ago. Dr. Keaton had fallen in his room again. She imagined his aged, fragile body sprawled out on the hard, barren floor.

Had his heart given out?

Ayanna took in a deep breath to try to calm herself, but it did little good. She could still feel her heart banging against her rib cage as she snatched a tattered stethoscope from the aluminum shelf next to the metal door and wrapped her fingers around the steel handle, jerking it open.

The metal scraped against the concrete and focused her mind. Blood pressure, temperature, heart rate, pulse, consciousness, airway. Blood pressure, temperature, heart rate, pulse, consciousness, airway. The emergency triage protocol rattled in her brain as a well-rehearsed mantra, and she repeated it as she made her way across the hall to her mentor's quarters.

The hallway's cool air prickled her skin, and a single LED light buzzed on and off, lighting her way through the concrete sub-basement corridor.

She reached Dr. Keaton's room in ten strides and used both hands to push against his door without knocking. It made only the slightest budge. Dr. Keaton was probably pressed against the other side of the door, blocking her entrance. She could hear him trying to breathe. The noise came out in short, quick gasps as the air escaped his lungs in shallow, desperate wisps. She didn't have much time.

"Dr. Keaton, can you move?" she called out. A moan answered from the other side of the door. He was still conscious. That was a good sign at least.

"If you can hear me, try to move away from the door. If only a little," said Ayanna. Her voice sounded strained, even to herself. *I need to control that, for the sake of the patient*, she thought. Her mind quickly harkened back to her training. "When treating the sick, it is important to remain calm and levelheaded," Dr. Keaton had told her in a raspy voice.

Ayanna took in another deep breath. She would try to do as she was taught and mask her terror, but that wasn't going to be easy. What if Dr. Keaton died this time? What if she couldn't save him? What would happen to Terra? What would happen to her?

Ayanna did not want Dr. Keaton to die. He was her friend. He was her teacher, and he was one of the few people in her life who didn't resent her for her father's mistake of helping to destroy the world—well, not exactly. It was the dragons that had destroyed the world. Her father had only invited them in to do it. Unwittingly. But she didn't have time to think about how and why people hated her father right now. Dr. Keaton needed her help.

Ayanna placed her ear against the doorframe and listened. After a few seconds, she heard Dr. Keaton make an effort to roll away from the entrance. Ayanna gave the door a shove and squeezed her thin body through the crack.

She stumbled into the tiny room and fumbled for the light. Dr. Keaton was faceup on the floor, just as she had imagined him. He struggled for breath with his chest rising and falling in short, sporadic bursts. At least there was some oxygen coursing through his body.

Dr. Keaton's gray hair clung to his sweat-covered forehead, and his long legs lay sprawled beneath him. His pale, wrinkled skin tightened around his light blue eyes. It made him look a great deal older than sixty-five. His eyes found Ayanna, and her heart sank. She felt profound sadness looking into Dr. Keaton's eyes. He looked desperate and very, very frightened.

Ayanna scampered to Dr. Keaton's side. She found his wrist and slid her slender fingers around it as she looked at her watch and counted to herself. She quickly did the math in her head and lifted her stethoscope from around her neck and placed the diaphragm to Dr. Keaton's chest just above his heart. She listened and shifted the instrument to his lungs.

Dr. Keaton wheezed in what seemed like an attempt to speak.

"No, don't talk," she said. "I think you have pleural effusion, and I need to drain your lungs. Can you sit up?" She slid her arm beneath Dr. Keaton's back and worked to lift him so his back rested against his cot. This took a lot of effort. It was like trying to move a water-soaked log, but she managed to position his body upright.

Dr. Keaton formed a tight smile. "Good diag . . . nosis, Young Doc. Could not . . . d . . . done better . . . myself." He struggled through his words.

Ayanna pursed her lips as a lump formed in her throat. She forced it down with a hard swallow. "Please, don't," she begged. "I'll be right back."

Ayanna lifted herself from the floor and ran into the hallway. Her long legs carried her past four concrete-reinforced rooms. She crossed Dr. Keaton's makeshift laboratory and finally entered the space that Terra's council had deemed the compound's infirmary inside the Clear Areas Metro Station.

The short sprint down the dimly lit hall made Ayanna think of how quickly her life had changed from relatively ordinary to surreal. Ayanna had spent over a year in the underground station and, out of necessity, had become intimately aware of every tunnel, pathway, and track inside the structure. Terra was small. Only 120 people lived in the basement community under the city, and the subway suited the community's need to hide.

Before the Fire Sky War, the sparsely furnished rooms had served as offices for the City of Tropeck's metro railway workers. The rooms were equipped with power outlets to route electricity from the compound's solar powered generators, sinks to siphon water through the pipes, and plenty of cabinets, desks, and tables that, with the addition of a few cots, allowed Dr. Keaton and Ayanna to use the space as a clinic.

Before the dragon infestation, she had never seen the

basement of any metro station, let alone dreamt of living in one. And she could count on one hand the number of times she had taken public transportation. Her family had been a member of the "Black elite," or so she was told. She had never needed to hop on the train to travel across town, as Maya did, in order to make it to Mrs. McLeod's sophomore biology class at Sacred Heart Academy. And on her fifteenth birthday, she had passed her driver's exam and received her first car in one exciting blur.

That was all before her father had opened a wormhole and ushered dragons into the world. Ayanna shook her head. *I don't have time to think about that*, she told herself. She needed to concentrate on the task in front of her. She had to drain Dr. Keaton's lungs. She had to save him.

Ayanna considered how unfair life had been to Dr. Keaton. Before the dragons, Dr. Keaton had been a trusted friend and colleague of her mother, Dr. Naomi Grace. Her mother and Dr. Keaton had both worked as doctors at Dixon Lee Memorial Hospital. And from what Ayanna could tell, Dr. Keaton had had a very happy life, a wife, and two teenage daughters. But the dragons had destroyed everything good in Dr. Keaton's life. The creatures had killed his wife and both his daughters, and despite his having survived the war against the dragons, his failing health was trying to kill him too.

Ayanna walked into the clinic. She passed her sunlamp lit herb garden. She would come back later to steep turmeric, angelica archangelica, and dandelion root into a tea for Dr. Keaton. The combination of herbs would relieve some of the pressure in his chest, but they would not be enough on their own. She tore through the wooden cabinets. She knew exactly what she needed. This was not the first time she had performed this procedure.

She yanked a small canvas bag from a shelf and threw into it a scalpel, a bottle of ethyl alcohol, a square plastic container, a syringe, clean gauze, some cotton balls, and a tiny plastic tube. Her hands shook as she stuffed the equipment into the bag, so she balled her left hand into a fist, trying to control the motion. It didn't help.

Ayanna paused and stared at her trembling hand for a fraction of a second. She was nervous. It was no wonder. She knew the truth that she and Dr. Keaton had been avoiding for too long: he was dying. Sure, she would drain the fluid from his lungs this time, but it wouldn't fix the problem. His failing heart would give out sooner rather than later, and then what? Who would take care of Terra's clinic? Her?

Don't be stupid, she thought. She was not qualified to run the clinic, even if there was no one else to do it. She had not learned enough. She had not practiced enough. She was not enough.

Ayanna hurried back to Dr. Keaton's quarters. Good. He hadn't tried to move. His body sat slumped where she had left him with his eyes closed. But his body was so still that her breath caught in her throat. Ayanna's eyes blinked slowly. Was she too late? No. His chest continued to rise and fall with small movements, she realized with a sigh of relief.

"I've got everything," she said.

Dr. Keaton tried to look up at her, but his head barely left his chest.

Ayanna kneeled down and started her work. Again, she struggled to move Dr. Keaton's body. He was so much heavier than she, but she managed to lean his body forward. She took the syringe from the bag and lifted Dr. Keaton's nightshirt in the back. He felt cold. She wished she had something to numb the skin, but nothing in her garden could help with that right now. She knew from experience it was best to insert the needle in the back, at the bottom of the rib cage. She used the cotton balls and ethyl alcohol to sanitize the area.

"This is going to sting," she said.

Dr. Keaton nodded weakly. Ayanna took a syringe and stabbed it into the space between his ribs. She pulled back the plunger and watched as a semi-clear fluid filled the syringe. Dr. Keaton's breathing eased.

"Good job, Young Doc. Good job," he said. His voice trembled, but he sounded relieved. Ayanna relaxed and slumped on the floor as she continued to drain Dr. Keaton's lungs.

Her eyes quickly scanned the small utility closet now used as a bedroom. Dr. Keaton's standard military issued cot was the largest item in the space, and medical books were piled high in a corner.

Seeing the pile of books reminded Ayanna of the hundreds of books that had filled her parents' study in the house where she grew up. Three large mahogany bookshelves had lined the walls, but there still had not been enough room for all their volumes. Tall piles of books had lain stacked in each corner of the room. The books had been read so frequently that they hadn't had time to collect dust. The memory brought a small smile to the corner of Ayanna's mouth.

That was gone now, she quickly remembered. She felt the smile drop from her face. The pleasant memory from her childhood vanished and reality set back in. Yes, Ayanna had been happy as a child, but that was before cancer had killed her mother and dragons had burned away the rest of her childhood. Dragons had burned her house to ashes. They had burned her city to smoldering pillars. They had forced her to give up her life and move underground. And perhaps most memorable of all, dragons had killed her father.

Ayanna shifted her weight and tried to push the thought away. Even if she had the time now, she didn't want to think about her father's death. But maybe there was no point in trying to fight it. No matter what she did, it seemed like her father was always on her mind.

Ayanna walked back to the lab slowly. She had bandaged Dr. Keaton's wound and helped him get back onto his cot. Her arms ached from the effort. She didn't know how many more times she could go through that.

Ayanna glanced at her herb garden again as she passed by, and an old idea formed in her mind that, until now, she had never taken seriously. Looters had wiped the shelves of the city's pharmacies and grocery stores clean at least a year ago, but there was one place where she might still find medicine.

For the first time in the night, Ayanna allowed her mind to linger on the memory of her father. She remembered that when she was a little girl, her father had taken her to visit Tropeck's Botanical Gardens. The average tourist trap sat on the shores of the Upper Savannah River near the border between Georgia and South Carolina. Even if dragons had burned the garden's outer walls to dust, the seeds of the plants were still bound to be around. There, in the scorched earth, she might find digitalis, and digitalis might work to treat Dr. Keaton's heart. At the very least, it might keep him alive longer.

She had good reason to believe this. Dr. Keaton had spent all year teaching Ayanna how to use plants as medicine. And even though the Watchers forbade anyone outside of Terra's militia, known as the Protectorate, to travel to the surface, she had made five unauthorized trips outside the compound.

On her trips, she had managed to bring back different treasures: lavender for wounds, chamomile for nerves, and wild indigo to fight infection. But she had never traveled more than half a mile beyond the compound for the obvious reason that the risk of encountering dragons in flight was very real.

Attempting to travel to the Savannah River would be

incredibly foolish because it was five miles away, and it was the very place where the dragons spent the daylight hours while they waited for night. The very thought sent shivers up her spine.

Dragons were just animals, no smarter than a wolf or a crocodile, but certainly larger, faster, and more vicious. Ayanna was no soldier. She knew what the massive creatures could do. Their armored skin and claws alone often destroyed their victims long before they blew out a deadly flame to finish the job.

She had never come close to killing a dragon. She had never even tried. If it weren't for all the time she had spent treating the wounded soldiers who had, she would not have thought it was even possible to kill one. *But I've outrun them*, she thought. *More than once.*

Ayanna shook her head. She wanted to push back against the ridiculous plan that threatened to possess her. She had no desire to be a martyr and traveling to the Savannah River to search for digitalis seemed an awful lot like that. The very notion reminded her of one of those god-awful fairytales where the hero took up a sword and shield and marched out to slay the monster in order to rescue the village.

The idea made her stomach turn. She had seen enough people brutally ripped to shreds, bitten in half, or burned to ash while their loved ones screamed in helpless agony to know that she was not living in any stupid fairy tale. Dragons were not a made-up myth.

Not to mention, she reminded herself, that guardsmen had already caught her leaving Terra twice and reported her directly to the Watchers Council. She did not want to relive anymore of the Watchers' punishments. Ayanna winced at the thought.

Terra's leaders viewed defying their rules and traveling to the surface as pretty much signing a death warrant to the rest of the group. And they made sure that anyone who thought about leaving knew what was at risk if they did.

The last time Ayanna had been caught, it was because she had gotten careless. Sneaking out was always easier than sneaking back in, and on that day, Ayanna had forgotten to avoid the cameras on the outer western wall when she returned to the compound.

To clarify their point about following the rules, the Watchers had locked Ayanna in a closet with water but no food for three days. She had no visitors, no toilet, except for a bucket, no shower, and she didn't even have her books to keep from going stir crazy.

Before slamming the closet door in her face and turning the key, the Watchers had told her that she should experience what her life would be like on the surface if she were left outside of Terra's walls for good. Those three days had felt close to torture, and they had been enough to make her think twice about leaving again.

Still, despite the Watchers and the dragons, Dr. Keaton needed digitalis. Ayanna threw her supplies back into the cabinet. Deadly dragons or not, she did not want to hold 119 lives in her hands. No one in Terra had come across any other doctor in over a year. Dr. Keaton was all they had. What other choice did she have but to try to keep him alive?

Ayanna swung open another cabinet and tossed her unused, clean gauze into it, slamming the door shut. She knew the answer, even if she did not want to admit it. There was no other choice.

Ayanna glanced at her watch. It was only one in the morning and still dark outside. No one, not even Terra's militia leader, would leave the compound in the dark. Her plan may be dumb, but she wasn't.

She had decided. She would leave for the Savannah River when the sun came up.

CHAPTER **2**

Ayanna moved a cardboard box from her shelf and placed it on her bed. She opened the lid and removed a knife covered in a leather sheath that she attached to her belt. Then, she reached for a silver charm bracelet and placed it on her left wrist. The bracelet was a gift her father had given her, and she liked to think that it brought her luck.

Ayanna lightly touched her fingers across the silver bracelet and let out a sigh. She choked back a lump that had formed in her throat. It was hard to think of her father. She missed him so much, but sometimes that made her feel guilty. People hated him, and she knew why. And even though she didn't agree with them, she still struggled to understand what he had done.

His name, Professor Jonathan Grace, PhD, had been in news articles, scrolled across cable television screens, and written all over the Internet from the moment he had decided to join the government's project to complete the world's largest spherical exotic matter shell, or SEMS, device.

Ayanna remembered watching a news show on television reporting that astrophysicists like her father had called the SEMS device a traversable wormhole creator. Scientists everywhere were clamoring to work with Jonathan Grace, world famous for having successfully tunneled a magnetic field through space that linked two different points in the space-time continuum. Her father's fame grew even more after the project appeared to be a great success.

But in only a short time, his fame turned into infamy. When the SEMS device was finally activated, it opened a wormhole just like it was supposed to. But it wasn't supposed to accidentally form a doorway to the Draconus Planetary System and usher dragons into the world.

With a wave of hysteria, newspapers, cable networks, and radio stations all reported that dragons had begun to flood through the wormhole and occupy Earth by the thousands. The same scientists and government officials who had at first been thrilled with the creation of the SEMS device later blamed the arrival of the dragons solely on Ayanna's father.

People from all directions had demanded answers from her father on how to close the wormhole, and it was no surprise when the headlines started to call the arrival of the dragons "The Mess that Grace Made."

It had all been unfair, of course, at least in Ayanna's view. Her father was a scientist. He made new discoveries. That was his job. There was no way he could have known what would happen.

But perhaps he, along with the government and the military that funded his work, should have considered what might have happened when they managed to create the largest manmade wormhole ever known. But her father hadn't meant to usher in the dragons, she knew. Ayanna, at least, had never blamed him. It didn't feel right to start now, especially since he was gone.

"Don't speak ill of the dead," her mother had told her when she was a little girl. And because they were both dead, the idea seemed doubly wrong.

Ayanna moved one of her father's black-and-white composition science notebooks to the side. She had saved over a dozen of them and had spent countless hours combing through the lined sheets every night. She was searching for some clue, some equation that might make sense of what had happened. But she knew better than anyone that her father's complicated notes were meant for someone much smarter than she. She could barely follow one page without having to look up a dozen words. It didn't really matter anyway. Nothing in his journals could help her with what she had to do now. Nothing in his journals could teach her how to face dragons.

She reached for a metal water bottle and stuffed it into her black backpack before pulling three sorghum bars from the shelf and tossing them into the bag. Miriam, the head of the rations team, had handed her the protein-filled morsels after a bit of an argument. Miriam had asked why Ayanna needed them. It was a perfectly good question that Ayanna had not intended to answer. Instead, she told Miriam that she would be working on replicating a new medicine in the lab this week, so she would not be able to make her way to the cafeteria for her designated mealtimes. This was mostly true, and it had softened Miriam's heart enough for her to fork over the tasteless bars.

The last item Ayanna reached for was a small blue hair tie that she used to haphazardly wrestle her long, thick, kinky, coiled tresses into a ponytail. She knew better than to think the small elastic band would do anything to corral her hair in the long run, but it would work well enough to keep it from falling into her eyes.

As she touched her messy ponytail one last time, she could practically hear Maya's voice in her head. Maya would be appalled to see her like this. She would insist that Ayanna at least take a swipe at her hair with a hard-bristled brush and maybe massage a few drops of coconut oil into her roots before walking around for everyone to see. Things like that still mattered to Maya, even though the world had ended two years ago.

Maya always kept her tightly curled, reddish-brown tendrils neatly braided.

The hair oil she used had been nearly impossible to come by, and Ayanna had sought it out especially for Maya's seventeenth birthday. Maya guarded it like a treasure, partly because it was. Everything ran low at Terra. There were at least a few girls who would gladly trade their leather belts for a few ounces.

Satisfied with her meager preparations, Ayanna placed her hand on her bunker door and swung it open with a strong *whoosh*, only to come face-to-face with Maya herself.

"Hey."

Ayanna jumped back. "Crap! My, you scared me!"

"Sorry. I knocked . . . you didn't answer," said Maya.

Maya scanned Ayanna from top to bottom. She seemed to take note of the black backpack Ayanna wore strapped to her back. "Where are you going?" said Maya.

Ayanna heard the twinge of panic in Maya's voice. *Lie*, she thought. It would be the easiest, fastest, and safest way out of this. If she lied, then Maya would not have to worry about explaining to anyone, especially to the Watchers Council, about Ayanna's whereabouts.

Perfectly good explanations tumbled around in Ayanna's head: She was just moving things into the lab and did not want to make two trips. Dr. Keaton had asked her to check on Quentin's broken arm. She was finally getting around to handing her old boots over to the militia. All sounded believable, and she was sure Maya would accept one of them.

Maya stood patiently as she looked up at Ayanna with sad, cool, brown eyes. Her bottom lip quivered a little, making her appear even more innocent than her tiny stature did. Ayanna hesitated. From this angle, Maya looked almost like a baby doll. Her golden-brown complexion with orange-red freckles that sprinkled her small, round face worked to exaggerate her cherubic features. Her expression made Ayanna think of Maya's younger brother, Malik—although Ayanna was sure that if Malik had been watching them, he would point out for the millionth time that it was she who could be mistaken for his older sister, not Maya. Ayanna's skin matched Malik's onyx-colored skin tone. Ayanna had smooth, dark-brown skin with cool, jeweled undertones and wide, umber eyes. Maya was the odd one out.

Still, standing next to each other, one could easily assume that Ayanna and Maya were cousins at the very least. Ayanna liked whenever people mistook her and Maya and Malik Sanders for relatives. Maya was, after all, the closest thing to a sibling she would ever have. This was why Ayanna had trouble shaping her mouth into a lie.

"I'm going to make a run to the surface. I'll be back in no time," Ayanna confessed.

Maya gaped. She shook her head with vigor. "No. Not again. Don't . . . you can't . . . I mean, you shouldn't. What if you get stuck out there at night?"

Ayanna thought for a moment. Should she tell Maya everything? That Dr. Keaton was very ill? That things were not fine? That his dying would be dangerous for everyone at Terra? And what about going to the river?

Ayanna bit the inside of her cheek. Telling Maya any of this would be a mistake. It was not that she did not trust Maya to keep a secret. Maya was quite good at secret keeping; she had even helped Ayanna travel to the surface before. But Ayanna did not want to force Maya to have to do it. The guilt of secret keeping weighed on Maya in a way that it never did for Ayanna.

"It'll be OK, Maya. Really it will. I won't be gone more than a few hours. I've done it before. Right?" she said.

Maya crossed her arms over her chest. She seemed torn

between fighting Ayanna and bursting into tears. "At least let me braid your hair before you leave. You don't want it sticking up every which way," she offered.

Ayanna smiled. She had known that Maya wouldn't be able to stand her appearance. Maya liked to control the things she was able to control. "When I come home," Ayanna said. "I promise." She took a step past Maya and pulled the bunker door behind her.

"But you'll miss Eight in Eighteen," said Maya, as if she had just remembered what she had come to tell Ayanna in the first place.

"It's optional, My. You know that."

Maya huffed and Ayanna held back a smile. Maya hated militia-led trainings, especially Eight in Eighteens. That was when Terra members had eighteen minutes to finish eight different circuits. Maya only participated when Ayanna did, stumbling through the obstacle courses and never volunteering to practice sparring. Ayanna wished she would, though. The outside world was too dangerous to walk through without knowing how to fight.

Ayanna took two steps toward the exit. She stopped and stood under a light that flickered in the corridor. "You're helping Taylor rewire the generators today, yeah?"

"Yeah," Maya answered. Her tone remained shaky.

"Great, I'll be back before you're done."

Ayanna turned to leave, but Maya spoke up again. "Ayanna, what about Captain Daniels?"

Ayanna stopped. Richard of course. His face flashed into her mind, and an anxious feeling filled her abdomen. She had gone four days without thinking about Richard. That was a new record.

She and Richard used to be friends, or maybe they had been more than that, but that had been before the war, and before Richard had returned home different from how he used to be. Instead of smiling and being full of life, he was now serious, humorless—sad.

Ayanna tightened her lips. "What about him?" she asked, trying to keep her voice calm.

"It's just . . ." Maya hesitated. "It's just he's in charge of security now. He tends to know where people are. . . ." Her voice fell. She looked pained, and Ayanna knew where she was headed. "I mean, he's bound to notice if *you're* gone too long."

There was an unmistakable emphasis on the "you're," and Ayanna took in a slow breath. She wished with every cell in her body that she could definitively say that she did not care what the young militia leader would think if he realized she had gone to the surface without the council's permission. But wishing for this was as dumb as wishing that dragons had never flown from the wormhole.

"I'll handle the captain," Ayanna said.

"But what if he asks me? You know how Malik worships him. I'd probably be the first one he'd ask."

"Tell him you don't know."

Maya's eyes fell and Ayanna sighed. "Listen, he won't take you in for a reprimand or try to make you tell him. He *won't*," Ayanna added with force. "He's not like that, My. He's just . . . I'll be back before anyone even notices I'm gone, OK?"

"Before sundown?" Maya asked. The fear she had seemed to momentarily suppress crept back into her voice.

"Before sundown. I promise."

Maya closed the space between them, flinging her arms around her friend for a full body hug. Before she had time to protest, Ayanna gave in and wrapped her right arm around Maya's back.

"You should get to your post," she said quietly. Maya pulled away and nodded slowly.

Ayanna watched her best friend walk away before heading to the access tunnel that led to the surface.

CHAPTER 3

Heat bounced off the scorched ground and formed a wavy pattern in Ayanna's view. Sweat dripped from her skin and pooled at her waistline, soaking into her gray T-shirt. The feeling made her grimace. She would be drenched by the time she made it to the river.

The shades she wore did little to protect her eyes from the arrogant sun. It sat high in the cloudless sky, surrounded by a sea of blue. It seemed to mock her, as if to say in no uncertain terms, "I could kill you."

She did not doubt its power. The sun could dehydrate her and leave her delirious and blind. She would have cursed the damn thing, were it not her only ally on the surface. The sun kept the dragons at bay.

When the universities and military bases were still operating, scientists had endlessly sought to discover more about the atmosphere of the dragons' home, the Draconus Planetary System, but most of what they knew was conjecture. Humans couldn't travel to Draconus, at least not yet, but given that dragons could travel to Earth and survive, it must have meant that the atmosphere on their home planet was somewhat like Earth's. And the one thing that must have been the same was water. Dragons loved the water.

Once the dragons made their way into the rivers, lakes, and swamps, they became impossible to wipe out. If there was water, they were there: breeding, growing, feeding, and destroying. In a short time, the dragons had taken over. But, like any animal, they had some weaknesses.

Dragons were nocturnal. They could tolerate the sun, and sometimes they did, but for the most part, their breed avoided it. They had perfect vision in the dark, but the sun's rays refracted in their eyes in a way that nearly blinded them. And their raised body temperature meant that in extreme heat, they had as much chance of overheating as any person did. These genetic defects were on the short list of small favors that nature had granted Ayanna for her journey.

What would Ayanna give for an easier route to downtown Tropeck than Highway 87? She groaned as she looked ahead at the huge cracks in the street that littered her path. She angled her feet to walk around the edge of truck-sized sinkholes and tried her best not to slip in. This latest hole she passed was the third one she had nearly fallen into since she'd started her trek two hours earlier. Her long legs were not carrying her far enough fast enough, and the broken pavement, mixed with the sea of abandoned and wrecked cars that crowded every inch of the highway's six lanes, slowed her pace to a crawl.

She surveyed the cars jammed together and bit her bottom lip. She did not see an easy way to escape if she needed to. The underside of a car made for a pretty crappy hiding spot from dragons or people, she realized. Her stomach sank. Dehydration, dragons, and sinkholes were not the only thing that could kill her on the surface; a random wanderer was just as likely to do the job, or a bomb left over from the war.

Ayanna looked around. From what she could see, she was

alone. That both scared and comforted her. At least she didn't have anyone to take care of out here. But that also meant that there was no one to take care of her.

She raised her head and spotted a green-and-white highway marker that hung from its post by one rusted bolt. Dirt and ash caked the face of the sign, but through a squint she could make out a few letters. *Exit 38, two miles.* She had walked three of the five miles to the river. Two more were manageable, she decided. They would have to be. Even if she turned back now, it would take her twice as long to shuffle back through the metal maze that stood between her and Terra.

Before her, she could see the ruins of the skyscrapers that had once made up downtown Tropeck. All she needed to do was make it past the burnt-out college campus, the long-forgotten restaurants, and the looted shopping plazas to get to First Street. That led to the Cypress Bridge that spanned the Savannah River. That was her plan, even if it was dangerous to the point of foolhardiness.

A bead of sweat dripped down Ayanna's forehead and landed in her eye. She swung her backpack around and fished out her water bottle. Her hand trembled as she wrestled with the steel top. Great. If her nerves made her feel this unsteady already, what was going to happen when she got to the river?

She held the canteen in her left hand and made a fist with her right. Maybe the movement would help calm her nervous twitching. She needed to get it together. With a jerk, she managed to lift the canteen top off and take a swig of water. The water slid down her throat, relieving the feeling of sandpaper that had nearly choked her seconds earlier. This was progress.

Her boots brought her another twenty feet. A mangled car blocked her path, and she moved to walk through the tight space between it and a neighboring military jeep. What was left of the car resembled the charred frame of a station wagon—a family car. There was no point in questioning what had happened to its owners. Dragons had burned them to dust, no doubt. The melted steel had coiled onto itself, and gaping holes remained where the windows had been. Had this family had children? Had they suffered or gone quickly?

Ayanna did not want to imagine the former, and she had witnessed the latter exactly six times. One second, a person was there. The next, they were not.

Her throat tightened, and she forced down a deep breath of hot air. She still had a ways to go before she got to the river.

CHAPTER 4

Ayanna walked in the shadows of the office buildings. Vagrant brick and concrete structures towered over her as she made her way through the gridded city streets. Everything dwarfed her. Large and small blocks of red and gray spread through the deserted road, and shattered glass crumpled beneath her feet, making crackling noises that echoed against the buildings' facades. *Crunch, crunch, crunch,* her boots sang with each hurried step.

The debris explained the huge missing sections of most of the buildings' roofs. But even though the top halves of the business towers had taken a beating, most of their frames stood intact. Ayanna looked for the blue light of the sky through the holes that the broken towers formed. A tiny shiver ran up her spine. It was important to keep one eye on the sky at all times, even with the sun shining brightly, and even if there were plenty of buildings to hide in if she had to. Buildings were not foolproof. There was no guarantee that she would be alone if she scurried into one. Unless there was a barrier that kept them out, dragons could, and would, go into any building they wanted.

Ayanna ignored the gnawing fear that ate away at her stomach. Daylight still worked in her favor. She could not forget this. She counted on it.

She pulled a city map from her back pocket without slowing her stride and turned the map upright. Back when the government was still working, and Tropeck's mayor was trying to encourage visitors to spend money downtown, she had had City Hall print a few thousand of these small maps on glossy paper with bright colors. The mayor had even gone as far as to post ads on the sides of city buses encouraging people to stop by City Hall to pick up a copy. It had been a wasted effort, in Ayanna's view.

Ayanna's eyes scanned the lines that crossed the page and made a sharp right turn onto Main Street. She was close. She remembered these streets. She was not far from the Dixon Lee Memorial Hospital where her mother and Dr. Keaton had worked long before the Fire Sky War. It was also the place where her mother had died when Ayanna was twelve years old.

Ayanna shook the thought from her head. There was no sense thinking about Dixon Lee Memorial Hospital. Nothing was left of the building except for rubble and ash.

Ayanna stopped at the end of Main Street. She heard the gentle flow of the water before she saw it. The rippling waves sounded like a hushed conversation between friends. Under a different circumstance, the serene sound would have soothed her. But she knew better than to be fooled. Nothing good came out of the river. Not now. Not anymore.

She took a few more steps, and the office buildings gave way to a miles-long stretch of burned-out waterfront stores and scorched soil. In what seemed like a few hundred feet from where she stood, she could see her goal, the Cypress Bridge.

Ayanna craned her neck to the side. Two center pillars that held the bridge up had three large cracks in their posts, but the structure was intact.

Beneath the bridge, the river water sparkled majestically in the sun's rays, giving a false impression of tranquility. The riverbed stretched at least fifty feet across, transferring fast-flowing dark water south toward a distant location.

Ayanna felt her breath hitch. Realization hit suddenly. She had made it, but now what? Her heart started to pound, and the shaking she had tried to get rid of earlier was back. There was a good chance it was not going anywhere this time. She had been certain all morning that this was what she had to do, but now her doubt seemed overwhelming.

Ayanna shook her head. She was doing this. She might as well do her best to stay alive. She raised her hand to look at the map that now lay crumpled in her sweaty palm. She turned it upright and squinted at the lines and curves of the page, but she could not get her mind to focus. This city map wasn't going to help anyway, as it did not list the landmarks she needed. She crushed the paper into a ball and stuffed it back into her pocket. She would have to guess from memory where the waterfront gardens used to be.

Ayanna closed her eyes and tried to imagine glimpses of her childhood. There had been boutiques, restaurants, a small museum. Her mother had particularly liked to take her to a French bakery with large glass windows. Flashes of images came to her. Ayanna remembered the smell of confectioners' sugar that wafted from inside the bakery when they entered and the dozens of rows of pastries, cakes, and pies that filled the shelves of the shop. She decided to walk to the right. But there was nothing left of how things used to look and no real way to tell if she were traveling in the right direction. What used to be a store was now just a pile of blackened timber and ash, indistinguishable from the rest.

She moved along the waterfront with delicate steps. Any bricks that had once paved a path were now scattered to the wind or ground to dust, and the loose soil that remained shifted beneath her boots, slowing her pace.

There was no sign of any wildlife, not even birds, but Ayanna had expected this. The smoke from the fires the dragons had set and the rain of bullets and bombs the army had fired made it impossible for most natural creatures to survive anywhere near the river.

Ayanna turned her head to the side to check that she was alone. On her left, something in the water drew her attention. She stopped and stared into the riverbed. The water flowed in two paths at a fork in the center. It was strange. Anything could block the water's flow with the amount of debris that scattered over everything, she guessed, but this seemed different. This seemed deliberate.

Ayanna followed the fork and saw huge chunks of dead tree trunks and misshapen, square concrete blocks sticking out from the water. She squinted. The tree limbs and rocks formed a tall structure that only seemed to grow in size from the far side of the river.

She wanted to study the blockade, but a loud echo drew her attention away. She heard something that reminded her of a flag flapping in the wind during a thunderstorm. The sound grew louder with each passing second and a dark object cast a shadow across the ground on the other side of the riverbank. Ayanna froze. A dragon flew overhead. She hadn't seen it, but she knew it was there. It let out a high-pitched cry followed by a snarl. Ayanna's mind fought with her body. She pressed her feet into her boots and willed herself not to run. There was a chance that it had not spotted her. *After all, you came all this way*, one part of her brain argued. *Yes, and what good will it do when you're dead?* snapped another.

The argument in her head ceased to matter when the dragon dove from the sky into the river. Water splashed high into the air, and Ayanna felt cool droplets hit her face. She waited and listened. One second, two, three. If the dragon had seen her, she would know it. Horrible memories flashed in her mind of mangled, bloodied bodies. That was what happened when a dragon hunted someone. This dragon was far from alone, she was sure. The rest were submerged and sleeping on the river floor.

But heading back was not much safer than going ahead. Ayanna steeled herself and pressed forward.

CHAPTER 5

A yanna checked her watch. She had been walking for at least twenty minutes since seeing the dragon. She looked behind her. The battered government building that marked her exit from Main Street did not seem more than half a mile away. It was no wonder—her boots sank into the earth, making everything harder, and the way the boot leather pinched her big toe made her hyper-aware of each step she took, slowing her pace to a crawl.

Ayanna felt her strength waver as the sun beat down on her head, reminding her of just how frail her body was. Her sweat-drenched shirt stuck to her skin, and she considered that dehydration, only a vague threat before, seemed just around the corner if she did not make progress soon. Her foolish plan to come to the waterfront was threatening to become a suicide mission.

Had Maya been right? Should she have not come at all? The memory she had conjured in her mind of a plentiful garden with thousands of plants might well have been a hallucination. There was no sign that the garden she remembered had ever existed, let alone that any of the plants it harbored had survived. And what about Dr. Keaton? Would she fail him and everyone else at Terra by her foolish actions?

Don't forget about your own death, the mocking voice in her head sang. *There is a pretty good chance that this whole stupid trip will be for nothing, and you will just end up dead.*

Ayanna pushed back against the cruel thoughts. There was no time for these doubts. Either the gardens existed, or they did not, but now was the time to find out.

She swiveled her head, searching for any sign, any glimmer of hope that would tell her what to do, and—as if she had been given a miracle—she spotted a tiny field of green peeking from beneath a darkened steel beam just ahead. The oasis of new life contrasted boldly against the dark soil. She felt a bolt of energy shoot through her at the sight, and she lifted her legs high to push faster over the unsteady earth.

Just then, Ayanna heard a new snarl from behind her. The muscles in her shoulders tightened.

Another dragon had come up to the surface, she knew—but she was too close to her prize to turn back. She continued on, and as her path made a gentle curve, a full view of the plants that were growing wildly in the fertile soil came into focus. She had not imagined it. The seeds of the gardens had survived, just as she had hoped. Native and exotic plants created patches of bright green, white, yellow, red, and purple twenty feet in front of her.

Ayanna could barely contain her excitement. Her thoughts jumped to how she would need to make space in her herb box for her new treasures. She was so caught up in her discovery that she barely registered the sound of another growl that reached her ears. She had to ignore it, if only for a second. She was so close.

Sharp steel beams and rods made up the remnants of the former garden house. They fell into themselves, leaving only the vague memory of a structure around which the new garden grew. Through the melted metal pieces, Ayanna spotted a large green plant with purple flowers that took on the shape of small tubes turned upside down. From where she stood, the plant looked exactly like the picture of foxglove she had seen in Dr. Keaton's botany book. She felt her mouth curl into a smile.

To reach it, Ayanna needed to climb between the beams that crisscrossed her path and into the center of the garden. Her eyes darted back and forth as she tried to figure out the best way to get under the largest beam. She was raising her foot for her next step when she suddenly felt the land beneath her give way and her body lift from the ground.

She kicked her legs and screamed a loud, terrified cry that came from deep in her stomach as a dragon pierced her backpack with its talon. Her hands grasped wildly for anything that could stop her from rising into the air, making contact with a steel rod that scraped across her skin with a sharp, painful sting. Ayanna felt three fingernails break from the force of trying to hold onto her only anchor to the ground, but it was useless. Blue sky replaced the black soil in her vision, and blood pulsed to her head as her heart pounded in her ears.

Hot air slammed into Ayanna's face, and her stomach jolted with the ascent. The heights mixed with her terror as vomit rose to her throat. Panic consumed her. Only the nearing sight of water beneath her focused her mind. Her legs dangled at least eight feet off the ground. If the dragon dropped her in the river, there was no chance of survival. Dozens of other dragons waited just below the surface of the water, ready to rip her limb from limb to share in an easy meal.

She writhed, trying to break free, but the straps of her bag had tightened and twisted around her arms, forming into a painful straitjacket. Ayanna stretched and reached for her belt. She ignored the burning in her palm and moved her fingers from memory. She pulled her silver-handled knife from its holder and with a desperate, sloppy motion, she stabbed at the dragon's ankle. The dragon kept its grip on her as it flapped its wings and climbed higher into the sky.

She removed the knife from its scaly skin and pierced its flesh again. This time, the dragon loosened its grip. This was all Ayanna needed. She took another swipe with her knife, but now, she sliced through the straps of her backpack, holding onto the bag as she kicked her legs to create enough propulsion to rip herself from the dragon's grasp. She held her breath as she fell from the sky, crashing to the soil below, her pack landing only a few feet away.

The force of the blow knocked the wind from her lungs. She opened her mouth to breathe, but her breath felt like tiny razors scraping against her lungs. Ayanna's eyes darted around. The dragon had flown her back toward the city. How would she get the digitalis now?

Ayanna located the dragon. It was too close for her to even consider trying for the plants again. She watched as the dragon circled around to come back for her. Its long tail, adorned with three spikes at the end, glided behind its thick body. This was a male, smaller than the females, but not by much. The dragon made an attempt to dive for Ayanna, but it missed her, its hardened middle talon scraping the air far above her.

Ayanna knew that the sun had saved her. The glare it caused had probably temporarily blinded the dragon. But would it give up?

She stiffened her torso. She could not stay out in the open like this. Bracing her hands beneath her, she tried to lift herself. Pain stabbed her ribs, and she let out a loud yelp. The fall had bruised her rib cage, she was sure.

Everything hurt. The world started to move in circles before her eyes, but she tried lifting herself up again by pressing her bloody hands to the ground. Her arms gave way, and she collapsed from the effort. What was she going to do?

Ayanna stretched her arms with a wince and reached for her bag. The miraculous save gave her hope, at least, and she cradled the ripped canvas to her chest as she looked around. Her vision blurred, but in her line of sight, she made out a rusted, military truck abandoned by the side of the road. It was at least fifty feet away from where she had landed. What other choice did she have?

Ayanna gripped her bag, took in a few more painful breaths, and managed to crawl from the riverbank to the road. Panting, she squeezed her eyes shut before rolling her body toward the truck. She stopped to catch her breath, then she rolled a second time. Each round hurt more than the one before it. The heated pavement burned her skin, and loose rocks scraped her arms.

She felt as though acid were burning her inside and out, but she was almost there. At last, she rolled the final two feet and felt the truck cast a cool shadow above her. The relief was instant. It would not last, but she stretched her arms out to relish her unsavory, temporary shelter.

Ayanna needed a plan. She had to get out of the city, but the adrenaline that had fueled her escape from the dragon had started to wane and her eyelids started to close. *No*, she thought. She could not lose consciousness. *No*. She was not safe. Things were not OK. *No*.

She fought with her eyes. She needed to keep them open. Objects flashed from white to red to black. She lost. Her eyes won. Darkness overcame her.

CHAPTER 6

Ayanna's eyes blinked open. She moved her arm that felt numb from sleep and let out a loud moan. The blood on her arms and hands had dried and formed tiny, gelled splotches on her skin.

As she turned to reach for her pack, her midsection screamed with pain. But her breath came out easier than it had before. Ayanna was sure her ribs were just bruised, not broken. She reached in her bag and pulled out her water bottle. Thank goodness she had held onto it. She took a long gulp of water that soothed her throat and replaced the bottle in her bag.

Ayanna's eyes strained from trying to focus under the shadow of the truck. The sunlight she had worked so hard to escape seemed dimmer now. She raised her wrist close to her eyes, squinting to read the face of her watch. Six o'clock. *Dammit.* She had been out for four hours. She took three short breaths to prepare herself for the pain and rolled out from under the truck, dragging her strapless bag with her.

A glance at the skyline told her it was clear. Her legs were just beginning to feel more inclined to work, so she lifted her body from the hard concrete with only a slight stumble, trying to gain her bearings. She did not know what street she had ended up on, and from where she stood, she could not tell how far she was from Main Street.

Her shades had fallen to some unknown place, but they were the least of her problems. The glaring sunlight she remembered from before she passed out had morphed into a steady glow close to the horizon. This was worse than any nightmare she could have conjured up in her basement closet. Not only did Ayanna not have time to try to go back for the medicine she had nearly died for, but she did not know if she had enough time to make it back to Terra before the sun set—or before the lone dragon she had met earlier turned into a swarm.

Ayanna looked back at the river. Digitalis was there. She had seen it with her own eyes. That precious purple-and-green foxglove plant existed, and it offered Terra a new hope. How in hell was she ever going to get another chance to get it? Maybe she could come back when she had more time? Some weapons? A car?

She shook her head. It did not matter right now. She had to abandon the medicine if she wanted to save her own life.

She reached in her pocket and unfolded the crumpled map she had stored there. Maybe there was some shortcut through the city. Something she had not thought of before. Tears pricked her eyes and threatened to fall. She was scared. No—*terrified* was a better word. Ayanna squeezed her eyes shut and took in three deep breaths, blowing them out slowly. Being scared was not going to help her out of this. She knew she had to fight it. *Just start walking*, she decided.

The sun reflected a reddish-orange glow off the ruins of the skyscrapers. Five miles separated her from Terra. She searched for the strength to press her legs forward as fast as she could, but the pain she felt was relentless. She needed something, anything to dull the stabbing pain shooting through her if she were going to have a chance at getting home.

She shuffled through the city. It was quiet except for the occasional crash of concrete falling from the side of a building. The beams of light that had peeked through the spaces of the buildings were shorter and fainter than they had been when she'd arrived. *Just keep walking*, she reminded herself. But the ache of her ribs and the pulsing of her wounds slowed her progress, and her only ally seemed farther away with each step.

After what seemed like forever, Ayanna passed the River View Pharmacy. Her eyes scanned the doorframe of the building. A landmark. Good. She was not far from the remains of City Hall. That meant she knew where she was headed. From the looks of the pharmacy, it had been ransacked. Picked clean. She would not find any supplies there. That was not surprising. Its location on a major city street had been too inviting for the survivors and soldiers alike to resist after the army abandoned the city and left behind the stragglers who had been too late getting to the drop point.

Truth be told, the army had left early, their convoys pulling away with half-empty trucks. At least, that was how Ayanna remembered it: bombs exploding around her head; her father and Richard scrambling to help load people onto green-and-gray trucks; the dragons attacking; her father running for his life; Richard's arms wrapping too tightly around her middle, forcing her back as he dragged her from the site. The memories flooded her senses. She could almost feel the weight of Richard's hands gripping her so close to his body that she could barely find enough breath to scream; his gruff voice that should have belonged to someone much older than his years, echoing against her eardrum as he shouted into his intercom to try to force his commanders to come back for them; and the tears—Maya's tears,

Ayanna's tears, pouring out and scalding her cheeks like dry ice against bare skin.

Ayanna stopped in the street and bent over in anguish, resting her elbows on her thighs. The memories only added to her current agony, and she felt vomit rise in her throat before she could stop it. Her body worked to purge the images from her mind as she gasped for air. After a few seconds, her breathing calmed. She stood up straight, swiped her mouth with the back of her hand, and took another step.

If not this pharmacy, maybe—maybe—the one on Glorious Way, her body urged. It was tucked away in an alley, out of easy sight. It might still have something. All the life-saving drugs would be gone for sure, but maybe—just maybe—she could find aspirin, even oxycodone, if she were lucky.

Ayanna looked behind her. She had to hurry. The detour was out of the way, yes, but the aching . . . the aching she felt insisted that she try.

CHAPTER 7

Ayanna smelled smoke rising from a building with a broken blue sign leaning from its facade. The sign was missing the letters "D" and "Y," but Ayanna could see that it used to be a dry cleaner. She turned a corner past the dry cleaner and walked to the end of the block. She remembered this block because she had ridden in her father's car down this street when she was eleven years old. The pharmacy was down the side street ahead.

This pharmacy was not far from Dixon Lee Memorial Hospital. On their drive there, Ayanna's father had told her that her mother preferred this store because she often spent long hours working at the hospital, and it had been a convenient place for her to stop before she came home. At first, Ayanna hadn't given that much thought. But when they arrived, Ayanna realized what everything meant. She and her father were going to the pharmacy instead of her mother because the cancer had made Ayanna's mother too sick to work, and she could no longer pick up her own medications.

Ayanna remembered the pharmacist who had helped them, a quiet, patient man with a long gray beard but no mustache. This feature had caused her to stare at his face for a long time. She recalled the solemn, sad look he had given her father when he handed him the paper bags filled with her mother's pills. It was then that Ayanna first realized that her mother wasn't going to get better.

Ayanna felt some relief when she arrived at the entrance to the pharmacy. There was a chance she might find something useful. A steel frame marked the door, and burn marks scorched the walls. Empty shelves littered the room.

Ayanna moved behind the cashier's counter and pulled open the drawers with frantic motions. She found some gauze, cotton balls, tape. She unzipped her bag and tossed the supplies in before moving to the next drawer. The room was desolate, and broken glass littered the floor.

She eyed the street outside. The sunlight she craved barely clung to the day, and Ayanna tried to weigh her pain against her need to run. Images of what would happen when the night finally took hold and the dragons emerged from the river played out in her mind. A dragon talon could slice through skin with the same ease as scissors slicing through paper. If a single talon were to cut her, through an artery in her leg perhaps, she would bleed out and die before she even had time to put up a fight.

She yanked open another drawer. There, stuffed between a bagged syringe and an ankle brace, she spotted a small white bottle. She lifted the bottle and read the label, acetylsalicylic acid. Ayanna could feel the drug's pain-numbing effects already.

She popped the top of the bottle. It was filled to the brim. She felt a smile widen across her face. She could imagine the relief this medicine would bring. She took two pills from the container, crushing them between her teeth before shoving the bottle and the rest of the drawer's contents into her ragged bag.

She rushed for the exit. As she walked out of the building, the broken glass crackled under her boots, causing her to notice when the sound stopped. She had stepped on a newspaper clipping, singed around the edges. Ayanna reached for it and read the headline: "*Thousands More Killed as the Dragon Population Surges.*" The date on the corner of the clipping was May 3, 2048. The paper was two years old. She folded the clipping and put it in her pocket. Then, she looked up toward the sun again. The sky was now purple, and the sun barely showed over the horizon.

This is not going to work, she thought. She needed a place to hide.

Ayanna looked back toward the open pharmacy. The dilapidated building scarcely remained standing. The roof had a giant hole in it, and plaster fell from the remaining walls. There was no way she could hole up in there for the night.

She stumbled into the street, panicking at the truth she faced. She was trapped on the surface at night, just as Maya had feared. She shuffled down the street, trying to use her memory to think of a decent hiding spot.

Ayanna tried to scan the area, but it was hard to see. The protective glow of the sun was gone, and darkness had taken over the sky. The only available light came from the moon's reflection.

From the dark quiet, an ominous figure swooped down just above her head. She heard a fluttering noise. It was exactly like the winged flapping she had heard on the banks of the river. Her time was up. She felt beads of sweat form on her forehead.

She looked at the sky in a useless attempt to spot the dragon she was certain was there, but she could not see anything. The figure had disappeared just as quickly as it had arrived.

Ayanna had no other options. She had to run. She took in a long breath. Pain shot through her body, but she ran. She ran despite the pain. She ran over the cracked streets, even as her muscles ached, and her already battered lungs burned.

As she approached Jefferson Boulevard, she stopped running. She paused and listened. She could only hear the beating of her heart and the sound of her lungs filling with air as she worked to draw breath. *I told you that you were going to die. Wiped out, burned to dust, chopped into pieces.* Her cruel, unhelpful thoughts had returned.

Again, an object descended over her like a bird sizing up its prey. Was this the same dragon? Or a new one? Did it matter?

Either way, it was hunting her.

CHAPTER 8

Ayanna's heart pounded erratically against her rib cage. It seemed to want to escape its home. How could she blame it? She wanted to escape too.

Her eyes darted between buildings. Nowhere seemed right. Gaping holes marred almost every building, leaving her with limited options.

Suddenly, Ayanna spotted a cracked door on the side of a red brick structure. It still had four walls and a roof. It would do. She gathered her strength and ran at full speed toward it. She ducked into the space just as she heard a loud growl and felt a stream of fire engulf the street behind her.

She glanced back just long enough to see the dragon fly over the roof of the building. She pushed her way through the door into the dark room, pulling it closed behind her. Her eyes adjusted to the darkness, and she saw ash-covered tables and overturned chairs. Hundreds of books, some burned, some not, lined at least fifteen rows of bookshelves. A bookstore? Books were low on the list of things for people to loot, she supposed.

Ayanna heard the dragon land on the roof. Each footstep made a loud thud. The dragon let out a cry. It was a shrill sound that pierced her eardrums, and her hands flew to the sides of her head. The sound was deafening and familiar.

She waited, listening as the dragon's large feet stomped above her head. Softball-sized pieces of plaster fell from the ceiling, adding more dust to the air. Dragons were smart. She had seen them lie in wait to ambush people before. This one knew she was here. Would it bring down the building to flush her out? Or worse, would it set the entire bookstore ablaze and make her run for the street?

Ayanna worked to stay quiet, but staccato breaths escaped her mouth. She listened through the wisps of air. The pain in her side had lessened, and she was grateful for the painkillers that were clearly working. That was something. *Not everything is against me*, she thought.

Suddenly, the dragon fell silent. What in the hell was it doing up there? Ayanna lifted her boots to look frantically around her hiding spot. Maybe there was a basement.

She made a short circle around the shelves. Hope swelled in her chest when she spotted a metal door behind the reference section, only for it to be dashed seconds later when she realized it led back outside to an alley. This bookstore sat on one level. Of course it did.

Ayanna shook her head. She needed to think. Should she try to run for a safer spot? Maybe she could make it into the sewer? *Dammit!* Now seemed like a good time to chastise herself. Guilt circulated in her chest, accenting her panic. She had broken her promise to Maya. Was she there in the basement tunnels, pacing . . . waiting for Ayanna to come back?

Ayanna had known this might happen. She just had not expected it to happen like this. She had imagined everything differently, somehow. She had always thought of herself as brave. At least, that was how her father had described her. But the fear that was seeping into her veins and pulsing through her body now, replacing her blood, made her feel as though she were cruelly betraying his view of her. Was there anybody she would not disappoint today?

More importantly, what was she going to do? The question felt so heavy that she almost did not register an odd sound coming from outside. It was too faint to be another dragon, and the noise had a rhythmic tone to it. Like . . . it sounded like footsteps walking in the street over broken glass.

Ayanna moved to the front of the bookstore and looked out the window. She focused her eyes past the popping crackle the fire created as it burned the already torched city and listened harder. *Was someone walking in the street? Who could it be?* she wondered. *Had one of the Protectorate followed her to the surface? Richard? That didn't seem likely. Would he have taken a risk like that just to bring her back?*

Her hands trembled, and she held them to her sides. Her eyes strained. Only the soft glow of inflamed objects lit her view, and she blinked slowly to take in whatever was in the street.

Ayanna's eyes widened at what she saw. Was this real? Maybe she was imagining it. She had taken a very nasty blow to the head earlier when she'd fallen from the sky. She probably had a concussion. But had it caused permanent brain damage?

If it had not, then her eyes were right, and there was a boy walking in the street. Ayanna's eyes focused on him as his left foot followed his right in a slow, steady march to his doom.

Ayanna shifted her body to get a closer look. The boy looked around her age, if not a few years older. He was around six feet, and his shoulders looked strong, like he could hold one of the militia's training weights over his head without blinking. His hair was cut close to his scalp, and he wore a black T-shirt that revealed a single tattoo on his left arm that contrasted against his light brown skin.

Ayanna felt confused. He did not seem to care about the dragon that hovered above the bookstore. From where he stood, she was sure he could see it. She watched with fascination and horror. What was he doing?

Ayanna felt her heart pounding again. It pumped with the pace of his march. She wanted to look away. She feared what she might see next: an innocent boy slaughtered by a ruthless creature. No. No, she couldn't take that. But she could not tear her eyes from him either. Was this bravery or stupidity? Was he crazy? Drunk perhaps?

Ayanna heard the dragon lift its body from the roof. The boy was obviously easier prey. She watched as it landed deftly on the ground and headed toward the stranger.

It approached him from behind, and she saw the full length of its body for the first time. It was at least as long as a city bus, and it stood taller than a grown man standing on another's shoulders. She could tell by the way the ground shook when it walked that it was heavy . . . and strong. It was a female. No horns on its head.

It walked on its four legs and folded its leathery wings back. Massive scales covered its body and protected it like armor. Its long tail, decorated with unforgiving spikes, knocked against the side of the buildings, causing bricks to fall. There was no hope of killing this dragon, even if Ayanna had had a proper weapon with her.

Ayanna watched as the boy turned to face it. His face was strikingly handsome and utterly serene. He spread out his arms and leaned his head back as if to invite the dragon to devour him.

Ayanna opened the front door to the bookstore. If she could not stand to watch him die, maybe she could stop it from happening.

She walked out into the street. Her mind screamed that she owed no allegiance to this suicidal fool, but could she just stand there and let someone else die in such a horrible way, even if he was an idiot?

"Hey!" she called out. The dragon turned its head away from the boy. With a whip of its tail, it moved to face Ayanna. She was the one it had really wanted, after all. But she felt absolute horror at the realization that she now had the dragon's full attention.

Ayanna looked to see which path she would take to run back, but she had wandered farther than she thought from her refuge, and the dragon moved faster than she had hoped. What were the chances she would make it back to the bookstore before the dragon's flame engulfed her? The odds were not good. The dragon stood so close that the putrid smell of its sulfurous breath invaded her senses. The creature took two steps toward her. It moved slowly, but it could launch at her with a sudden jolt of speed at any moment. Maybe she could summon one more burst of adrenaline—one more push to save herself.

Ayanna started to move, but instead of running, her legs stiffened into weights, terror having seemed to melt the ground into wet asphalt just as it stopped time. Her eyes drifted from the dragon, and the handsome boy fell into her sightline next. He seemed as stunned by the moment as she. They stared at each other for what must have been a few seconds, but each second stretched like pulled saltwater taffy, and it seemed as if they had an eternity to spare. Maybe death could freeze time? The idea reminded her of a faintly remembered fable she had heard years before in school.

The boy's expression looked as if he held a thousand questions, and his eyes seemed filled with longing. Did he hope Ayanna could answer them? How could she, right when death had finally finished taunting her and had decided to end their day-long dance?

The boy appeared to use every moment they had left to study Ayanna. He looked first at her hair, then her eyes, her face, and her body. His lips parted, and he mouthed something that she could not quite make out, but it looked like the word *beautiful*.

In a sudden sense of urgency, he broke his gaze from her. His eyes shot to the dragon. His head panned gently from right to left as his eyes traveled from the dragon to Ayanna and then back to the massive creature, and his face contorted as if he had just been hit in the stomach by an invisible force. Ayanna understood. He must have realized that she had placed her life in danger trying to help him. From the looks of things, there was a good chance she was going to die because of it.

CHAPTER 9

Ayanna closed her eyes and waited for the dragon's flame to incinerate her. Things did not seem so scary anymore. Maybe it helped that she was not alone.

Her eyes flew open when she felt the strong blow of the boy's body tackle her to the ground. It immediately reminded her of the wounds she had already endured that morning, and she let out a loud yelp as their bodies fell with a hard crash to the pavement. The dragon's breath soared just above their heads, the heat from the flame singeing the ends of her hair. Then, the dragon took flight. It would surely come back to destroy them, but Ayanna lay on the ground, dazed from the blow and shocked to be alive.

She only emerged from her stupor when she felt the boy grab her hand and pull her up. They ran hand-in-hand for the open bookstore door and crashed into the room, moving instantly to the window frames to peer outside. They watched the dragon fly overhead, gaining height as it screeched and flapped its leathery wings. It thrashed its tail against the outside wall, and Ayanna felt the ground shake beneath her.

"Do you think it will—?"

Ayanna and the boy ducked to the ground just as the dragon opened its mouth and shot a streaming flame of fire at the building. The boy was on her again, hovering so his body shielded her from the heat.

The brick facade absorbed most of the flames, and only a few flares made it into the bookstore, but those few were enough to activate the sprinkler system. A cascade of water poured from the ceiling. Ayanna blinked repeatedly, trying to see through the unexpected shower. The water felt cool on her skin, and the sensation helped her focus on the next step. Would the dragon try to wait them out? Or would it move on to easier prey?

Ayanna did not have to wait long for an answer. From perhaps a block away, she heard an explosion, followed by what sounded like a building collapsing. No person had caused that noise at this hour. Another dragon might have broken a live gas main in one of the other buildings. Maybe her choice of shelter was not so bad after all.

Whatever had caused it, the noise was enough to interest the dragon that stalked just outside. She heard it snarl before it flew off to investigate the commotion.

Ayanna felt cooler and realized that the boy had lifted his body from hers. The lack of heat left her feeling damp, and she saw that her clothes were soaked through—just what she needed to make this terrible day feel even longer.

The boy walked back to the window, presumably to check that they were safe. Ayanna watched him silently. She felt too many emotions to think straight, let alone say anything that would make sense.

The sprinklers calmed down before Ayanna's mind did. As their stream transformed into a slow drip, she tried to follow their lead. She was so confused that it was a struggle to steady her heavy breathing. She was not quite sure what to believe. Had he saved her? Or she him? Perhaps neither?

The boy seemed to sense Ayanna watching him, and he

turned to look at her. His eyes made one swipe of her body and he frowned. "You OK?" he asked.

Ayanna's mouth opened, but nothing came out.

"I said, are you OK?" he asked again. He took a step toward her, and she flinched. She lifted herself off the ground. She wanted to keep distance between them.

The boy stopped moving. "I think it's gone; not sure if it'll come back, though. There might be others. We oughta stay here," he suggested.

Ayanna knew he had spoken, but his words seemed distant and unimportant. "What—what were you doing out there? Who are you?" She heard her voice break. "You almost got us killed. I almost died because of you!" Ayanna screamed before he could answer.

Her body started to tremble; she couldn't stop it. Her lungs felt short of oxygen, and she gasped, unable to find a breath. Tears welled in her eyes. She hated the feeling. Tears were useless and stupid right now, but there was nothing she could do to keep them from forming. "I'm in shock," she squeaked out as warm droplets touched her cheeks.

Through her tears, Ayanna saw the boy walking toward her. He held his palms up and moved in a slow, steady stride. She tried to back away, but he moved closer to her before she could get far, his hands reaching out for her.

"I know how to kill you!" she threatened between gasps.

The boy nodded and paused. But he continued to watch her.

"I believe you," he said quietly, before closing the space between them and pulling her close to his chest. "Shh," he whispered, "it's all right. You're all right."

Ayanna stiffened, but her body shivered, and she craved his warmth. Despite everything, she was unable to resist wrapping her arms around him. She held him tightly, and her muscles relaxed. The air she needed found its way to her lungs, and for a brief moment, she felt safe.

Ayanna's control started to come back, and it vaguely occurred to her that she should move. She had let him hold her for over a minute. She had no reason to remain in his arms. Being in them at all was insane. This boy was a complete stranger. She knew nothing about him.

But she did not leave. Instead, she looked up and met his soft hazel eyes. Sadness filled them. Whatever story they held probably explained a lot. She felt lost as she continued to stare, and the boy stared back. Had time frozen again?

Finally, the boy lifted his hand and gently rubbed a stray hair from Ayanna's face. He let his hand stop at her cheek and carefully wipe away the remnants of a tear. He touched Ayanna as if he had always known her. But he did not know her at all.

And she did not know him, she reminded herself. Why was she allowing this? She shifted and pulled away from his embrace. What in the world was she thinking?

"I'm better, thank you," she said as she took several steps away from him. "I'm sorry. I was just upset. I'm Ayanna. What's your name?"

"Ayanna?" he said to himself. "Got a last name, Ayanna?" The boy did not seem in any hurry to answer her question. With all the trouble he had caused her, she would think he could at least tell her his name, but apparently not. Maybe if she answered his question, he might get around to answering hers.

"Yes, it's Grace, but what does that—?"

"Ayanna Grace . . . I Yawn Na Grace," he repeated slowly. "It's got a nice ring to it."

Unbelievable. "Thanks, I guess. But what's your—?" Ayanna began, trying hard to hide her annoyance.

"Yeah . . . yeah, I like that," he said, nodding as if he had just made a major decision about his life.

"That's great." She could not quite see why it would matter to him either way.

"I'm Jackson. Jackson Kyle," he finally said with a smile. His wide, bright smile softened his features, and Ayanna forgot her annoyance.

But if she was not going to be annoyed with Jackson, maybe she could be afraid of him. She knew she should be. There was something untamed and disorderly about him. His friendly tone could all be an act, and he could hurt her if he wanted to. There was nowhere she could escape to at the moment. And she had a very good reason to think that he was crazy. Only a few minutes earlier, he had been out in the middle of the street taunting a dragon.

But then again, had she not been doing the same thing at the river this morning?

Ayanna sighed. She did not want to think about this morning's failure, how much trouble she was going to be in tomorrow, or how frightened Maya would be tonight when she did not come back to Terra. She shook her head and moved to the bookshelves. It seemed all right to turn her back on Jackson, at least for a moment. Fear was not the emotion he stirred in her. She was curious about him and attracted to him, though she wished she could push back against that fact. Her training and the messages put out by the Watchers had taught her over and over to be wary of strangers. The war had changed people, and anyone without a home might act desperately or even violently, the council had warned. But Jackson didn't seem the least bit interested in attacking her. He had already moved back to stand guard at the window. She might as well try to find something to help them dry their clothes.

"So, Jackson," Ayanna said as she moved through the aisles of bookshelves, "I take it you aren't from around here."

"Huh? Oh, yeah. You take it right," he said. "I'm just passing through. I'm headed out West. Hear there are fewer of them out there."

Ayanna stopped her search. "Really? Where'd you hear that?" she asked.

"Just from people. You know, around," he said. "People I come across as I go."

"Do you come across a lot of people? . . . I mean, have you seen a lot of survivors?" Ayanna peered around the shelves to catch Jackson's eye. She was excited at the possibility. Maybe he had found another compound, maybe in Charleston. Maybe he had passed through there on his way to Tropeck.

"Naw, not really," he said.

Ayanna frowned and returned to her search. The sudden movement caused her to remember the pain in her side. She sighed, aware that she would need to take more aspirin soon to make it through the night.

Carefully, she pulled some books from a shelf. "*Superbowl Highlights Past and Present: See the Ball, Be the Ball*," she said, reading the title of the first book aloud in an exaggerated fashion. "These seem to still be dry. They should burn all right." Ayanna walked back toward Jackson with what she hoped made for decent kindling.

"What? You don't like football?" Jackson asked, with a smirk that came in close second to his perfect smile. Ayanna's stomach did a tiny somersault. *Where did that come from?* she wondered, shaking her head. There was no way she had time to entertain whatever theatrics were going on inside. She needed to focus. She needed to stay warm enough to make it through the night, and then, when the sun came up, she had to rush back to Terra before the Protectorate learned she was missing.

She shrugged at Jackson's question. "The games were fun

I guess, and my dad was into it. He used to play in college. He taught me all the rules. I just don't see any other way for this kind of book to help us, or anybody else, right now."

Jackson nodded. Ayanna grabbed her backpack from the floor. She was hoping her flint had not gotten too soaked by the sprinklers to work when Jackson asked, "Your dad went to college?"

It was strange which things Jackson cared about. He seemed to want to know about her past, but he wasn't too keen on trying to keep them warm for the night. Ayanna nodded. "Yes, and he became a professor. He was a physicist at TroTech," she said, thinking that she could guess what Jackson's next question would be.

"And your daddy, he's still around?" Jackson asked. "I mean . . . with everything." He gestured toward outside.

Ayanna looked over at Jackson briefly, then back into her bag. She didn't know if she should answer any more of these questions, especially about her father.

Terra's citizens weren't the only people who blamed her father for the infestation of dragons. She couldn't see how talking about him now with Jackson would help her.

"No," she finally answered, "he's not around anymore."

"I'm sorry," said Jackson.

Ayanna cleared her throat, trying to ignore the knot there. "So what about your dad?" she asked. "Did he teach you about football?"

"Never met him," Jackson answered quickly. "But my social worker used to take me to games sometimes, before, you know . . . everything went to hell."

Ayanna felt air pass over her lips, and she realized her mouth had dropped open. She wanted to ask another question. Actually, she wanted to ask a lot more questions, but she had gotten herself into enough trouble for one day. She needed to keep quiet.

Ayanna found her flint and moved to drag an overturned garbage can near a window frame. She ripped some pages from the spine of the book and crushed them into balls before she tossed them into the can. "Still, it's a shame to burn books," she said as she struck the flint. Its spark lit the remaining paper she held.

"I wouldn't worry too much about that," said Jackson. "It's not like we'll ever get a chance to watch football again."

"We might . . ."

"Oh, yeah? When?" Jackson asked. Ayanna heard the disbelief in his voice.

She lifted her eyes from her fire that burned brightly and looked back at Jackson. He seemed to expect an answer. "I don't know. After all this is over, I guess. After we figure out how to get rid of the dragons," she added.

"Yeah, well. I wouldn't hold my breath," Jackson said. His voice was calm, but Ayanna heard the frustration it held. She let her eyes fall back to the fire. There was no point in arguing with him.

"We should probably sit low, if we don't want to suffocate," Ayanna said. "Most of the smoke should travel out this broken window, though, so we'll probably be OK."

Ayanna heard Jackson move. She looked back and saw him headed toward the tables and chairs. He dragged two chairs from their place and brought them over to the fire, placing one beside Ayanna. "Thanks," she said taking a seat.

"Thanks for this," he said, sitting down in the other chair so close to Ayanna that they almost touched. She thought about moving her seat, but who was she kidding? Whatever last-minute hope she had of keeping her distance from him was gone.

"I thought we were going to have to spend the night wet *and* hungry. Now, it's just hungry." He let out a short, resigned sigh. How many hungry nights had he seen?

Ayanna reached for her bag and pulled out two misshapen square bars wrapped in cloth. "Here. They're a little wet, but they're still edible." She handed one of the bars to Jackson.

"What is it?"

"Sorghum bar. We grow it at Terra. It doesn't taste like much, but it holds back the hunger."

"Thanks."

"You're welcome," Ayanna said.

Jackson took the bar from her with a little hesitation. He squinted. His expression held more questions, but he didn't ask them. He bit into the bar and made a face. Ayanna guessed he didn't care much for the taste. No one did, really.

She bit into her own bar and let her eyes return to the fire. It felt warm on her skin, and she could feel the moisture leaving her shirt. She needed this moment to relax, she knew. Her body ached from taking so many hits.

Ayanna watched the flames dance. It was odd that she didn't fear fire. She should. It destroyed everything it touched, but it didn't scare her. Not like this, anyway—controlled. It had been a part of her life for too long. Fire found Ayanna wherever she was.

Jackson laughed suddenly.

"What?"

"Nothing, it's just . . ."

"What?"

"It's just, you're good at this stuff," he said.

"At what stuff?"

"Surviving. It's like your thing," he said.

Ayanna blinked. That wasn't how she thought about it. And she did not understand Jackson. He had survived this long. Otherwise, he wouldn't be here now on the surface. What was so special about the way she did it?

She thought of Maya's cherubic face. "I've had help," she said.

"At Terra?" Jackson asked. He seemed to be studying Ayanna again.

Ayanna waited to answer. How many questions would follow this one? And what did he hope to learn? Should she be telling anyone about Terra? Probably not. Would Jackson want to come there? Would he be welcomed? Ayanna had no say on whom the council allowed to shelter at Terra. Mrs. Johnson led the Watchers, and she seemed paranoid at the idea of allowing strangers anywhere near the group. Was it even safe for him to know about it? He might come back with others and put the whole compound in danger.

Still, she had to say something. "It's a sanctuary. Started during the war, after we lost the city . . ." Ayanna trailed off. Jackson seemed innocent enough to tell that much to; besides, it looked like he was alone. How much harm could one person do?

Jackson nodded. Her answer seemed to satisfy his curiosity.

Ayanna had questions too. "So . . . what were you doing out there in the street like that? You have a death wish or something?" she asked.

Jackson laughed. Of all his possible reactions, laughter was the strangest one. "I wouldn't say that. I just think that whatever will be will be. Kay seray, or whatever the saying is," he said after a long pause.

Ayanna tilted her head to the side. She was confused. "That seems a bit absurd if you ask me. We each choose our own destiny."

Jackson's eyes met hers. Ayanna recognized the sadness sitting just behind them. She had seen it in others and had known it in herself. Which day had broken his heart? Something told her it was before the dragons swarmed.

"If you say so," said Jackson. "And what would you say you're doing around here? Just sightseeing?"

Ayanna grimaced. "Point taken. I guess you're right. We all take our share of risks for whatever we think is important."

"So, what was so important you risked your life for it?" Jackson asked.

Ayanna lowered her eyes. She just wanted to forget about this morning. "Actually, I didn't get what I came for," she said. "But I did get something I needed." She reached into her bag again and pulled out her bottle of painkillers.

"Aspirin?"

"It's hard to come by. I'm sure you get that."

"Yeah, I get that. But it's worth you dying for?" Jackson asked incredulously.

Ayanna breathed out a sigh. "Like I said, I didn't get what I came for. And what is it that *you* almost died for?" she asked. She still did not understand what he'd been doing in the street like that.

"Well, from where I sit, it looks like the answer would be you."

Ayanna gaped. Wait. What? She tore her gaze from him and looked out the window. It *was* true that the dragon would have burned her to death if he had not knocked her out of the way. "Well, thanks for pushing me out of the way of that flame. But you still didn't answer my question."

Jackson turned his bright smile on her, and her stomach jumped again. It was harder to ignore this time.

"You're welcome . . . no, I guess I didn't."

Ayanna waited, but Jackson did not go on. She could press him, but that did not seem like it would get her far. Besides, she had way too many other, more important things to worry about than a handsome stranger's weird game of dragon chicken.

Ayanna sighed and leaned back against her seat. With any luck, she could get right back to those things as soon as the sun came up.

CHAPTER 10

Ayanna woke with a start. She lifted her head from the hard table where it rested and looked around. Light from the sun shone through the windows and reflected off the shattered glass on the floor. A moan escaped her lips as she straightened her back against her chair. Her shoulder hurt like crazy. She remembered that she had landed hard on it when she hit the ground the night before, not to mention the blows she had taken when the dragon dropped her from the sky.

She raised her hand to massage her shoulder, kneading her thin fingers into the muscle, but it did not help. Aching riddled her body, and nothing short of some warm compresses would make a difference. *That's probably a long way off*, she thought. *This discomfort is likely just the start of the day's punishments.*

Ayanna stood up and walked toward the open window frame. Her boots crunched over the glass and chunks of fallen plaster that matted into the still wet and blackened carpet. At least she had lived long enough to see the sun come up. She could not complain about that.

She shifted her eyes to find her companion. She had not forgotten about Jackson, not even for a second. He was both the one who had almost gotten her killed and the one who had saved her life in a weird how-in-the-world-did-that-happen sort of way.

He sat in a corner near the front window with his eyes closed and his head resting on the wall, right where she had last seen him. She felt like adding another check to the plus side of things in her book. She had survived dragons and a random wanderer. All that was left was to not die of heatstroke before she made it back to Terra. Still, it was hard to not feel defeated. She had been so close to the digitalis. When would she get another opportunity like that again? And how long could Dr. Keaton hang on without it?

Ayanna paused to watch Jackson sleep. His chest rose and fell, and he looked different in the light. It was strange. Last night, he had seemed indestructible, but now, he looked almost vulnerable. Maybe it was the sun that made the difference. The light accentuated the shape of his features. He had a strong, chiseled jaw that took on a square shape, and his face was smooth, giving him a youthful look. *Stunning. That's a good word to describe him*, she thought. But stunning or not, he looked worn out, just like everyone else she knew. No one could have survived this long without signs of suffering on their face.

Ayanna knew she should stop staring. Not only was it rude, but she didn't have time for it. Still, she let her eyes scan Jackson's body, taking in the details. His wide shoulders extended to well-defined arms, and Ayanna squinted to make out the shape of the tattoo that decorated his left arm. His black T-shirt covered most of it. But she recognized the symbol from one of the history books she had read at Sacred Heart. It was a taijitu symbol representing the concept of yin and yang.

She wondered why Jackson had chosen it. Maybe she would ask him. She nodded, pleased at the thought of having something to talk to him about, but then she stopped. *Wait*, Ayanna huffed, scolding herself. . . . Jackson's tattoo had not seemed important to her last night. And it was not important now. She needed to get back to Terra. She shook her head, annoyed with how she had let his beauty distract her. Still, should she invite him to come back with her? Would it be safe to do that? She needed to decide—quickly.

Unexpectedly, Jackson opened his eyes. Ayanna shuffled her feet. *Dammit.* He had caught her staring at him. She cleared her throat and looked away.

"I didn't mean to sleep this long," he said, looking at Ayanna with what appeared to be a satisfied smirk.

"Neither did I. People will be looking for me. I need to get back," Ayanna said. She glanced out the window frame again to see if it was safe to leave.

"The dragons should be gone now," said Jackson, standing up. He stretched his arms to the sky, and Ayanna forced herself not to admire the way his shirt tightened itself onto his sculpted torso. "They don't really like the sunlight," he added as he took a step. He grunted and reached for his leg.

Ayanna squinted. "Are you hurt?" she asked.

Jackson tried to take another step and stumbled backward into his chair.

She moved toward him. "Let me see," Ayanna offered.

"It's nothing," he said. He lifted his hands into the air to resist her attempt to investigate. "Just a cut. Nothing I can't handle."

"You might think differently if it gets infected," Ayanna said sharply, edging closer to him. "Come on, let me see." She kneeled, and he winced as she took his right leg in her hands. She then rolled up his jeans, revealing a layer of dried blood that stained his skin. A long cut sliced down his shin, leaving a deep wound.

"Nothing, really? And how long were you going to walk around with an open wound?" Ayanna asked. "Or maybe I should ask, how long did you think you would?"

"You're one to talk," said Jackson. He gestured toward the fresh scratches that littered her arms and hands.

"They're not deep," she said dismissively.

Jackson sighed and sat still as Ayanna examined him. "I don't see any glass in there. That's good, but I need to clean it."

Ayanna rose from the floor and walked across the room, searching for her bag. When she found it, she pulled out another bundle of cloth. She unwrapped it to reveal a small plastic bottle.

"What's that?"

"Grain alcohol. It'll kill the bacteria or give you a buzz, depending on your preference. Now hold still; this is going to hurt a little bit." Ayanna poured half of the bottle over Jackson's cut, and he winced again.

"That hurts!" he shouted.

"I'm sorry," she said meeting his eyes. Jackson held her gaze and nodded his head. Was that an acceptance of her apology?

Ayanna pulled some white gauze from her bag and wrapped it around his cut three times, tying it off at the ends. "Truth is you probably need stitches, but I don't have any thread with me."

"You're pretty good at that," Jackson said leaning forward. "What are you, some kind of nurse?"

"You're welcome," Ayanna said, pushing up from the ground and backing away from him. For some reason, Jackson's question bothered her. Was she some kind of nurse? Or some kind of doctor? Or some kind of phony? She moved to her bag and started to organize her things for her trip back home.

"Something like that. I work in the infirmary at Terra. I study whatever medical books I can get my hands on. There might even be a few here I can take back with me," she noted. "Everything else, Dr. Keaton teaches me."

"I didn't mean nothing by that," Jackson said. He used the chair to prop himself up and walked toward her with a slight limp. Ayanna wasn't sure what he was about to do, but she didn't back away.

Should she? She didn't know anymore.

Jackson placed his hand on Ayanna's shoulder. "Thank you," he said, sounding apologetic. "I meant what I said—you're good at it."

"Thanks," she said, before moving away from him. That was enough of that. Jackson's touch was too warm, too familiar. The last thing she needed was to fall into another one of his embraces. "And I'm not offended, it's just . . . never mind."

"What?" Jackson asked.

She had said too much, but she wasn't finished. Her words sat impatiently in the back of her throat. She wanted to tell him everything. She wanted to talk to him about why she was on the surface, about how she feared what would happen when she returned home, about how she feared what her failure would mean in the long run. Why? Why did she want to tell him any of this? She didn't know him. But maybe that was the reason. He was a stranger. He wouldn't judge her. He couldn't expect anything from her. To Jackson, she was a blank slate with no baggage at all.

Ayanna shook her head and zipped up her bag.

"You should probably come back to Terra and let Dr. Keaton monitor you, just in case," she said. The words slipped from her mouth before she had time to stop them. Even though it didn't make sense, she hoped he would accept her offer and return with her.

"Naw, thanks, but I think I'll be moving on," he said.

"Oh?" Ayanna tried to hide the disappointment in her voice. "Where will you go?"

"I told you, I'm headed out West. Texas maybe," said Jackson. "There's nothing here for me. For a while, I thought I might run into someone, but that ain't likely now."

"Someone?" Ayanna asked. "Like who?"

Jackson's eyes fell to the ground. He seemed pensive. "I was told I might run into someone my mom used to know around Tropeck, but with the way it looks out there, I doubt they could've survived. Plus, like I said, I hear there are fewer dragons out West, something about the weather, not enough water or something like that. I don't know, but the way I figure it, it's got to be better than hanging around here," he said.

"Your mom's friend? But last night you said—"

"She died a long while back," Jackson interrupted. There was an edge to his voice. It sounded even stronger than what she had heard the previous night, when they'd talked about life before the war. "Foster care came after that . . . and then, well, you know," he said, jutting his head toward the window.

"I see," she said. "My mom died too . . . I mean, before . . . cancer."

Ayanna's voice trailed off. Jackson stared at her, his sad, pale eyes watching her with an intense focus. She knew exactly how Jackson felt, but the only thing worse than swapping dead mom stories was talking about deaths that happened a long time before the war.

She wanted nothing more than to drop the subject. "Aren't you afraid you'll run out of water or food before you get out there?" she asked. She was curious about Jackson's trip. Maybe there was a reason to hope that things were different farther out. Jackson's plan to go to Texas was not all that far-fetched. A lot of people thought there was a better chance of survival out West, but no one at Terra knew what the conditions looked like beyond the borders of Tropeck, and neither the Watchers nor the militia wanted to risk lives to find out.

Jackson shrugged. "I'll take my chances," he said.

Ayanna nodded, but she did not understand. It seemed like a

pretty big gamble. "I used to have dreams of going out West when I was little," she said. "I wanted to be a cowgirl. Ride horses and live on a ranch."

Jackson smiled at Ayanna's story. "Oh yeah?"

"Yeah. I used to read books about the pioneers and the Plains Indians and about the buffalo soldiers who moved out West after the Civil War. I'd sit for hours and imagine riding a horse and having a ranch." Ayanna smiled at the memory for a second before letting it fade.

"But that's just a dream. No Wild West adventure to set out on anymore.

But sometimes . . . sometimes, you know, I can still see what it would be like. Still imagine a place where you can feel the sun on your face without fear."

Jackson was standing by Ayanna again. She had not noticed that he'd moved.

"So, why don't you go?"

Ayanna scoffed. "It's not that easy."

"Why not?"

She shook her head at the thought. "People are counting on me. Counting on me to take over for Dr. Keaton when . . . in case . . . people just expect me to be there to treat them when they get sick," Ayanna said.

"And that's what you want? To help sick people at your— what's it called? Terra?" he asked.

Ayanna paused. She took a deep breath and allowed her eyes to fall back to her bag. "Sometimes. Sometimes not," she said. "I mean, I like the science. The books, learning about medicine. It's just . . ."

"What?" asked Jackson. He followed her with his eyes. Ayanna met Jackson's eyes as they danced from green to brown in the light. Why did he care? Maybe he felt the same way about her as she did about him. Maybe the fact that she was a stranger made talking about everything that was going on seem easier. She didn't know, but he seemed interested in her thoughts. She could go on. She could tell him.

"It's just that sometimes, I feel like getting away from everything and having to take care of everyone," she confessed. "I don't want it to be my fault if things . . . if things don't go well."

Jackson nodded. She wondered why. Did he understand, or was he just trying to be sympathetic? She had so many questions when it came to this boy, but no time to think them over.

Ayanna brushed her hair out of her face. Her blue hair tie was all but useless at this point. The movement of her hand made her think of Maya. She needed to get back home. "Why did I just tell you all that? I don't even know you," she blurted out. Jackson's presence affected her and that irked her. She shook her head. It was time to go.

"Maybe that's the point," said Jackson. His voice was gentle, and she could hear the compassion in it. The sound made Ayanna relax a little.

"Yeah, maybe. Well . . . I've gotta get out of here. I'm sure someone has asked about me by now. I wasn't supposed to leave."

"Supposed to?" Jackson asked.

"Yeah, it's against the rules to leave Terra without permission."

Jackson raised an eyebrow like he wanted to ask a question, but instead, he tilted his head upward. She took that to mean he had heard her.

She opened the front door of the bookstore and stepped out onto the pavement. She should have kept going, but her desire to spend more time with Jackson made her pause. What did she want? He had already turned down her offer to come back with her.

But as she looked back at Jackson, she understood. She wanted him to stop her. She wanted him to tell her that he had changed his mind and would follow her back to Terra.

She stared at him for a long moment. He looked back at her and gave no sign that his plans had changed. But why would she have expected them to? She was the only one going around trusting strangers.

"Good-bye, Ayanna," he said. Ayanna took in Jackson's face. It looked serene, resolved.

She swallowed her disappointment. She felt like there was more she wanted to say. There seemed to be more to learn from him, more to learn about him. But she had to go home.

"Good-bye, Jackson," she said softly.

CHAPTER 11

Ayanna walked away from the bookstore, her mind twisting into knots. Everything was wrong. Yesterday had been nothing short of a disaster. As much as she wanted to return to the river, she knew she couldn't. Maya would be panicked. Dr. Keaton would have noticed her absence by now. Not to mention the aching in her body made it impossible.

She had not gotten a single thing that she had come for, except for the knowledge that there was foxglove growing on the banks of the Savannah River—and she hadn't a clue how to get to it without getting herself killed. And most disturbing to her list of worries was the fact that Jackson's face continued to flash into her mind. She remembered his sad, beautiful eyes and strong arms. An involuntary smile crept onto her lips.

Ayanna would never see him again. She was sure. And that made her sad. Wait. No. Why was she thinking of this reckless stranger? He had almost cost her her life. She should forget that she had ever met him.

She blew out a breath and tried to focus on her journey. She would be back home soon. She had found some aspirin. That was always useful. She could not wait to show Dr. Keaton. Ayanna also wanted to tell Maya about her night, although Maya would be more than a little upset with her.

Poor Maya. There was no telling if she had gotten any sleep at all worrying about Ayanna. But she had not meant to make her worry. Still, she needed to do better by her friend.

Ayanna passed through the five-mile-long sea of cars without incident. She was low on water, but she would be home soon. The slope started to incline. Terra was just over the hill.

The sun started to heat the surface as it always did, and Ayanna looked at her watch. Nine o'clock. She made her way down the hill and walked to the south entrance and the secret passageway she had taken to leave. Comfort washed over her. Overgrown branches hid a steel door covering the entrance into the city's subway system. Ayanna pulled the brush away from the hidden door and took two more steps.

"Grace, what are you doing out here?"

Ayanna stood still as an electric shock ran through her. Every nerve in her body stood on edge. She would recognize that deep, rhythmic voice in a crowd of dozens, soothing and harsh in the same breath. Richard. The very idea of him flooded her with too many emotions to process: hurt, anger, comfort, sadness, affection, regret.

Her father was dead. But had it really been Richard's fault? This was the question that had looped in her mind for over a year. She had blamed him, scorned him, yelled at him, cursed him. But she also remembered she needed to add shame to the list of emotions that Richard stirred in her.

Ayanna steeled herself as he repeated her name, this time a bit louder. This was just what she had dreaded, for him to be the one to find her on the surface. Of course he was. Had she been naïve enough to expect something different?

Immediately, she thought of Maya again. Had he gone asking her where her friend was? Had Maya gotten in trouble with the council? Ayanna had promised Maya that wouldn't happen. But maybe she had overestimated what she knew about Richard.

Ayanna took in a breath. She let her shoulders rise and fall before she turned and faced him. Her hand shot up to block out the sun that almost blinded her.

"Captain . . ." she said. Richard stood tall. He towered above everything around him, dwarfing Ayanna with his height. He held his back rigid, and every muscle in his body seemed to tighten.

He looked as if he were prepared to kill a dragon at a moment's notice. She did not doubt that he could. After all, he was the only person Ayanna knew who had managed to pull off that task without artillery. It was a feat that everyone knew of, but one that Richard refused to talk about. Ayanna had often wondered why he didn't like to bring up the dragon's nest he had destroyed at Hamer Swamp. She understood why he would not want to talk to *her* about it, because, well, they didn't talk as friends. Not anymore. But she thought it was strange that he refused to talk to anyone else about it either.

That victory in the first few months of the war is what had earned Richard the title of captain. And it was what had kept Richard's name on everyone's tongue: Tropeck's very own, fighting on the front lines to defend the nation from its worst fears. Anyone else would have been thrilled to have a reputation like that. But not Richard. Admittedly, it was something she wondered about.

Ayanna stepped forward and positioned herself a few inches in front of the captain. Her head rested over half a foot below his. She looked up. Richard reminded her of an Olympic athlete, his strong body sculpted to perfection. His height, combined with the breadth of his shoulders, made him appear intimidating to anyone who had a reason to fear him. But this was not the case for her. There was no circumstance, real or imaginary, where Richard would hurt Ayanna.

She stood so close to him that they were almost touching. If this had been three years ago, before the wormhole had let in the dragons and before Richard had gone off to fight them in the war, she would have been thrilled to be this close to him. And she was certain she would have reached up and hugged him on sight. But that seemed like forever ago.

They never shared the same space anymore. And they never, ever touched. It was one of the many unspoken rules that Ayanna had made up, and Richard had silently agreed to. Touch was just something else that had died between them along with her father.

Richard squared his wide shoulders with hers as he looked at her sternly. His clean-shaven skin—rich and brown, the color of the earth—contrasted perfectly against his gray fatigues, and Ayanna unwittingly thought that she couldn't remember a time when she hadn't found him impossibly handsome. His jaw formed a hard edge, and his full lips rested in a straight line. The expression hid the youth of his nineteen years, and it seemed as though he had forgotten how to feel any emotion that did not resemble pain. He probably had.

She met his dark eyes, and he gave her an intense look that mimicked everything else about him, but his gaze toward her was always strangely warm—even in moments like this, when he likely intended it to be cold. Ayanna's emotions stirred in her again. Hurt, anger, comfort, sadness, affection, regret. They were all there.

She had so much to say to Richard, and yet nothing at all. They stared at each other for several seconds without speaking, until Ayanna looked away. Experience had taught her that

Richard's eyes could pierce through her and touch her still bleeding wounds, even if she tried her best to cover them.

He shifted his body. Did he feel it too? The weight of being this close to one another when there was so much left unresolved between them?

"I didn't expect to see you here," she finally said, breaking the silence.

Richard blinked. "And what exactly are you doing here?" he asked. He sounded confused, but unsure if he should be alarmed just yet. That was a good sign. That meant he had not been out looking for her. But it was also a bit surprising. How had Richard gone a full night without knowing she had left Terra and not returned?

"Maybe she came to try to get water from the pump?" said a shaky voice from behind Richard.

Ayanna looked past the captain and saw that Malik stood with his weapon held firmly in his hand. He had been dispersed in a small unit of the militia that consisted of five men, two women, and two boys, of which he was one. Some of them held solar panels, copper wire, and scrap metal. Terra's engineers would be happy about that. Of course. This was a scouting day, Ayanna remembered.

Malik was one of the newest members of the Protectorate. He had been excited to be assigned to Richard's team. Ayanna admired how hard he worked to fit in. But Malik's age of fourteen showed as he mingled into the mix-match band of more disciplined, older, and stronger soldiers who had been fighting dragons since the start of the war. His scrawny arms barely fit into his borrowed military uniform, but Ayanna knew better than to think that Malik would ever let such a minor detail deter his efforts.

She gave Malik a small smile as a thank-you for trying to defend her presence on the surface. But there was no need to get him involved. This was between Richard and her.

Ayanna took in another breath. How was she going to get out of this situation? She could lie. She was just outside their gates. She could make up a story as to why she needed to come to the surface. Malik's suggestion about the water pump did not sound half bad. And there surely was no need to mention her little trek to the river.

Richard scanned her body with a hard stare. "And why are you injured?" he asked pointedly.

He had seen the scratches on her arms and hands. She had forgotten to try to hide them. So much for making up a story.

It was probably for the best anyway. Lying would have been the easiest thing to do and maybe the fastest, but there was a risk involved with lying to Terra's militia leader, despite the fact that he was Richard. Or maybe because he was Richard.

It was not so much that Ayanna had to answer to Richard. She didn't. But she did have to answer to the council, and there was no way that Richard would go against the council. She doubted if he would even know where to start. He was the most disciplined person Ayanna had ever met. Lying would only make everything harder on her when he inevitably brought her before the Watchers.

"Captain, I . . ."

Richard's brow furrowed, and he still looked confused. He lingered over the scrapes that littered her skin before lifting his head to scan the area around them. His hand motioned for the gun he wore on his hip, and he seemed to be looking for what or who had caused her wounds.

Ayanna frowned. The truth would be her best bet. "I came to the surface without permission. I'm just returning to camp. I know my actions put everyone at risk, and I'm prepared to face whatever punishment the Watchers have for me. I do have a good reason though," she added for good measure.

Ayanna had foreseen what would happen next: Richard's eyes widened, the muscles in his face contracted, and he was quiet for several seconds.

"Ramirez?" Richard said, turning his head back to his unit.

"Yes, sir," answered Ramirez. Ayanna glanced over at Richard's second-in-command. He was almost as tall as Richard. He looked nearly as strong too. His steely gray eyes moved with sharp, quick scans, as if he could digest an entire landscape in a matter of seconds.

"Radio down to the Watchers and tell them we're coming back early," said Richard. His voice was cold, detached.

Richard met Ayanna's eyes again. She matched his look, refusing to glance away this time. Ayanna wondered what thoughts were rolling around in his head, but there was no chance he would tell her.

"Please come with me, Grace," he said in a cool, calm voice.

Ayanna nodded. She was in no position to argue. "Sure, Captain," she said. Nothing else had gone her way. What was one more thing?

CHAPTER 12

Ayanna ducked her head under the large, metal-framed sign that marked the entrance to the Clear Areas Metro Center.

She pulled a small flashlight from her bag and held it against the darkness, being careful to watch her step as she moved down short concrete stairs that led to the foyer. The foyer of the station had taken a beating during the war, and mainly broken, gray tiles covered the floor. A few lone white letters showed from the barely visible signs covered with a thick layer of soot, ash, and dirt. Ayanna lifted her head long enough to look up at the abstract art murals that plastered the cracked and faded walls. The paintings had been completed by the city's youth years before as a gesture to promote urban development and engage the community.

Ayanna remembered that her mother had found the city's efforts halfhearted at best and patronizing at worst. At least, that was how she had described it. What the youth needed from the city was a safe place to gather and activities to do, her mother had noted. She had felt strongly about the matter.

Ayanna and her parents had lived outside of the city in the suburbs, and most of her after-school activities came in the form of Sam and Sally Club meetings. Ayanna was on the fence about hanging out with the kids in that group. They were well-off, like her, and the organization had a legacy as far back as Emancipation, but she found some of the members to be rather vapid, if not completely shallow. What Ayanna liked much better were the Science and Math League competitions that filled most of her weekends. Both she and Maya were on Sacred Heart's team, and they had led the group to more than one trophy.

Mrs. Sanders, Maya and Malik's grandmother, always had a lot to say about Tropeck's youth, though—even more than Ayanna's mother. She worried herself sick because Malik had so few options for after-school activities in the city, even though the small family lived right in the heart of Tropeck. Unlike Maya, he did not have a scholarship to attend Sacred Heart.

Mrs. Sanders lived in Terra with her grandchildren, and she had tried to steer Malik away from joining the Protectorate. She had hoped he would take up with the agriculturalists and learn to grow crops, but Malik would not hear of it. He had been adamant about becoming a militiaman, and now that he was old enough to join, Ayanna imagined that Mrs. Sanders was anxiously waiting for his return underground.

Ayanna took another step. From this level, two sets of escalators stood motionless. Three-foot slabs of concrete surrounded the structure on all sides, and the hard metal stairs descended one hundred feet underground.

She held up her flashlight and started her slow descent. Richard's unit walked ahead of her, but Richard trailed behind. His pace was measured, and he remained silent. Maybe she should talk to him? Try to figure out what he was thinking?

Ayanna heard the crackle of an intercom, followed by a voice speaking words she could not make out.

"That's affirmative, we're coming back now," one of Richard's men answered.

The dark, slow descent by escalator led to the first of the

sublevels. The last step from the bottom of the escalators entered a pathway that opened into an enormous train terminal. The terminal occupied a giant space that thousands of commuters used to pass through daily, guided by blue signs with white lettering that told them where to go: *Train Platform Straight Ahead. Metrorail Downstairs.* Large, broken ticket dispensers lined the walls, and turnstiles blocked the passageway. Next to the turnstiles, operator booths acted as guard posts, and video cameras surveyed the length of the room, while motion detectors scanned the area. Terra had gotten most of its equipment from abandoned military tanks and armored vehicles left behind after the war.

It was thirty-five feet from the bottom of the first escalators to the checkpoint before entering Terra—Ayanna had measured it before. When Ayanna and the militia arrived at the checkpoint, Josiah Audrey shot up but relaxed when he recognized their figures.

Josiah was fifteen. He had short, brown hair, dark brown skin, and innocent eyes. It was his first year in the militia, and he proudly wore a tattered gray uniform, where patches repaired the pants and the jacket was missing two buttons.

He caught Ayanna's eye and gave her a curious look. She shook her head at him and continued. He didn't want to know. Ayanna's stomach churned. The three days in isolation she had served during her last punishment had made an impression on her. She would not want anyone else to face that.

Past the turnstiles, a short set of escalators descended to a lower sublevel and followed a hallway to the remnants of a large gallery. Shops and tourist kiosks filled the space, and empty stores sported barren shelves and missing storefront windows. Beyond the kiosks, toward the rear of the gallery, rows of tables and chairs covered the floor of a cafeteria. A set of large double doors rested at the edge of the cafeteria, leading to the train tracks.

The group turned right and headed through the doors. This part of the station contained a platform, on either side of which lay train tracks that carved their way throughout. Electric-powered tracks covered the floor of the tunnels, and sheath-covered wires lined the walls of the subway routes. Square lights illuminated the walls of the tunnels, and water flowed through buried pipes. The tunnels went on for miles in four directions, covering the distance of the entire city. Several doors within the tunnels led to hidden storage closets, control rooms, and access shafts to other parts of the underground system.

They stopped in front of the Watchers' chamber. Ayanna took in a deep breath. She was not looking forward to this. She imagined that right now the council was sitting in the former operations room trying to decide what was next to address on the daily list of issues Terra faced.

It occurred to her that it might be a good time to tell them that Dr. Keaton was fatally ill and they should consider coming up with a plan to deal with that. Had he even made it through the night? What if he hadn't? She didn't know what she would do then.

But Ayanna went cold. Dr. Keaton still seemed to be in denial—and what if the Watchers' plan consisted of just telling her to more quickly prepare for the inevitable?

Nope. That was not going to happen. She was better off keeping this information to herself for now. At least until she figured out a way to treat Dr. Keaton's heart.

Ayanna watched as Richard's unit dispersed all at once, leaving her alone with Richard in the hallway. Malik leaned in close to her ear and said, "I hope they go easy on you."

"Thanks, Malik," she said. He gave her a limp wave as he dashed back to his station.

The door to the chamber opened, and a young woman came

out. Several names bounced around in Ayanna's mind, but she couldn't remember the one that belonged to the girl. Sasha, Sequoia, Sarah maybe? Ayanna knew she was an electrician, like Maya, but she couldn't place her name.

The girl smiled when she saw Richard. "It'll be a few minutes, Captain," she said. She ignored Ayanna. Richard nodded and the girl whose name began with "S" turned back into the room. She seemed disappointed at Richard's lack of response, and Ayanna fought back a smirk. Something like that shouldn't have given her so much satisfaction, but it did.

Ayanna stood with her back pressed against the wall and contemplated her fate, her arms crossed in front of her body. She did not look forward to the manual labor, ration deprivation, solitary confinement, or banishment that waited for her on the other side of that door. Ayanna cringed at the thought.

No, she was pretty sure that the Watchers wouldn't banish her from Terra. Sure, she had broken a serious rule, but no one had been hurt because of her, and they still needed a medic. Didn't they?

They could replace her as Dr. Keaton's assistant, she guessed, but that didn't seem likely either. Frankly, few others were up to the task. Of the 120 people at Terra, Ayanna was one of the few available to study medicine. People were generally too old, too young, or too busy for the assignment. With all the problems of keeping the lights on, recycling the air, and growing the food, the engineers and electricians were stretched thin as it was. The council greedily recruited the girls and an occasional boy for the task. The militia monopolized most of the boys, and the teachers and agriculturalists swallowed up the rest.

No, Ayanna doubted that they would send her away so easily. *And what would Richard think if the idea of banishment came up?* she wondered. Would he go along with the council on that issue?

If Ayanna got to choose her punishment, she would pick ration deprivation. She was used to living on an almost empty stomach, and she had enough sorghum bars stored away to make it through a few days.

She snuck a glance at Richard. He was deep in thought. What about? It was impossible to guess. What did he think about her being on the surface? And how long could he keep his opinion inside?

Ayanna examined him closer. He looked exhausted, a consequence of fighting for so long, she imagined. But this seemed different somehow. Worse. He was unquestionably as handsome as he had always been, but his otherwise even, dark skin gave way to circles beneath his eyes.

"I could give you something to help you sleep," Ayanna proffered. Richard blinked. He seemed startled that she had knocked him out of his near trance. He turned and moved slowly toward her. He met her eyes and took in a long breath, releasing it quickly.

Ayanna waited for him to answer her. Abruptly, Richard reached his hand toward her. "May I?" he asked.

She nodded without moving her body. What was he doing? The motion seemed unlike him. But she could not think of any reason to protest it. They used to touch all the time, she remembered. Ayanna had known Richard since she was twelve and he was fourteen. They had been neighbors and friends—best friends, she might once have said.

Since Richard was two years older than Ayanna and tall as a basketball player, no one in their neighborhood had ever known what to make of their friendship. Some assumed that Richard was Ayanna's older brother. Others thought he was her boyfriend. She had never cared to correct them and explain that neither was true.

That was when things had been easy, and touching had come naturally to them. Everything had been simple, light, playful. It had been a handhold here, a hug there. Whenever they hugged, Richard had always held Ayanna so closely that he lifted her feet off the ground. It was like a little game between them that Ayanna had found thrilling.

She shifted her weight as a pang of longing shot through her stomach. In that moment, she wished she hadn't told Richard it was his fault her father was dead. She wished she hadn't told him she hated him; she didn't, really. And how different would things be between them now if she hadn't told him never to touch her again?

Richard pulled the knife that rested on her hip from its sheath. She watched carefully as he held it flat in his palm. She felt her lower lip drop into a curious pout.

"Captain?" Ayanna asked quietly.

Richard gripped the knife and brought the blade closer to his face. "It's dull," he said. "You didn't sharpen it before you left?"

Ayanna couldn't tell what emotion his voice held. "No, I was in a bit of a hurry," she said.

"But the weight's good," he went on.

Ayanna felt her eyebrows raise. What was he getting at?

"You saw some action," he said as he lifted his uniform jacket and wiped the deep red dragon blood from the blade.

"Nothing I couldn't handle."

Richard's eyes found Ayanna's battered arms and hands as his lips folded into a frown. Slowly, he placed the knife back into its sheath. His hand was careful not to touch her. He always remembered their understanding, even when Ayanna forgot.

Richard turned away from her and crossed his arms in front of himself. "No, thank you. I've managed to sleep just fine," he said.

He seemed morose. Ayanna gaped. She had forgotten her original question, and now she remembered just how easily Richard's obstinance could annoy her. She sighed. She didn't know why he had gone on about her knife, but she didn't have time to figure him out right now. She had too many other things to worry about.

Still, it bothered her that she didn't know what he was thinking. It bothered her that Richard kept so much to himself . . . kept so much *from her*, she admitted in the back of her mind.

"Captain, I really do have a good reason for being on the surface last night. Maybe you don't have to take me before the council. I'm not exactly on their good side."

Richard raised his eyebrows, showing the first sign of feeling she had seen from him all morning. This was a long shot. She doubted she could persuade him to break protocol. He seemed to live and breathe order, and according to his influence on Malik, he believed in order because for Terra, order meant safety.

"You see . . . well, Dr. Keaton, he . . ." Ayanna took in a slow breath. Richard waited.

Just then, she heard the door open. It was the electrician again. "They are ready for you, Captain Daniels," the girl said. She smiled at Richard before walking down the hall. He did not notice.

Richard broke his concentration with Ayanna and turned toward the door.

"After you, Grace."

CHAPTER 13

Ayanna sighed and walked into the chamber. She needed a plan for what she was going to say and when she would say it. Was it better to blurt out everything—her trek to the river, the fact that a dragon attacked her, and Jackson? What should she tell the council about Jackson? *Nothing*! her mind screamed at her.

From the moment she had decided to leave, she knew that she might end up answering for her actions. There was nothing surprising about any of this, really. She just wished that she had something to show for it besides bruised ribs and ugly scratches that would probably take weeks to heal. She had found painkillers. That was something.

Ayanna inched farther into the room and blinked from the bright LED lights that gave off a slight buzzing sound. Everything was as she had remembered it. Rows of long desks were elevated on four platforms that resembled stadium seating and extended from the back wall. On the other side of the room, hanging on the wall, three large panels of electronic switchboards rested below three giant projection screens. Open space separated the two halves of the room, and three council members sat on the first level of the platform with two members each sitting on a row above the other. Large, Plexiglas windows surrounded the space, and file cabinets lined the room.

All nine of the Watchers sat there. This was not a good sign. She would not escape this situation unscathed.

Most people at Terra suspected, and resented, that the council met so often simply because they wanted to stand out from everyone else. Their habit reminded everyone that no one had elected the council. They had just been the ones to keep the people alive after the government failed to completely evacuate Tropeck. Everyone left behind had problems, and the Watchers had stepped up with answers. So just like that, they became Terra's leaders.

Ayanna hadn't minded so much. She thought that most of the council's decisions made sense. They had come up with a plan for generating and conserving electricity. They had organized the Protectorate, and they had given everyone a job in the compound so that the work was evenly divided up. Most importantly, in Ayanna's view anyway, they had kept the group together.

But not everyone at Terra agreed with this logic. She had heard rumblings. She knew that some people weren't at all happy with the council. The reasons seemed pretty clear to her. Within the first six months after the abandoned group fled underground, some people were calling for elections and others wanted a place on the council, but somehow, the elections never happened. Several people were still angry about that.

Ayanna moved forward and noticed that Richard stayed near the door. It was silly for her to have assumed he would remain by her side. Besides, how could she expect Richard's presence to comfort her when it made her anxious at the same time?

She shook her head. Later. Maybe she would think about that later.

Ayanna walked to the center of the room and stood with her hands pressed to her sides as she awaited her punishment. She held her head up and met the Watchers' faces. She knew them all well. She had memorized their disapproving looks. She could see the disappointment churning behind the soulful brown eyes of Mrs. Latasha Johnson, who sat in the middle of the table on the first level platform as the senior councilmember. Her expression indicated that she wasn't surprised to see Ayanna there. Of course not. How many times was this now? Three . . . four?

Mrs. Johnson took her leadership role seriously. She had enforced all of Ayanna's past punishments, and Ayanna knew she had a reason to be afraid. Still, how could she not respect someone so stern? It was a quality worth having, in her opinion: not taking anyone's crap just because that is what they offered up.

Ayanna studied the older woman for a few seconds and noted that she wore her dark hair pulled up into a formal bun. With her hair off her neck, Ayanna was able to notice the few strands of gray that scattered throughout. Was it just her age that had grayed her hair? Or was it the stress of her life? And her face used to be fuller, Ayanna thought, with plumper cheeks. But really, what *could* one expect surviving on sorghum and canned food the way they did? Ayanna's own weight had dwindled a bit over the year. Even now she could feel her stomach growling. She had not eaten anything since last night.

To the right of Mrs. Johnson sat Harold Christy. Mr. Christy had been an entrepreneur and a business tycoon. He knew the most about the city's transportation system because his iron ore company had invested millions of dollars in the creation of Tropeck's subway, and he had learned everything about "the mechanics of his investment," as he repeated on numerous occasions.

The other council members were Jacob Frye, Carol Morgan, Dolores Alvarez, Hector Sanchez, Nefertiti Abaka, Sharita Evans, and Colonel William Daniels.

Colonel Daniels was Richard's father. Richard got his height from him, although the older man's build was smaller than his son's. His dark brown complexion accented his hazel eyes, and he carried a full head of gray hair, cut to the scalp. He was handsome, like Richard. But unlike Richard, the colonel and Ayanna had never been close. In fact, she could barely tolerate him. She found him rude, arrogant, and lacking in anything resembling compassion. He wasn't going to make this easy for her, she was sure.

The primary teachers had made it a point to "educate" the children at Terra on the colonel's accomplishments. They went on about how he had been a highly decorated soldier in the military long before the Fire Sky War. He had lived all over the world and spoke four languages. He had worked as an analyst, and when he finished his tour, he returned to Tropeck to perform top-secret military work for the government. Colonel Daniels never smiled. He lacked any sense of humor, and he lauded his commitment to the army to anyone who would listen.

But Ayanna knew another side to the colonel. Colonel Daniels and Richard's mother, Ella, had married young and settled in Tropeck. At the beginning of their marriage, they were happy. But soon, Colonel Daniels started to spend most of his time away from home. From then on, Colonel Daniels only returned to Tropeck on occasion, and Richard and his mother spent most of their time alone. Ella, Colonel Daniels, and Richard all lived at Terra now, and there was a fragile truce between Ella and the colonel.

Ayanna remembered how hard the colonel's absence had been on Richard when they were younger. Richard had always been smart. He had a box filled with awards to prove it. He had been a member of the math team, and, like his father, had studied languages, but apparently Colonel Daniels's travels kept him from noticing any of his son's accomplishments.

Lately, though, the colonel had appeared very interested in

Richard. Ayanna wasn't sure exactly what had changed. She only knew that these days, the colonel hovered over his son, freely criticizing his decisions, even in front of others.

It was no surprise that Ayanna heard his voice first. "You again, Miss Grace? I'm starting to think that we should set up a separate council just to deal with your infractions," said Colonel Daniels. He turned his mouth into a deep frown.

"We are very disappointed Miss Grace," Mrs. Johnson chimed in with a sincere voice. "We expected that you, of all people, having such an important job here, would set a good example and follow the rules we have put in place for the safety of the group."

Ayanna jumped to her own defense. "Council, the safety of the group is exactly what I was thinking about when I decided to leave. I know I broke the rules by going to the surface without permission and by staying out past dark. And I realize that my actions could have placed Terra in danger and at risk of an attack. . . ." Ayanna paused. This was not coming out right. Whatever happened to that plan she was supposed to have come up with before she just started blathering? Ayanna took a breath and tried again.

"But in my heart, I believe that the health of all of us here and our survival is dependent on Terra's ability to protect ourselves against disease and to have the medications that we need," she said. It made for a halfway decent argument, at least.

"Nonetheless, your behavior was reckless and irresponsible. Do you not think, Miss Grace?" asked Colonel Daniels. Ayanna examined the colonel, who wore an immobile mask. He would be the toughest obstacle on the council to overcome. Should she even bother to answer?

She took a deep breath and let her words come out slowly. "Looking at it from the council's perspective, I can see how you might think that, but as I said, I acted for the good of the group."

"Really, Miss Grace? I did not realize that you were the one who should determine what would be best for all of us," retorted Colonel Daniels. "Why bother having a council at all if the great Ayanna Grace has all the answers? Like father, like daughter I guess."

Blood rushed to Ayanna's face, and she felt angry tears prickle at her eyes. Her feelings were torn between humiliation and fury. Ayanna swallowed the frustration that had built in her throat. This was not the time to argue, and she really wanted to earn leniency from the council. But Colonel Daniels's tone was even more biting than usual.

She heard Richard shift behind her. "Colonel, I don't think that's called for," Richard said. Ayanna blinked, surprised that he had defended her against his father's cruelty. She couldn't deny that he made her feel a little less alone.

Colonel Daniels gave his son a warning stare, and Ayanna took in a shallow breath. The colonel looked furious, but Richard glared back at his father. She wasn't sure what to make of their exchange. But the moment between the two men was interrupted when Mr. Frye spoke.

"What do you think would be a fitting punishment, Ayanna? A week transporting the sewage to the outer line? That seems fair," said Mr. Frye. He was a short, balding man with a calm demeanor. His tone was matter of fact.

Before Ayanna was able to respond, Mrs. Johnson interrupted. "I believe Miss Grace understands the seriousness of her actions and doesn't intend any further infractions. I move that we excuse Miss Grace's violation and get on to more urgent matters." She gave Mr. Frye a pointed look, and he nodded his head in agreement.

Wait. What was going on? Ayanna was not being punished? She must have missed something. And what was with that look from Mrs. Johnson? Nothing was adding up.

"Richard, thank you for handling this matter personally. We know how busy you are," said Mr. Christy.

"Do you have anything to add, Captain?" asked Mrs. Johnson.

Richard stepped forward and cleared his throat. Ayanna raised her eyebrows. She clenched her fists tighter, waiting for him to speak again. This was his chance to tell her and everyone else what he thought about finding her on the surface.

He turned his head. Ayanna could not read his expression. Of course she couldn't. He kept everything so well hidden. He met her eyes and stared. For several seconds he looked as if he did not recognize her. Richard seemed fascinated by something he saw in her face, but Ayanna had no idea what. She was confused and surprised when she saw his breath catch in his throat. The moment dragged on, and Ayanna realized that she desperately wanted him to break his gaze and speak. Richard made the tiniest movement with his head, like he was trying to clear it. What was he holding back? And more importantly, why?

When he looked away, Ayanna let out the breath she'd been holding. Richard looked back at the council, and she finally heard his voice. It was low and deep.

"No, I agree with Mrs. Johnson's motion. I'm sure Miss Grace understands how serious this all is," he said. Ayanna looked down and unclenched her fists. What was this? Did Richard not have any annoying words for her about how following the rules keeps everyone safe?

Her body ignored her brain as the corner of her mouth pulled up into a smile. For a second, Richard smiled back, but it faded at the sound of Mrs. Johnson's voice. He straightened his posture.

"Fine," said Mrs. Johnson. "Miss Grace, please understand that this council does not take your actions lightly. We will be paying close attention to you, but for now, there are other, more pressing issues that we need to discuss."

Some of the council members started to nod their heads. Ayanna tried to stand up taller, but the aching in her ribs made it difficult.

"Before I go on, I want to ask you about Marcus. How is he? I hope his fatigue has passed. We had planned to ask him to this briefing, but he reminded us that he had several patients to see today," she said.

Ayanna cleared her throat. "Dr. Keaton is . . ." She didn't know how she should answer this question. There were so many versions of the truth.

"Dr. Keaton is fine. He's working hard to keep Terra healthy," she finished. Her voice strained when she said this, and Richard looked over at her, but Mrs. Johnson didn't seem to notice. Mrs. Johnson nodded. Ayanna could see Richard continue to stare at her from the corner of her eye. Could he see through her reply? Probably. Out of everyone there, he would know there was more to her story than she was sharing. Ayanna looked away to avoid his eye.

"Good," said Mrs. Johnson. "Miss Grace, you have been asked to remain in this council meeting because we feel that Terra may be facing an emergency and we will require Dr. Keaton's and your assistance. We expect that you will provide Marcus with a full report but know this: nothing you hear in this room today is to be repeated to the general population until the time when this council deems it necessary. Do you understand?"

"I understand."

A clamoring noise made Ayanna turn around quickly. She wished she hadn't. Her abdomen ached with the movement as she saw the chamber door open. Malcolm Channing entered the room with a clipboard gripped to his chest, fumbling to find a spot by the door.

"Malcolm, I'm glad you're here. Please come in and tell us what you have to report," said Mr. Christy.

"Forgive me for being late," said Malcolm. Everyone in the room looked at Terra's lead engineer. "Unfortunately, I do not have good news." He pressed his glasses to his nose and brought the clipboard up to his face.

As Ayanna scanned the room, she noticed that Mr. Christy was sitting at the edge of his chair. Colonel Daniels had narrowed his eyes and was listening as if Malcolm were the most interesting person in the world, and Mrs. Johnson seemed to be holding her breath. Ayanna stared at Malcolm. He did not seem that interesting to her. He was nervous, certainly, but no more than any other time Ayanna had seen him. She leaned forward, wondering what everyone was worried about.

"My team and I have checked the reservoir levels again, and from my calculations, Terra's stored clean water is now at a thousand gallons," he said, "which means that we have about a week and a half of potable water remaining."

Ayanna heard Mr. Frye gasp slightly. She watched the faces of the council, trying to understand what they had just heard. Terra got its water from two sources: the rain and the river. Ayanna didn't understand what Malcolm was trying to tell the council. Surely, she was missing some vital piece of information.

"So, what are we saying here?" asked Mr. Frye.

"We're running out of water," said Malcolm.

"What do you mean?" Ayanna asked, interrupting Malcolm. "We live beneath a river."

Her tone shocked her. She didn't mean to sound so flippant, but she could feel the growing anxiety in the room, and she really wanted to figure out what was going on.

"It seems . . . well, you see . . . ," said Malcolm, "our access to the river water has been greatly reduced over the past month and a half."

"Reduced? How is that possible?" asked Mr. Frye.

"I don't know, but the underground pipes have stopped delivering water into our tanks. The flow of water has slowed exponentially. There have been ebbs in the flow of water before, but we usually were able to ignore them because the rainwater would make up for the difference," he said.

"So we will simply wait for it to rain. I mean, it obviously is going to rain," said Mr. Frye.

"Captain?" asked Mrs. Johnson. "How are the rain vats today?"

Richard spoke up. "The Protectorate checked the water bins when we were out, but unfortunately, they remain dry," he said.

"That's the fifteenth day this month," said Mr. Frye, in a small voice.

"Well, based on the wind patterns and the lack of rain, I think that it is possible that Tropeck may be experiencing another drought," said Malcolm.

"Another drought?" Ayanna asked, still trying to piece together the urgency that she heard in the council members' voices.

"Yes, they are more frequent during the summer months. We used to get them all the time before . . . but of course, we hardly noticed. That is to say, we had more options back then."

"OK, but I don't think we should start to panic," said Mr. Frye. "It is going to rain, and Malcolm has told us that we still have at least a week and a half of water remaining. It will surely rain within a week."

"Well, we all hope so but—" said Mrs. Johnson.

"Miss Grace," interrupted Mr. Christy. "You were asked to stay for this meeting because we want you to explain to the council exactly how much water a person needs to survive."

All the council members turned and stared at Ayanna. She scanned the room and felt a hard lump form in her throat. She knew the answer. Right? *Of course*, she thought. There was a long pause before she spoke.

"Well, that depends." Ayanna shifted her weight. "Children, sick people, pregnant women, and the elderly are more vulnerable than the rest of the population when it comes to the risk of dehydration. These groups will need to drink about a gallon of water every day," Ayanna said.

"And we have to remember Terra uses water for more than just basic hydration. We also use the water for cooking, cleaning, and maintaining sanitary conditions. If any one of these stops, it could hamper our ability to control disease from spreading in the population," she added.

"Yes, yes, but we need a hard number, Miss Grace. We need to know the minimal amount for each person to drink before he or she dies from dehydration," said Mr. Christy.

"An average person outside of one of the vulnerable groups would drink two liters of water per day," Ayanna said reluctantly. "But—"

"Thank you, Miss Grace. We may have to rely on this number if it doesn't rain soon."

"But, Council, like I said, I'm not sure that this amount is—"

"Miss Grace, may I remind you that you are not a member of this council," said Colonel Daniels. "We are at war for life. No water, no life. It is that simple."

Ayanna swallowed hard but spoke again. This was too important. "Of course, I understand. But there is just one other thing that I think the council should know."

Colonel Daniels seemed to forcibly hold in a sigh.

"When I was on the surface yesterday, I went to the Savannah...."

Richard's eyes darted toward her. His face was a mix of shock and anger. He would never take his unit that far from Terra's base. She ignored him.

"The Savannah River feeds our pipes," said Malcolm.

"Yes, we know," said Mrs. Johnson.

"When I was on the riverbank, I saw something weird about the water," Ayanna said. She paused and dared to look over at Richard. He narrowed his eyes and his face turned to stone, resembling his father's.

"Well, go on Miss Grace," said Mrs. Johnson.

"It seems as if the dragons have built some sort of mound in the river made of rocks and tree limbs. The structure was very large, and it might be what's blocking the water from flowing in its usual direction. I think this may be the cause of the shortfall in the pipes," she said.

"Miss Grace, are you suggesting that the dragons are making a dam?" said Mr. Frye.

"That's what it looked like."

"They couldn't possibly be that intelligent. Besides, why would they need a dam?"

"Well Mr. Frye, even beavers know how to build dams, and I'm sure that dragons are smarter than that. And as for the reason—"

Richard's voice overpowered hers. "Miss Grace is right, they certainly have the intelligence to build large structures," he said. "I wouldn't put it past them to organize something like this. With the council's permission, I would like to take a reconnaissance team to the river to view the structure."

"No," said Colonel Daniels. "We shouldn't lead forces on some wild goose chase based on what Miss Grace may or may not have seen."

Ayanna let her frustration travel from her head, through her body, and down to her legs, finally pressing into her feet and to the floor.

"Then, I will go alone," said Richard. Colonel Daniels looked at his son with a clenched jaw and then at Mrs. Johnson. His eyes burned into her, but she seemed to ignore him with a turn of her head.

"Malcolm, will a downpour solve our problem?" asked Mrs. Johnson.

"Yes, if it rains within a day or two, we should be able to replenish the supplies," he said.

Richard stepped closer to the council. "Council, I truly think that the more information we have, the better prepared we can be," he said. Mrs. Johnson gave Richard a smile. It was genuine, and it was clear that she did not want to argue with him.

"Captain, you know that Terra places our safety in your hands every day, but right now, there is no need to place you or the militia in danger. We will wait for the rain," she said.

"I'm inclined to agree," said Mr. Christy. "I don't think that we'll gain much from such a dangerous mission as going to where the dragons populate."

The muscles in Richard's neck tightened, and he looked like he wanted to say something else. Maybe he was ready to press them on this? But then his body relaxed. He had lost this argument, it seemed. "Yes, Council. I understand," he said.

Ayanna looked down. The ache in her body reminded her of why she had gone to the surface in the first place, and she was eager to return to the clinic. As if the council had heard her thoughts, Mr. Frye spoke up. "That will be all, Miss Grace. We trust that you will keep your vow about what we've discussed here today and tell only Dr. Keaton about this situation."

"I will," Ayanna promised. Then, from habit, she added, "To Terra."

"To Terra," the council responded in unison.

Ayanna picked up her tattered bag from the ground and started to walk out of the Watchers' chamber, passing Richard. She sensed that he had more questions. But he just watched her leave.

Ayanna pulled the door behind her. She started to move away but she could hear Mr. Christy go on. "Captain, we'll need to control the flow of information that Terra's population receives. . . ."

She slowed down. She wanted to eavesdrop. She shouldn't, but there was nothing wrong with moving slowly. Was there?

After a few seconds, Richard emerged from the chamber. His eyes wandered down the pathway toward her, and his lips parted. Of course, there was something he wanted to say. She knew it. He probably wanted to know more about her trip to the river. He might ask her how she had managed to sneak past the interior guards so easily and why she had risked such a dangerous expedition.

As his body began to shift in her direction, Ayanna cursed herself for lingering behind. She braced herself for yet another interrogation, but in a fluid motion, Richard stopped, turned, and continued back toward his unit. She took her opportunity to quickly head back to the safe confines of the clinic.

CHAPTER 14

Ayanna walked through a metal door into the railway tunnels toward the clinic. It was not far, maybe a hundred feet or so from the start of the corridor to her destination. She had made the trip so many times she knew the pathway by heart. The same two half-broken lights that she had left untouched hung on the wall above her, emitting an annoying buzz. Their chaotic flashing pattern made shadows dance across the walls.

Ayanna turned into the laboratory of the clinic to look for Dr. Keaton, but she didn't find him there. He must be on his rounds around Terra, checking on patients. Terra was lucky. There hadn't been any serious germ-born illnesses there, but the people had a lot of trouble with chronic illnesses like hypertension, gout, and asthma, as well as work-related injuries. Every week, it seemed like someone had gotten cut, burned, or injured in some way. Ayanna suspected this was because the power went out so frequently at Terra, causing accidents.

Ayanna wanted to talk to Dr. Keaton. She needed to check on his condition and warn him about the water problem the Watchers had found. But she didn't know where he was—plus, she knew Maya would be looking for her. There was just one thing she needed to do before she visited her.

Ayanna walked into the clinic. She put down her bag and headed to the sink to clean her wounds. Without warning, Jackson popped into her mind. She wondered where he was now, and if he were safe. His plan to head out West was not the worst one she had ever heard. What would that be like—to drop everything, leave Tropeck, and follow him out there?

Ayanna huffed. What a ridiculous idea! She shouldn't even entertain it. It was pointless and wouldn't get her anywhere. She had work to do. She wasn't going to spend another second thinking about that reckless stranger. Besides, she would never see him again, so there was no point.

Ayanna grabbed a bottle of alcohol from the wooden cabinet, took a cotton ball, and dabbed it onto her cuts. The slight sting made her wince.

Next, she plucked one of the lavender leaves from her garden and crumbled it, squeezing the plant's moisture onto her wounds. The task calmed her. She would go make amends to Maya and figure out the rest later. No more thoughts of Jackson, she decided.

Ayanna hurried through the tunnels toward the Sanderses' quarters. She turned the corner not a moment too soon because she saw Maya pacing in the hallway, wringing her hands in a pattern that she must have perfected from hours of practice. Ayanna felt guilty about Maya's worry. She had broken her promise.

Maya, who seemed to possess an uncanny sixth sense, spotted her immediately. It was a wonder she hadn't come to the lab earlier. A blur filled Ayanna's sight and the next thing she felt were Maya's arms wrapped tightly around her still-aching midsection. She could feel the air struggling to enter her lungs, but she didn't resist Maya's hug and instead held in a grimace. It was the least she deserved. After all, she was the one who had broken her promise to return yesterday and caused Maya so much worry.

Ayanna brought her right arm up and hugged Maya back. But then Maya pulled away suddenly, her relief visibly giving way to some other emotion that Ayanna hadn't figured out just yet. Maya let out a short, exasperated breath as she scanned Ayanna, her mouth forming a deep pout as she seemed to make the connection between the night before and the white bandages that now covered Ayanna's palms.

"You OK?" Ayanna asked. Maybe she could keep the attention away from herself for a few minutes.

Maya gaped. Obviously not.

"Me? I'm fine. I'm not the one traipsing off to the surface every five minutes," Maya scolded.

"I'm fine, Maya. See? Back in one piece," she said.

Maya shook her head. She linked her arm with Ayanna's and tugged gently, leading her into her family's shelled-out train car. Three cots occupied the small space, and a wooden box acted as a night table in the corner of the car. Three lit candles in the room provided enough light to maneuver, as the dim tunnel lamps did nothing to help.

"Thank goodness you're back, even though I had to hear it from Malik," she said.

"I know. I'm sorry I didn't come find you sooner. It's just that I had a few mishaps to tend to first," Ayanna said. It was a pathetic answer, but true.

"You can't imagine how worried I was about you," Maya said.

"About me?" Ayanna joked. "Come now, Maya. You know I can take care of myself."

"Take care of yourself or not, when you didn't come back last night, I didn't know what to think."

Ayanna frowned. The feeling of guilt crept back into her stomach. She really did feel bad for having frightened Maya.

"Everything is all right now, OK?" she said. Although Ayanna didn't know if everything was OK, what with everything she had learned in the Watchers' chamber.

Ayanna was about to ask if anything had happened while she was away when Maya and Malik's grandmother walked into the room. Mrs. Arletta Sanders was fifty-eight years old. She was short with rounded hips and a full bosom, the kind a toddler might comfortably rest her head on for a perfect day's nap, and she sported neatly organized two-strand twists that sculpted her face and accented her serious brown eyes.

She smiled at them both as she placed a book she was carrying onto the wooden box. "Hi, honey," she said to Maya. "Ayanna, I'm glad to see you. We missed you last night. You must've been working in your lab for hours. Couldn't you have snuck away for a few minutes to let us know that you were all right?" She went over to Maya's cot and waited for her to stand before scooping her up into a hug. After a long moment, she repeated the process with Ayanna and took a place on her own cot.

"I know. I was just apologizing to Maya for not coming by last night," Ayanna said.

"I just hope that you haven't been working on anything dangerous. I'm worried enough about Maya being around electricity all day and Malik keeping up with the militiamen. I worry about all of you so much," she said.

Maya frowned and bit her bottom lip.

"Everything's OK," Ayanna said. Ayanna knew where Maya got her disposition, but before Ayanna could find the right words to make both of them feel better, Malik rushed through the door.

"Hey, guys!" he greeted them excitedly.

"Malik—I'm so glad you're back, but I must admit that I

thought the militia would have you out there longer," said Mrs. Sanders, standing to hug her grandson.

Mrs. Sanders ran her hand over Malik's closely cut hair. He groaned and gently moved her hand, but he gave his grandmother a quick hug before walking over to sit next to Ayanna. He was smiling brightly, no doubt still beaming from the mission to the surface and his opportunity to travel with Richard.

"Yeah, I thought we'd be out there longer too. Everything was going fine, but the captain turned us back early," he said. "Looked like the Watchers called him back for something, but I'm not sure what."

He gave Ayanna a knowing look. Ayanna thanked Malik in her head and looked down, but she could feel Maya watching her. The three of them knew exactly why the Watchers had called Richard's team back early.

"Well, I, for one, am glad. I still think it's too soon for you to be traveling to the surface," replied Mrs. Sanders.

Malik's face sank. Mrs. Sanders had always kept a close watch on Malik, especially when he was a small boy. When he was little, he'd tried to imitate Maya. He spent most of his energy keeping track of her day-to-day activities and following her around, but when they moved underground, Maya became too busy studying as an apprentice to Taylor Weaver, Terra's chief electrician, to pay attention to her younger brother.

After a while, he'd turned his attention to trying to trail behind Ayanna. He knew she often ventured to the surface, despite the council's strict prohibition on the unauthorized activity, but Ayanna was too clever for Malik to catch her. She had always found secret passageways and tunnels to sneak through, leaving Malik behind with the children in the primary program.

But Malik had told his family and Ayanna many times that he didn't feel like he belonged with the other children. He had always said that he thought most kids his age lacked courage. He frequently went on about how the other children seemed to be happy hiding underground in fear forever, but he wanted to distinguish himself from the rest of the group, and he wished he'd been old enough to fight when the dragons first arrived. Ayanna did not have to guess why Malik thought this way. Only former members of the official military were Protectorate leaders, and she knew he wanted to be in charge one day.

Whenever Maya and Ayanna pressed him as to *why* he wanted this, he never came up with a good reason, in Ayanna's opinion. "I just think I'd be good at it," was the only thing that he would say.

"Come on, Grandma. Don't worry so much. This is what they train me for, remember?" Malik stared at Mrs. Sanders with wide eyes. He looked as if he hoped she would side with him on this, although he must have known she wouldn't.

"Right," said Mrs. Sanders. "Training . . . that's what you need more of. You're only fourteen, and you've only been training for three months. I hardly think it's time for you to be parading up to the surface with dragons skulking about. Tell him, My," she said, turning to Maya.

Maya tugged the end of one of her long braids that reached her shoulders. "It *has* only been three months, Malik. Maybe you should ask to be reassigned. You know, to the interior guard. I'm sure there are other boys . . . boys with more training who could take your place," she said.

Malik huffed. "I can't believe this. Betrayed by my own sister. Ayanna, you'll back me up, won't you?" He turned to Ayanna with wide, hopeful eyes. His naïvety struck her. He wore it like a badge, and given the way his deep brown eyes and innocent face were watching her, she wanted to assign him the same title of "cherub" that she had given Maya earlier.

She had almost been killed last night on the surface by a dragon's flame. The idea of little Malik Sanders facing one of those deadly monsters sent chills down her spine.

"We know how brave you are, Malik. That's all that really matters," she said, giving him a small smile.

Malik sighed. "I'm not sure what that means," he said, "but, I'll take it."

Ayanna shook her head. Nothing could discourage Malik, it seemed. She just hoped that he was right and the rest of them were wrong. Maybe he *was* ready to fight dragons.

"Goodness, I nearly forgot," said Maya. Her voice rose excitedly.

Ayanna's eyes tightened, unsure of what Maya was about to do, until she saw her friend reach for a small box that she readily recognized. The simple cardboard container was what Maya had been passing off as a cosmetics caddy for a year now. Ayanna wanted to groan as Maya pulled out a tiny bottle of Natural Elegance Essentials hair oil, a wide-toothed comb, and a brush with the hardest bristles she'd been able to get her hands on, but instead of groaning, Ayanna silently slunk from the cot and took her space on the floor in front of Maya's legs.

She sat quietly as Maya worked her hands through her hair: brush, part, braid, repeat. There was no need for a mirror. She was sure the finished product would be perfect, not to mention neat. So she let Maya complete her favorite pastime without complaining, listening as her friend babbled on about the alarm that she had missed last night and about Malik's ambition to lead the reconnaissance team. From time to time, Malik and Mrs. Sanders chimed in, too, and Ayanna relaxed. She was home, and in the moment, that was all that mattered.

CHAPTER **15**

Ayanna liked the morning calm. The new day provided hope. Everyone, perhaps naïvely, believed that the danger from the sky lessened with the rising of the sun.

Ayanna let out a wide yawn before pushing herself out of bed. She was up in time to make it to the showers before they got too crowded.

At the showers, Ayanna turned the faucet, and a spray of cold water fell from the sprinklers. The cold water soothed her bruises, and she was happy to have a chance to remove the layer of dirt that had collected on her skin. She grabbed a bar of soap, cleverly made by the agriculturalists from the plants in their gardens. It was less effective against bacteria than the soap that Ayanna remembered from before the infestation, and it did not smell as nice, but it worked to keep up hygiene.

Ayanna dressed quickly and ticked off the list of things she needed to do today in her head. She had to talk with Dr. Keaton, first about the possibility of a water shortage, and second about what they were planning to do about his heart. This would not be easy. She knew Dr. Keaton had trouble facing up to the fact that it was becoming increasingly difficult for him to complete his work.

Should she suggest that he ask the council for an additional assistant? Even though most people were very busy with other work, there might be an agriculturalist who could be spared.

Ayanna frowned. She knew that to even get to the point of asking the council for more help in the lab, Dr. Keaton would have to accept the truth about his health. Every time she had tried to broach the subject in the past, he always assured her that he would be fine. She didn't know if today's conversation would go any better.

Ayanna walked into the laboratory. She looked for Dr. Keaton, but he must already have started on his rounds. She made her way to the bookshelf and picked up one of her father's old composition notebooks. Opening it to the middle pages, Ayanna ran her index finger over her father's handwriting. His writing was neat with fully formed letters and nearly completely straight lines. She wished that seeing his words comforted her, but instead she felt conflicted. It was this work that had helped lead to so much destruction. And she had no way of knowing whether her father's words could help her figure out what she needed to know. Sure, there might be something in his writings that could explain how to get rid of the dragons, or at least explain more about how they were able to come through the wormhole. But in the back of her mind, she felt a sinking feeling of regret. *Why hadn't he thought through what might happen in his quest for discovery?* she wondered. *Why hadn't he thought to protect her?* Ayanna shook her head and pushed the thought away. It felt too much like blame. She didn't want to be like the others around her who blamed her father for everything that had happened. She didn't want to feel anything but love and understanding for him, and that meant trying to understand his work. She looked at the notebook's opened page:

As the general theory of relativity postulates, the three dimen-
sions of space and the one dimension of time can be fused into a
single four-dimensional continuum.
  The resultant wormhole creates a bridge.

Ayanna shook her head. She could only pretend to understand what these writings meant. She could tell that the words
wormhole and *bridge* were important. For months, the news had
aired stories about the bridge that had connected her universe
with another. She just didn't have a clue about what to do with
the rest of the writing.

She closed the notebook and sighed. Somebody else was
going to have to figure this out, preferably a scientist—a real one.

Ayanna turned on the small ultraviolet lamp that hovered
above the petite, rectangular, soil-filled box she called her garden.
Dr. Keaton had taught her everything he knew about horticul-
ture. She liked watching him with the garden because it was very
entertaining. He believed that the gardener had to love the plants
if he wanted them to grow, so he often hovered over them, speaking softly to them as if they were delicate babies.

He was a lot better at growing things than she, but Ayanna
had done her best. Her angelica archangelica was growing tall,
which was promising because she could never have too many
remedies for stomach problems. And the chamomile was almost
ready for harvest. Ayanna could hardly keep track of the number of people who came looking for that particular gem to help
them sleep. But her wild indigo didn't look like it would survive.
At least she still had a healthy patch of lavender for cuts.

She heard a quiet tap on the laboratory's doorframe and turned.
She blinked twice and tried to hide her surprise when she saw
Richard standing there. He held his hand close to his body, smears
of blood stained his fatigues, and Ayanna imagined that the now-
red cloth he had wrapped around his palm had once been white.

Seeing him hurt made her forget to hold up the formal wall that normally rested between them. She staggered toward him with her hands outstretched and her palms turned up. "Richard," she gasped.

"I was hoping you might help me," he said.

Her hands made contact with Richard's forearm. She could feel how strong he was, but he didn't resist her pull as she led him through the lab into the adjoining infirmary. She frowned. It was a bad sign that so much blood had gushed from his hand, so she ordered him to take a seat on her examination table.

Ayanna moved quickly to the water basin and turned on the faucet. The water flowed out freely. The council had to make sure that they didn't lose this. What would happen if they did? She shook her head at the notion. That wasn't going to happen.

Ayanna washed her hands and turned back toward Richard. He had removed his uniform jacket, and now wore a long-sleeved, black, fitted shirt that outlined his fit body. Ayanna noted the breadth of his shoulders, remembering how easily others might fear the captain. She felt small next to him, but she was not sure if it was his size alone that caused that feeling. Maybe it was how Richard could be these days—distant, sometimes cold. *Is it only to me*, she wondered, *or has he become that way with everyone?*

Ayanna imagined that anything that bled so much had to hurt, but Richard did not flinch as she took his hand in her own and unwrapped the cloth covering his wound. His dark brown skin matched hers, but his hand was much stronger and larger. Its rough texture reflected what Ayanna already knew—he worked with his hands daily.

She examined the wound. He had tried to apply pressure. That was good, but it was not enough. His cut sliced almost to the bone.

Ayanna raised her eyes and realized how close their heads

were. Richard seemed to realize it too. He blinked slowly and appeared to be stunned by their proximity. It was the way they had been earlier, on the surface, except he seemed caught off guard this time. Like a deer in the road, he looked uncertain whether to stay or run. His eyes were unintentionally expressive, and unspoken words seemed to dance behind them. *I miss you.*

Ayanna was stunned. She felt confused—with herself and with Richard. How long had he felt it too? This painful space between them that she seemed to both hate and need.

Richard's throat caught. Ayanna swallowed. This was the most she had touched Richard in over a year, and memories of her body being near his threatened to distract her from her task.

She used to know exactly how it felt to lazily rest her head in the crook of Richard's shoulder between his arm and neck. Sometimes, on warm summer nights, she would even fall asleep there while listening to one of his long, and admittedly boring, lessons about the planets and constellations.

"The Big Dipper is easy to spot, see, Ayanna?" he had said.

"Uh-huh," she had replied sleepily. He'd been fascinated by that sort of thing, and she hadn't minded letting him go on about it.

Another memory of the past flashed in her mind, and she recalled that Richard had been the one to carry her home to her father when she had broken her ankle after a stupid attempt to ride Samuel Thompson's skateboard.

The memory of that day seemed fresh. Richard had lifted Ayanna from the ground so quickly that she hadn't even had time to register the blinding pain that clouded her senses. She remembered pleading with him to put her down. She was convinced that she didn't need his help. But Richard had distracted her with a joke.

"Why was the tomato blushing?"

"I don't know, why?"

"Because it saw the salad dressing."

Richard had smiled, and that made Ayanna smile, despite her pain. The absurdity of it all had temporarily made her forget her anguish, and when they arrived home, Richard had insisted that carrying her home had been for his benefit, not hers, something about her body weight having saved him a trip to the gym.

Ayanna tried to shake the flood of memories from her head. That was forever ago. There was nothing left of who Richard and Ayanna used to be. Dragons had burned their relationship away. Still, her eyes fell on his frame again. She couldn't help it. He was so beautiful.

Ayanna shifted Richard's hand in hers. "You need stitches to close this," she said. She waited for him to answer. His dark eyes stared at her for a long moment, and it occurred to her that he might still want to question her about her trip to the surface. It was a strange time to do it, really. How could he even tolerate the pain that he must be feeling? Richard's wound was deep. Ayanna's cuts had only been scratches, but even those still ached.

"Go ahead," he said.

She nodded and turned her back to him to search her cabinets for the right supplies. "I don't have much by way of numbing agents, but I think there's a little—"

"No." His deep voice reverberated through Ayanna's body, and she quickly turned her head in surprise. Richard averted his eyes. He seemed embarrassed at having raised his voice at her. Ayanna had no idea what expression she wore.

"I'm sorry. I just mean . . . save it . . . save it for the others," he said softly.

Ayanna felt her head bob up and down in agreement. She

didn't understand his resistance, but he had apologized for yelling at her. She accepted it. She wasn't going to try to force pain medication on him if he didn't want it.

It took Ayanna thirty minutes to clean Richard's wound and sew it up. They sat in silence as she worked. She could have forced small talk, but that was stupid. Meaningless words would never do; besides, the silence seemed to suit Richard.

But Ayanna had lots of questions: Why hadn't Richard asked her about the surface? Why had he defended her from his father? And why hadn't he been sleeping? She could tell he hadn't been.

"Can you make a fist?" she asked. Richard moved his fingers slowly. He strained but managed to crumple his fingers into a ball. His expression remained stern, and he took in steady breaths. He seemed resolved not to show any pain.

"Good. But let me check one more thing to make sure you don't have any nerve damage." Ayanna reached to roll Richard's sleeve back and felt him tense. Had she hurt him?

"Sorry," she said as she rolled back the black cotton that covered his arm. "I just need to—"

Ayanna held in a gasp when she saw that no fewer than seven scars sliced into Richard's arm. The largest one followed a discolored pink-and-light-brown pattern of a dragon's talon that had buried itself deep into the muscle. It led up to Richard's shoulder, where his arm must have been nearly severed. The injury looked painful. It would have taken months to heal.

She felt her stomach drop. More questions filled her mind. Had he gotten these during the war? What happened at Hamer Swamp? How did he get away from whatever had caused this? Why had he never told her about it?

Ayanna kept quiet. He hadn't told her about it because she'd been avoiding him most of the time. She felt guilty, and she also felt an aching sensation that she wanted something from Richard that she could no longer have. She wanted him to confide in her. She wanted him to explain everything that had happened over the past two years. But at the same time, she knew it was impossible. The distance between them was something Ayanna had wanted because she had blamed him for her father's death.

This was what she believed. Or at least this was what she told herself—but was it true? She didn't know anymore.

Richard shifted in his seat, and Ayanna rolled his sleeve back down. "There. That should take care of it. I think you'll be all right," she said, fixing a final strip of gauze over his hand. She was slow to meet Richard's eyes again.

"Thank you." His voice was deep and low in his throat.

"Do they hurt? The scars?" She couldn't help asking. Not knowing about Richard's time in the war drove her crazy. And the answer felt important to her.

Richard studied Ayanna's face. He was quiet for a long time, and Ayanna wondered if he would answer her. "No," he said, finally. "Not anymore."

He moved slowly to get up, then reached for his uniform jacket. Ayanna watched him wince for the first time as he put it on.

She moved toward her basin. "I was going to say before, I can give you something for the pain. An herb, I mean, if you don't want pills. There's enough for that. There is," she said. There was a persistence in her voice that she wanted him to hear.

Richard's face softened, which made him look younger. She hadn't seen that expression on him in what seemed like years. "Right, from your garden."

Ayanna paused. She felt her eyebrows knit. Was he making fun of her?

"Yeah . . ."

"You love it. Don't you?" he asked.

"What?" she asked.

"This." Richard raised his uninjured arm and waved it around the room. "The medicine, the books . . . the science. It's what you used to talk about. What you and your mom talked about."

Ayanna opened her mouth to answer and then closed it again. She swallowed hard. She hadn't expected to think about her mother. Her time with her mother, and the slow, painful journey to her death was yet another thing that Ayanna tried not to think about much these days. But isn't this what she had asked for? If she wanted Richard to tell her about his wounds, she would have to talk about hers in exchange, she supposed. It was only fair.

Richard was right, she did love the science, but he was also wrong. It was the rest of it that came along with this work—the pressure, the responsibility, the fear of letting everyone down. She didn't love that part. In fact, she hated it.

"Dr. Keaton is lucky to have you. We're all lucky to have you," he said.

Ayanna didn't know what to say.

"Richard . . . Captain . . . you know that Terra wouldn't work without you, don't you? I mean, none of us would even be here if it weren't for—" Ayanna choked on the words. An image of her father's brutal death flashed into her mind. She felt tears prick her eyes, and she quickly turned to her basin to clean her instruments.

She knew it wasn't fair to blame Richard. She had always known it. She knew that her father would have made the same choice Richard had made on the day the city fell. To save her life, to drag her to safety instead of him, but she still didn't know how to move past it.

Richard took in a deep breath, as if he knew what she was thinking. She expected him to leave, but he stood still. What else did he have to say?

"I'm glad to see that you have some materials to study," he

said, his voice breaking their silence. Ayanna lifted her head and saw Richard eyeing her bookshelves.

"Yeah, me too. I try to read every medical and scientific book I can get my hands on. Some things I understand, and others are harder, but with Dr. Keaton's help, I think I'm starting to get the hang of things. I try to be prepared for whatever comes my way, especially when things are so unpredictable."

"Yeah, they are," Richard said with a sigh. He ran his fingers across the spines of the books thoughtfully. "How'd you manage to get your hands on all these anyway? I mean, I go out on reconnaissance missions, and it's always nice when we come across books—it makes the teachers happy—but I don't remember many trips turning up with *Human Anatomy* and *Medicinal Treatments for Blood Disorders*."

He paused. He seemed to be processing an idea. What was he getting at?

"About your trips to the surface . . ."

Here it came. This was what she had expected all along. Richard was a lot of things, but never coy. Ayanna stopped cleaning and looked over at him. His face was as perfect and serene as it had ever been, and he remained relaxed. She couldn't tell what he was going to say next.

"This is the third time the Watchers have caught you up there, isn't it?"

Ayanna didn't respond. She had been to the surface more than three times, but she would never tell Richard that.

"Why?" he asked. The question was sincere, and Ayanna considered answering honestly. There was something in his voice. Not judgment or chastisement, but concern.

She shifted her weight from one leg to the other, continuing to stare at him. "I do what I have to do. I mean, we all have our responsibilities, right? My responsibility is to maintain the health of Terra, and sometimes that means sacrificing for the good of the group."

Richard's mouth formed a thin shape that looked like the beginning of a smile. "I guess our primary program is effective after all," he said.

Ayanna didn't understand. She felt her eyebrows raise. When he didn't go on, she pushed. "What are you talking about?"

"It's just that that idea was one of the lessons my father and the Watchers convinced the teachers to drill into the kids. It seems like the message spread to you too."

Ayanna moved closer to Richard. She wanted to see where he was going with this. "And you don't believe that? That the group is more important than any one of us?" she asked.

He took the tiniest step backward. Only then did Ayanna notice that they were inches away from each other. She followed suit and moved slightly to the right. Richard turned away from her and continued to look at the bookshelf.

"Of course, I believe it. It's my duty. You're right. We each must do what is right for the whole. That's all that matters. Even if it's not what we would choose for ourselves," he said.

His voice was solemn. Ayanna hadn't missed what he implied. Richard hated it too—the pressure of trying to keep everyone safe. This surprised her. He had always talked about honor and duty, even before the war—*especially* before the war.

But maybe things had changed. That would make sense. He had been fighting for a long time, and he carried the responsibility of Terra's safety on his back.

"It must be hard for you," she said. She was prying to see how far he would let her go with these questions. "I mean, having so much responsibility."

He shifted away from her. He must have realized he had expressed more than he meant to. "No, I am my father's son. No

Daniels has ever shirked his responsibilities. I must stay steadfast and dutiful," he recited.

Ayanna took in a quick breath. She was ready to challenge his sudden change in attitude. She didn't believe him for a second. This life was too much: the war, the responsibility, constantly taking care of others. She knew he felt it too. He had to. She wanted him to tell her. It mattered that she was not the only one. But it wasn't as if she could make him confess, and his tone most likely meant he wanted to close the subject.

Richard glanced over at her and rested his eyes on her face. "I have one question for you, and one request," he said.

Ayanna took a breath. She had no idea what he would ask of her, but she didn't see why she should refuse him just yet. His voice had hardened, and he seemed to be asking from his role as captain.

"I'll start with the question," she said.

"How large was the structure you saw on the river?"

Ayanna blinked. That was not what she had expected. But it seemed like a question she could answer.

"Oh, that. Well, it was pretty wide. I'd say it was about three-fourths the size of the riverbank, and tall enough to sit at least six feet out of the water.

"So, you believe me?" she asked before he could move on. Richard shook his head lightly. Her question seemed to confuse him.

"It's just that your father—I mean, Colonel Daniels—he didn't seem to believe what I was trying to tell the council about the dam."

Richard made a noise in the back of his throat that was midway between a groan and a sigh. *What was that about?* she wondered. He had always been obedient to his father. Was the colonel's constant criticism of his son wearing on him?

"I'm sure he has his own reasons for doubting you, but I don't have any reason not to believe you," he said. "The dragons are probably spawning. I've seen it before...."

At Hamer Swamp? she wanted to ask, but she let him go on without interrupting.

"They need the dam to hide their eggs and hatchlings," he said.

Ayanna nodded. Richard studied her face again. His lips parted as if he had something else to say. "What about the request?" she said.

"Look, it's the Protectorate's job to bring back medicine, clothes, and weapons, so if you tell me what you need in the clinic, I can try to bring it back for you. The request is that you ask me first before you go off to any more dangerous places."

Ayanna thought for a moment. She didn't want to promise to do this, but she didn't want to bluntly refuse Richard either. She decided to be noncommittal.

"Thank you," she said, "that's a generous offer."

"You're welcome. Good-bye, Grace." Richard met her eyes one last time before heading to the door of the clinic.

"Good-bye, Captain," she said, "and be careful of your stitches."

Ayanna turned back into the clinic. Her eyes quickly registered her box of herbs, and she realized that she had not given him anything for his pain.

"Richard," she called after him. But he had vanished back into Terra. Ayanna sighed and returned to her work.

Four days. Four days had been her record for not thinking about her endlessly complicated relationship with Richard. But knowing he was in pain and knowing his insistence on pushing through, she was sure there was no hope of beating that record. Richard would not be leaving her thoughts any time soon.

CHAPTER 16

D r. Keaton walked into the clinic in his tattered white coat carrying one of his thick medical books. Ayanna studied the gray-haired man. Yes, a little color had returned to his face, and he seemed to be moving about just fine, but he still looked frail. She thought about his heart condition and her failure to bring back the digitalis from the Savannah River. This weighed on her mind.

"Ayanna, my dear. I'm glad to see you. We have to prepare for Mrs. Sadiq's checkup today," he said. He wore a soft smile on his face.

"OK," said Ayanna. She walked to a supply cabinet that sat in the corner of the clinic, pulled out an old sonogram machine, and plugged it into a wall socket. Then she pulled out the supplies she and Dr. Keaton would need to monitor Mrs. Sadiq's progress during her pregnancy.

But Ayanna's mind drifted over to what she planned to say to Dr. Keaton about the river. She looked up from her work and saw Dr. Keaton staring at her with a pensive look on his face. "Young Doc, Mr. Frye tells me that you have been traveling to the surface."

Ayanna lowered her eyes. She nodded.

"Why on earth have you been doing such a thing?"

She could hear the worry in his voice. She raised her eyes and met Dr. Keaton's. "You need digitalis, and the surface is the only place where I might be able to find it."

Dr. Keaton frowned. "Young Doc, we've been through this, and I'm going to be fine. The dandelion root has been helping with my breathing, and as long as I get enough rest, I should be able to perform my duties. Not to mention, I know that Terra will be fine as long as it has you. You are an excellent student. I couldn't have asked for better. There's no need for you to worry yourself, and there is definitely no need for you to go risking your life on the surface," he said.

Ayanna sighed. Nothing he had said was comforting. Of course, she worried about whether Dr. Keaton lived or died. In fact, she worried about it so much that she was convinced it was driving her a little insane. She had figured that their conversation would go like this. But she wasn't sure what to say next. It wasn't true that he would be fine. None of the medical books she had read said anything about congestive heart failure healing without treatment. Dr. Keaton must have known that. Why did he deny it? Maybe he was scared, she considered.

Or maybe he was just saying what he thought she wanted to hear to make her feel better. Older people tended to do that, she had learned a while back. The practice reminded her of when her mother had first been diagnosed with cancer. Everyone around her—her father, her mother, the nurses, the doctors, even her teachers at school—all had lied and told her everything would be fine. But of course it wasn't.

On top of that, the idea that Terra would thrive as long as it had her as its medic didn't ring true either. How could it? There were an endless number of things she didn't know, procedures she couldn't perform. How could she possibly be enough?

Dr. Keaton blinked suddenly, as if he had just remembered

something. "That reminds me. Mr. Frye tells me there may be trouble brewing with the water supply."

Ayanna sat up. She had hoped that something had changed since she had learned about the water blockage, but it didn't seem like it had.

"Yes," she said. "I wanted to talk to you about that. Mr. Channing sounded worried when he appeared before the council. He said that Tropeck is experiencing a drought, and something is blocking the water from coming down from the Savannah River."

She closed her mouth quickly. She didn't want to mention to Dr. Keaton that she knew that something was a dam that the dragons were building. No one she had told about going to the river had reacted well to the information. She thought it was best if she kept that part to herself.

Dr. Keaton scratched his head. He sat down on a chair near their microscope and became quiet.

"Should we be concerned? I mean, about dehydration or sanitation?" she asked.

"Well, your mind is in the right place, but I think we should give it a few days before we start panicking. There is a good chance that it will rain," he said.

Ayanna agreed. The rain would come, and everyone could forget about this problem in a few days' time. With everything else she had to worry about, she needed this to be true.

She moved to the worktable and stopped in front of a stack of medical journals. Dr. Keaton had kept all sorts from his time working at Dixon Lee Memorial with her mother. He had several that covered emergency triage and medical training for field dressings. Ayanna picked up one of the books and flipped through it.

"Yes, yes. The rain will come. You know, there is always hope that today will be better than yesterday. We should simply focus on today's tasks," Dr. Keaton said.

Ayanna nodded and gave him a small smile before turning another page in the book. "By the way," she said eagerly, "I found some pain killers when I was on the surface."

Dr. Keaton sat up in his chair. "That's wonderful news," he said. "Replicating the medication should be our top priority for the month. But we'll need more bonding agents to replicate the medicine. The ones we've been using aren't stable enough."

Ayanna felt her excitement wane. She sighed. Terra was running out of supplies, especially medical supplies. The Protectorate returned with fewer items each time they left. Although Dr. Keaton didn't say so, he knew it was a problem too. Without the right chemicals, they couldn't make the medicines that Terra needed.

Everything Ayanna needed to do swirled through her head and formed a never-ending, winding road for her to travel. The only catch was that the road didn't lead anywhere except to one more challenge.

She wished she could get out somehow, escape. But that was just a silly dream. There was no out. No escape. This was just the way it was. Dr. Keaton, Maya, the council. They needed her.

Dr. Keaton seemed to notice her disappointment. "You know what, Young Doc? I think I have another chemistry book in my quarters. Maybe there's something we can try to work around the bonding agents."

Ayanna nodded and gave Dr. Keaton another little smile. Trying was all they had for the moment, so she might as well make the best of it.

CHAPTER 17

Ayanna journeyed to the common area of the compound and searched for Maya. Maya would be completing her daily rotation, checking the generators' wiring. Terra's wiring was always in need of repair.

As Ayanna walked toward the gallery, three militia soldiers ran past her in the same direction, nearly pushing her against the wall. What was their hurry?

Ayanna stopped David James as he passed. He was the only soldier she knew would stop. "What's going on?"

"I'm sure you heard the news, Ayanna," he said.

Ayanna shook her head. "No, what news?"

"Captain Daniels said to tell everybody I see we have an emergency meeting at seventeen hundred hours in the gallery."

"Emergency meeting? About what? Did something happen?"

"I don't know yet, but everybody should make their way to midlevel. I know I can't wait to find out what's going on around here."

Ayanna picked up her pace as she followed David and the rest of the soldiers into the large space of the gallery. Within fifteen minutes, teachers, engineers, council members, students, and militia had crowded into the area. Everyone seemed on edge as they waited for the announcement, and Ayanna noticed the conversations around her grow louder as the minutes ticked by. Council members Johnson, Abaka, Christy, and Colonel Daniels stood talking near the head of the crowd. They looked serious and worried. Ayanna watched them, trying to figure out what was going on.

She needed to find Maya. She turned to look behind her and ran straight into Richard.

His muscular chest made the impact jarring. Ayanna stumbled back slightly and looked up into his eyes. He stretched out his arms. His large hands gently held her by the shoulders. An almost imperceptible smile played around the corners of his mouth and then faded. Ayanna regained her balance and Richard dropped his arms to the side.

"Are you OK?" he asked.

"I'm fine," Ayanna said. "More embarrassed than anything."

His forehead wrinkled. "I'm sorry. I'll be more careful next time."

"It's all right. I'm fine. Don't worry about it. You should probably get to your post."

Richard's eyes flashed up toward the front of the room as if Ayanna had just reminded him of where he was headed.

"Yes, I should. Please excuse me." He sidestepped her and walked over to Mrs. Johnson and his father. He and the colonel shared a brief exchange, and then he went to the control booth that was elevated above the gallery floor. The booth housed one of Terra's intercom systems. An anxious feeling spread through Ayanna's abdomen. She had a feeling she knew what Richard was about to announce, and it would not be good.

Pressing a black button, Richard spoke into the microphone, and the amplifiers on the walls carried his deep voice throughout the compound.

"Occupants of Terra," he began. The amplifier screeched and beeped. He adjusted the equipment and began again.

"Occupants of Terra, as you know, I am Captain Richard Daniels, and I am in charge of Terra's security. As some of you may also know, Tropeck has experienced dry weather over the past twenty days. We are in the middle of a drought. The engineering team has also come across a problem with our access to the river. In short, Terra is running out of water."

Several of the members of the crowd started to whisper, and people turned their heads to look around at each other. Most people in the room seemed surprised. Ayanna shifted her weight anxiously.

"As of today, the Watchers have ordered that Terra ration its remaining water supply. Therefore, each person will be allotted two liters of drinking water per day until the end of this drought.

"Due to these events, the council would also like to remind all members of Terra that all trips to the surface are banned except for approved personnel. Anyone in violation of this order will appear before the Watchers for immediate discipline. We expect your cooperation, and we appreciate your loyalty to the group."

Richard stepped out of the control booth and returned to his father's side. The crowd started to buzz with energy. People talked in loud, nervous bursts. Ayanna looked for Maya again.

Then, from behind her, she heard her friend's voice. "Can you believe this?"

Ayanna turned. Maya wore a frown and her lip quivered slightly. She stretched out her arms, and Ayanna moved in for a hug.

"I can," Ayanna said. "I found out a few days ago, but I promised not to say anything about it."

Maya's eyes widened in surprise, and she started to protest, but then she seemed to change her mind. She understood how promises worked.

"I just wonder how bad things will get. There's no way to determine how long this drought will last. I don't think the people will do very well with water rations," she said.

Ayanna looked into the sea of bodies that surrounded her. Maya might be right. Some of the members of the group stood with their arms crossed. Their expressions were angry, and their shouts rang in her ears. A smaller group formed in front of Mrs. Johnson. They seemed to have a lot of questions, but Ayanna could not make out all their words.

". . . arbitrary abuse of power," she overheard Raheem Campbell say as he raised his voice. His hands flew in the air as he spoke.

Maya leaned in closer to Ayanna. "Malik says he's heard that some people are talking about leaving Terra, for good," she whispered.

"Leave Terra? Why?"

"I don't know. Something about how we're not really safe here. I bet they'll take this sort of thing as just another sign of that. It's hard to say if they're serious. You know Malik. He swears that he has his ear to the ground."

"Yeah, I know," Ayanna said. "I'll be right back."

"Wait. Where are you—"

"Don't worry," Ayanna said.

Ayanna left Maya and tried to make her way toward Richard. She approached the council members and saw that Richard was speaking with Mr. Christy, but then in an instant, he turned his back to her and walked away before she could reach him.

"Richard!" Ayanna called after him. But he continued to walk away. He seemed unable to hear her over the noise coming from the crowd.

"Captain Daniels, may I please speak with you?"

Ayanna pushed and squeezed through the crowded room.

She followed Richard into an empty corridor and the sound transformed into a distant hum. Quickly, he turned around, having heard her last call.

"Grace?" he said, surprised. "I'm sorry, I didn't hear you."

"It's all right," Ayanna said. "It's just . . ."

Richard looked at her attentively, waiting for her to continue.

"It's just that I haven't heard anything from the council . . . that is until today . . . about the situation. I was wondering if you could update me. I mean, your announcement just now was a bit of a shock, even to me. Do you mean nothing has gotten better in five days?"

Richard stared at her. Ayanna could see from the way his body tensed that he was negotiating with himself. His eyes shifted toward the gallery, then back toward her. She imagined he was weighing whether he should tell her anything without the council's permission.

Ayanna's toes pressed into her boots as she waited on edge for Richard to speak. He was quiet for so long that Ayanna was convinced that he had decided not to tell her. Finally, Richard's voice broke the silence.

"Unfortunately, it seems that the situation has only gotten worse. There's still no indication that it will rain, and we must plan for Terra's future."

"But, Captain, rationing water won't work for very long," Ayanna said. She didn't need medical training to know it was not a very good plan for solving their drought problem.

"As of now, it's the only option that we have."

"Won't you at least talk to the council again about going to see that dam at the river?" she pleaded. "Maybe there's a way to clear the blockage."

Richard opened his mouth to say something, but a group of four people from the gallery were making their way toward them. Richard straightened his back and stood taller as the others approached.

"You know I'm willing to go, but that decision isn't up to me, Ayanna. We have to wait on the council," he said. "I'm sorry. But it's up to them, not us. We'll just have to wait and see. To Terra," he added.

Ayanna was about to speak again, but the group of four practically pushed Ayanna out of the way as they gathered around Richard, demanding his attention. She moved to the side to make room for the circle they formed.

"To Terra," she whispered to herself before going back to find Maya.

CHAPTER **18**

Ayanna blew out a long breath. She didn't want to endure another day like yesterday. Everyone was tired, dirty, and thirsty. The water crisis had been particularly troublesome for the Sanderses. The Protectorate was working Malik to the point of exhaustion as they were the ones trying to enforce the water rationing.

The whole ordeal was taking its toll on Mrs. Sanders too. Maya had rushed her grandmother to the clinic because she was showing signs of dehydration. Ayanna discovered that Mrs. Sanders had not been drinking her allotment of water because she was attempting to hoard it in case the family ran out. This, of course, had only increased Maya's anxiety, and both of them had been brought to tears, leaving Ayanna feeling desperate to help find a solution to Terra's problem.

This was more than the Watchers had felt the need to do, it seemed. Ayanna was under the distinct impression that the Watchers were in hiding. No one had heard from or seen most of the leaders in days. The council seemed to have left the bulk of overseeing the water rationing to Richard and his team. And her sympathy for Richard had grown with every passing hour. He was always running around Terra dealing with one crisis or another.

On top of that, people seemed to blame Richard for everything that was happening.

Any remaining criticism had been reserved for her and Dr. Keaton. In the past thirty-two hours, six people had come to her complaining of two dozen illnesses ranging from insomnia to heart palpitations, but Ayanna's only diagnosis was that the water shortage made people anxious and angry.

Dr. Keaton had managed to track down Mrs. Johnson and Mr. Frye to explain that the clinic needed more water than the allotment the others had been assigned. The clinic had to worry about anyone who came through the doors, not just water for Dr. Keaton and Ayanna. They had to keep their equipment sterile, make medications, and continually wash their hands. Mrs. Johnson agreed. Still, neither of the Watchers' most influential members seemed to have any clue about how to solve any problem beyond this.

When Ayanna went to collect her rations yesterday, she had waited in the cafeteria like everyone else. Richard made three announcements to the group crowded there, and each announcement seemed to make the group more anxious than the previous one. The first two times he spoke, he informed the crowd about the new rules the Watchers had put in place. Apparently, everyone was supposed to meet in the cafeteria at seven in the morning and four in the afternoon for rations, and meals had been rearranged from shifts based on duties to shifts based on age and infirmity.

People asked questions, but Richard didn't answer them. That only made everyone angrier. After both announcements, he had hurried off to his post, leaving the crowd to talk among themselves. Ayanna had overheard more than one furious conversation. Some people felt Richard was keeping quiet to maintain his dominance over the group.

Ayanna had trouble seeing it this way. Richard was duty

bound, not power hungry, she knew. Most people wouldn't be able to understand this about him, but then again, they had only known him as the captain. It was easier for Ayanna to realize that the reason Richard didn't answer the crowd's questions was because he didn't have any answers. He tended to speak only when he had something useful to say.

Still, Ayanna's willingness to understand Richard hadn't prepared her for his third and final announcement of the day, and she found herself shocked along with everyone else. His announcement started off like all the others. Richard approached the front of the cafeteria calmly. He looked tired, and his dark hair had grown out more than usual. He must have been too busy to cut it, Ayanna thought. Although people had grown more and more agitated throughout the day, almost everyone in the room stopped to listen to him.

Ayanna had expected Richard to declare yet another rule the Watchers had thought up. Maybe they planned to put some kind of lottery system in place to decide who should receive water, she thought wildly. Even with strange possibilities like this bouncing around in her head, she had not expected to hear what came next.

"Fellow citizens of Terra . . ." Richard started. His voice sounded strained, and Ayanna moved closer to the front of the crowd to hear him better.

"The Protectorate has been working to keep us safe, and part of that duty has entailed keeping a census and tracking how much water we have been distributing."

Ayanna heard groans coming from the crowd, but most people continued to listen. She did too. There must be more. So far, Richard hadn't said anything that she hadn't figured out by herself.

"As of the census check at fourteen hundred hours today, three members of Terra are missing. Specifically, no one has seen the Lincoln family in two days. We have no idea what has happened to them," he concluded.

After that, a shockwave traveled through the group. Reactions varied. Several people said the family had left Terra, and dragons had killed them. Others added that the Protectorate had recovered the bodies but refused to tell the people to prevent panic. And some expressed the belief that the Lincolns had the right idea by leaving and had found a safer place to hide, although the Lincolns' friends denied knowing about any plans the family had made to leave Terra.

Ayanna didn't know what to believe. Who in their right mind would up and leave Terra? They could travel out West, she supposed. But where? To what? She guessed they *could* look for some mythical home that Jackson had spoken about. . . .

Jackson.

The thought of him stopped Ayanna in her tracks, but she tried to push it away. She hadn't had time to worry about Jackson, not with everything else that was going on. Besides, she remembered, she was never going to see him again, and maybe he had managed to fare better on his own than anyone else in the moment. If he had come back to Terra with her like she had wanted, then he would be in the same predicament as the rest of them. *And who knew, maybe he was safe. Maybe he was even happy*, she thought. She would want that for him.

But Ayanna couldn't linger on the thought. All that mattered was that more days of water rationing were approaching, and it was obvious that the people were growing restless.

The noise of the crowd grew louder as Ayanna approached the cafeteria. A long line had already formed as people stood to receive water rations. They waited with their plastic and glass containers, chatting to each other, as each person approached

Miriam, who—having had previous experience with fairly distributing the food—had been charged with overseeing the water rations as well. Ayanna joined the line.

"Can you believe this crap?" said Darian Shakur. "Who do they think they are anyway, telling us what we can and cannot have?"

"Yeah," said Frida Janes, "this is definitely a pain, but we have to trust in the Watchers' judgment. After all, they have kept us safe this long."

Darian huffed. "Safe? I guess you could call this safe. But they can't even figure out what to do when there is a drought, and these are the people that we are supposed to trust with our lives. I don't know about that."

Ayanna watched as Benjamin Herndon walked past in a hurry, bumping into Darian.

"Hey, where do you think you're going?" asked Darian. "The line starts back there."

"I know, I know. It's just that I need to get back to the crops and I was hoping—"

"You were hoping? I don't give a damn about what you were hoping. The line starts back there," Darian shouted.

"Calm down, D," said Frida.

"Calm down? This guy thinks he's just going to waltz in here and cut in front of all of us without waiting his turn, and I'm the one who needs to calm down? Screw that." Darian moved closer to Benjamin, nearly touching chests.

"So what, Herndon, you think that there's something here that makes *you* special? What makes *your* need so much more important than any of the rest of us?"

Benjamin pushed Darian with his hand. "Get out of my face."

"*You* get out of *my* face."

Benjamin swung his fist and punched Darian in his mouth. The impact of Benjamin's knuckles to Darian's jaw made a sick crutching noise. Darian staggered, but he regained his balance. He drew his fist back and with a rounded motion punched Benjamin in the face. The two men then collapsed in a brawl on the floor.

Ayanna stepped back as she heard someone call for help, and two militiamen arrived to break up the fight. She was fully aware that it would not help anyone for her to get in the middle of two grown men beating each other up. But she felt agitated. She had not seen a fight at Terra in months. It was far from the norm. They had gotten along rather peacefully. Of course, they had also had enough water and food until now.

Officer Geoffrey, another soldier from the Fire Sky War, managed to subdue the men, pulling them apart. Ayanna wanted to see if either Darian or Benjamin was hurt, but the men's dangerous scowls warned her away. They seemed ready for another brawl with anyone who came near. She decided to wait.

But just as the fight broke up, her attention shifted to a large crowd forming in the center of the cafeteria. She scanned the room and caught a glimpse of Malik standing on the outskirts of the group with his arms folded. Ayanna left her position and moved closer to him.

"Are you OK?" she asked. Malik laughed an incredulous laugh. It sounded foreign coming from him.

"Me? I'm fine. You don't have to worry about me, Ayanna. I can take care of myself," he said. "But it doesn't seem like folks are taking too good to rations."

"I agree. It's not going very well."

Ayanna registered when Richard walked into the cafeteria. He was hard to miss. He flowed through the crowd with ease due partly to his height and partly to the way people made room for him without him having to ask. Richard the Dragon Killer. *Why did he never talk about that?* she wondered again, studying his face.

He looked so tired, worse than before. His sleep problem, the one that he had denied, seemed not to have gotten any better.

She watched as he did a brief scan of the room and seemed to find the same thing Ayanna was seeing: the beginning of chaos. His square shoulders moved swiftly through the crowd, like he knew where he was going. He walked up to Officer Stevens, and the two men talked briefly.

Ayanna tore her eyes from Richard and drew her attention to the crowd. A group of about fifteen men and women were now standing around the center of the cafeteria, and Rafael Rudd had climbed up on one of the tables. Rafael was thin and average height. His dark skin tone matched Ayanna's, and he wore his hair cut close to his scalp, but he sported a thick black beard that made him look older than he was. Rafael started to give a speech, and his friend Oluwale—a larger young man who looked like he was more brawn than brains—stood beside him with his arms folded, scanning the crowd as if to protect his friend.

"The Watchers arbitrarily tell us what we can and can't do. They claim that they know what's best for all of us, but did anyone from the council come down here and ask us what we thought about them taking away our water?" said Rafael.

Some members of the crowd answered. "No. No one asked me what I thought!" said one male in the group, and the crowd clapped and nodded in agreement.

"Sanders, what's going on here?" Richard asked from behind Ayanna and Malik, startling her.

Malik stood up straight. "I'm not really sure, sir. First, there was a fight between Shakur and Herndon. Then, Rafael got up there and started yapping on about something."

Ayanna thought about asking Richard for an update from the council, but she could see he was eager to figure out what was happening with the crowd. She held back her question as

Richard moved closer to the front of the crowd. Ayanna guessed he wanted to hear Rafael's speech for himself.

Rafael noticed Richard and frowned, shifting his eyes from Richard to Oluwale, then back to Richard. He stuttered over his words but went on with his speech. "I know that our leaders mean well, but they don't know what the hell they're talking about. They can't just dictate and expect us to follow their orders without question like this forever. No.

"Don't take it any longer. We need to let the council know. We're not the enemy. The enemy is out there, not in here. No to rations. We're not farm animals. We're human beings!" Rafael shouted.

"Yeah!" yelled some in the crowd.

"That's right!" said others.

Energy ran through the room. Ayanna saw Richard swivel his head to look around at the many men and women who were nodding their heads in agreement with Rafael. Then, Richard pushed his way forward, so he could stand in front of him. Richard's first lieutenant, Ramirez, approached from the hallway too. A sense of unease enveloped Ayanna. Ramirez's strong-bodied stance mimicked Richard's rigid positioning, and she could feel the tension building all around her. The room was like a balloon that had been filled with too much air.

Oluwale stood up taller. He shifted toward Richard with his fists clenched, but Rafael shook his head. Oluwale relaxed his hands and stepped back.

"How can I help you, Captain?" said Rafael, stepping down from the table.

Richard's hard face did not ease with Rafael's false pleasant tone. "For starters, you can disperse whatever it is you have going on here. Then, you can come with me." There was something in Richard's voice that Ayanna had never heard before. His tone was eerily calm, deadly.

Rafael hesitated. Richard remained composed, fearless. He kept his eyes glued to Rafael and squared his shoulders with the smaller man. His feet seemed planted in the ground, and it was clear he wasn't going to move until Rafael complied with his order.

Ayanna suddenly felt frightened for Rafael. She didn't know if her fear was justified, but the look on Richard's face told her that neither Rafael nor his friend Oluwale could take the captain if they tried.

Rafael tightened his eyes. He jutted his head up once. "All right, Cap'n, I don't have a problem with that," he said. Richard nodded once and stepped aside, allowing room for Rafael to walk out. The smaller man held his head up high and headed for the door. His friend Oluwale sneered toward Richard but followed Rafael out of the cafeteria.

Ayanna felt her diaphragm relax. The crowd broke up. Lieutenant Ramirez came up to Benjamin and Darian, and the men followed behind Richard's group as well. Ayanna noticed that Darian had a large cut on his head. *He'll need stitches*, she thought.

"I guess Rudd's not a complete idiot," said Malik. "The captain would've destroyed him."

Malik had been watching the scene unfold so quietly next to Ayanna that she had forgotten he was there. Ayanna shook her head in disbelief. What was that whole thing about? And what would it have led to?

"I guess he's not," she said. "I'll see you later, OK? I've gotta go check on Darian. That cut on his head looks bad."

"Yeah, OK. See ya," said Malik.

Ayanna stuffed a suture kit into her bag and headed for the militia base unit. That is where Benjamin and Darian would likely be. Ayanna walked down the tunnel, lit only by a few lights in the distance. She felt unsettled. Water rationing was not working, and the council was short on solutions. It was really just a matter of removing that dam she had seen in the river. Ayanna was sure it was the source of their problems. There had to be a way to destroy it.

She passed through access door thirty-three and into the hallway headed toward the militia rooms. Ayanna turned the corner and saw Colonel Daniels stumbling into his quarters. This was the first she had seen of him in days. He looked unkempt, and he hadn't shaved recently. He closed the door to his quarters behind him with a slam, followed by a loud crash. This was very strange. Ayanna didn't want to, but she felt that she should check to see if he was OK.

After knocking on the door, she called out, "Colonel Daniels, are you all right?"

No one answered. That was not good.

Ayanna really didn't want to do what she was about to do. To say that she was not Colonel Daniels's favorite person was an extreme understatement, but Ayanna could not just let the Colonel lie in his room, possibly injured, could she?

She knocked again. No answer. She turned the handle and pushed the door open.

"Colonel, are you . . ." Ayanna turned on the light and stopped short when she saw Colonel Daniels lying facedown on his bed. His limbs were flung out to the side, and he was taking in air with a loud snore.

How could Colonel Daniels be awake one minute and unconscious the next?

Ayanna closed the door behind her and looked around. His room contained a bed, a small aluminum desk with two drawers, a wooden chair, and a slender cabinet positioned against the wall in the corner.

A small wooden picture frame with a broken glass face rested on the corner of his desk, and an old, wrinkled photo of a boy sat in the frame. It was a picture of Richard when he was a little boy, around the age of eight. A cracked, leatherbound notebook sat on the edge of the desk.

As Ayanna approached the colonel, the pungent smell of alcohol slammed into her nostrils. Was Colonel Daniels drunk? That would explain his behavior. She should leave, but she could not resist the urge to search his room a little. She had no idea what she might find, but she would never be there again. She moved closer to the desk and picked up the framed photo of Richard. The little boy in the photo had the same soulful, dark eyes, but unlike now, he carried a crooked, happy smile.

Unexpectedly, the corner of another picture slipped out from the bottom of the frame. This picture was older, more worn, with wrinkled lines crossing through the paper. Colonel Daniels made a snorting sound in his sleep. Ayanna paused. He took in a long gasp before his breathing returned to normal.

Ayanna tugged at the picture gently, and it fell into her hand. She studied the image. It was a picture of a young white woman. She had brown, straight hair and sad, blue eyes. She seemed distant, as if she were unaware that someone was taking her picture. Ayanna wondered who she was. Obviously, this was not Ella, Richard's mother. Maybe she was related to the colonel somehow.

Just then, Ayanna heard voices in the hallway. It was time to leave.

She moved to place the photo back into the frame, but it dropped from her hands and fell on the floor. She kneeled to pick it up and noticed the desk drawer was ajar. A large, square, glass bottle of whiskey and two small shot glasses sat in the drawer. This explained the colonel's condition.

The voices in the hall grew louder. She had done enough

snooping for one day. She knew she needed to get out of there. But questions flooded her mind. Why was Colonel Daniels drinking in the middle of a crisis? Who was that woman in the photo? Would the colonel know that someone had been in his room when he woke up? How often did he do this?

She didn't have time to wonder much longer about the answers to any of these questions. No, Ayanna needed to get to Darian and Benjamin and make sure that they were OK. Everything else would have to wait.

CHAPTER 19

Ayanna walked toward the east quarters. She needed to check on Sampson Carter's broken leg. He was one of Ayanna's favorite patients.

For a ten-year-old kid, he knew a lot about life. He seemed to have tons of insight about everything that had happened during the war, and as far as Ayanna could tell, he'd come up with his own way to deal with it.

Sampson had broken his leg two weeks earlier while helping reinforce the southern interior wall. That was the same rotation Malik used to be on when he was in the ten-to-thirteen-year-old group. No one considered the work dangerous, but the kids had to be careful of loose bricks that might tumble as they worked.

That was exactly what had happened to Sampson while he was patching a hole in the wall. A heavy brick had landed on his leg and snapped his tibia in two. Ayanna had set his leg and made him a plaster cast, but she needed to check that he was healing properly.

She entered the family's quarters in a tiny train car that reminded her of the Sanderses' room: small, a bit cramped, and with three cots and an aluminum desk to furnish the space. Sampson's father, Jamal, stood in the corner of the room and gave

Ayanna space to sit by his son. Jamal was a short man with dark hair and light brown skin. Sampson resembled his father a lot—in looks, at least. But Jamal was an agriculturalist, and Ayanna knew that Sampson had his sights set on the militia, just as Malik did. The young boys were all so eager to fight dragons, it seemed. Naïve was the word that came to mind.

"Should we wait for Roberta?" Ayanna asked. She knew Sampson's mother would want to be there for the exam. The woman normally hovered over her son like a worried hawk guarding her nest. Ayanna understood this. The Carters had already lost their daughter, Tasha, during the infestation, and Ayanna knew how much they adored Sampson. The idea of anything happening to him was probably too unbearable for them to consider.

"No, go ahead," said Jamal. "She'll be along soon."

"How are you feeling?" Ayanna asked Sampson.

He looked up from the sketchpad he held in his hands, lifting his pencil from the paper. "I'm OK, I guess," he said. "I think I'm getting better . . . at drawing at least." Sampson gestured toward his sketchpad. He lifted it for Ayanna to see.

She reached her hand toward the drawing and looked over the picture. Sampson had drawn a building with what looked like flames shooting out of it. There was a girl lying on the ground, covered in what Ayanna assumed was fire. And a small boy stood in the corner of the sketch covering his face with his arm, shielding his eyes from the sight. In the corner of the page, Sampson had drawn what looked like a truck driving away from the scene.

Sampson's talent was real, but the image was horrible and frightening. Ayanna handed the picture back to him. What should she say? There was no way to remove those memories from his mind. And the image, as horrible as it was, was not unique. Ayanna had seen similar things the year before.

"Do you know what I think, Ayanna?" asked Sampson.

"No, tell me. What do you think?"

"I think they left us here. . . ."

"They?" said Ayanna. She wasn't sure what he meant.

Sampson nodded his head. "Yep, the people in charge. They said that there were too many people on the trucks already, and they would have to come back with more later, but I think they lied. I don't think they were ever gonna come back, you know? I think they left us here, and they didn't care what happened after that. They didn't care if we died."

Ayanna nodded. Sampson's memory of what happened the day of the evacuation was not too far off from what she remembered. Ayanna didn't want to relive the events of the evacuation, but the images came to her mind anyway.

Tropeck had not yet been overtaken by dragons. But many of their neighboring cities were losing ground to the creatures, and people had to flee their homes on a moment's notice. There were too many dragons. They bred too quickly, and they burned too many areas at once. The dragons had overrun most of the Mississippi River Valley, and they were headed down into Florida and north to the Great Lakes. Only areas where fresh water was scarce or those cities that had fought and won to keep the dragons from breeding in their waterways still stood.

Individual army units had retreated all over the southeast, and the plan had been to evacuate whatever citizens were still left to the remaining military bases in the central and southwestern United States.

Ayanna and her father were told that local army units would evacuate Tropeck. But given how central her father was to the entire ordeal, the regional commanders planned to provide him with a personal escort team. Not surprisingly, their escort team included Richard, who had returned to Tropeck after having fought dragons throughout Georgia and Alabama.

On the morning of the evacuation, anyone who wanted to leave Tropeck met on Main Street at noon. Thousands of people waited to enter one of the canvas-covered military trucks that had lined the streets. Fatigue-uniformed soldiers assisted old and young people into the back of the trucks. When Ayanna saw that Maya, Malik, and Mrs. Sanders had made it onto a truck, she felt a wave of relief.

Ayanna, her father, the mayor of Tropeck, Richard, and a handful of other high-ranking military officials from the army base had piled into a hard-topped Hummer jeep in the exodus caravan line.

Ayanna was nervous but hopeful. After months of worrying that the city would fall, she had finally believed that everyone was going to be OK. She believed that everyone she cared about was going to make it to a safer place, somewhere with more weapons, more equipment, more soldiers.

"You're very brave, Ayanna," her father had told her. "I'm proud of you." He had smiled at her with a gentle expression. Ayanna had searched his face and she saw that he too seemed to have hope that they would be safe.

Then, suddenly, the soldiers' two-way radios started to crackle and pop. Frantic shouts came through the receivers, and panic erupted on the street. A swarm of twenty, maybe thirty dragons appeared. Fire engulfed Main Street. People screamed and ran in all directions. Bodies were snatched from the ground into the sky, and blood poured onto the streets.

Trucks started to pull away only half full, and a huge flame that felt like a fireball slammed into the jeep that carried Ayanna and flipped it over onto its roof.

Ayanna swallowed hard. She felt tears prickle her eyes. She didn't want the memory to continue.

"You know that the Protectorate and the Watchers will do

everything that they can to protect you here, right?" Ayanna said.

"Cap'n Daniels?" Sampson asked.

"Right . . . Rich . . . Captain Daniels is going to do everything he can to keep you safe. He'll keep us all safe," she said. Ayanna didn't know if she was right to say this. She didn't know if it were true. But she wanted it to be.

Sampson nodded his head. "Yeah, he didn't leave us. The captain would never leave us behind," he said.

Sampson's words were true. Richard had not abandoned them. In fact, he had brought his unit back to Tropeck specifically to get his family and friends out. This had included Ayanna and her father. She knew that. It just had not worked out the way any of them had hoped.

"He's a dragon-killer, you know? My friend Calvin says the captain has killed ten, fifteen, maybe even twenty dragons by hand," said Sampson.

Ayanna thought about these words. Richard's celebrity with the kids did not surprise her. She knew how all the boys in camp admired him . . . and how all the girls had a crush on him.

Ayanna gave Sampson a small smile and nodded her head. "Yeah, I know," she said softly. "I'm going to check your heart now."

Sampson shrugged his shoulders. "OK."

Ayanna took out her stethoscope and began her examination. "Now, breathe deeply . . ." she instructed. She lowered her stethoscope to Sampson's lungs. ". . . and again.

And how is your leg feeling? Would it be OK if I took a look at your setting, to make sure that everything is healing the way it should?"

Sampson nodded with his bottom lip jutting out, forming a small pout. She knew his leg likely hurt. She wanted to treat his pain, but she didn't have enough pills to use only on one patient, so she also had to give him an herb tonic from the plants in her garden.

Ayanna ran her hand across the top of his head as an apology. But she frowned when her hand made contact. His forehead was warm.

"Jamal, can you come here, please?" she called out.

"Hey, Ayanna, how's he doing?" asked Jamal.

"Have you and Roberta been changing Sampson's dressing every day, like I asked?"

Jamal lowered his eyebrows. "Absolutely," he said. "What's wrong?"

"I'm not sure yet."

Roberta walked into the room and stood behind Jamal. She wore her dark, black hair pulled back into a braid and away from her rounded face. She looked stricken. Her dry, cracked lips whispered a greeting. "Ayanna, we're so glad you're here," she said, holding one hand to her stomach and clutching for the wall with her other.

"Roberta, are you feeling OK?" Ayanna asked.

"I think I have a little fever," she said.

Ayanna stood up and placed the back of her hand on Roberta's forehead. "How long have you had a fever?"

"Not long, just a day or so now," said Roberta.

"You should sit down."

Ayanna placed two fingers on Roberta's wrist. "Your pulse is fast. Look into my eyes." Ayanna pressed her thumbs just beneath Roberta's eye sockets and pulled gently, widening her own eyes so she could see better. "Your pupils are dilated."

Ayanna scanned the room. She only had a faint idea of what she was looking for, but she could feel her own pulse quickening. Something was wrong, and she just hoped that it wasn't as bad as she feared.

Her eyes stopped on a glass of water sitting on a shelf.

"Where did you get that water?"

"What?" asked Jamal.

"This water. Did you get it with your rations?" Ayanna asked, not sure that she wanted to hear the answer to her question. She felt like spiders had started to climb up her spine. Anxiety threatened to overcome her.

Roberta lowered her eyes, avoiding Ayanna's. Then, Jamal and Roberta looked at each other, and Jamal frowned. Ayanna knew that this was not going to be good.

"Please," Ayanna said, "it's important. I need to know."

Roberta shifted her eyes from her husband. "Cafferty's giving it out," she said.

"What? What do you mean giving it out? This didn't come from the rations? Where is he getting it from?"

The couple hesitated. Both sets of eyes found the floor.

"He tapped the pipes," said Jamal.

Ayanna's eyes widened. "He tapped the . . . ? Don't use any more water that doesn't come from the Protectorate's rations," she said. "It's not safe! I'll be back." She jetted for the door and stumbled into the hallway.

"But what about Sampson and Roberta?" asked Jamal.

"Don't worry, I will help them. I promise!" she yelled as she took off down the hall.

Ayanna searched for Dr. Keaton. She didn't know what else to do. She had a bad feeling.

She found him in his room. "Dr. Keaton? Dr. Keaton we need to talk," she said when she walked in. As soon as Ayanna looked at Dr. Keaton, though, her panic increased. He looked terrible. His face was sunken in, and dark circles had formed under his eyes. Beads of sweat drenched his forehead. He was not breathing normally, and it showed.

"I'm fine, just fine, Young Doc. What's going on?" Dr. Keaton sat up from his cot slowly. He seemed to be trying to brush off Ayanna's concerned look. He probably didn't want to worry her, but she didn't want him to pretend that he felt better than he did. How would that help anyone?

Ayanna stopped. The words she wanted to speak sat in the back of her throat. She needed his help. Terra needed his help, but he clearly needed to rest.

She swallowed before she spoke. "The water situation has just gotten worse," she said, siding with the side of her brain that demanded that she get help. "I just went to see the Carters, and they told me that someone on the compound has been giving out unclean water. It hasn't been treated, and it's not coming from the river. I think they may be getting it from the sewage. At least two people are showing symptoms of infection."

Dr. Keaton ran his hand through his gray hair. "What are their symptoms?" he said.

Ayanna took in a short breath. "High fever, stomach cramps, clammy skin."

Dr. Keaton nodded. "You're right. This is very serious. It could be dysentery. I'll check in on the Carters," he said. He moved to get up, but sat back down, almost toppling onto the bed again. Ayanna took a quick step toward him, but he lifted his arm to stop her.

"I need you to go find all the antibiotics we have. Measure them and tell me how many doses are left. After that, go before the council and alert them to the situation," said Dr. Keaton.

On his second try, he got up and gathered his medical bag. Ayanna looked back at him. Maybe it was not the best idea for him to be moving around. He looked terrible. Couldn't she figure out what to do by herself? What else had all her training been for?

"Hurry, Young Doc, we have to get in front of this thing," he said.

Ayanna shook her head. She felt undecided. Was it too late to change what she had already done? "All right, but are you sure that you're feeling up to it? I mean, I think I should be able to administer the antibiotics we have left," she said, although she was not sure at all.

"I'll be fine. Now go on, and hurry. We don't have any time to lose," said Dr. Keaton.

Ayanna nodded and walked toward the clinic. Her count only took a few minutes. There were not many antibiotics to choose from. They had a few—very few—antibiotics that they could use to treat four, maybe five people for a few days, but certainly not more than that. Would these antibiotics even work? She had no way of knowing. Not to mention that if Roberta and Sampson were suffering from dysentery, the biggest threat to them was dehydration.

When she had finished in the clinic, Ayanna walked toward the council's chamber. She planned to walk into the chamber without knocking or waiting to be announced. There was no telling who would even be there. She did not know their meeting schedules, but she would have to risk it. If no one else, Mrs. Johnson was probably in there working, or at least trying to work. Mrs. Johnson could call the others.

Yes, Ayanna nodded, the meager plan started to come together in her mind. Maybe Terra could get ahead of this. Maybe things were not as bad as she feared.

CHAPTER **20**

Ayanna burst through the doors of the Watchers' chamber with a small stumble. Her nerves threatened to get the best of her, but she recovered quickly and straightened her back. She stepped in front of three members of the council who seemed to be arguing among themselves. Richard was already standing before them, his dark face drawn and unshaven. He looked exhausted.

"Miss Grace, what are you doing here?" asked Mr. Christy. He appeared appalled at her interruption.

Richard looked over to Ayanna and stared, as if he too couldn't seem to work out why she was there. But the muscles in his arm tensed as if he were preparing to take a blow. He was not wrong. Ayanna was there to add to his problems.

She didn't stop for breath. Though she had no idea what she was going to say, she just started to speak. "We have a bigger problem than we thought," Ayanna blurted out. "The people have been drinking water from the sewer. They are being exposed to all sorts of bacteria."

Mrs. Johnson opened her mouth in shock and then closed it again.

"How? How is that possible?" asked Mr. Christy.

"Someone has been giving out water. The pipes in the lower parts of Terra lead out, and somehow, they have been tapping the water flow. I guess they don't know the water is undrinkable. Or maybe they haven't been boiling it long enough. Either way, we have to tell them. Anyone who's drinking it is going to get sick," she said.

"Fine," said Colonel Daniels, "but I don't know if it's enough to stop them. We are going to have to find out who has been giving out the contaminated water and deal with him. How is it that you discovered this, Miss Grace?"

Ayanna hesitated. She wanted the council to have enough information to protect Terra, but she did not want to be responsible for getting anyone in trouble. The people were just scared. Would it help for anybody to be punished or expelled?

"One of my patients showed signs of an infection that came from a waterborne pathogen, probably dysentery, but we're not sure. After some pushing, they admitted that they got the water from someone in the compound. They didn't say who," Ayanna lied. She didn't know if this was the right thing to do. Cafferty was passing out water, but maybe if the council told everyone about what was happening, he would just stop.

"Has anyone else become sick?" asked Mrs. Johnson.

"So far, there are two people who have high fevers. I'm afraid that the situation will only get worse before it gets better," Ayanna said. She was confident that this was true. She doubted that the Carters were the only ones exposing themselves to the tainted water.

"Any ideas as to what you want to do?" Mrs. Johnson said to no one in particular.

The room fell silent, and Ayanna became annoyed. Deliberating seemed unnecessary to her when the solution, at least to one of their many problems, seemed obvious. She stepped forward to answer before anyone else spoke. "With respect, Council, I don't think that it is fair to keep the population in danger like this when you could simply send the Protectorate out to destroy the dam that is blocking the water flow."

"Miss Grace, you need to concentrate on healing the sick, and we will concentrate on keeping Terra safe. You will do what you are asked," said Colonel Daniels.

Ayanna examined the colonel. He looked different to her after what she had seen in his room. Would he be so smug if he knew what she had witnessed, him passed out, facedown, reeking of alcohol?

She gritted her teeth. "But . . ."

Ayanna looked at Richard. She didn't know what she expected to find. She hoped for support, but she could have just as easily found disapproval. There was neither in his face. His expression hid his mind. His brown eyes were contemplative, distant. He did not move from his position. *Richard, help me,* she thought.

But she did not say this aloud. "Yes, I understand," she finally said, before walking out of the chamber and heading back to the infirmary.

But it made no sense. What was the point of having a council that refused to act? Why were she and the rest of the people forced to accept things as they were, without complaining? She balled up her fists as she grew more and more frustrated. Wait. What was happening? The voice in her head sounded familiar, but it didn't belong to her. It sounded like Rafael, standing on that table trying to rile the group. No, Ayanna did not think like that. She knew the value of the Watchers. She knew all that they had done to organize the people and help keep them safe. She just didn't understand what was happening now. Why wouldn't they act?

And Richard? Why wouldn't he fight them? He believed her. He had told her he did. Ayanna shook her head. She needed to get back to the clinic and Dr. Keaton.

Ayanna turned the corner and saw Adam Frey pacing the clinic floor. "Ayanna, Tamara has terrible stomach pain. Please help her," said Adam. His voice trembled with fear. Tears brimmed in his eyes.

Tamara leaned against the wall. She held her arms around her stomach and leaned forward with her head almost to her knees, bellowing in agony. Ayanna rushed to Tamara. "Here, lie down," she said, helping Tamara onto a cot in the clinic. "When did the pain start?"

"This morning," she yelped, "after breakfast."

"Did you eat breakfast in the cafeteria?" Ayanna asked.

"No," said Tamara, "in my room."

"I'll be right back. I just need to get some medicine from the other room. Adam, stay with her please."

"I'm not going anywhere," he said, grabbing Tamara's hand.

Ayanna hurried into the laboratory and went to the cabinet. She pulled down some sodium bicarbonate and a glass beaker. She reached for her water rations and was about to pour the water into the beaker when she stopped, set down the water, and ran back into the infirmary.

"Tamara where did you get the water—" she started to say but was interrupted when she found Donna Burrows now sitting in the room.

"Oh, Ayanna, thank goodness you're here," said Donna. "The pain is getting worse."

Ayanna hurried to Donna's side, placed two fingers on her wrist, and counted. She shook her head. Next, she placed the back of her hand across Donna's forehead. "You're burning up. Here, lie down over here," she said, guiding her to another empty cot.

"How many others have these symptoms?" Ayanna asked Donna.

"I don't know. What . . . what is it?"

Ayanna frowned. She knew what this meant.

An hour later, a boy in the primary program named Angelo and his mom entered into the clinic complaining of pain. The clinic was now filled with patients.

She was relieved when Dr. Keaton shuffled into the room and looked around. "Oh, Ayanna, we have a growing problem here. We need to sort out the various degrees of illness and assess the incubation time for the disease. I also want you to take some fluids from the patients so we can try to determine what is going on, but I think you're right. It looks like a waterborne pathogen." Dr. Keaton moved to the medicine cabinet, and Ayanna saw him grip the countertop and lean forward.

"Are you OK?" she asked, rushing to help steady him.

He nodded slowly, and his lips made a strained smile. "I'll be fine," he said quickly.

She wanted to protest, but there was not much she could do under the circumstances. Ayanna was not any closer to helping treat him than she was to helping the people in the clinic. She felt like a failure. She had to find a way to treat Dr. Keaton's heart. People at Terra needed him. She needed him too.

"Maybe you should lie down. I mean, I'm sure I'll be able to handle things here," she said. This was far from true. Ayanna was terrified. An outbreak of disease could be deadly, and Terra lacked the supplies she and Dr. Keaton needed to treat everyone. There was not enough clean water, there were not enough antibiotics, and there was not enough space in the clinic. Not to mention, their infection would lead to dehydration. If the disease didn't kill them, dehydration would.

"Listen to me, Young Doc, don't think of me again, just the patients. Helping them is all that matters now," said Dr. Keaton. His voice was stern.

Ayanna nodded her head reluctantly. What else could she do?

CHAPTER **21**

A yanna looked at her watch. One in the morning. She craned her neck and rubbed her eyes. Everything ached, and she was exhausted. She couldn't stand too much more of this. She yawned and looked around the infirmary. Eleven people now occupied the small room. They each suffered from slightly different symptoms, but pathogens coursed through their blood streams, and they all needed more water.

For hours, she had tried to reduce fevers, apply cold compresses, and divvy out aspirin. But nothing was enough. There were children in the clinic with high fevers that had spiked throughout the night. Sampson was among them. She worried the most for him. A 104-degree fever had held him hostage for six hours. Ayanna felt desperate to bring it down.

And even though most of the other patients didn't have a fever, which was a blessing, they all complained of terrible cramping, diarrhea, and vomiting. People throughout the compound volunteered their water rations, and Dr. Keaton and Ayanna gave up their own for the sick, but as the number of sick grew, it became harder to hydrate everyone.

Dr. Keaton was asleep not far from where she sat, slouched in his chair with his head against the wall and his mouth slightly open. Ayanna started to take out four glasses, avoiding making any noise so as not to wake him. She used a teaspoon to scoop crushed aspirin from its container and placed a small amount in each glass. Then, she walked over to her rations of clean water in the corner of the room, the liquid sloshing in the glass container. Only two liters remained. If they used up the emergency reserves, what would they do?

Tamara moaned from the infirmary. Ayanna's remedies had done little to lessen the excruciating cramping in the woman's stomach. A feeling of helplessness came over Ayanna in waves, but she forced herself not to let it overtake her. She had to keep trying. There must be something she could do.

She walked to the bookshelf, pulled a book from it, and flipped through the pages, trying to find the answer—any answer—to help the people writhing in agony in the other room. But nothing stood out to her.

Finally, Ayanna sat in a chair and rested her head against the wall. Without meaning to, she drifted off to sleep.

When she awoke, Josiah was standing above her. Ayanna jumped, startled. "Josiah, you scared me," she whispered. She looked at her watch. Two hours had passed

"I'm sorry, Ayanna. Mrs. Johnson sent me," he said as he looked around the room at all the disheveled, sleeping bodies. "She wanted me to ask Dr. Keaton to come and speak to the council."

Ayanna stood up. Her neck ached. She stretched to the side. "Come and speak to them? The Watchers are up at this hour?"

Josiah nodded his head.

"Dr. Keaton shouldn't leave his patients. Just tell them that he will have to come another time."

"You see, that's the thing," said Josiah. "They told me to stay down here to help you and Dr. Keaton, so that he could report to the council."

Ayanna looked at the sleeping, frail man with his stethoscope hung around his neck. She hadn't checked his vitals in days, but she could tell by looking that they couldn't be good. If anyone needed rest, it was the doctor.

"I'll go," she said. She walked to her work table and held up a bottle. "Everyone is going to need their medicine when they wake. If anyone wakes up before I get back, I want you to give them this to drink. Only use the water from this container. Do you understand?"

Josiah frowned as he reached for the bottle. He held it as if the plastic burned his hand.

Ayanna frowned but relaxed her stance when he nodded. "I'll be back as soon as possible."

Ayanna took heavy steps into the chamber. She did not see the point in being there. Several frizzy curls escaped from her hair tie and fell in her face. Her lips felt dry, and she imagined that her eyes were bloodshot.

She walked in and looked toward the council members, then waited with her arms crossed. Her mind wandered back to the clinic. She was anxious about leaving. The council members looked tired too. Apparently, even they were suffering through the night. Hopefully, the situation was as critical to them as to everyone else.

Ayanna was not surprised to find Richard there as well. It seemed that the Watchers relied on him more than any other person at Terra. She stood beside him, studying him. He looked even more weary and stressed than he had a few hours earlier, and she wished that they were alone. She wanted to know what he thought. He of all people had to have a plan. Everyone was counting on him, but he seemed very restrained in this atmosphere, with the council watching him so closely and turning to him for answers. Ayanna doubted she could get him to reveal his mind to her here.

"Miss Grace, how are the patients? I've received reports that twelve people are now sick," said Mr. Christy.

"Thirteen," Ayanna corrected. "But I sent two back to their quarters because their symptoms were minor compared to the others. As for everyone else, they're not doing well. I'm running low on everything. So far, the antibiotics could be working, but we only have a limited amount, so it's hard to tell." Ayanna wondered if they could hear the near panic in her voice, or if they even cared.

"Miss Grace, we have discovered that Cafferty was the person who distributed the tainted water," said Mrs. Johnson.

"Really?" Ayanna feigned ignorance. It didn't matter that she had lied earlier. Besides, this information would not help them now. What good would come from punishing Cafferty? Would it help anyone or improve their health? Ayanna could feel heat rising up her spine. She was becoming more and more frustrated with the council's misplaced priorities.

"Yes, he was brought before the council and admitted that he, in fact, distributed water from the pipes leading from the sewer," said Ms. Evans.

Ayanna shook her head. "OK, but that doesn't change anything. Our friends won't survive if we don't get more water. Several are suffering from dehydration. I have to have more water. I'm afraid that most of our patients will become delirious soon, especially the children," she said.

"Children? How many are sick?" asked Mrs. Johnson. She sounded worried.

"Three," Ayanna said, "Esteban, Angelo, and Sampson."

"It still has not rained, and the reserves are now at a critical point, but we can have one of the Protectorate bring more clean water to the clinic," said Mrs. Johnson.

"Thank you," Ayanna said. "Council . . ." She hesitated. She knew the temperament of the council, and she knew that she had failed to sway them before.

Ayanna looked to Richard for help. His eyes were patient and filled with concern, but she lost her courage. She sighed. Was this why they'd asked for Dr. Keaton? To hear more of the same? "I need to get back," she said.

"Please do," said Mrs. Johnson. She nodded her head slowly, and Ayanna recognized that Mrs. Johnson, out of all the council members, seemed the most concerned about the situation.

Ayanna turned and made her way back to the clinic, her thoughts scattered. There was a solution. Why wouldn't the council act?

When Ayanna arrived back in the clinic, she found Dr. Keaton standing above Sampson with his stethoscope pressed to the boy's chest. Jamal sat next to him, holding his hand. Ayanna approached slowly.

"He's worse," said Dr. Keaton. "It's dehydration. What did the council say?"

Ayanna looked over at Jamal and she felt a panic shoot through her. His face was drawn in, and dread filled his eyes at the sight of his son's condition.

"Not much."

Sampson moaned and shifted on the cot. His eyes blinked open, and a small whisper escaped his mouth. "Water," he said.

Ayanna walked to the counter and poured the last of the ration supply that she had into a small glass, then handed it to Jamal. Jamal cradled his son's head and lifted it from the sweat-covered pillow on the cot. "Here, Son, drink this. Take it slow," he said.

Sampson took small sips. He coughed a little and lay his head back down on the pillow.

"Dad?" he asked with a strained voice.

"Yes, Son."

"I want Mom," he said.

Jamal looked pained. "Your mother is resting right now, Son. She wants to be with you, I know she does, and she'll come to you as soon as she feels better."

Sampson pouted, and a small sigh escaped his lips. "Is Mom going to die?" he asked.

Jamal looked up at Ayanna. Fear and anguish swam in his eyes. She wanted to look away, but she forced herself not to. The truth was that she didn't know if Roberta was going to die, or if Sampson was going to die. She didn't know what would happen to any of the sick or even the healthy without water.

Jamal blinked and turned back to his son. He rested his hand on his son's forehead. "No, Son, your mother is not going to die. You are not going to die. You are going to be just fine," he said.

Someone cleared his throat at the door, and Ayanna, Jamal, and Dr. Keaton looked up. Richard stood in the doorway with a stoic look on his face.

Ayanna stared, surprised to see him there. Jamal shifted in his seat to allow Sampson a clear view of the door.

"Look, Son," he said, "Captain Daniels has come to see about you."

Richard nodded politely and stepped farther into the room. "Mr. Carter, Dr. Keaton, Miss Grace," he said with a formal tone. Ayanna studied him. A sad frown washed over his face when his eyes landed on Sampson's frail body. He moved closer to Sampson, and the little boy smiled weakly.

"Captain Daniels?" His voice came out softly.

"Hello, Sampson. The doc tells me that you've been very brave. I'm glad to hear it because the Protectorate needs good soldiers to fight the dragons," said Richard.

"Like you?" Sampson said.

Richard nodded his head gently. "Yeah," he said. His voice was barely audible. "Like me."

Dr. Keaton slowly walked out of the room and into the hallway. He gestured for Ayanna and Richard to follow him.

"Captain Daniels, what brought you down here? Is there any news?" asked Dr. Keaton.

Richard shook his head. "No, I just wanted to see for myself how people are doing," said Richard.

"Well, we're doing the best that we can, Captain. But what we need is water. We're lost without it," he said. Dr. Keaton seemed to be pleading with Richard.

Richard nodded his head. "I understand. The council seems . . . stuck," he said. "I'm hoping to get their permission to travel to the surface," he said. "But they need some convincing."

A feeling of anger flashed through Ayanna. She couldn't let this happen. She had failed to demand that the council do something to change this, but she wasn't going to be quiet anymore. She did not want Sampson or anyone else to die because of their inaction.

Besides, it didn't make any sense. They acted when they wanted to, decreeing rules and meting out punishments. They could act now. They should. Otherwise, what purpose did they have? This defiant thought scared Ayanna. Again, she recognized that it echoed Rafael. Had there been any truth to what he had said in his speech? She worried about what agreeing with him might mean for her. But for now, she pushed that worry aside.

"I have an idea," she said suddenly. She turned back into the clinic.

"Jamal?" she said softly.

Jamal's eyes shot up toward Ayanna, startled. "Yes."

"I need your help . . . for Sampson."

"Anything," he said.

"I need you to come with us. You see, the council, they don't understand what's happening down here. They won't listen to us . . . but they might listen to you."

Jamal looked at his son's fragile body. "What do you need me to do?"

Before Dr. Keaton could speak again, they were gone. Ayanna would take Jamal to the Watchers, and this time, she would force them to listen.

CHAPTER 22

Jamal, Ayanna, and Richard walked through the chamber doors. Richard stood beside Ayanna. She felt overwhelmed by the need to speak.

"Miss Grace, what's happened?" said Mrs. Johnson. She eyed Jamal standing there.

"Listen. I respect this council and I believe that you have Terra's best interest in mind, but I'm here because the people are suffering. We have to destroy the dam that I know is blocking the water flow," she said. "We can't continue like this much longer. Sampson may not make it through the night."

Ayanna turned her head to Jamal and gave him a small, encouraging smile.

He took a labored step forward. "Council," he began. He swallowed hard, but he looked emboldened. Richard raised his eyes to Jamal and listened carefully.

"My son, Sampson, is very sick. Ayanna and the doc tell me he'll die from dehydration if we don't get more water soon. I'm begging you . . . please don't let that happen. His mama is sick too and . . . and we've already lost our little girl." Jamal's voice cracked. "Please, Mrs. Johnson. If there's anything that you can do, then do it."

Mrs. Johnson opened her mouth to speak, her eyes brimming with tears. She was clearly moved by Jamal's words.

Mr. Christy interrupted before Mrs. Johnson could say anything. "Malcolm, has there been any progress on the water flow?"

Ayanna just noticed that Malcolm was now in the room. He must have walked in moments earlier. Malcolm shook his head. "Sadly no," he said. "The water from the river has stopped flowing altogether, and there are no signs that it will rain anytime soon."

"Captain, what do you think?" asked Mrs. Johnson.

Richard moved forward eagerly. "Miss Grace is saying what I think we all know," he said. "Things aren't going to get better on their own. The people are restless and fighting each other. The farmers tell me that the sorghum is beginning to suffer. If those plants die . . . so will Terra. If something isn't done soon, more people will be hurt, if not killed."

Ayanna felt a surge of relief. They would listen to Richard, she was certain. And Richard was on her side.

"Latasha, we need a solution now," said Mr. Christy to Mrs. Johnson.

Mrs. Johnson brought her hand to her head and rubbed her temple. It was rare to see her this vulnerable. Colonel Daniels remained silent.

"Captain, do you believe Miss Grace's description of what she saw in the river?" asked Mr. Christy. Ayanna opened her mouth but closed it quickly. She was too relieved that the council was considering sending the Protectorate out to be offended by the suggestion that she had made the whole thing up.

Richard needed no time to think over the question. "Yes."

"Well, Miss Grace, it looks like you and Captain Daniels agree on this matter," said Mrs. Johnson. "All right, Captain, I will leave the details of the mission up to you."

"OK. We will leave at first light," said Richard.

"That's not good enough," Ayanna said.

"Why not, Miss Grace?" asked Mr. Christy.

"Because the people lying in the clinic need fluids now. If we wait until sunrise, they might not all make it."

"It's too dangerous," said Mr. Frye. "Traveling to the surface in the dark is a terrible idea."

"But I agree with Miss Grace that the situation with the sick people is urgent," said Mrs. Johnson. Richard looked at the two council members. He seemed undecided about their assessments. Ayanna hoped Mrs. Johnson could sway him.

"Can it be done, Captain?" asked Mr. Frye.

"Possibly, if we move swiftly," said Richard.

Yes. He was willing to try.

"There's something else. I would need to go to show them where the blockage is located," Ayanna said abruptly.

Richard looked sharply at her. He stepped forward and spoke with authority. "With all due respect, Council, Miss Grace's presence might jeopardize the mission."

Ayanna glared at him and then looked back at the council.

"And with all due respect, Captain, letting your team go out to the river blindly won't help. I know where the dam is. The only way to make sure your mission is successful is if I come with the militia."

"My team hardly needs Miss Grace to show us where the Savannah River is located," Richard said, raising his voice slightly. His jaw clenched. Ayanna wasn't sure, but she thought she saw his hand tremble as he spoke. He seemed almost frightened. Ayanna shook her head. That was not possible.

Richard eyed her too. But Ayanna stood firm. She intended to go with the Protectorate. She needed to get the water flowing again, and she needed the digitalis for Dr. Keaton. That was the only way she could ensure that everyone made it out alive. Dr. Keaton was the one the patients needed, not her.

Richard looked over at his father, and Colonel Daniels nodded. "I don't see any reason why Miss Grace should go to the surface," said Colonel Daniels. Ayanna blew out a quick breath. "I'm sure that her knowledge can be conveyed on paper. Certainly, Captain Daniels knows what would be best for his mission. You said it yourself, Latasha. He is the one in charge of it."

"Of course Captain Daniels is in charge of his own mission, but I tend to agree with Miss Grace," said Mrs. Johnson. "The mission will be most successful if she simply shows the team where she identified the dam."

Ayanna allowed herself a small smile. Mrs. Johnson carried the most sway.

In that instant, Richard's expression resembled panic. Ayanna was certain this time. His eyes widened, and he raised his eyebrows. It was an unusual expression for him. Ayanna had never imagined that Richard could be afraid of anything. She didn't understand it. He was not afraid of the surface or of facing dragons. No, this was something else.

Richard again spoke up in opposition. "Council, this isn't a simple trek to the surface. We're talking about approaching the dragons on their territory *in the dark* . . . ," he said with emphasis, "setting charges and blowing up their dam, all before they realize that we're there. Only the senior members of the Alpha Team should come with me, and I'm pretty sure that some of us won't return. Having Miss Grace there . . ." Richard stopped. His next words were obvious.

"Captain," Ayanna said, "I can take care of myself. I don't need a babysitter or a protector. I'm going."

"Council, I strongly feel that—"

"We understand your position, Captain, but Miss Grace is more than capable, as she has shown us so defiantly in the past. I think that she should accompany your team to the surface," said

Mr. Christy. "Let us put it to a vote then. All in favor of Miss Grace showing the Protectorate where she spotted the dam, say 'aye,' all opposed 'nay.'"

The council members spoke in unison.

"The 'ayes' have it. Miss Grace goes," said Mr. Christy. Richard drew in a deep breath.

"Captain, when will you be ready to leave?" asked Mrs. Johnson.

"We will be prepped to leave at oh four hundred hours, ma'am," said Richard.

"Very good." said Mrs. Johnson. "To Terra."

Richard nodded his head.

The council dismissed Ayanna, Richard, Jamal, and Malcolm. Ayanna quickly headed for the door. Before she reached the exit, she felt a hand grab her arm and spin her around.

"Ayanna, what do you think you're doing? I won't be able to protect you out there if something goes wrong," said Richard.

Ayanna stood up tall in front of him. "Richard, I have an infirmary full of sick patients. Do you really think that I'm going on this mission to have it fail? I don't need you to protect me. Trust me. I can handle myself," she said confidently.

Richard stared into her eyes. He seemed to be searching for something. His frown deepened, but he nodded and released her arm.

"I'll expect you to be prepared and ready to leave at oh three thirty," Richard said sternly.

"I understand, Captain. I'll be ready."

Ayanna left and headed back to the clinic. She had finally gotten through to the council. Getting to that dam was the right thing for everyone. She would not waste this trip. This was her chance to collect the digitalis plant that she needed for Dr. Keaton's heart, but she felt a familiar sensation in her solar plexus.

Fear. The last time that Ayanna had been to the surface, she was almost devoured by a dragon, and this time would only be worse.

The team would be leaving soon, while it was still dark, and they needed to travel to the river in order to destroy the dam. It was what needed to happen. She pushed her fear aside. She would do whatever she had to do to save her patients and Dr. Keaton.

Ayanna stood by her bunk and placed a white cloth and a knife in the new backpack she had snagged from one of the storage closets. She tested the batteries in her flashlight and added it to her other items. She was so distracted packing her things that she nearly jumped out of her skin when Malik burst through the door.

"Where is the captain taking you?" he demanded. He looked furious. His eyes were red and moist from what seemed like frustrated tears just on the brink of falling. His little boy features were covered with an angry scowl.

Ayanna could not remember the last time she had seen him like this. Maybe right after they had first been forced underground, and everyone realized the military transports had left, with no intention of returning to help them.

"What? Malik, how did you . . . you know I can't tell you anything like that," Ayanna said.

"Captain Daniels just walked into base and chose five of the top guys in the unit to go with him on a secret mission. Now, I come down here and see you preparing to leave with him too. What is this all about?"

Ayanna closed her backpack and walked over to Malik. She sighed and placed her hand on his shoulder. His body was rigid, and he seemed to concentrate on controlling his breathing.

"The council has instructed me not to talk about this with anyone. Look around you, Malik. People are dying. The Protectorate and the Watchers aren't just going to sit around and let that happen, and neither am I. If Captain Daniels wanted you to come with him, then I'm sure he would've picked you. I bet he needs you here, protecting the people at home."

"I . . ." Malik's face shifted between anger and disbelief. "I can't believe this crap! Why would he choose you over me? You're not even a soldier!"

Ayanna could see the hurt in his eyes, and she felt bad for him. Ayanna knew how important things like this were to Malik, but she could not comfort him right now. There was no time. "Look, Malik, I can't talk about it, OK? Everything is going to work out fine. You'll see. Now please, report to your station. I have to go," she said.

Ayanna picked up her bag and started to leave her room. Malik let out a deep huff as he walked past her. He kicked the concrete wall and shook his head as he left. Ayanna sighed and followed behind him in the direction of the Alpha Team.

CHAPTER **23**

Ayanna took slow steps to the militia base, carrying only the essentials. She did not want anything to slow the mission.

But Malik's angry words pressed on her mind. "Why would he choose you over me? You're not even a soldier." It was true, Ayanna wasn't a soldier. Was she really the one who had to go? And besides, was she even sure she knew why she was going?

Yes, she thought. She knew why. She had to. She couldn't risk being left alone to take care of all the sick people in the clinic. She wasn't a real doctor. She didn't know enough. What if someone died because of her? She couldn't risk that. She was going to do whatever it took to help them, but that meant helping Dr. Keaton.

Still, her legs were a little heavier than they should be. Ayanna wanted to go with Richard's team . . . well, she needed to go. She had to return to the banks of the Savannah River, but she sensed that this time would be different. This time would be even harder. Not only did Ayanna have to deal with dragons, but she would have to get onto the riverbank and collect the digitalis before the Protectorate set off their charges, and while evading Richard's watchful eye.

With each step, she considered the consequences of her

decision. Maybe Richard was right. Maybe she didn't need to go. Ayanna reviewed the possibilities. She could forget the mission and ask Richard to retrieve the plant she needed. She remembered his request that she ask him first before doing anything dangerous. He might consider taking on this job for her if she told him why it was so important.

However, this plan could backfire. Ayanna understood Richard. This mission had a very specific task. He was taking his team out to destroy the dragons' dam. Richard was not likely to deviate and risk many for the benefit of one. He didn't think like that. If Ayanna revealed her other intentions, he would try to stop her.

No. She needed to risk the danger, Richard's anger, and the anger of the council to get the medication that Dr. Keaton needed to stay alive.

Ayanna walked to the place where the Alpha Team was supposed to meet and stopped. She suddenly regretted the words she had spoken to Malik, and she wished she had said good-bye to Maya. It was not that she thought she would never see them again. It was just that it occurred to her now, more than it had thirty minutes ago, that there was a chance she might not return.

As Ayanna waited in the tunnel, she spotted Richard in the doorway. He stood still with his arms crossed, resembling an onyx statue. He stared ahead, concentrating on the prep work his team performed. Ayanna looked around. The men in Richard's unit had serious faces. They moved back and forth across the space, packing equipment and exchanging brief phrases. They were all business. Each movement made it easy to tell why they had been selected for this mission.

Ayanna knew all their names, but she was only really familiar with two of them. Officer Latif was a stocky man, only five feet, eight inches tall, but wide. He had thick neck muscles and arms like tree trunks, and he lifted heavy boxes of materials without straining. His mouth was set in a straight line; he was neither frowning nor smiling.

And then there was Juan Ramirez. Ayanna knew the most about him. He had known Richard since the start of the war. He was from Georgia, and it was only by chance that he had found his way to Tropeck. His parents had died when the dragons appeared, but there was still a chance his sister and cousin had made it to an evacuation checkpoint. Even so, there was no way of finding them now.

Ramirez had fluid and precise movements. If Ayanna had never seen him before, his stoic expression matched with his strong and tall features would have made him seem completely unapproachable.

Ayanna walked silently toward Richard. His commanding presence reminded her why she and everyone else trusted him to keep Terra safe.

He glanced over his shoulder and said, "Come with me please." He moved toward a wooden box containing supplies and began to pack a bag for the mission. Ayanna followed him to the box, which held guns, grenades, yellow squares of C4, and bullets. Ayanna knew that Terra kept a small weapons locker at the end of the compound that contained everything the soldiers had managed to recover from the abandoned tanks. She didn't know a lot about weapons except for the basic operations of a handgun, but she knew from Malik that at least two of the members of the Alpha Team had been experienced explosives technicians during the war. Ayanna figured that one of these men would be coming with them.

Richard slid a knife into the sheath on his waist belt and loaded a gun with a clip of bullets, sliding it into a holder on his hip. Then, he removed a piece of paper from a pile on the box, unfolded it in front of him, and began to study it. It looked like a map.

Ayanna stood as still as she could, trying not to interfere, but her patience was wearing thin. It annoyed her that Richard was taking so long to say anything. What exactly did he want her to know? Only a few weeks back, Ayanna had associated this behavior with him. She tightened her hands into fists by her sides. She was about to demand his attention when Colonel Daniels's voice startled her.

"Captain, I came to see how the preparations for the mission are coming along."

Richard stopped his perusal of the map and looked up at his father. He looked startled. "Colonel, everything is going fine, sir. We'll leave on schedule," he said.

Colonel Daniels looked over Richard's shoulder and saw Ayanna standing there. He eyed her and frowned but did not speak to her. Ayanna looked between Richard and his father. She let out a sigh and backed away from the box, moving to the corner to recheck her bag of supplies.

When the colonel was satisfied that she was far enough away, he addressed Richard, but she could still hear him. "You know how important this mission is to Terra, Son. I know we can count on you. You are your father's son."

Richard nodded his head.

"Well . . . ," said Colonel Daniels, pausing.

Richard looked at his father with what seemed to be anticipation. There was a long break, and Ayanna could not help wondering what he was going to say.

"You're a good soldier," Colonel Daniels said finally. The words sounded foreign in his throat, and he seemed to strain to get them out.

It seemed odd to Ayanna, not the sort of thing she would expect a father to say to his son. She thought perhaps Colonel Daniels might have gentler words for his son who was about to go out on a deadly mission. Maybe she expected him to tell Richard that he loved him, and that he was proud of the job he was doing.

Richard's face softened, and he looked surprised. He faced his father and stared at him for a few seconds. Ayanna could tell that Richard was searching for the right words to say in return. It occurred to her that she had misjudged him again. She had almost forgotten how strained things must be between Richard and his father.

"Thank you, sir," he finally said. Colonel Daniels turned and quickly walked toward the hall. He turned back briefly, and the men looked at each other. Richard waited with a faint look of anticipation, but Colonel Daniels did not speak. Richard nodded once, the colonel passed through the doorway, and that was the end of the exchange.

Ayanna stood up from kneeling over her bag and reclaimed her position at Richard's side, taking a deep breath before she said anything. She wasn't afraid of Richard's judgment, but she knew he disapproved of her coming with the Protectorate. A whimsical wish flashed through her. She wanted him to have confidence in her ability to take care of herself.

This was probably based on a memory from when they were children. She remembered how Richard used to be so impressed with almost everything she did: winning awards, acing her tests, or helping him fix the lenses in the telescope he had accidently knocked over and broken. She thought she had gotten over that feeling, but apparently she was wrong.

"I'm ready whenever you are, Captain," Ayanna said.

Richard broke his gaze from the path his father had taken and turned to face her. She looked into his eyes. They were stern, but warm.

"Grace, it's no secret that I would prefer you not to go on this mission," he said.

Ayanna had expected him to be direct. His words were harsh, but his voice was calm, and it lacked the biting tone necessary for his declaration to sting. She said nothing. She already knew this.

"But the council seems to think otherwise, and the council represents Terra, and I have pledged my loyalty to Terra. So, it is Terra I obey. I would only ask that you might show the same level of loyalty to me . . . for Terra's sake," he said.

Ayanna raised her eyebrows. "What do you mean?"

"I need your word that you will follow any instructions I give you. If I tell you to run, you run. If I ask you to hide, you hide. I need you to do exactly as I tell you. What do you say, Ayanna?"

Ayanna could feel the blood rising to her face. She was grateful that Richard would not be able to notice it beneath her skin tone. She didn't want to lie. He had a sincere desire to keep her safe. She felt guilty about denying him another request, but she knew she would not follow his orders. She had plans of her own.

"I need your word."

"Richard, I—"

"Excuse me, Captain Daniels, but we're ready for you to take a look at the detonators now," said Officer Gomez.

"OK, I'll be right there. Excuse me, Miss Grace."

"Of course, Captain." Ayanna held in a sigh of relief.

After a few moments of talking with his team, Richard gave the signal that it was time for them to leave. They started their trek through the dark subway tunnels. Ayanna moved in conjunction with the group. The men jogged at a steady pace, and she stayed close to the front, following the small light that their flashlights provided and maintaining steady and quiet breaths. She deliberately kept up with Richard, who kept looking in her direction every few seconds. He had been clear about his feelings, and she hoped that when he saw that she could take care of herself, he would abandon the cautious watch he kept over her.

After moving through the tunnel for twenty minutes, Richard stopped and pointed his flashlight up. Her eyes moved to a small access door.

"This is where we will enter the street."

Gomez and the soldier named Henry moved forward, and Gomez picked the lock. The door opened to a steep set of concrete stairs leading up to the surface. It was completely dark.

"Grace, come up with Ramirez," Richard instructed.

Ayanna looked around and acknowledged Ramirez, who now stood beside her. Richard began the ascent to the city first. Ramirez and Ayanna waited for the others to climb the stairs, and then they followed closely behind.

The team and Ayanna came out at the edge of the city, four miles from the river. No one spoke. There was no way to know if they would immediately encounter dragons.

Richard removed the pistol from his hip and walked out onto the street. He periodically checked the skyline. The night was clear, and the moon and stars provided a dim light. A warm breeze kissed Ayanna's skin.

Richard's head moved back and forth to scan the area. It was dark, and Ayanna could not make out more than a few figures on the street. She recognized the shapes of the buildings and the blackened and broken light posts.

Despite the darkness, Richard's team seemed to anticipate each other's movements. They traveled as a well-trained unit. Richard gestured to the other men, and they understood his orders.

Ayanna tried to follow. Richard walked over and leaned close to her, almost touching her ear with his lips. He whispered, "OK, Ayanna, it's time to find this dam."

The calmness of Richard's voice reassured her, and she relaxed, letting out a long breath. "Let's go," she said, pointing east in the direction of the riverbank.

CHAPTER **24**

Richard walked so close to Ayanna that she could hear his controlled breathing. He kept his body a few inches in front of hers as they moved quietly through the city streets. The only sounds came from the scratching noises that echoed from a department store with broken windows and burnt walls. The fact that they were not alone sent a tingling sensation up the back of Ayanna's neck.

The swift and agile movement of Richard's team surprised her. No one had ever accompanied her on her trips to the surface, and the team's presence made her feel both safe and nervous at the same time. Like most days of her life, Ayanna realized that others were counting on her. This time, she had volunteered to point out the exact location of the dam. The realization started to wash over her and her heart beat faster. But taking Richard to the dam would be relatively easy compared to what would follow. How had Ayanna come all this way without a sensible plan for getting the digitalis?

Think, Ayanna commanded herself.

Richard paused suddenly. His surprise movement focused her attention. The team approached the open land, leaving the confines of the skyscrapers. Ayanna glanced at Richard, whose face wore a frown.

"Wha—?"

Richard brought his finger to his lips. Ayanna closed her mouth with a slight pop. Her breath rang loud in her ears. What did he see that she didn't? A dragon? She waited for Richard to move. After a few seconds, he motioned ahead. Whatever it was seemed to have moved on, and the team stopped in front of two massive blocks covered with a canvas tarp. Gomez and Ramirez approached the wide figures and pulled back the canvas sheet to reveal two military jeeps.

"Grace, ride with me," said Richard.

Ayanna felt relieved. She hadn't realized the Protectorate had hidden vehicles nearby. But then again, there was no reason for anyone to have told her.

She squeezed into the back of Richard's jeep. Richard took the wheel, and Officer Gomez sat beside him, while Lieutenant Ramirez rode in the back with her. The other men climbed into the second jeep, and they continued to the riverfront.

Richard sped over the open road. Only a few cars sat abandoned in the streets. The jeep's tires rolling over gravel mixed with the roar of the engine, drowning out most of the night's sounds. Ayanna could not see beyond the first two hundred feet in front of the jeep, but she knew the dragons flew high above them. The night was their time.

Richard brought the jeep to a bumpy halt and turned off the engine a half mile before the riverbank. The second jeep did the same. The men got out with their weapons drawn, and Richard stood beside her again before Ayanna realized he had moved.

"If we get separated for any reason, I want you to take a jeep and return to the Scion building. Do you understand?" Richard said.

"I understand," Ayanna said.

The group approached the bridge overlooking the Savannah.

Ayanna remembered the last time she had been at the mouth of the bridge and sucked in a quick breath. Everything had gone wrong then.

Ayanna gestured with her hands, indicating that they needed to crawl over the side of the bridge and lower themselves onto the riverbank. Richard nodded and left her side to take the lead. Before climbing over the edge, he pointed to Gomez and Latif. The men became alert and watched as Richard motioned with his fingers that they cross the bridge. They nodded silently and started jogging across the waterway.

"OK, Grace, how much farther?" whispered Richard. The sound of his voice broke her attempt to view the patch of green waiting for her at the far end of the riverbank.

"Thirty feet or so. Here, follow me," Ayanna said.

Ayanna moved to swing her leg over the side of the bridge and Richard hesitated, blocking her way. She started to protest. She needed to get to those plants.

"I've done this before," she reminded him. He looked at Ramirez and Samuels. They waited with their guns drawn and their heads facing the water. Richard nodded in agreement and moved onto the soil, allowing space for her to follow.

As Ayanna moved onto the soil, her feet sank into the earth. She gritted her teeth, hoping the soil did not disturb the water. This was crazy. Before, it had felt reasonable and necessary, but now that they were so close to their goal, the entire mission seemed insane. Ayanna closed her eyes, pushed her fear down past her feet, and opened her eyes again.

She began to fight her way through the loose soil. Richard and Ramirez followed closely behind her while Samuels stayed on the bridge. After twenty feet, Ayanna stopped in her tracks and turned to the water. "There," she said pointing.

Richard tightened his eyes as he struggled to see. His

expression changed as he started to recognize a massive layer of concrete, wood, and dirt protruding from the river.

"Damn," said Ramirez. "Are you sure two blasts will be enough?" he asked Richard.

Richard ignored Ramirez's question and turned to Ayanna. "Grace, I can take it from here. You and Samuels go back to the city. Wait in the Scion building for one of us to come for you. You can expect us in two hours."

"Captain, I—"Ayanna started to speak, but Richard cut her off.

"That's an order," Richard said bluntly.

Ayanna frowned, but Richard could not see her face in the darkness. She needed to go farther down the riverbank to get to her digitalis.

There was no way to convince Samuels to defy Richard. He, like Ramirez, had fought in the Fire Sky War. They were trained government soldiers, and they seemed to believe in orders as much as Richard did.

Ayanna entertained the wild thought of breaking into a run and escaping Richard's team, but the idea seemed ridiculous under the circumstances. Maybe she should just come clean and tell Richard what she needed. Now was as good a time as any.

"Richard, I . . ."

"Sir—" Ramirez interrupted.

"What is it?" Richard asked.

"I thought we needed Samuels to detonate," Ramirez reminded him, "but this dam is a lot bigger than you or I could have anticipated. If we're gonna have any chance of bringing it down, we're gonna have to get out there and put a charge in the center of that baby."

Richard's muscles hardened into stone. He dropped down on one knee and looked out over the water. He studied what dimensions he could see and took in a heavy breath.

"You're right," he said after a long pause. "I'm going to have to swim out there to set the other charges."

Ayanna's stomach sank, even as her heart jumped. This was the moment she had been waiting for: she was going to be left unsupervised long enough to collect the digitalis. But the idea of anyone, let alone Richard, swimming in dragon-infested water crushed her happiness. "Wait, you're going to swim? Out there?" she repeated in disbelief.

Richard nodded. "Grace, I've changed my mind. I want you to head back to the Scion building alone and wait there, just like I said. We'll be there to collect you in two hours. Do you understand?"

His tone was more a statement than a question. Ayanna's hands balled into fists. She wanted to challenge him, but she didn't know if she could influence Richard right now. His voice was hard and serious. He would accept only one answer. Besides, this was the chance that she needed, Ayanna realized, and trying to change Richard's mind might backfire.

She pointed her flashlight at her wrist. "I understand. Two hours," she said. She turned and started to back away from the soldiers.

"All right, listen up. As soon as these charges are in place, we'd better be ready to run," Richard said to Ramirez. "They'll swarm us, and there's no way around it."

Ayanna moved back toward the bridge as Richard and Ramirez approached the water's edge. She waited until she passed Samuels walking to join his team before she changed direction. She hoped the team would be too distracted, and the darkness too encompassing, for them to notice her movements.

When it was clear they could no longer see her, Ayanna pushed her way through the soil toward the oasis. She had no more than twenty minutes to get the plant, get back on the bridge, and return to the Scion building before Richard set off his charges.

Adrenaline masked the terror that coursed through Ayanna's veins. She was not sure what she had imagined would happen when they made it to the banks of the Savannah, but she was certain this was not it. Maybe she had believed they could throw the explosives onto the dam without having to get near it. She should have known better.

Ayanna walked into the dark, trying her best not to make a sound. The small lights that the militia carried shone just enough for her to see Richard step into the water. Wasn't there something else he could do? Anything else? This was not a good plan. Dragons swam even better than they flew.

Ayanna wished that one of Richard's men would volunteer to place the explosives, but then immediately felt guilty. Of course, she didn't want anyone to die, but what would Terra do without its militia leader? She knew each of them had to pay a price for survival, and she was willing to do whatever it took to save Dr. Keaton and the people who relied on him. But it didn't seem fair to her that Terra should suffer even more if something happened to Richard too.

And there was also a quiet, subtle undercurrent that Ayanna could not ignore. What would *she* do without Richard? The question didn't have any place in this moment, and yet, there it was. She could not deny it. Ayanna didn't want to lose Richard.

She turned and looked back toward Richard and his team and watched them, all the while trying to force her feet forward to the digitalis. From afar, she saw Richard check his bag for the explosives.

"How's it look?" Richard called to Samuels, moving toward the water.

"Seems clear, sir."

Richard took three short breaths to prepare himself for the chill of the water; then, with his bag on his back, he started to wade silently into the cold dark of the river.

Ayanna watched with awe and dread. In theory, the dragons would have cleared the water to go out and hunt, but Ayanna didn't think Richard should risk his life to test this.

Her eyes struggled to see, but her ears remained alert. Ayanna listened and immediately regretted this decision. She heard movement from every corner. Wings flapped in the distance, mixed with intermittent squawks and low growls, all with the backdrop of the sound of water flowing over rock.

Gomez stood on the other bank of the river. He flicked a flashlight three times, and it was not until Ayanna saw a light coming from the center of the dam that she realized Richard had made it all the way out into the middle of the river.

Richard removed his backpack and took out two square bars of explosives. He held out a flashlight and clicked it on and off two times. He waited, and after five seconds, Ayanna saw two flashes of light from across the river on the other end of the dam.

A part of her—most of her—wanted to watch. She needed to know that Richard wasn't going to be eaten or blown up, but the rest of her needed to collect the digitalis and get to the Scion building before any of them realized she was missing. She tore her attention from the scene and trudged toward the patch of green waiting on the beach that rested a few hundred feet south of the dam. When she arrived, she pulled a knife from its holder and clipped all the flowers from the patch of digitalis. Then, she stuffed the plants in her bag and turned to run back.

Everything after that happened so fast that Ayanna could barely tell what was going on. She was knocked backward. She heard the deafening roar of an explosion and saw a large plume of fire shoot into the air. She ducked and held her arm up to her head in a futile attempt to protect herself from flying debris.

She was in trouble. She had ventured far from Richard and his team, and she was nowhere near the jeep. She had so concentrated on reaching the coveted plant that she had forgotten to plan an escape route.

Horrible screeches sounded, and Ayanna felt the shift in the air as an unknown number of winged creatures started circling above the river. Sounds came from everywhere.

Bright firelight replaced the darkness, and Ayanna could see clearly for the first time. In the near distance, the small glow of rounds being fired from the soldiers' weapons created tiny sparks in her vision, followed by the popping sound of the gunshots. The dragons flew overhead and spewed out fiery streams toward the men as they raced for the bridge.

There were at least four of them in the sky above the river. Their wings thrummed through the air in a rhythmic fashion as they alternated between flight and dives toward the earth, barely missing Richard's team with each attempt.

Richard was back on the beach now. Ayanna watched as a dragon landed in front of one of his men and grabbed him with its claws. Richard ran toward the creature from behind with unbridled fury and unloaded repeated rounds at the base of the dragon's neck. The dragon released the soldier, but Ayanna was horrified when the soldier's body was flung through the air like a child's doll, landing limply on the soil. Without missing a step, the dragon squared off to attack Richard.

Ayanna lunged forward, unclear as to what she could do to help, but a dragon flew from the sky just above her head. She looked up and screamed when its long tail barely missed her. She wanted to make her way back toward the soldiers, but she couldn't cover the distance quickly enough, and now the dragons were coming from all directions. She ran instead, her hands grasping at the rocks and roots that came out of the side of the precipice, as she fought her way back up to the street.

The screeching was terrible. The creatures attempted to encircle her, two streams of fire forming trails around her. All Ayanna could think to do was keep running. The heat of their flames threatened to scorch her skin as they began to light the ground in front of her. She ran back toward the city; at least she hoped that was the direction she was running in. It was difficult to tell, as everything was chaotic. She needed to hide and tried to look for recognizable buildings in the distance, but it was hard to see even twenty feet in front of her.

Everything flashed past her eyes in a blur. Her urgency made the distance seem so far. She didn't know where to go. The jeeps that had brought the team to the river were too far now. A tall overpass entered her line of sight. The closest hiding place was in this concrete split in the wall of a highway. Ayanna charged for the entrance and slid through the crack.

CHAPTER 25

Ayanna lifted up her small flashlight, which barely provided enough light to see. She took in a shallow breath and held her hand to her nose as a putrid stench assaulted her nostrils. The air was thick with must and sulfur. She took three steps, her shoes sticking to the ground with each one. She lifted her leg slowly and discovered a gooey, thick substance on the bottom of her boots. She then noticed that the crack she'd slipped into opened into a wide, cavernous hole in the concrete.

Ayanna took another step before recognizing that something blocked the way. A large object filled the concrete structure from one wall to the other. She held up her light and strained her eyes to see, moving her flashlight from side to side to try to make out what stood in her way. Whatever it was, it was moving slowly up and down, almost as if it were breathing.

Breathing.

The realization of what was in the cavern with her overwhelmed her senses, and she gasped. She had stumbled upon a sleeping dragon.

Ayanna's eyes dashed back and forth as she looked for a way out, but she had journeyed too far into the cavern, and the creature had made a slight movement of its tail, blocking the exit. She wouldn't be able to leave the same way that she had come in.

The dragon stirred, and she held her breath, her mind shooting thoughts at her too fast for her to process. How long did dragons sleep? Could she make it out if she tried to run? Did it know that she was there? The smell of sulfur burned in her lungs as Ayanna forced air through her mouth in shallow gulps. She needed to escape, and fast. She also needed to know where the dragon's head lay—that knowledge would keep her alive—but the darkness made that difficult to figure out too.

Ayanna crept around the massive creature. She couldn't make out its full form with the little amount of light she had, but she knew its body had to rise at least twelve feet from the ground. She tried to calculate the path that she should take. Just beyond its body on the other side of the room was a crack in the wall similar to the one Ayanna had entered through. It seemed to lead back out onto the street.

The dragon took in long, steady breaths. Ayanna pressed her back against the concrete wall, walking as erectly as the space would allow. Her feet moved sideways, and her toes pushed down firmly before her heels hit the ground. She tried not to make any noise, but the rubber on her shoes made a pulling sound with each step. When the dragon drew in a long breath, she paused. She closed her eyes and listened, counting the seconds.

This was it, she thought. It would wake up and kill her.

One second, two. But then the dragon returned to its cadenced, low, rumbling breaths, and Ayanna continued to move toward the crack in the wall.

It was painfully slow work. Every step felt like an hour. But finally, she stood at the head of the creature, her light illuminating the space enough for her to see that its head stood taller than her body, and thick scales created patterns across its skin.

It had large slits in its neck that looked like gills, and nostrils on its face.

A small part of her wanted to touch the dragon, to study the contours of its skin. But the part of her brain that indulged in curiosity was no match for the part that screamed for her to escape. The two parts met when Ayanna surmised that if she did not leave soon, the dragon would smell her presence, even in its sleep.

If she could just pass by its head, she would make it through the exit. But she calculated all the ways that this move could go wrong. If the dragon woke up while Ayanna was crossing, she knew it would only need to open its mouth in order to finish her.

Sweat from her forehead dripped into her eyes. She took one step toward the animal, its hot breath escaping from its nostrils and hitting her face. The smell of rotting meat caused vomit to rise in her throat. Her breath locked in her airway as she continued to inch past the dragon, almost to the exit.

She had taken two more steps when she tripped over something that rested on the floor in front of her and went up to her waist. She looked at the dragon's head. Panic shot up her spine. Had she hit a part of its body? She waited, but the dragon did not move. It was not what was blocking her exit.

Ayanna's outstretched hand fumbled for the object. The same slime that covered everything else in the cavern was smeared across her fingers too. Beneath the slime, though, she could feel something leathery. She slid her hand down the side of whatever it was she was touching, making out what felt like an oval shape. Her eyes widened in vain as she tried to take in more light.

Suddenly, something in Ayanna's mind clicked, like a key in a lock. She was touching an egg. This was the first one she had ever seen.

She held her light above the translucent object. It had no markings or openings, and its texture gave slightly when she pressed against it. She lowered her light to the side of the egg next. Its contents stirred and Ayanna jumped back, falling on her backside. After a moment, she raised herself to her knees for a closer look, and she saw that the creature was suspended in a fluid that she assumed was keeping it alive.

Ayanna looked around. This was not a single egg. Dozens covered the ground.

She moved her eyes from the exit to the egg, to the dragon. She wanted to study the nest, to take in as much information as she could, but every muscle in her body knew it was time to leave.

The dragon's breathing shifted. Her time was up. Its huge, yellow eyes opened abruptly, and it lifted its head from the ground. Every terrible death she had ever witnessed because of a dragon flooded her mind. The same thing was about to happen to her. She could imagine her singed flesh, her ripped skin, her broken bones, her blood-soaked body. Terror took over and Ayanna made a desperate dash for the opening of the cavern. She slid between the tight sides of the concrete walls and let out a painful cry as shards of metal rods sliced into her arm. Warm blood oozed from her veins and down her hand.

Fresh air hit Ayanna's face. She took in a deep gulp when she realized she was back in the street. She looked for cover and ran, but the dragon would not ignore her presence in its nest. She had angered it. It sounded off as it expanded its wings and flew up through an opening at the top of the cavern that she hadn't realized existed.

Ayanna watched it emerge and perch itself above the overpass. It spotted her and made its way into the open street just as she ran for another concrete column that held up the highway overpass. It was not going to let her escape.

The dragon's cry stung her ears just before it shot a flame in her direction, covering the street behind her. She expected to feel the flames incinerate her. Instead, Ayanna felt herself fly through the air for a brief moment before smashing hard onto the ground. She tried to look up to see what happened. But her head throbbed, and her eyes became heavy. She blinked twice, and then everything went black.

CHAPTER 26

Ayanna lay with her eyes closed and wondered if she was still alive. She couldn't feel her body. Maybe she was dead, which was likely. Death seemed strangely peaceful.

As she mulled over the idea that she had died, she heard gunfire in the distance. The Protectorate was close. Ayanna wasn't dead. She was still on the surface. Dragons still surrounded her, though, and she was definitely still in danger. She opened her eyes and was shocked when she heard a nearby voice.

"You really are crazy, aren't you?"

Ayanna looked up and searched for the source of the voice. Her eyes widened in disbelief when she saw Jackson standing above her.

She moaned as she tried to stand, and a shooting pain stabbed through her nerve endings. She grabbed her left arm and cried out. Now, she remembered cutting it when she escaped the dragon's nest. The impact from her latest fall had only made the throbbing pain worse, and the bracelet her father had given her no longer dangled from her wrist.

She saw Jackson clearly, his bright hazel eyes glowing in the soft firelight, and his tattoo peering from beneath his T-shirt, contrasting sharply against his tawny skin.

"Hold on, let me help you," he said, moving toward her.

Ayanna felt confused. She had thought she was imagining him until she felt his warm hand gently touch her waist and lift her from the ground in one swift motion. She held onto Jackson's muscular forearm and stumbled against him as she tried to gain her balance. When her eyes met his, she was sure he was real.

Ayanna stared at him, and coherent thoughts abandoned her. The same stranger she had tried to forget now stood with his arm cradled behind her, providing her support. Her body gently pressed against his, and a familiar sensation of warmth and exhilaration washed over her. Had he saved her . . . again?

"What on earth are you doing here?" Ayanna asked.

Jackson smirked. "Good to see you too."

Ayanna winced in pain. Jackson released her carefully from his embrace and stepped back.

"How can you smile at a time like this?" she asked, annoyed at his flippancy.

He let out a quiet laugh, revealing an even brighter smile. "Can you think of a better time?"

Ayanna tilted her head to the side. She had no response. "Did you bring me here?" she asked, looking around at what appeared to be the inside of a factory.

"Yep, looked like you were in a bit of a jam. Figured I'd help you out, but you hit your head and passed out when I knocked you out of the way of that last flame.

You were out for about three minutes," he added, anticipating her next question.

"Thank you." Ayanna looked around at where they hid.

"You're hurt; you should take it easy." Jackson spoke in a matter-of fact tone. He seemed at ease, as if they hadn't almost been burned to death only minutes before.

"I'm fine." Ayanna tore the bottom of her T-shirt and used

the cloth to wrap around her wound. "My sample!" she remembered suddenly, before rushing to her bag. Her head pounded with her movements, but she ignored this latest sensation, using her good arm to open her backpack.

"What sample?" Jackson asked. He stayed rooted in his spot and checked the skyline.

"It's a plant I need. Digitalis . . . foxglove."

She reached in her bag frantically, found the cloth concealing the precious medicine she had risked her life for, and let out a sigh. "Oh, thank goodness," Ayanna said, holding the cloth tightly to her chest.

Jackson stared at her, then shook his head. He looked like he was trying to make a decision.

"I was right about you."

Ayanna allowed her eyes to leave her precious medicine and look up at him. She had seen this look before. "What are you talking about?" she asked as she carefully put the cloth back into her bag.

"Shh." Jackson abruptly held up his hand. He looked around the corner and out into the street. Ayanna took in a shallow breath and waited, expecting to hear the dragon just outside. After a beat, Jackson lowered his hand and turned back to her.

"When we first met, I pegged you as someone who would walk right out in the path of dragons and look them square in the face for no reason at all. Now, here you are proving me right. Unfortunately, you can't just go out there right now because there is more than one dragon waiting to kill us."

Ayanna shook her head. "Richard," she gasped, remembering the team that had accompanied her to the surface. "There may be dragons out there, but I need to get back to the others."

"You're here with other people?" asked Jackson.

"Yes, the Protectorate came out here and risked their lives to free up the water that was blocked by the dragon's dam. I have to find them so we can get out of here before one of them is killed."

"You need to rest. You're injured," he said, pointing to her arm.

"No, I'm fine," Ayanna insisted, shaking her head. "I need to get back. I don't want anyone dying because they stayed out here longer than they needed to. I won't have them risk their lives any more than they already have."

Jackson ran his eyes from her arm to her face. There was a long pause. "Well, if anyone can take care of themselves, it's you. Where are you supposed to meet your friends?"

"I am supposed to be in the Scion building."

"That's the really tall one that has a golden lion's head for a door?" he asked.

Ayanna nodded her head.

"That's not close."

"I know, but I need to get back there. Otherwise, they might keep looking for me, and the longer they're out here, the more chance they have of dying," she said. Worry and guilt crept into her mind.

Jackson frowned and clenched his jaw. Ayanna could tell he was considering what she told him. He looked outside again.

"All right, I'll help you get over there. I know a shortcut."

"No, I've put too many people in danger today. I won't ask you to risk your life for Terra. This is my responsibility," she said.

Jackson turned to her, looked into her eyes, and the seriousness left his face in an instant. A smirk replaced it. "Well, good news then. I won't be risking my life for Terra. I'll be risking it for you. Turns out, I'm pretty good at that."

"No, I'm serious." Ayanna shook her head defiantly.

"So am I." Jackson's smirk widened into a smile, and Ayanna felt defenseless against his expression. "Come on, get your stuff. We're going to have to make a run for it."

Ayanna wanted to argue with him. She didn't know if she could change his mind or not, but the idea of another person placing his life in danger made her ill.

"Why on earth would you do this?" she demanded.

"You're not used to people helping you, are you?" he asked, never letting his grin drop. This silenced her. It was an observation, not a question. When had he had time to learn anything so personal about her?

But Ayanna didn't have long to worry about that. The answer seemed irrelevant given the situation. She moved to pick up her bag. Her action seemed to satisfy him, and he waited calmly.

She held back a wince as she situated her backpack and held her injured arm close to her side. "OK, I'm ready." She met Jackson near the exit. He looked at her and nodded.

Ayanna took in a breath and Jackson grabbed her right hand. "All right, Ayanna Grace—let's see what you've got."

CHAPTER 27

Ayanna and Jackson ran under an overpass and took shelter after five hundred feet. Jackson looked around. The only signs of dragons came from the river, and that was at least a hundred feet away now.

"OK, the Scion building is west, and we can cross over Main Street to reach it. Fifth and Main is about three blocks from here. We're going to have to stay low and move fast. You ready?" he asked, with clear excitement on his face.

Ayanna nodded unconvincingly. "Ready."

They ran through the abandoned streets as quickly as their legs would allow, small fires lighting their paths through the city. They crossed over Olive and Third. When they got to Fourth Street, Jackson stopped suddenly.

"What is it? Do you see something?"

"I thought I heard something, but maybe not."

"You sure?" Ayanna was worried. She looked up at the sky but could see nothing.

"Yeah, I'm sure. Look, over there. We just need to make it onto that street," said Jackson.

"OK."

They fell through the broken doors of the Scion building.

Ayanna's chest heaved from exertion. She recovered within a few minutes and scanned the room. They had arrived in the lobby of what used to be a hotel with marble floors and high ceilings. Wiring from shattered chandeliers hung from the ceiling. The elevators stood immobile and broken in the lobby, but a long, elaborate stairwell led to the upper levels of the building.

Ayanna reached for her flashlight, and Jackson let out a small laugh.

"What?"

"You."

"What about me?"

"You're ready for anything," he said.

Ayanna shook her head. She didn't feel ready for anything. She felt nervous and out of control. Meanwhile, Jackson moved about carelessly. He didn't seem to have any plan. They walked through the lobby of the building side by side looking for signs of people, using just Ayanna's small light to find their way.

Jackson seemed calm, but Ayanna was frantic. She was worried about Richard and the others. She was worried about what was going on back at Terra. And she was worried about whether they were going to get out of this alive.

"So," said Jackson, "what's it like?"

"What's what like?" Ayanna asked, distracted. She wanted to check everywhere she could see to find the others.

"Having a purpose. What's that like?"

"What are you talking about, Jackson? Do you hear anyone?" Ayanna wanted him to focus on her task.

Jackson ignored her and continued his line of questioning. "I mean, knowing that you want to help people, knowing that you have a place in this world. It must be fascinating being you."

Ayanna stopped her search for a second and shined her light in Jackson's direction.

"I don't know anything except that I need to find Richard and his team and get back to Terra," she said, exasperated.

"All right, fine, just trying to make a little conversation." He raised both hands in the air.

"You want to talk, *now*?"

"Why do you keep thinking there's a better time for things? I mean look, if your friends are in here, then I'm sure you'll find them, but until then . . ."

"OK, fine. You want to talk, let's talk. I didn't always know that I wanted to help people. All that I knew was that I wanted to be like my mom. I wanted to study biology and organic chemistry in college and go to medical school so I could be like her," she said. She had raised her voice without meaning to.

"You don't like to talk about her. I shouldn't have brought it up."

"It's OK. It's not that I don't like to talk about her. . . . I mean, I think about her all the time, every day." Ayanna poked her head down a long hallway as she continued. "I remember. I remember everything, her smile, her voice, her laugh. I remember everything about her, and I guess . . ." She stopped.

"What?"

"It's hard is all. It hurts to remember. Sometimes, I wish I could forget, but then I feel guilty for wishing that. What kind of person wishes they could forget the one person who loved them more than anyone in the world?" Ayanna said. She started walking again. Jackson continued at her side but said nothing.

"What do you mean, anyway? 'What is it like to have purpose?' Don't you have a purpose?" she asked.

She couldn't see well in the dark, but she thought Jackson shook his head.

"No."

"But I don't understand. I mean, everybody—" Before she

could finish her thought, Ayanna heard a rumble come from somewhere in the building.

Jackson looked up and then in her direction.

"Is that them?" she asked.

"I don't think so. We should move a little faster to find your friends, OK?"

"Is that a—?"

"Just hurry."

"OK," Ayanna said. They started to jog through the huge lobby of the building.

The noise grew louder. Jackson stopped abruptly. Ayanna suspected that at least one dragon was inside the hotel.

"We've gotta figure out how to get out of here," he said.

"You think it's a dragon?"

"Willing to place a bet on it."

"So, what are we supposed to do now?" Ayanna asked.

"Well, I don't know if it knows we're here," said Jackson. "This building is pretty big, you know. Maybe he's just resting upstairs."

Ayanna looked at him, unimpressed with his theory. "Just resting?" she asked incredulously. "I wouldn't count on it. Their sense of smell is better than a dog's. If it doesn't know we're here yet, I'm sure it'll figure it out. We'd better think of something fast so we can find my friends and get out of here."

"We could just wait in another building until the sun comes up," said Jackson.

"Yeah, I guess. That is, unless it's hunting us."

"True. All right, so I guess waiting for its next move is out," he said.

Ayanna pointed her light at Jackson. He was smiling. He raised his hand to block the light from his eyes. "Is that a smile? Are you actually smiling again? This is *not* funny, Jackson. Our lives are in danger. I can't believe that you are smiling at a moment like this."

"Relax, Ayanna. I've gotten out of tougher spots than this before—and so have you, I might add. I bet it doesn't even know we're here. Just breathe. Let's just—"

A huge crash rang through the room. Jackson grabbed Ayanna's hand before she could tell what was going on and they scrambled to hide behind the large check-in counter. Jackson poked his head around the corner.

"What do you see?" Ayanna whispered.

"Well, there is definitely a dragon. That's for sure. But it's kind of small, looks young. Almost like a baby if you ask me."

"A baby? Really? I've never seen one of those before. What else do you see? Can we make it out of the lobby?"

"Hold on, let me check." Jackson looked around the counter again. "Not sure. I don't know what the little ones are capable of; never seen one before, either."

"Well, Dr. Keaton hypothesizes that the dragons don't develop their ability to shoot fire until they reach six months of age or two thousand pounds. So, if it is a baby, maybe it doesn't pose that big a threat."

"Really? Two thousand pounds? So you want to *weigh* this thing?" said Jackson.

"Sorry, but it's hard to think clearly while I'm waiting to be killed," Ayanna snapped.

"Relax, Ayanna, I won't let anything happen to you," said Jackson in a changed voice. Ayanna looked into his face. He wasn't joking anymore. He was serious, and Ayanna didn't know what to make of him.

"I believe you," Ayanna whispered, "and I'm not worried. I know we'll make it out of this. It's not like it's the first time that I've faced death with you,"

Jackson smiled again. "No, it isn't."

A different, louder noise pounded just outside the doors of the hotel. It was something much larger than the small dragon that threatened them inside. Ayanna heard that excruciating, screeching call and felt the building shake. Plaster fell from the ceiling.

"Oh man . . . another, *much larger*, dragon just landed outside," Jackson said slowly, emphasizing his words. Ayanna lifted her head from under the counter to observe. She watched in amazement as the smaller dragon made a wild dash for the street, clamoring through the doors of the hotel. The racket sounded like a car crash.

"What in the world is happening?"

"I don't know, but I don't think that it's going well for one of them," said Jackson.

Suddenly, the small, baby dragon cascaded to the ground in front of the window of the hotel. The larger adult followed swiftly. It grabbed the baby dragon in its talons, and the two struggled. Jackson and Ayanna watched in shock as the creatures fought outside of the window. The baby dragon stood little chance, as it was no match for the adult that brutally clawed and struck at it. Streams of blood splashed over the front of the building.

"I think this is our chance to escape."

"Are you insane?" Ayanna responded. "There are not one, but two dragons right outside."

"I know, Ayanna, I can see them clearly, but they're preoccupied with each other for the moment. If we wait for the big one to kill the little one, then we have no chance at all. I say we get to the other side of the building while they're busy."

Ayanna thought for a moment before deciding that Jackson was right. They'd be better off trying to escape while the dragons were distracted. If the large one remained preoccupied with killing his young competitor, he would not notice them.

"OK," Ayanna said. "Let's run for the back door."

Jackson took hold of her hand, and they leaped from behind the counter. Ayanna turned around just in time to see the large dragon burn the smaller one to ashes and roar above it in the street. It did not notice them at all.

They ran down a long corridor with their hands still locked together. In the distance, Ayanna noticed small lights coming from one of the rooms.

"There!" Ayanna said. "It's them. It's Richard!"

Jackson stopped and let go of her hand. Immediately, she felt the loss of his warmth and looked at him. She didn't understand. Her torso turned toward Richard's lights, but her head looked back to make sense of Jackson. She fought to study his expression in the dim light.

"Well, it looks like this is my stop," said Jackson.

"Wait. What?" Ayanna was baffled. "Aren't you coming back with us?"

He shook his head. "Nah, think I have to sit this one out. But it's been fun, like always."

Ayanna shook her head. She didn't want to understand what Jackson was saying to her. "But . . . but why not?" she asked in disbelief.

"Ah, I dare say you're going to miss me," Jackson said mockingly.

That did it. Ayanna snapped out of her disbelief. She tightened her fists and drew in a quick breath.

"Look, I was only trying to make sure you don't get your fool self killed out here."

Jackson showed her his smile, its brilliance visible despite the darkness. "Don't worry about me, Ayanna. I'm not one of the ones you've gotta save. I promise you that. Take care of yourself.

Oh, and do me a favor? Try to stay out of trouble, OK? Just in case I'm not around to save your life next time."

Ayanna tried to hold on to her anger, but a mix of emotions clouded her mind. She felt something that lingered between sadness, annoyance, and a third feeling that Ayanna couldn't identify. Loss, maybe?

"Well, you don't have to worry about me," she said defiantly. "I can take care of myself."

"I don't doubt it, Ayanna. I don't doubt it." Then, Jackson turned and jogged away toward the back exit of the building.

Ayanna watched his striking form disappear into the darkness. For a fraction of a second, she considered following him. Where was he going and why didn't he fear this world?

But then she heard voices shouting, and her brain clicked back into focus. It was Richard calling her name. "Grace? Grace!" shouted Richard from a distance. "Grace, is that you?"

"It's me," she said. And she took off, sprinting toward his light.

CHAPTER **28**

Ayanna stumbled through the dark, musty, underground passageway, cradling her left arm against her body. Pain throbbed and pulsed through it, but at least she had stopped the bleeding.

However, not even the pain of her injury could block out the emotions that flooded her mind. Ayanna felt conflicted. On the one hand, she was happy that she had the digitalis. She was also excited that the dam was gone. Now, Terra had a better chance of survival. But the mission had come with a heavy cost: two of Richard's men were badly hurt and needed immediate treatment.

Ayanna heard gentle moans come from Officers Samuels and Gomez, and she smelled the sulfur from the ashes that covered their clothes. She felt guilty. Maybe if she hadn't abandoned the team and wandered off, the men wouldn't have gotten hurt.

Then there was Jackson. It wasn't just that she was thinking about Jackson that bothered her. It was that although she had tried to forget about him, she had never been able to do it. Considering all the events of the early morning, worrying about him should have been at the bottom of her list of priorities, but it wasn't. He had been on her mind since they had met, but until tonight, Ayanna had been convinced she would never see him again. She had found relief in that fact, but now that relief was gone. Seeing him again and having him save her life again had permanently etched the sight and sound of him into her mind.

With luck, he would be safe. She had no way of knowing. And why hadn't he moved out West like he'd told her he would?

Richard's voice interrupted her swirling thoughts. "Ayanna, are you OK?" he asked. His voice was raspy from shouting and smoke. Ayanna hadn't realized it before, but she was very relieved that he was safe and had survived the dragon attack.

Small flashlights lit their path, and Ayanna could barely see. "I'm fine. Terra will have everything that it needs. Everything is going to be OK."

"Yes, we freed the water, but I meant your arm, you've been holding it like that the whole time. I thought you might be hurt." Richard's head shifted down to look at her left arm.

"It's nothing. All that matters is that Terra will be safe. Everything was worth it for that."

Richard held his flashlight up in her direction. "You're bleeding. . . . I know you're the medic, but it seems clear to me you're injured. Let me help you." He reached for her.

She shied away slowly. "I told you, Captain. I'm fine," Ayanna said. "There are more important things to worry about than me. Two of your men have burns."

Richard's head shifted behind them as he took in a heavy breath. "Yes. I'm just happy we all survived," he said.

"Me too." Ayanna paused. She needed to choose her next words carefully.

"I'm sorry," she said. She knew it wasn't nearly good enough, but she didn't know how else to express what she felt.

Ayanna couldn't see Richard's face in the darkness, but she could feel it when he turned to look at her. "Sorry for what?"

"Earlier, you asked me to go directly to the Scion building

and wait until your team returned from the river, and I didn't. I didn't mean to put you or your men in danger. It's just that I . . ."

Richard listened, waiting for her to finish. Ayanna took a breath. "There was just something that I needed to do, and I'm sorry I made you go out of your way looking for me."

Ayanna wished she could see his eyes so she could gauge the extent of his anger. Richard continued to walk in silence, and her stomach dropped further with each step.

Finally, he spoke. "It's true that I didn't want you to come on this mission, and you know that I ordered you to stay at the Scion building. . . ."

Here it came: Richard's condemnation. Ayanna wondered how severe it would be—would he immediately send her before the council so they could cast her into a laborious sentence for weeks on end? Maybe he would simply enumerate all the ways he was disappointed and how she had nearly caused their mission to fail.

". . . But, Ayanna, I accept your apology," Richard said.

She was so stunned that she wasn't sure she had heard him correctly. "Thank you," she said.

Richard stopped abruptly in the tunnel although his men continued down the path home. "But there is one thing that you need to understand."

Ayanna held her breath waiting.

"In terms of coming to look for you, that wasn't me going out of my way," Richard said, his voice lowered. "You know that, don't you?" He stated each word carefully. Ayanna opened her mouth to speak, but nothing came out.

"I would never have left you up there under any circumstance. No matter how long it took, I was going to find you," he said slowly. His words sounded sincere. It was impossible for her not to believe him.

Richard took a deep breath. "I realize things are difficult between us. And I know you don't understand why I did what I did before, with your father. I know you blame me for choosing your life over his. . . ."

Ayanna blinked. Richard was aware of the resentment she had held toward him, and she shouldn't have been surprised to hear his words. For months, she had only spoken to him when forced to. And before that, her words to him had been cruel and unforgiving. Still, it shocked her to hear him talk about it so openly. It made her remember how much she had come to regret the harsh things she'd said to Richard on the day her father died.

She had called him a coward and a liar. She had poured all her grief, anger, and anguish from losing her father and her mother and her home onto Richard that day, and he had simply taken it. He hadn't tried to defend himself or argue with her. He had just stared back at her, and her pain had only grown when she'd seen compassion and hurt looking down on her from his impossibly dark eyes.

Ayanna's mouth opened to speak. She wanted to say something, but Richard wasn't finished. "But I thought that by now you would've understood just how important you are to me . . . I mean, just how much I . . ." Richard let out a short breath. Ayanna wished so much that she could see his face clearly. He shifted. He seemed to have abandoned the thought. He turned and kept walking.

Ayanna stood still. She had only partially understood what just happened. What was Richard saying? What did he mean? She should know "just how much" . . . just how much *what*? She wasn't sure what to think. Slowly, she resumed her trek home.

CHAPTER **29**

T wo weeks had passed, and Ayanna walked into the clinic feeling lighter than she had in forever. Terra seemed warmer, the air cleaner. There was no noise. People weren't bursting into the clinic with one emergency or another. And there was a happy, calm buzz all over the compound. All the patients who had suffered from dehydration or infection had begun to recover. The color had returned to their faces, and their skin looked less ashen. Many people were still weak, but no one had died, and Ayanna was eternally grateful for that.

Officers Gomez and Samuels struggled with healing their burns, but they too would live. Terra had enough water. And even Dr. Keaton's symptoms had started to stabilize with each treatment of digitalis that she gave him. Terra was safe again, and everyone had started to relax—or at least gone back to how things had been before the drought.

Ayanna felt relieved. She still had many things to plan for, except now, she had time to think through her next steps. She considered what it meant that she had seen Jackson in the middle of all this, but he had turned down her offer to return to Terra with her . . . again.

There wasn't anything she could do about that now, though,

and too many things were finally going right. She didn't want to spend time sulking over the beautiful boy who clearly had his own agenda.

Instead, Ayanna chose to spend this day studying her father's work again. She turned on the light in her sleeping quarters and sat on her cot as she flipped through one of her father's composition notebooks.

"What are you doing?" asked Maya, smiling in the doorframe. Ayanna jumped and looked up from her book.

"Sorry, I didn't mean to scare you."

"It's OK. I'm just studying. What's up?"

"I've come to collect you for the celebration."

"What celebration?"

"Well, everyone is so happy the water is back on that they've gathered in the common area for a glass or two," said Maya.

"A water party?" Ayanna asked in disbelief. "Terra is having a water party? I think I'll pass." Everything at Terra up to this point had been about survival or training to survive. Ayanna couldn't remember a time when people had stopped to celebrate a victory or a time when they'd had any fun at all.

"Oh, come on, Ayanna. You need to get out of this basement and spend some time with us. I know my grandma misses you like crazy. It was really hard trying to convince her that you weren't in mortal danger when you decided to go to the surface with the Protectorate. Even though you were, and I climbed the walls all that morning with worry," said Maya.

Ayanna frowned. She knew that Maya's words were true.

"And Malik misses you too," Maya added.

"How is Malik, anyway? I know he was upset the last time I talked to him about not being able to go with the team to the surface," Ayanna said.

"Upset, really? He didn't mention anything to me about being upset. But you can ask him yourself when you come to the party. I mean, even Captain Daniels agreed to be there."

Ayanna shrugged her shoulders. "Of course he did. He's the hero of the day. Who knows where we'd be right now if he hadn't blown up that dam."

"Right. Well, I'm surprised, actually," said Maya.

"Why?" Ayanna asked.

"He just doesn't strike me as the social type. Look at him. He's just so . . . serious."

"Sure he is, but he's got to be. I mean look at all the pressure he's under," Ayanna said. She didn't realize she had become defensive until she saw Maya staring at her.

"What?"

"Nothing. I just didn't realize that the two of you were back to being friends."

"We're not. I mean . . . I don't know. I guess I just understand what he's going through, is all," said Ayanna.

"OK," said Maya. "Still—party?"

"My, I don't have time for parties, OK? I have work to do and—"

"Really? So, you're just going to sit in your room while everyone else is celebrating?"

Maya crossed her arms and waited. Ayanna knew this look. Her friend would not let this go easily. There was a sad gleam in her eyes, and Ayanna cringed at the idea that she'd hurt Maya's feelings yet again. "Fine, I'll come to the party, but only for a few minutes," Ayanna said.

Maya's smile returned instantly. She grabbed her friend's arm, practically skipping as they left for the upper level.

When Maya and Ayanna walked into the gallery, people filled every corner of the room, and most were smiling as they talked together. As they passed through the crowd, Ayanna overheard some of the conversations.

"I'm just so relieved. I didn't know what we were going to do," said Lee Simon.

"Well, I don't think this changes anything. The Watchers are still incompetent. I think we need to have elections, and soon, because if they can't even handle a simple drought, then what?" answered Catherine Blacksburg.

"I always knew we could count on that Captain Daniels. He's a war hero, you know? Both he and his father served in the Fire Sky War."

Ayanna relaxed into the crowd. She was glad Maya had convinced her to come. It was nice to be reminded that Terra was still a community and still her home. Miriam offered Ayanna a tin cup of clean water with a smile, and Ayanna smiled as she took it, holding the cup delicately in her hands. She was careful not to spill even a drop.

She noticed when Richard entered the room, dressed in uniform as always. His face was its usual stern, expressionless mask. But Ayanna knew there was more going on behind his eyes. There was always more. They had gone back to ignoring each other after releasing the water from the dam, and she wondered if it was because he regretted the conversation they'd had in the tunnels on their way back from the surface. She also imagined that, despite the recent success at the dam, Richard was still worried about his injured men and about Terra's safety.

Ayanna was about to greet him when two girls approached him from the side. Ayanna knew the first girl, Rasheeda Sawyer. She was an electrician who worked with Maya and Taylor. Ayanna only recognized the second girl's face. She was a schoolteacher in the primary program. They stood on either side of Richard, backing him into a corner. He looked tense and stood with his arms at his side and his jaw tightly locked. Occasionally, he nodded at the girls, acknowledging their comments.

Ayanna smiled with amusement. She watched for several seconds, surprised at how different Richard seemed here. Although he was normally confident and quite sure of himself, in this setting, he looked uncomfortable.

Rasheeda laughed cheerfully. She seemed to be telling him a story, and she placed her hand on Richard's shoulder whenever the opportunity presented itself. The other girl smiled brightly, trying hard to hold the captain's gaze. It was then that Ayanna realized the girls were flirting with Richard. She felt blood rush to her face. A nagging feeling of annoyance crept up her spine. She tried to ignore it and quickly shifted her eyes away.

Malik and Mrs. Sanders joined Maya and her in the corner. Malik took his place beside her and leaned against the wall.

"I'm glad you're safe," he said.

"Thanks. How are you? I know, before, you were up—"

"Me, I'm great. I'm not worried. I know I'll get my shot," said Malik. "I have no doubt about that."

"Malik, it's not a competition," she said.

"'Course not," he said.

"Excuse me," said a voice from behind. Ayanna, Malik, Mrs. Sanders, and Maya all turned toward Richard, who stood just outside their small circle.

"Captain Daniels, please let me be the first to say how grateful we all are to you for keeping us safe and for bringing Ayanna back to us in one piece. You're more than welcome to join us in the celebration if you'd like," said Mrs. Sanders. "I'm sure you know my grandchildren, Maya and Malik, and I am Mrs. Sanders."

"It's nice to meet you. I'm just glad that I could be of service to you and to your family," Richard said, shaking Mrs. Sanders's hand. He turned to Malik. "Private, how are you?"

"I'm doing great, Captain. Just glad you guys are back and Terra is safe," said Malik.

Malik turned toward his sister and grandmother, and Richard and Ayanna faced each other.

"How's your arm?" Ayanna swallowed hard at the reminder of their time on the surface. Even though Richard had forgiven her, she still felt guilty about putting his team in danger.

"It's better, thank you." He nodded his head, and his eyes remained fixed on her face. Ayanna felt her stomach tighten, and she concentrated on her glass of water. She wasn't sure what to say next.

"How's Dr. Keaton responding to the medicine?" he asked.

Ayanna's eyes shot up at him. "How did you . . . ?" She felt indignant. Had he known the entire time? Of course, he had figured it out. What else had she expected?

Ayanna faltered before speaking. "He's going to be OK. The digitalis seems to be working."

Richard never moved his eyes from her face. *How does he always stay so still?* she wondered. "Well, I hope he gets all his strength back."

"Thank you, Richard," Ayanna said. Several seconds of silence passed before she spoke again. "Captain, there is something else I forgot to mention about that night."

Richard shifted his torso, and Ayanna felt him lean in toward her. He was the only thing in her line of sight, and she found that she had no choice but to look into his onyx eyes. She considered backing away from Richard's gaze, but his eyes were soft and patient.

Ayanna shook her head gently. "When I ran to escape the swarm, I came across a dragon's nest."

"A nest?" he asked.

"Yes, it was in a concrete opening under an overpass about

five hundred feet from the river. It was hard to see, but it seemed to me that there were at least a dozen eggs in it and one very large sleeping dragon. I don't know why I didn't mention it before. I guess I just got so distracted with everything else that was going on."

"No, it's OK. Thank you. That is important information for me and the council to have. It means it wasn't enough just to destroy the dam. We'll need to go back and destroy the nest too. But that . . . that's really dangerous," said Richard in a soft voice. He looked down. He seemed to be thinking about something.

This made Ayanna curious. Since when was Richard afraid of anything? A few more seconds of silence passed before they heard a tin cup drop in the corner, followed by the sound of laughter.

Ayanna looked around. She listened as Mrs. Sanders seemed to be finishing a story about her third-grade class when Malik abruptly hugged his grandmother and sister. "If you don't mind, I'm going to go check on the guys. See you after my shift. I'll catch you later," he said, hurrying out of the party. Mrs. Sanders and Maya waved at Malik and continued to socialize with the rest of the group.

Ayanna returned her attention to Richard. "You deserve this, you know. You should enjoy it," she said.

"What's that?" asked Richard.

"This party. The praise. It's true. You're a hero."

"I don't know about that. I was just doing my duty." Richard's mouth turned upward. The expression softened his features, and for a fleeting moment, he resembled the young boy she remembered from a lifetime ago.

"Well, I do," Ayanna said, smiling. He started to speak again, but one of the militiamen came up to him and whispered something in his ear. Richard's face fell. He suddenly looked serious again.

"I'll be right there. Excuse me, Ayanna. I have to go," he said. He reached out his hand and touched her shoulder, a motion that seemed to surprise both of them. Then, Richard nodded his head once before rushing away.

She wondered where he was headed, but she dismissed the desire to follow him. She had to learn that knowing everything that went on at Terra wasn't always for the best. It had already caused her enough problems. Besides, Ayanna needed to get back to the lab.

After a few more minutes, she finished her glass of water, hugged Maya and Mrs. Sanders, and returned to work.

CHAPTER **30**

Ayanna paced impatiently outside the Watchers' chamber. Only thirty minutes earlier, Brenton Harvey had rushed into the clinic to tell her that the Watchers wanted to see her immediately. There was a stranger at the gate, and he had asked for her.

Had Jackson actually followed her back to the compound? Was this why Richard had been called from the water party so urgently? Ayanna couldn't believe it. Could this really be happening?

She needed to concentrate on breathing. One breath in. One breath out. Good. She had that part down pat. Now, she just needed to figure out what she was going to do about everything else. To this point, no one knew about Jackson but her. She hadn't even told Maya about him. And the whole time, she had told herself that she just didn't have any good reason to bring him up. He wasn't dangerous to them as far as Ayanna knew, and she thought that he would have moved on from Tropeck by now.

Brenton walked out of the Watchers' chamber. He wore a question on his face, but he didn't speak. Ayanna fixed her eyes on him and tried to will him into telling her what was going on in there. Instead, he headed back down the hall.

"We are ready to see you now," said Mrs. Johnson from inside the room.

Ayanna walked into the chamber. Her eyes fell on two guards, and then to the person who stood between them. Her pulse quickened. It was Jackson. He wore a black T-shirt and dark pants, and he looked the same as before.

Jackson smiled at her when she passed. Ayanna's breath caught in her throat, and her stomach performed a tiny somersault, but she gave him a shy smile before looking away to stare at the assembly of councilmembers in front of her.

Richard stood in the back of the room, his expression unreadable. *What in the world must he think of all this?* she wondered. *Was he angry?*

Colonel Daniels jumped straight in. "What can you tell us about this stranger that you encountered? What is his name?" he asked councilmember Christy.

"Jackson," Ayanna supplied, before Mr. Christy could check his notes.

"Yes. Jackson," Colonel Daniels repeated. "What can you tell us about him?"

Richard moved closer. She paused before answering, not knowing what she should say about Jackson. She didn't want him sent away, and yet, her mind couldn't form a reasonable excuse to protect him.

"Well Colonel, it's just as you said. He's a stranger. I met him on the street and he . . ." Ayanna thought for a moment, going over in her mind the time they had spent together. "He saved my life . . . twice." Ayanna's voice softened as she said this. The memories of almost dying were fresh in her mind. " He told me he planned to travel out West and that he was alone. That's all I know."

Colonel Daniels's frown deepened, and his hazel eyes bore down on her. He didn't believe her, she could tell. But he had no way of disputing her story, either.

Unexpectedly, her mind jumped to a memory of the colonel passed out in his room. Ayanna wondered if Richard knew about his father's habit. He must, right? Unless the space between them was so great that they didn't spend enough time together to notice.

"Uh-huh, that will be all, Miss Grace," said Colonel Daniels.

Ayanna looked toward Mrs. Johnson. She wore a deep, disapproving frown on her face. There was a long silence before she said, "Miss Grace, if you knew that this stranger was lurking about, then why didn't you report him to this council?"

Ayanna snuck a look toward Richard. She was sure he was thinking the same thing. It was a fair question. Why hadn't she told? Ayanna lowered her head. She didn't want to admit in front of everyone that her reasons had been selfish. She hadn't told anyone about Jackson because she had enjoyed having a secret that only she knew. Knowing he was out there on the surface had given her something to think about that wasn't all the worry and responsibility of Terra. Part of her had even considered what it might be like to run off out West with him, assuming that was really where he was going.

Ayanna lifted her head back up. "I guess I just didn't see him as much of a threat," she said. She looked at Jackson, who was smiling softly at her, and felt her face turn warm.

"That will be all, Miss Grace," said Mrs. Johnson. Her tone was brusque. She clearly did not want to hear any more from Ayanna.

Ayanna stammered before turning toward the exit. She wanted to ask the council what they would do with Jackson. She wondered if he would be invited to stay, but she also knew that no one on the council would tell her.

She looked over toward Richard. He appeared pensive. Was he angry that she hadn't told him? Should she have? She wasn't sure. But even if he would tell her what was on his mind, they would have to be alone.

Ayanna avoided Richard's eyes as she left the room. She waited down the hallway out of sight, bouncing from one leg to the other. She had to know what the council would do with Jackson, and the waiting was agony. Time seemed to drag on and on.

Finally, the council members dispersed. Colonel Daniels left the room first, Richard following close behind him with a strong hold on Jackson's arm. Jackson looked angry, but he didn't seem to be resisting.

Ayanna wasn't sure where they were going. She knew what she was about to do was senseless, but she couldn't help herself. She needed to know what would happen with Jackson. The lack of information was more than her curiosity could take. Plus, she wanted to talk to him. What in the world was he doing there? Why had he just shown up all of a sudden?

She waited a few more minutes hidden from view until all the council members had cleared the room, and then she quickly trailed behind Richard and Jackson. If she were extremely lucky, no one would notice she was following them.

This was stupid. There were ten thousand smarter ways to do this, she knew, but they all would require patience.

Ayanna didn't have patience. She stood behind a wall and poked her head out into the militia wing. She'd seen where Richard and Colonel Daniels had led Jackson. Terra had turned the metro train station's employee locker closet into a holding cell. The Watchers rarely authorized its use except for emergencies. The locker closet stood six feet by five feet with concrete walls and a large steel grate covering the opening.

There weren't many people walking through the militia base, so Ayanna moved closer to the locker room. She had no idea how she would explain what she was doing down there if she got caught. But she had to know what had happened.

She snuck up to the opened door of the entrance and stood just out of sight of Richard and his father. The room smelled old and musty. Cubbyholes lined the shelves of the closet, and spiderwebs covered each hole. A squeaking sound came from a hole in the cell, and a moment later, Ayanna noticed a mouse scurrying across the floor of the pen. Richard slammed the steel gate behind Jackson.

"Is this any kind of way to treat a guest?" Jackson asked.

"I don't know. Is that what you are? A guest?" said Richard.

Jackson walked up to the gate and stood in front of Richard. He looked him up and down, never dropping a smirk from his face. The two boys were nearly the same height, with Richard standing only slightly taller.

It was strange seeing Richard and Jackson next to each other. They were both incredibly attractive, but the similarities ended there. Richard stood tall and straight—all business. Jackson's shoulders hunched forward. He was clearly relaxed and amused. Richard was worried about Terra, whereas Jackson seemed irreverent.

"I'd like to think so," said Jackson.

"What are you doing here, sir?"

Jackson's eyes wandered past Richard to Colonel Daniels, who stood silently near the door. Richard turned his head and observed his father too. He nodded before continuing his questioning.

"Again, what are you doing here?"

Jackson's smirk widened into a smile. "My name's Jackson Kyle." He held out his hand. "I would shake your hand, but . . ." He gestured to the gate.

Richard didn't move.

"I guess they don't teach manners here at this Terra of yours," said Jackson.

Richard glanced at his father again, and then back to Jackson. "My name is Captain Richard Daniels. How is it that you know that name, Terra, Mr. Kyle?"

Jackson laughed. "Ah, now that's the million-dollar question, isn't it? Did you ever watch that show as a kid, *Million-Dollar Question? That* was quality entertainment."

Richard took in a deep breath. "Do you think this is some kind of game?"

Ayanna could hear the annoyance in his voice.

"Honestly, yes," said Jackson. "Life is a game. Sometimes you win, and sometimes you lose, but it is definitely just a game. Unfortunately, I'm not winning at the moment." He placed his fingers between the spaces in the gate. "But the good news is that I never had much to lose to begin with."

Richard glared at Jackson. Jackson laughed and dropped his hands from the gate. He seemed to be enjoying Richard's discomfort.

"Fine, Ayanna told me about it. However, I have to say that it's not living up to my expectations."

"She did?" said Richard, surprised.

"Speaking of Ayanna, I have a cut here on my leg that she helped me out with before. Do you think you could ask her to come and take a look at it?" Jackson pulled at his pant leg to show Richard.

"I will get you medical treatment in due time, but right now, I want you to answer my questions."

"Right . . . and what was the question again?" Jackson smiled.

Richard clenched his jaw. "Right, of course, Ayanna. You want to know how I know Ayanna Grace. You could say that we ran into each other on the street."

"And what were you doing out in the street? In fact, what are you doing in Tropeck at all?"

Jackson looked toward the door again. Colonel Daniels stood unmoving.

"What am I doing in Tropeck?" Jackson repeated. "You know, I've been asking myself that same question for a while now. This trip is turning out to be more trouble than I anticipated."

"So, you are on a trip? And where is your destination?"

"I'm just passing through. Heard there might be some camps of survivors. Looks like I was right about that part. Plus, I hear there are fewer of *them* around, the farther west I go. Tropeck was just one stop on my journey toward the desert," he said.

"Where are you coming from?" asked Richard.

"Here and there."

Richard folded his arms across his chest. Jackson suppressed a laugh. Ayanna could tell he was enjoying how easily he could irritate Richard.

"I'm from Rockport. You heard of it?"

Richard shook his head "no," but Colonel Daniels, who had previously not said a word, spoke up. "You are from Rockport?"

"Yeah, I was born there. My mom and I lived there until I was ten."

"Your mother?" asked Colonel Daniels. "And what about your father?"

Jackson's smirk returned. "Don't know much about him. He split when I was a baby. He was some military guy, like you two. Doesn't matter anyway; he died during one war or another. Not that I care. I guess he had more important things to do than to raise his kid," Jackson scoffed.

Richard started to speak again, but his father interrupted.

"Where is your mother now?" Colonel Daniels asked. Colonel Daniels shifted his weight and leaned forward.

"Dead," Jackson said. "Next question?"

"How did she die?" Colonel Daniels continued. He spoke in a low voice, and Ayanna could barely hear his words.

"Her heart gave out. Next."

Colonel Daniels ignored Jackson's quips. This time he moved closer to the steel gate of the locker. "You say that your mother told you that your father was in the military?"

"Yeah," Jackson said, annoyed.

"What else did she tell you?" asked Colonel Daniels.

Richard looked toward his father. He looked confused. Ayanna was confused too. What did Colonel Daniels hope to get from Jackson?

Jackson must have been wondering the same thing because he asked, "Where are you going with this?"

"Just answer the questions," Richard commanded, supporting his father's authority. "This is Colonel William Daniels, councilmember responsible for Terra's safety."

"You're Daniels too. Wait. Is this your old man?" Jackson asked. "Ah, how touching. Father and son working together like a team. That is really adorable."

"The question, Mr. Kyle," said Colonel Daniels.

"My mother . . . my mother met my father in Rockport. They'd been seeing each other for a while 'til his wife found out. Hey, everybody makes mistakes, right?" Colonel Daniels stepped back from the gate and nodded, seemingly satisfied with this answer.

Richard breathed in slowly. "Mr. Kyle, what is it that you want here at Terra? We have a limited amount of space and resources, and there are people out there who would love to take them from us. We can't just let strangers wander in off the street."

"But we might be willing to let you stay with us, under certain conditions," said Colonel Daniels quickly.

Richard looked at his father, dumbfounded. Ayanna was surprised too. She had never known Colonel Daniels to be generous about anything, let alone to offer a stranger a place at Terra.

"If you agree to join the militia, become one of us, and protect Terra with your life, then the council might be willing to let you stay," Colonel Daniels clarified.

Jackson stepped back from the gate and walked around the cell. He studied one of the cubbyholes as if he would find a hidden answer inside. He said nothing for several moments.

"So, you're saying I can stay here awhile, rest up, as long as I play along?"

"And follow our rules," added Richard.

"Of course, of course, and follow your rules. We can't forget that part, the most important thing," he said. There was a smile in his voice. "But to be fair, this Terra of yours certainly does seem to have a lot of rules."

"Your answer, Mr. Kyle. You heard the offer. Take it or leave it," said Colonel Daniels.

Jackson looked down at the ground. Apparently, the answer he was looking for had jumped out of the hole and was now somewhere in the cracks in the floor. He snapped his head back up to meet Richard's eyes.

"I guess I can put my plans on hold for a little while and see what this Terra has to offer," he said.

Richard took a key from his pocket and opened the gate wide. He stretched his arm in the direction of the exit. "After you," he said.

Jackson smiled and walked out from the locker closet.

"Just one more thing," said Colonel Daniels, "Kyle . . . that's your family name?"

Jackson slowly turned and looked back at the colonel. "Yeah, my mother's name."

"What was her first name?"

"Why are you so interested in my family tree?" said Jackson.

Richard and Jackson both seemed to be waiting for the colonel's answer. Ayanna realized that she was waiting too. "We just want to make sure you are who you say you are," said Colonel Daniels.

Jackson sighed. "Did anyone ever tell you guys that you're a paranoid bunch? My mother's name was Rebecca."

Colonel Daniels nodded once. He lowered his eyes and looked thoughtful. Ayanna had never seen him look like this before, and like Jackson, she wondered why he had been so interested in Jackson's family. But she was out of time. She took her opportunity to launch into a sprint back toward the clinic.

CHAPTER 31

Ayanna wrote carefully in her medical log, capturing every detail.

Any dosage that exceeds 0.03 mg daily is likely toxic to the system. Note: It is very easy to exceed a safe dosage.

She yawned and reached for her cup of tea. She hadn't slept well. She was tired, but she still needed to finish two books on chemical compounds before she could take a break. Ayanna took a few sips of the bitter tea and lowered her eyes back down to her work.

"So, this is where you hide out?" asked a voice from the doorway.

Ayanna jumped and looked up from the books sprawled in front of her. She was astonished to see Jackson standing there. She had expected the Protectorate to restrict his movements, and she still could think of no reason why he had accepted Colonel Daniels's invitation to stay. Had he abandoned his plan to go out West? Had he just gotten tired of trying to get by on his own?

Ayanna fought back a smile, but it didn't work. He looked cleaned up and rested in his fatigue pants and T-shirt, and she couldn't ignore the fact that his new look somehow made him even more handsome.

She wanted to jump up to greet him, but she managed to stay seated. "It's called working," Ayanna said, "not hiding."

"Oh, I see."

Jackson's almost constant grin adorned his face, and without invitation, he walked in and sat on the bench next to her. "And what are you *working* on?"

"I'm trying to make a medication," Ayanna said, turning the page of her book. She tried to pretend she wasn't excited to see him there. She even hoped to find some way of being irritated with him for showing up so unexpectedly. But it wasn't working. All she felt was excitement.

Jackson slid closer to her and stared at her books. Ayanna felt the warmth of his body near her own, and blood rushed to her face.

"*Hydrogen bonds*," he read aloud. "Do you really understand this stuff? Or have you just got everybody fooled?"

Ayanna tilted her head to the side, closed her eyes, and opened them slowly. "Has anyone ever told you that rude and interesting are not the same thing?" she asked.

Jackson leaned his head back and laughed, widening his perfect smile. "You're a funny girl, Ayanna Grace," he said. He pointed his index finger at her as he said it.

Ayanna raised her eyebrows and partially closed her lab book, using her arm as a placeholder. "To answer your question, I try very hard to understand as much about medicine as I can. I've read every book here at least ten times," she said. She gestured to the books stacked on the shelves of the clinic. "Before the infestation, I really liked chemistry in school, and now . . . well now, I learn from experience."

"Sometimes that's the best way. I know that's how I prefer it," said Jackson.

Ayanna rolled her eyes at him, intending to ignore his implication. "So, the Watchers are letting you stay here?" she asked.

She forced her voice to sound as disinterested as possible. She didn't want to let on that she knew all about his conversation with Richard and Colonel Daniels. She also didn't want him to know that she had hoped he would be invited to stay.

"They are letting me stay . . . under certain . . . conditions," he said. Jackson stood up in one swift movement. He seemed irritated as he walked around the clinic, and Ayanna followed him with her eyes as he examined the equipment. He reached for a beaker, looked at it, and put it back down.

"Conditions, like what?" Ayanna asked, although she already knew the answer.

"They say I have to follow their rules. Join their militia. Be a part of the team," he said. His voice was thick with sarcasm.

"Well, that's to be expected." Ayanna gave up on her work and closed her lab book.

"Is it?" Jackson confused her with this question. In fact, she noticed that he had confused her with all his questions. He challenged everything that Ayanna had taken as fact.

"Well, yes. We all work together here. We each do our part. It's how we survive."

Jackson stopped walking and turned and looked at her. She wasn't sure what he was about to say.

He laughed once to himself. "You really believe that don't you?"

Ayanna shrugged her shoulders. "Of course I do."

Jackson continued to stare, but this time, he moved closer to her, never breaking eye contact. He sat down only inches away from her.

"Then maybe you're right. I guess I'll give it a try. Besides, there's something about this place that seems to draw me in. I might even go as far as to say it has an irresistible hold over me."

Ayanna sat in place, unsure of what she should do. She felt a flutter in her stomach.

A satisfied smirk appeared on Jackson's face as he got up abruptly and moved toward the door. "Well, I need to go have a talk with the guy I'm bunking with, and I'm sure you have a lot of work to do," he said.

Ayanna wasn't ready for him to leave, but she worried about what he would think if she asked him to stay.

"And who is it that you bunk with, Ayanna?"

The question surprised her. She blinked her eyes several times as if it would help.

"Me?" Ayanna stuttered. "No one . . . that is to say, I sleep in that room down the hall so I can be near the clinic, in case Dr. Keaton needs help with anything," she said.

Jackson smiled.

"Why do you ask?" Ayanna said. Her tone was suspicious.

Jackson let out another laugh. He was making fun of her and enjoying it, she knew.

"Relax, Ayanna," he said, his grin widening. "Just wondering who keeps you company at night, is all."

Ayanna felt her mouth open. The thought of anyone keeping her company at night had never even crossed her mind. She wanted to try to force Jackson to clarify his interest in how she slept, but no words came to her. In the next moment, he was gone.

Ayanna worked all day preparing her compounds and testing her samples. If one experiment failed, she tried again.

Before she knew it, the day had slipped away from her, and it was night. At seven o'clock, she pulled herself away from her work and went to find Maya. They hadn't had an opportunity to really talk since the party, and Ayanna was eager to find out what her friend thought about Jackson's appearance.

She figured Maya might be in the cafeteria for the final meal of the day. She headed there, but Maya was nowhere to be found.

Ayanna decided to eat while she had the chance. Miriam was serving the usual boiled sorghum mush, so Ayanna helped herself to a small portion of the unappetizing gray substance and sat at a table in the corner alone.

She ate her meal quietly and made a list of chemicals she still needed to replicate the medication. The people at the table next to her were speaking loudly, and Ayanna couldn't help listening.

"So, who is he?" asked Sarafina Rutledge, one of the teenage girls on the compound. Sarafina was training to be an agriculturalist. She was sixteen and thin, with thickly coiled black hair. Ayanna didn't have many reasons to interact with Sarafina, but she knew her face.

"I don't know," answered Katrina Sully. "But I hear he is young and not from around here, and the Watchers have invited him to stay. The council approved his entry into the compound. I haven't seen him yet."

"How's Josiah?" Sarafina asked, changing the subject. "Are you two still talking about getting married?"

"Well, yes, but lately . . ." She paused, looking around to see if anyone was listening. Ayanna concentrated on her meal. She didn't want the two girls to realize she was eavesdropping. "Lately, Josiah has been complaining about Terra. He says that we don't take enough action. He talks as if he wants to go fight the dragons. He worries me."

"Don't worry, Katrina, he's just talking. You know how much he loves you. He would never do anything so crazy," she said.

"I know," Katrina replied. "It's just . . . well, some people say that the drought was a sign that we aren't safe here anymore. Josiah says that we should consider moving on from Terra, or if not, we should at least try to fight. And now, with this stranger arriving, I don't know what to think. I mean, is he alone, or do you think there will be more?"

"I think Josiah is just being paranoid. Is that all you've heard about the stranger?" Sarafina asked.

"Yes. Hopefully, I can find out more soon," said Katrina.

Sarafina nodded as if satisfied with her friend's response. Ayanna allowed her attention to leave Katrina and Sarafina. Of course they were talking about Jackson. What had everyone else heard about his appearance in the compound? She realized that out of everyone at Terra, she knew the most about Jackson, and yet, she knew hardly anything at all.

CHAPTER **32**

Ayanna rested on Maya's cot and told her the story of Seema Sadiq's delivery. "Yes, Maya, it was amazing. I helped deliver him, six pounds, seven ounces. Seema and Khan were so excited when I announced that it was a healthy baby boy. They both cried," Ayanna said.

"Really? So you, like, performed a real-life miracle?" said Maya.

Ayanna smiled. "Well, I wouldn't go that far. I mean, Seema *did* do most of the work," she admitted.

Just then, Malik walked into the family's quarters and plopped down on his cot. He sighed and lay back to rest. "Wow, what a day," he said.

"What's that all about?" asked Maya.

"The captain has us working double-duty now that we're having more sightings. I have another shift in an hour, and I'm already exhausted.

There's talk, too. . . ." Malik looked around and lowered his voice, as if to check whether anyone else was listening. "Talk that the dragons are on the offensive because their food supply is running short. Folks, important folks, are thinking that Terra is in a lot more danger than ever. And most people don't know this, but

Josiah picked up a radio communication. They must have been close by to be in range and, well . . . well, some people are suggesting that we should pack up and move. You know, follow the tunnels to a new location."

Maya and Ayanna looked at each other. They knew that Malik tended to exaggerate, and with everything that had just happened with the drought, they were both highly skeptical of what he said.

"Why haven't we heard any of this 'talk' Malik?" asked Maya, not believing her little brother. "I mean, I work directly with Taylor Weaver, and she meets with the Watchers weekly. She's never once mentioned us packing up and going anywhere."

"Just 'cause she doesn't talk about it with her subordinates, doesn't mean that she doesn't talk about it at all," Malik snapped back.

Maya frowned at him.

"Besides, you don't believe anything I say anyway. What do you think, Ayanna?"

"Well," Ayanna began, "I don't think it sounds very—"

"Oh yeah, that reminds me," Malik interrupted.

"Reminds you of what?" Ayanna said.

"The new guy, Jackson, he asks about you a lot," said Malik. "He said that you were friends, and he thought I might know you. I don't know how he knew that, but he's always talking about you."

Ayanna commanded her body to suppress her excitement. She had waited to hear news about Jackson, and now she was learning for the first time that he'd been asking about her, but she wondered why he didn't simply come to see her in the clinic. She held back a smile and tried to deflect Malik's comment back to the subject of Terra. But before Ayanna could speak, there was a knock at the door.

Malik looked at Maya and refused to budge from his comfortable position on the bed. Rolling her eyes, Maya uncrossed her legs and got up to slide the train car doors apart. When the doors opened, everyone was stunned to find Jackson standing in the doorway with his hand poised to knock again.

Maya tripped over her words. "Hi . . . hi there," she said. She turned and smiled conspicuously at Ayanna. "I didn't expect to find *you* at my door. What brings you by?"

"I'm sorry if I'm interrupting," said Jackson. "It's Maya, right?" He looked at her, then scanned the tiny room, stopping when he saw Ayanna sitting on one of the cots. Jackson smiled and looked happy to see her.

"You're Malik's sister, right? I was just hoping to have a word with Malik," Jackson said, looking at Maya again.

"Oh, of course, and you're right. I am Maya. You're Jackson, if I remember correctly. Forgive me, but I've heard a lot about you. You've caused quite a stir here," she said.

Ayanna's eyes widened. What was Maya doing? Ayanna stared at Maya, but her friend ignored her.

"Have I?" Jackson asked, but this time he was looking at Ayanna.

Malik hopped up from his bunk and held out his hand to greet Jackson. "Hey, man. What brings you to this side of the compound?" he asked, trying to deepen his voice.

Ayanna felt like laughing. She guessed Malik was trying to appear older in front of Jackson.

"Well, I was hoping that maybe we could switch shifts. I mean, I was kinda hoping for a break right now. I'd be happy to take your station tonight, if you could cover me now."

Malik showed obvious excitement at the idea of doing Jackson a favor. It seemed like he too was impressed with the new arrival.

"Switch shifts with you?"

"Yeah. You'd be doing me a big favor. I'd owe you one."

Malik responded without having to think. "I'd be happy to switch shifts with you. That would be great. Man, you were pretty cool in training today. The way you decimated that stand in was awesome." Malik beamed with admiration.

"OK, Malik," said Maya, "he gets the point. You're a fan."

Malik frowned at his sister. "I'm not a fan, Maya. I just think Jackson has what it takes, you know? What it takes to fight the enemy," he added.

"Well, thanks guy, I really appreciate that. And I appreciate you helping me out like this. You're really going out of your way, and I won't forget it," said Jackson.

"Hey, don't even worry about it. Glad to do it. You're on the south corner, right?" asked Malik.

"Yeah, that's right," said Jackson.

Malik looked excited about his new task. "Catch you later, Sis . . .'Yanna," he said. He gave a quick wave to Maya and Ayanna and rushed out of the door to get to Jackson's post.

Jackson turned and faced Ayanna. Maya looked around and shuffled her feet.

"OK . . . well, you know, I just remembered I need to help Taylor check the meters. Hey, it'd be nice if we had lights tomorrow, right?" she mumbled, swinging her arms and edging toward the exit. Ayanna gave Maya a curious look, but her friend continued to hurry.

"Hey, you just pull the doors when you're done in here . . . I mean, when you've finished . . . I mean, talking. Finished *talking* in here . . . just pull the doors," she stammered as she left the room. Jackson watched Maya slide the doors behind her. Then, slowly, he moved to sit next to Ayanna.

They were alone. Ayanna had imagined this moment for

weeks now. She had wanted to look into his hazel eyes again, and she had entertained the idea that she might end up back in his strong arms. She remembered the heat that radiated from his body the first time he had held her close to his chest, and her skin tingled at the possibility she could feel his warmth again.

Now that Jackson was here in front of her, she didn't know what to say to the boy who had saved her life twice and stolen her focus at least once a day ever since they'd met. She straightened her back and placed both of her feet on the ground.

"Hey," he said with his usual grin.

"Hey," Ayanna said, raising her eyebrows. She didn't know much about Jackson, but from what she did know, it wasn't like him to hesitate before speaking.

"So, I haven't seen you in a while. How've you been?" Jackson sat next to her on the cot.

"I've been fine. How about you? How's everything going? How have things been for you?" Ayanna was nervous and couldn't stop talking.

"I can honestly say things just got a heck of a lot better in the past ten minutes," he said. As usual, Jackson had caught her off guard with his comment.

"So . . . ," Ayanna began.

At the same time, Jackson began to speak. "I was wondering . . ." He paused. "Go ahead."

"No, you first," Ayanna said. Why was she nervous? Hadn't they been alone together more than once?

Jackson paused for another moment before continuing. "I was wondering if you'd like to go get something to drink with me. I'm on break, thanks to our friend, Malik, and I thought maybe you and I could catch up. You know, find out what I've missed," he said. Jackson smiled slightly and scanned Ayanna's body before returning his eyes to meet hers.

Ayanna felt blood rushing to her face. She didn't know how to hide her enthusiasm.

"Go get a drink?"

Jackson smirked at her hesitation. "Yeah, wet stuff. I hear people need it from time to time to live, and apparently, your mad scientists figured out how to grow tea of some sort in this place, at your infamous Terra."

His voice held his familiar sarcasm, and Ayanna snapped out of her reverie. "Yeah, of course they did. That sounds like an OK idea. I wouldn't mind having tea, though I have to admit . . ." Ayanna stopped, thinking about what she was about to say, but then changed her mind. "Oh, never mind."

"No, tell me. What is it you have to say? Miss me, did you? It's OK, you can admit it," said Jackson, his mouth curled into that wonderful smile of his.

Jackson shocked Ayanna with how well he knew her. But she didn't want to admit this to him. She didn't want him to know she had spent weeks looking for him. "Oh, please. Don't be ridiculous. Of *course*, I didn't miss you. I don't even really know you. You're just some foolish guy whose life I had to save."

Ayanna looked away from him, and he took the opportunity to move closer to her. His arm briefly brushed against hers, and Ayanna felt his warmth. His proximity made her look into his eyes without calculating the consequences, and she was captivated . . . again.

Dammit. She had forgotten what she wanted to say.

Jackson leaned in closer, his face so close that she almost forgot to breathe. "Is that really who I am?" he asked, his voice low. "Because I could've sworn that events occurred a little differently."

"Well, maybe things were a little different," Ayanna mumbled.

"So that is a yes, then?"

"Yes. I mean . . . what?"

"Something to drink? That is a yes? You will go get something to drink with me?" Jackson took his right hand and brushed a strand of hair back from her face.

"Yes. Yes. A drink. That sounds like a good idea. You and I should go and get some tea, right now," she answered. Ayanna hopped up and headed for the door.

Jackson smirked again. She was starting to recognize it. It was the expression he wore when he seemed to know he had gotten to her. He always knew when he'd made her nervous. She could swear it pleased him.

She hated and loved it at the same time.

Jackson followed her and waited, stretching his arm in the direction of the door. "After you," he said.

Ayanna walked swiftly out of Maya's bunker, and Jackson followed, pulling the doors closed behind him.

CHAPTER 33

Ayanna and Jackson entered a nearly empty cafeteria. They had missed dinner, but tea was still available. They sat at a secluded table in the corner of the hall, and Ayanna watched as people passed by. No one seemed to notice them.

For several minutes, they sat in silence. Ayanna held her tin cup tightly and stared at its contents as if there were liquid gold floating there.

Jackson, on the other hand, stared directly at her. "I take it you like the tea," he said, causing Ayanna to realize how tightly she was gripping her cup. She set it down on the table and looked up.

"No," she said, "not really. I've never actually cared for the bitter taste. These days, I just drink it because it helps me stay awake so I can study."

Jackson leaned forward. Ayanna took this as encouragement that he was interested. "You do that a lot, huh?" he asked.

"What?"

"Study. The last time I saw you, that's what you were doing. Studying."

"Yeah, I guess you could say that. I have to. I mean, one day, I'll take over as Terra's medic, and I need to know what I'm doing.

Even now, I have people's lives in my hands, and I need to know how to help them," Ayanna said.

Jackson sat back in his seat, pensive. "You seem to take the weight of the world and place it right on top of your shoulders, Ayanna," he said. "Why? Why are you always worried about everyone else? Don't you ever just worry about yourself?"

Ayanna tilted her head to the side. She thought about the question. Really, she had thought about the question a million times before. She used to know the answer, that she had to worry about everyone else because it was her duty. It was her job. But now, she wasn't so sure.

Weeks had gone by without an emergency. Dr. Keaton was getting better. His strength was returning so he could care for the people at Terra. And the terror she had felt about having to be responsible for everyone had started to fade. Maybe Jackson was right. Maybe the way he saw life had a point. He didn't appear to worry about what would happen the next day or the day after that, and it seemed to bring him peace.

Why did she try so hard to fix everything? Was it because her mother had healed the sick? Or was it because she felt guilty for her father's invention that had unleashed hell on Earth? Even if that had been true for them, they weren't Ayanna, and she wasn't them. They were both dead, and they hadn't told her what she should do.

"I've never known anyone like you, Jackson. You act like there's a choice. Like there's some other way of being. I mean, how can there be in this world? How can we not worry about each other?" Ayanna asked.

Jackson sighed. "Maybe you're right. Maybe there is no other way to be. Maybe I spend too much time worrying about what's in it for me."

Ayanna was silent for a few seconds. "You are the only one

who knows if that's true. But isn't there anyone else you care about?"

"Ayanna . . . ," he said. Her eyes widened, and she waited for him to speak. The pause lingered, and Ayanna leaned in closer to Jackson. "I've been wandering around for a long time now. I've seen things. Crazy things and crazy people, and I haven't cared about anything for a while."

Ayanna looked back down at her cup.

"That is," he continued, "until now, at least."

Suddenly, there was a loud clattering of dishes as if someone had dropped a pan on the floor. Jackson and Ayanna both turned toward the noise. It was one of the electricians who worked with Maya.

Ayanna took a deep breath and decided on a new line of questioning. "So, how's everything going with the militia?" she asked. "Malik says that you guys have been really busy."

Jackson sighed again and shook his head.

"Well, Malik tends to exaggerate a little bit," Ayanna said.

"No, it's not Malik at all. He's a good kid. Honest and loyal, believes in what he's doing. It's just . . . this place has a lot of crap that just makes it barely tolerable. Just look at today. During the morning routine, I'm going along about my business when I notice that this jackass—Michael, I think is his name—he starts picking on this kid. Some scrawny kid with freckles who basically has twigs for arms—"

"You mean Kevin. He has always been pretty small."

"Yeah well, I guess Michael feels like it's his job to give this kid, Kevin, a hard time, because every time Kevin finishes repairing his section of the inner wall, Michael finds a way to tear it back down. So, after watching this for like the fifth time, I decide to say something to Michael. I get in his face about picking on people smaller than him, and we push back and forth a bit."

"What happened after that?"

"Well, the commanding officer on duty, Geoffrey, he comes over to see what the commotion is all about, and he ends up sending both me and Michael in for reprimand.

So, I'm thinking, fine. I'll just tell my side of the story, and we'll let Captain Daniels work it out. That seemed only fair, right?"

Ayanna nodded in agreement.

"Well, apparently, Daniels doesn't understand the meaning of the word *fair*. Instead of punishing Michael for being an ass or both of us for fighting, he accuses me of being a troublemaker and sentences me to clean out the latrines for a week," said Jackson angrily. "Can you believe that crap?"

Ayanna tilted her head again. She wanted to find compassionate words for Jackson. Before she could say anything, though, he said, "You're a good listener, you know that?"

"Thank you. You're a good talker." Ayanna gave Jackson a shy smile, and he seemed to forget his anger. He laughed.

"Beautiful *and* funny."

Ayanna shifted. She felt heat rise to her face.

"I'm glad we're friends," he said after a beat.

"Me too," Ayanna said softly.

"Who knows, I might just stick around."

This announcement startled her. It hadn't occurred to her that Jackson had considered leaving.

Jackson hesitated, looking around the room to see if anyone was listening. Then, he moved closer to her. "It is just that damn Captain Daniels. He's the biggest hypocritical jerk that I've ever known, and I've known quite a few, believe me."

Ayanna's eyes widened, and her mouth opened in shock. She had never heard anyone at Terra speak about Richard like that, not even his detractors.

"Do you know him?" asked Jackson. He looked quizzical and Ayanna could tell his question was sincere.

"Richard?"

Jackson nodded.

"Yes, he . . ." Ayanna felt her heart speed up in her chest. She had no idea how to handle this. She knew how Richard could seem to some people, but she knew better than anyone not to judge his strict persona. Richard cared deeply about keeping everyone safe. He would give his life for Terra. If he didn't get along with Jackson, it would only be because he didn't trust him. If they could get to know each other, things would be different. She was sure of this.

"And his father, Colonel Daniels . . ." Jackson huffed. "I think he might be even worse. He's always lurking about. I swear, he watches me like a hawk."

Ayanna appreciated the out. She had no problem talking about how much she disliked the colonel. "I can see how that could be true about the colonel. I seem to only deal with him when I'm in trouble. People around here respect him for his service in the military, but I think he's too strict and really rude. His wife lives at Terra too, you know, but I don't think they see much of each other. In fact, I've even heard rumors that they barely speak."

"Oh yeah? Why's that?"

"I'm not sure, exactly, but I think it is from something that happened before the war," Ayanna said.

"That doesn't surprise me. The guy's an ass."

"He is. But Jackson, Colonel Daniels and Richard are not the same. Maybe you should give Richard another chance, even if you don't like his father," Ayanna said. She couldn't resist. She didn't like the idea of Jackson hating Richard unfairly.

"Look, I don't mind giving the guy a chance, but he won't get off my case, and he has no idea about what's going on around here."

"What do you mean?"

"This supposed well-oiled machine that you guys have going on isn't that at all. Truth be told, I don't think the militia could handle a dragon attack if there really was one. Don't get me wrong, it's a great effort, I admit, but I think everyone is just fooling themselves."

Ayanna leaned forward, and her shoulders tensed. She was about to speak, but Jackson wasn't finished.

"And I've heard rumors of my own. Rumors that the dragons are getting hungrier and fiercer. Some even say that they know where this little hideout is located and that they are just biding their time before they come to destroy it. But none of the military types ever speak about that. Instead, they preach protocol and rules. I don't think there will be much use for rules if the dragons finally get tired of letting this place stand," he said.

Ayanna cringed as heat rose in her stomach. She wanted to deny what Jackson said, but now she wondered if Malik's warning was true. Were they less safe than she thought? Were some people really thinking of leaving Terra, like the Lincolns had?

"Besides, I don't know how safe it is for you if others find out you're living down here," said Jackson.

Ayanna tightened her eyes. "What do you mean? Why does it matter if I'm here?" She didn't know what expression she wore on her face. *And what did Jackson mean about* others, *what others?* she wondered.

Jackson swallowed hard and took in a short breath. For the first time, Ayanna couldn't read him. "I just mean, with your father being who he was and all," he said. "Some people might try to use that against you."

Ayanna was confused. How long had Jackson known who her father was? And what people would care about her living at Terra? "I didn't realize you knew who my dad was," she said. Her voice was soft. She hoped she could hide her disappointment in Jackson having found out. It had been nice thinking that she had been talking to someone who didn't know her family's history.

"Some of the guys told me. It's not like it's much of a secret, and I was able to put the names together. Your dad's face was all over the TV screen for two years, you know? 'Scientist opens portal to other world: genius or madness? You decide.' That sort of thing, you know?"

"Yeah, I know," Ayanna whispered. She wished she didn't. But she had seen hundreds of headlines like that. She knew how the world had felt about her father's discovery. She knew how easy it had been for everyone to blame him for what happened next, namely dragons passing through the wormhole and entering this world.

Ayanna had more questions for Jackson. What did he mean by, "People might try to use the knowledge of who her father was against her"? What people? Everyone at Terra already knew who she was. She was about to speak again when she heard a high-pitched beeping.

It was Jackson's watch. "Well, looks like my break is up," he said. Had two hours passed already?

"I guess I'll catch you later, huh? Thanks for the talk."

"Yeah, I'm glad . . . I'm glad you asked. Maybe we can do it again sometime."

"Oh, I'm sure we can," he said. He flashed her his signature smile and got up from his seat. Jackson walked toward the door of the cafeteria, and Ayanna followed him with her eyes. A strange feeling permeated her body. It was unfamiliar, and she didn't know how to label it. Although she had previously tried to deny it, she couldn't anymore. She wanted to know everything there was to know about him. She liked him.

More than that, she *wanted* him. And she didn't know what to do about that.

CHAPTER **34**

Ayanna pressed a towel to Jackson's head. "Hold this here while I get some supplies," she instructed.

She moved to the clinic's cabinets and pulled down a suture kit. She used a clean, sterile cloth to clean blood away from a large gash on Jackson's forehead and started to sew up his cut.

"So, aren't you going to ask me for my side of the story?" he asked playfully.

"Hold still." Ayanna sighed. "Your side of the story? Well, seeing as you are the one in the infirmary, I'm guessing that your side is not the good one."

Jackson smiled with a wince. "That's what I love about you Ayanna. You've got perspective."

She stopped sewing the cut and raised her eyebrows at him. "How did you get hurt, Jackson?"

"Did anyone ever tell you that you've got pretty eyes?" he said. She rolled her eyes.

"Seriously, they remind me of something warm and peaceful," he said.

Ayanna blinked. "You've been drinking," she said.

Jackson shrugged. "Doesn't change the fact that you're beautiful."

Ayanna frowned, and Jackson let out a small laugh. "OK, which story do you want? The one from this morning or the one from tonight?" he said.

Ayanna took in a deep breath and let it out slowly. This couldn't possibly be good.

He didn't wait for her to answer. "Let's start with this morning and the bastard you call a militia leader."

Ayanna bit her tongue. The impulse to defend Richard was almost uncontrollable. She wanted to ask another question, but she needed to know where Jackson was going with this. She could see why Richard and Jackson would clash. They were polar opposites, at least when it came to rules and order. But Richard was the calmest person Ayanna had ever met, and although he wore his seriousness like impenetrable armor, she knew that he was kind. Jackson's cavalier attitude probably drove Richard crazy.

"As seems to be the norm these days, I found myself in front of the precious Captain Daniels again . . . ," Jackson said.

"Go on. Why were you reprimanded?"

Jackson looked up to the ceiling, pretending to try to remember. "You know what? Come to think of it, I have no idea. Either way, I found myself sentenced unjustly again. Sewage detail, of all things. You got some twisted rules in this place. Order and rules, rules and order. Please . . . but I digress."

Ayanna nodded her head, encouraging him to continue.

"After having such a rough day, I decided to blow off some steam in the north tunnel."

"What's in the north tunnel?" Ayanna asked, confused.

"Ah, could it be that *I* know something about Terra you don't?" he asked mockingly.

Ayanna rolled her eyes again. "Are you going to tell me or not?"

Jackson pointed his index finger at her. "You're funny when you're mad."

Ayanna swiped his finger away. "And you're even more annoying when you're drunk," she retorted.

Jackson laughed. "All right, fine. The north tunnel is where a few of us guys go to drink some of your finest moonshine, gamble, and talk trash. But it's sort of an exclusive crowd. Only the right kind of people allowed," he said.

"Uh-huh. So, something tells me that this 'right crowd' led to this," Ayanna said, pointing at Jackson's bleeding skull.

"I just got into a little tiff with one of the boys over a pair of kings. He claims I was dealing from under the deck."

"Were you?"

Jackson feigned a gasp. Ayanna shook her head and resumed stitching up his cut. "Ayanna, you should know better by now," he said.

"Should I?"

"Yeah, you don't deal from the bottom of the deck, you deal from under the table."

Ayanna stared at him. He tried hard not to smile. The pain seemed to keep his expression in check. "You're impossible," she said, fighting back a smile of her own. "You should try to stay out of the clinic, OK?"

"Don't you like seeing me?" asked Jackson. His voice turned serious.

Ayanna tilted her head to the side. "Yes, I like seeing you," she said. Jackson had no idea just how much she liked seeing him. He also had no idea how much she thought about him throughout the day. She thought about talking to him. She thought about touching him. She thought about wanting to kiss him. She just wished he were happier at Terra.

"I want you to try to stay out of trouble. Will you?" she said.

"You're one to talk. You don't always stay out of trouble," he said. Ayanna's eyes widened at the accusation, and her mouth gaped. She wanted to deny what he had said, but she couldn't.

"In fact, I could've sworn that I found you out on the surface after dark. That's one of the Watchers' big rules, isn't it? Although they have so many, who can tell the big ones from the little ones? But it goes to show you don't always follow the rules, like you're trying to convince me now. Sometimes, you do what you feel."

Being on the surface in search of digitalis had been reckless and dangerous, but Ayanna couldn't hold back a smile at the memory of meeting Jackson. "OK. You're right. So, sometimes, I do bend the rules a bit. But only for a good cause," Ayanna protested.

She considered this for a second. She believed that Terra's rules had kept them safe even if she hadn't agreed with all of them. But Jackson was also right. Many times, her gut feeling was the right one. And more and more, being with Jackson was what felt right.

Ayanna completed the last stitch on Jackson's forehead and moved her equipment to the basin. Jackson hopped up from the exam table.

"So, I guess things here are not going that well for you, then?" she asked.

Jackson sighed. "They're going. This is an interesting place, your Terra, but I'm afraid that being near you is the only thing I like here," he said.

"Well, maybe you should try to make some friends," she said.

Jackson walked over to the basin and stood beside her. "I thought we were friends."

"We *are* friends, Jackson. Of course, I just mean that you might have an easier time if you tried to get along. You know, if you stopped fighting it all the time."

"And what is it that I'm fighting all the time, Ayanna?"

"Belonging. Having a place to call home. Try it—you never know, you might like it."

Ayanna smiled at Jackson and turned to face him. Unexpectedly, he brushed her hair off her face and let his hand rest there. His thumb made tiny circles on her skin.

They looked at each other for a few seconds, and Jackson leaned in slowly. Ayanna felt her lips part and her body tensed with anticipation. Then, Jackson's eyes shifted toward the door. Ayanna turned around and, to her surprise, saw Mrs. Johnson standing in the doorway.

"Evening, Mrs. Johnson," Jackson said, dropping his hand to his side. "I think I should get going. Thank you, Ayanna."

Ayanna watched as Jackson walked from the clinic, stumbling slightly when he reached the door. Mrs. Johnson stared disapprovingly at Jackson as he made his way past her.

"Miss Grace, may I have a word with you?" asked Mrs. Johnson.

"Of course," Ayanna said. "Are you feeling OK? Dr. Keaton is available if you want me to get him."

"No, I am feeling fine. I don't need a doctor. I actually wanted to talk to you about Mr. Kyle," she said.

"Really? What about him?"

"You see, it is my understanding that Mr. Kyle is having some trouble with the other members of his unit," she said. Mrs. Johnson paused before continuing.

"Miss Grace, you are one of Terra's most talented and important attributes."

"Thank you, Mrs. Johnson," Ayanna said.

"And I know you have had to overcome quite a bit, what with your family's legacy and all," said Mrs. Johnson. Ayanna held in a sigh.

"But you are also very young . . . ," she continued.

Ayanna waited impatiently, trying to understand where this conversation was going.

"I see that you and Mr. Kyle have become friends."

Ayanna nodded. "Yes, I mean, he has saved my life twice now, and I—"

"It's just that I imagine you've not had a lot of experience with young men. Especially those from outside Terra. Before the war, did you ever speak with your mother about . . ."

"My mother died," Ayanna said, faster than she intended to.

"Oh, I see," said Mrs. Johnson. "It's just that—"

"Mrs. Johnson, I don't mean to be rude, but I'm not sure I understand what you are trying to say," Ayanna said. "Is there something about Jackson . . . Mr. Kyle that I should know?"

Mrs. Johnson took a deep breath. "He just seems to be a troublemaker," she said, "and I don't think that he is the type of person you should befriend. That is to say, I don't believe he can be trusted."

"Thank you for your concern, Mrs. Johnson, but I don't really think you know much about him. Besides, I'm more than capable of knowing who is and isn't a friend."

Ayanna knew she was being rude now, but she didn't need Mrs. Johnson or anyone else telling her who she could associate with.

Mrs. Johnson took a deep breath and nodded before turning for the door. "I hope you're right, Miss Grace, but people are not always who they pretend to be. Some people have secrets that they don't want anyone to know about. You should be careful."

Before Ayanna could respond, she was gone.

CHAPTER 35

Ayanna felt uneasy. Something was going on at Terra, and she didn't know what. Malik, of course, had insisted for weeks that people's attitudes had been changing. According to him, at least four people had confided in him that they were thinking about packing up and leaving Terra. She didn't know if she should take these rumors seriously. Ayanna thought that much of Terra's unhappiness had passed after the Protectorate successfully destroyed the dam, but she had been wrong before, and she guessed she might be wrong now.

She needed to talk to Richard. If he knew what was happening, he might tell her. But they hadn't spoken much since Jackson's arrival. This was her fault. She had been avoiding Richard again, and, like always, he hadn't tried to force anything between them.

She felt foolish. She didn't have a good reason to avoid Richard. Why was she? Maybe it was because she'd been spending time with Jackson. She liked Jackson. She liked the way he made her feel, excited and nervous. She liked how every time she looked into his eyes, she thought about kissing him and pulling him against her body. She thought about the warmth of Jackson's body pressed against hers. But Jackson and Richard seemed to oppose each other, even in her mind.

And even though she was sure how she felt about Jackson, and she knew how much she wanted him, she was not sure about Richard. Her feelings about him had been muddled for a long time, and she hadn't known what to make of their past few interactions.

She thought she must have misinterpreted what Richard had been trying to tell her in the tunnels on their way back from the surface after they had destroyed the dam. He had told her that he would never have left her up on the surface under any circumstance. Why had he said that? Was it because of what she used to mean to him? She used to be important to him. It couldn't be because Richard loved her. How could he after everything that had happened between them?

And how about what she felt for Richard? She had never thought to put it into words. All Ayanna knew was that she did not want to imagine life without him. She pushed the thought from her mind.

Ayanna sighed. Whether or not she understood their conversation in the tunnel or where they stood now, she still needed to talk to Richard alone. She suspected the Protectorate would stay underground today. It wasn't one of their usual times to journey to the surface.

As Ayanna walked past the cafeteria, she saw a crowd of at least twenty people standing around one of the tables, upon which Rafael stood. The scene reminded her of the rations debacle, and she was surprised that he still had more to say. She had forgotten all about him now that the water shortage was over.

Ayanna watched from the entrance and tried to figure out what was going on. Three people pushed past her, nearly knocking her over in order to squeeze into the group. The crowd grew louder, and people began shouting.

What was going on? And why wasn't anyone stopping this?

But then again, why *should* it be stopped? No one was fighting.

She moved closer to get a better look.

"I've had enough!" Rafael shouted. "The war is over. Why have we allowed the same nine people to lead for this long? Before *they* arrived, we lived in a democracy. This is *still* a democracy if you ask me. I call for elections!"

"I agree!" shouted a woman from the crowd. Three other voices joined hers.

"This isn't a prison, and despite what Captain Daniels thinks, it isn't the military. I don't know about you, but I'm sick and tired of the Watchers and their little lap dog, Daniels, making decrees, calling all the shots, and refusing to ask us what we want," he continued.

Rafael's expression shone hot with anger. Ayanna couldn't tell if this was an impromptu meeting or if he had been planning it for some time, but based on the number of people in the crowd, it seemed organized. She didn't know what to do. Should she call a militiaman and try to stop Rafael's speech? That didn't seem right. She couldn't think of a reason why she should stop him. Rafael, or anyone else, was free to talk about whatever he wanted.

She understood why Rafael was still angry. Restoring the water to Terra hadn't changed anything about the way the Watchers ruled. Elections still had not been called. They hadn't reformed the rules. Their punishments were still too harsh, and they hadn't sent anyone to learn about the grievances in the compound. Rafael was right in many ways.

Ayanna thought of Jackson. She looked around, but she didn't see him in the crowd. She imagined he would agree with Rafael. He had complained about some of these same problems with the Watchers.

But Jackson and Rafael were both wrong about one thing: Terra was not like a prison. People could leave whenever they wanted as long as they didn't intend to return, but why would they? What else was out there? She moved closer to the crowd. Maybe someone would tell her what Rafael hoped to achieve with his speech.

"Now, I'm not saying that I could do a better job than the Watchers—" he began.

Robin Wiser cried, "Yes, you could!"

This seemed to energize Rafael. He smiled and continued with his speech. "Thank you, Robin. I appreciate that, but more importantly, what we are talking about here is a need for fair and effective leadership. The current council members have had their shot. It's time for some new folks to try their hand at it," he concluded.

"Yeah!" the crowd cheered.

Ayanna stood with her arms crossed over her chest and surveyed the faces in the crowd. Of the 120 people at Terra, this group represented at least one person from every walk of life, except for the militia.

"Well, looky here," said Rafael. He stopped his speech and pointed directly at Ayanna. "Ladies and gentlemen, we have been graced, excuse the pun, by none other than our fine medic."

Ayanna wanted to turn away and run out of the door, but it was too late. People surrounded her on either side.

"You're connected to almost everyone here, Ayanna. Don't you think that the people have the right to have their voices heard?" Rafael asked. Dozens of eyes bore down on her. She didn't understand what was happening.

She felt her throat tighten and her heart started to beat faster. "I . . . I—"

"Miss Grace doesn't have to answer to you."

Ayanna heard Richard's authoritative voice boom from the doorway, surprising her. She hadn't noticed him walk in, and apparently, neither had Rafael, because his face dropped when he saw him.

Ayanna was relieved to see Richard, but she was also conflicted. If he hadn't arrived at that moment, what would she have said to Rafael? She did think that people had a right to have their voices heard. The Watchers promised elections that never came. They made rules and just expected everyone to follow them. Blood rushed to Ayanna's face. She didn't know what would happen next.

Rafael crossed his arms and stepped down from the table. The crowd parted and made room for him.

"Captain Daniels, I assumed you would show up sooner or later," he said, moving toward Richard.

"What's going on here, Rafael?" Richard asked.

Rafael shrugged his shoulders. "Nothing, just having a chat with my people," he said. His voice barely hid his anger.

"At it again, I see. I think it's time that you moved on, don't you? In fact, I think it's time for all of you to move on," said Richard, addressing the crowd so everyone could hear him.

By now, ten militiamen, including Malik, had shown up and sprawled around the room. Ayanna didn't like the look of this. There was an unusual tension in the air, and it was obvious that the group was divided into "us" versus "them." The only problem was that Ayanna didn't know which side she was on.

Some people started to walk out voluntarily, seeming uninterested in taking sides, but many stood their ground.

"Rafael, you heard me the first time," Richard said.

Rafael's eyes tightened in anger, and he lost whatever control he had over himself. "Now hold up a minute," he said, pointing his finger at Richard's chest. In reaction, Richard grabbed Rafael's arm and threw him to the ground, pinning him there. Ayanna jumped back, frightened at how quickly Richard moved. Rafael's top supporters, Olawale, Stanley, and John moved forward. She guessed they wanted to pull Richard off Rafael. But the militiamen reacted immediately, and six of them restrained Rafael's men, while the rest ushered the people toward the exit.

"Look. I didn't come here to fight," said Rafael, with his face pressed brutally against the ground.

"I'm not so sure about that," said Richard. "All of you are coming with us, now!" Richard pulled Rafael up and held his hands behind his back. The militiamen did the same to Rafael's supporters as they led them out of the cafeteria. Richard caught her eye when he passed. His face was cold, but his eyes gave him away. Ayanna could still see the person she knew he was beneath the perfect soldier.

She stood with her mouth agape. She couldn't believe what was happening. This couldn't be right. The people shouldn't fear the Protectorate.

After most of the people had dispersed, Malik came and stood next to her. "Are you OK?" he said. She nodded her head. She still couldn't decipher her feelings about the scene she had just witnessed.

"Where will he take them?" she said.

"The holding pen, most likely, but if it was up to me, I'd kick 'em all out on their asses tonight," said Malik. Ayanna looked over at him, shocked. He looked weary. She shifted her eyes back to the table where Rafael had given his speech.

After several seconds of silence, Ayanna looked at Malik again. He seemed to be concentrating hard on something. His eyes were narrowed, and he seemed frustrated. She couldn't tell if he remembered she was there.

Finally, he spoke. "I can't believe the way that these people are so quick to challenge the captain after all that he has done for them," said Malik, his voice angry.

Ayanna stared at him. She worried about how seriously Malik took the protesters, but she agreed with him. It was true. Richard *had* helped protect Terra from its beginning. He had helped devise the security system and organize the militia. It seemed unfair to accuse him of abusing his new position as the head of security when he had served the people so selflessly.

Malik wasn't finished. "These people need to understand everything the Protectorate does for them. Then, maybe, they'd show some respect. I mean, we put our lives in danger every day to keep them safe. They act like they've forgotten that there's an enemy waiting to kill them just outside these walls," he said.

Malik no longer seemed to be talking to her. "What the captain needs is a victory against the dragons. Now *that* would give these folks some perspective."

Ayanna perked up. "A victory against the dragons? How is he supposed to do that? Even the whole military couldn't pull that off," she scoffed. "Besides, Richard had a victory when he freed the water from the dam. Plenty of people remember that."

Malik shook his head defiantly. "Not enough, apparently . . . look, I gotta go. You sure you're all right?"

It was strange to hear him say these words to her. Ayanna had asked him the same question many times before, but everything about him seemed different now. He looked angry and older. There was an edge to him that she didn't recognize.

"I'm sure, Malik," she said. His body was tense, eager to leave.

"Cool. See ya," said Malik.

"See—" He was gone before Ayanna could even get the words out.

A few seconds later, Ayanna followed Malik out of the cafeteria, but she wasn't going back to her lab. She needed to talk to Richard more than ever. She needed answers about what was really going on.

CHAPTER 36

"Come in."

Ayanna took a deep breath. She pulled the lever down and opened the door to Richard's room.

"Grace?" He looked up with a start. Richard sat on a cot with a blanket neatly folded over its sides, his chin resting on folded hands. He looked like she was the last person he had expected to see at his door.

She felt her courage waver. She wasn't sure what she wanted to say.

"Richard," Ayanna began. Her voice was quiet. She felt the distance between them, but she knew she had created it.

"I'm sorry . . . I was hoping I could talk to you about the . . . I guess you could call them *protesters*."

Richard rose from the bed and walked slowly toward her, stopping directly in front of her. Ayanna gazed up into his dark eyes and felt her body relax.

He shook his head. "Grace, what is there to talk about?"

"Captain, I want to talk about what they're saying . . . about what they want."

Richard raised his hand to his chest to interrupt her. He shook his head again. Then his face softened, and some of the seriousness faded. The expression made him look younger. Or rather, it made him look his age. Ayanna, like everyone else, it seemed, always forgot that Richard was only nineteen. There was a weariness in his features that he rarely let show.

"Look, my first duty is to Terra. You know that. I can't just allow a small group of people to disrupt our lives here. It's dangerous for all of us," he said.

"But what will you do with them? They haven't hurt anyone. Don't you think that keeping people quiet just because you don't like what they say is unfair?" Ayanna asked. Richard sighed and paced across the room.

"Come on, Ayanna. I know you remember what life was like during the infestation, the chaos, the panic. Everything was a struggle. We struggled to live every day. It was hell."

Ayanna felt a shudder run down her spine. She did remember. It *was* horrible. No one knew if they would live or die. There wasn't enough food. There wasn't enough electricity or medicine. It was hell. They both fell silent.

"Let me ask you something. What would you do with them if it were up to you?" His voice was sincere, and Ayanna could see that he expected an answer.

She dropped her head, let out a heavy breath, and settled on Richard's cot. Her shoulders slumped. How had she again managed to forget what all this was like for Richard? Yes, he was a soldier and a natural leader, but he didn't have a rulebook to follow. He was barely older than she, and he had to figure everything out as he went along. They were in the same situation. So many people turned to them for answers that they just didn't have.

"I'm sorry," Ayanna whispered.

Richard frowned. A crease formed in his forehead. He looked like he didn't understand her response.

"I just mean, you're right. I have no idea what I would do. I guess . . . I guess I would try to make the decision that was best for all of Terra."

Richard fixed his eyes on her. She couldn't read his expression, but he gave her a sad half smile. Then, he took in a deep breath. Ayanna saw that he had more to say, and this surprised her. She couldn't remember the last time he had just wanted to *talk* to her. She waited for him to continue, wanting to hear his thoughts.

"It's hard . . . having lives in your hands," he said in a low tone. "Damn near impossible."

"Yes, I know, but you're different from me, Richard. You know how to lead. You were born for this. Everyone trusts you."

"They shouldn't."

Ayanna shifted her weight, and her eyes narrowed. She didn't understand what he meant.

Richard moved away from her. "People always wonder if the stories about me during the war are true. Do you?"

Ayanna sat still, uncertain how to answer. She very much wanted to know about Richard's time in the war, but she couldn't say that she had ever doubted the stories were true. Exaggerated, perhaps. After all, his name had practically become legend at Terra.

"I . . . I know how eager you were your senior year to go fight. I just assumed that whatever you did impressed your commanders," she said.

Richard scoffed and shook his head. He stopped pacing and moved over to a small aluminum closet in the corner of the room. He leaned onto it and folded his arms across his chest. Ayanna stood up and took a tentative step forward, trying to read his body language. He let her hold his gaze, and she saw a sadness in Richard's eyes that she hadn't recognized before.

"It's true I've killed dragons, maybe more than any man in the war. I don't know. I even lured some into a trap and killed them by hand like people say, but I'm no hero."

"Come on, Richard, of course you—"

"Ten. That's the number of men who died following me on my . . . I'm not sure what you would call it. Quest?"

Ayanna blinked. She didn't understand. She felt confused and searched for words, but none came. She took in a heavy breath.

"Ten men died?" she asked in a strained voice. "Because of you?"

Richard nodded his head. He unfolded his arms and took a step closer to her. Ayanna stood still, too stunned to react.

"It was after the dragons had overtaken Columbus. Everyone knew we were outnumbered. The commanders had ordered us to stop our assaults and to put all our firepower into defending the areas that hadn't been overrun. But that wasn't good enough for me.

"I thought I knew better. I thought I understood the enemy. I knew how the dragons lived, how they moved, where they bred.

"I guess I wanted to prove I wasn't afraid. So instead of standing down, I led my men to destroy a nest at Hamer Swamp. We killed seven dragons and took out their eggs. Problem was, I got us cornered into an estuary.

"The dragons swarmed, overtook my men and killed all but one." Richard pointed at himself and his eyes watered. He blinked to keep his tears from falling. Then he cleared his throat and continued to talk.

"But back at command, no one seemed to see it for what it was . . . blind stupidity. Instead, I was lauded as a dragon-killer and a war hero. The commanders even gave me the rank of captain." He let out a humorless laugh.

"But why? I mean, why did you lead them into the fight if you knew you couldn't get out?" Ayanna's voice came out small.

Richard shook his head. "Did you know my father graduated from the military academy at age twenty, with honors?"

"I . . . I . . . ," Ayanna stuttered.

Richard sighed. It was a heavy sound. His eyes fell from her face, and he turned his back to her. The seconds passed, and Ayanna thought about filling the silence, but anything she said would be just noise.

"My whole life, I've wanted to be like him, to impress him. I guess you should be careful what you wish for."

Ayanna shifted forward. Richard sensed her approach and turned around to face her. He wore a tortured look. His pain was tangible, overlying his normally stoic expression. Ayanna wanted to soothe him, but she didn't know how.

She dropped her eyes from his face. She wasn't sure what to think. Richard had led others to their death? She turned the idea over in her mind. It seemed impossible. He was always so careful, so precise, so sure of his actions. He was a leader. Everyone trusted him to lead. Ayanna trusted him.

She looked back up and met his agonized expression. A storm was brewing within him, raging just below the surface. Ayanna had only seen glimpses of it before, but he'd momentarily forgotten to shut her out, and now she could see it all: his remorse, his guilt, his torture.

Ayanna understood. Responsibility brought these feelings. The possibility of failure lingered like a specter, always threatening to attack.

She found her voice and leaned in close. She reached out her hands to Richard's face, and he leaned into her touch. His face was warm, and his cool breath came out in slow, steady beats. Ayanna blinked slowly. They hadn't touched each other like this in years, but her hands remembered. She remembered.

Her words came out in a whisper. "Richard, I wasn't there during the war. Everything was so . . . Listen . . . all that matters is what you've done here and now, for Terra. For over a year, you've kept us safe, and that means something to people here. It means everything to me."

Richard peered into her face. His eyes softened as he reached for her hand, brought it up to his lips, and placed a soft kiss on the back of it. His thumb glided gently over the back of her hand. Ayanna felt as if she had just stepped into a warm bath. His delicate gesture reminded her of something he used to do when they were younger. The wall between them crumbled into nothingness.

"Thank you, Ayanna," he said. She smiled at him. She couldn't help it. The moment felt too familiar, and she had missed him too much. "You're welcome, Richard," Ayanna said.

A knock came at the door.

"Who is it?" said Richard.

"We need to talk," said a gruff voice on the other side of the door. Richard straightened and his entire body stiffened. He let go of Ayanna's hand and moved around her to open the door.

Colonel Daniels stood in the doorframe. He looked at Richard and then at Ayanna. Richard turned his body back to her. He didn't speak, but she understood his meaning. She nodded. "Good-bye, Captain," she said, before heading for the door.

"Miss Grace," said Colonel Daniels, clearly not pleased to see her talking to Richard.

"Colonel," Ayanna said, brushing past him.

Richard closed the door behind her.

CHAPTER **37**

*B*ang, bang, bang.

A loud knocking jolted Ayanna out of her sleep. She shot straight up in bed and looked around. The knocking continued, with more urgency this time. She made her way to the aluminum door.

"Who is it?"

"It's me," responded a curt voice. Jackson.

She turned on the light and pulled the door open.

"Ayanna!" Jackson shouted.

"Shh!" He looked terrible. His eyes were bloodshot. "What's going on?" she asked, concerned. "Are you OK?"

She reached for him. His hands were so cold they made her shiver. "People will hear you. Hurry up and get in here." She quickly ushered Jackson into her room.

He stumbled in and sat down on her bed. "Oh, Ayanna, let them hear," he said, staring at her. "Forget these people and their damn rules! I'm so sick of everyone acting like they can't have a little fun."

Frustration and sadness filled his eyes as he placed his hand on her forearm. Ayanna leaned into him, even though his palm was cool. She took in a deep breath.

Jackson let his hand fall and, in a disorderly fashion, he pulled a tin flask from his pocket and took a drink. Ayanna assumed the flask held more of the moonshine he had told her about before. She reached for Jackson's hand, trying to stop him from drinking.

"I think you've had enough, don't you?" she asked, taking the flask and sniffing. "What is this? It smells terrible. It's almost certainly destroying your liver, you know."

Jackson stumbled toward her, playfully trying to snatch up his flask, but she held it behind her back. Pointing at her, he said, "That, my lovely Ayanna Grace, is a quality alcoholic beverage, distilled two months. You should try some. It will make you feel a lot better, I promise." He reached for the flask again.

She was determined not to give it back, and after his third attempt, he gave up. He fell heavily onto Ayanna's bed and leaned back.

"I don't need to feel better, I'm fine. You, on the other hand, I'm worried about," Ayanna said. She sat next to Jackson on the bed and placed her hand on his chest. He played with her fingers, gently lifting them up and down.

"What is it? What's wrong? Why are you drinking like this?"

"Because I'm bored," said Jackson.

"Bored—really? Are you sure that there isn't something else going on with you?" Ayanna leaned down and moved her head closer to his. "What is it? Please, I want to help," she said.

Jackson stared into her eyes, ignoring her question.

"You're the best friend I've ever had, you know that?"

His declaration surprised her, and Ayanna sat up and smiled halfheartedly. "Oh, no, you aren't going to get out of this one so easily. Come on, Jackson—tell me what's going on."

"Don't you ever get tired of this place?"

Her head fell to the side. And her eyebrows furrowed. It was an odd question. She couldn't imagine where she would be without

Terra. She had no idea how any of them would have survived if they hadn't come together. Terra was her home. Everyone that Ayanna cared about lived there. It was her only connection to normalcy.

She tried to find something to say to Jackson that would make him feel better, but before she could speak, he continued.

"Everyone here is about rules. And for what? The dragons are still out there. They don't give a crap about all these damn rules. They strike when they want to, kill whoever is standing, and burn everything in their way. How does following rules protect anyone? No one is safe. This compound has a militia, and it doesn't even go after them. It just sits back and waits, waits for them to come in and kill us all. And they will, you know. Those dragons will come tearing through here, biting, clawing, crushing, and burning, and they will kill each and every person at Terra."

Ayanna shook her head. She tried to block out the image that Jackson's words stirred in her mind. The idea terrified her. She had lived through a dragon attack. She knew what it meant for them to kill and destroy. She remembered how they burned and burned until there was nothing left.

"Jackson, don't say those things. You're just talking nonsense. We are safe. This is our home. My home. Your home. We are happy here."

Jackson turned his head away from her and faced the wall. "Happy here? Ayanna, I'll never be happy . . . anywhere," he said, his voice barely audible. He inched his body closer to the wall, leaving room for her on the cot. She hesitated. She had never had a boy in her bed, but she took a breath and squeezed next to him.

Ayanna's heart sank. She had seen Jackson sad before, but she had never seen him despondent. She hated it. She felt bad for him and afraid. Why was he having such a hard time here? Maybe it was better if she didn't understand. She blinked slowly, took a deep breath, and tried to forget what he had said.

She gently rubbed her hand across his back. "You just need to rest now. Everything will be OK in the morning, I promise. Just rest," she said. She didn't know if this was true, but she hoped it was. Jackson scoffed and cradled his body against the wall.

She removed Jackson's shoes and pulled the sheet over him. Then she turned out the light and crawled onto her cot beside him. For several minutes, she lay on her back and looked up at the ceiling, trying not to think about Jackson's words.

The room grew quiet, and she listened to the night. Beyond Jackson's breathing, Terra rumbled. She heard a thud that sounded like something heavy hitting the ground over and over. Her mind jumped to the most frightening thought she could imagine: a dragon approaching the compound. Panic struck. Ayanna shot up and swung her legs to the floor. She was prepared to wake Jackson and run to her post, but she waited, listening for sirens. None came. She shook her head, angry with herself for letting her imagination run wild. It was most likely the generator she had heard.

She slid back into bed, frustrated by her fear, and let out a sigh. Then she turned to Jackson, who breathed in a steady rhythm. Why had he said those things?

Ayanna shuddered at the thought of Jackson wanting to leave Terra. He stirred something in her that no one else ever had. He seemed so free. He reminded her of what could have been if the portal had never been opened. He made her think of what her life had been before, when she was a normal teenage girl . . . before she had so many responsibilities.

Ayanna sighed. She needed him to stay.

She closed her eyes and decided not to think about anything anymore. She was tired, and she had a lot of material to read when she woke up. She would rest, and everything would be better in the morning.

CHAPTER **38**

Ayanna woke suddenly. She reached out, found an empty space beside her, and sighed. At least Jackson had gotten some rest.

She had no idea how to ease his unhappiness. She didn't even know if it could be fixed. He didn't look at Terra, or life for that matter, the same way that she did. He struggled to fit in, he hated the compound's rules, and he didn't seem to have any real plans. Ayanna, on the other hand, couldn't imagine a better way to live, considering the shape the world was in.

She got out of bed and threw on a T-shirt and jeans. She pushed her feet into her boots and stood up. She was about to get started on her work when she heard a loud clattering noise coming from the clinic. Maybe Jackson hadn't left like she had thought . . . but what could he need in the clinic?

Ayanna crossed the twenty feet into her laboratory, and dread knocked the wind out of her. Dr. Keaton lay facedown on the floor.

She ran to him and turned him onto his back. A small amount of blood covered his nose from the fall. He hadn't even put his hands out to catch himself.

Ayanna reached her head down and placed her ear near his mouth. He wasn't breathing. "Dr. Keaton, can you hear me?" she said. There was no response.

Ayanna placed her fingers on Dr. Keaton's neck, but she couldn't feel a pulse.

"Help me!" she screamed. Pointless. No one would hear her. She needed to . . . what?

She formed her hands into a crisscrossed shape and pressed them firmly against Dr. Keaton's chest. "One, two, three," she said as she applied chest compressions, trying to make his heart beat. Her movements were frantic but correct. Her hands remembered her training, even if her brain refused to form a coherent thought as she desperately tried to restart his heart. "One, two, three. One, two, three. One, two, three. Come on!" she urged him, the pressure in her palms turning violent.

She was now pounding on his chest. "Don't do this!" she begged Dr. Keaton. "Help me!"

Ayanna screamed for help again—this time, to anyone who might hear her—but her voice cracked under the strain. No one was coming.

"One, two, three."

Reason started to creep to the forefront of her mind and the rational part of her knew . . . even if she could restart his heart, then what? There was no proper medication, no defibrillator, no open-heart surgery. There was nothing, nothing that *she* could do.

Her brain knew . . . it knew.

She placed her ear to Dr. Keaton's mouth again. Nothing. She stopped her compressions and opened his mouth with her hands, cleared his air passage, took in a breath, then blew into Dr. Keaton's lungs. Again.

She returned to her compressions. Tears streamed from her eyes faster than she could stop them, blurring her vision. Ayanna trembled.

There was nothing. Nothing . . .

She pushed up from the ground and tore through the drawers.

She found a syringe. She took her solution of digitalis and filled the syringe with it. An amount this large could be fatal, but it was her last hope. She injected Dr. Keaton with the medication and started the chest compressions again.

"One, two, three," she said. "Please . . . please hold on. I will save you. I promise. You are going to make it."

Again, she searched for a pulse, but there was none.

Ayanna . . . knew.

Her heart beat faster as she tried to choke back her pain. She couldn't see because tears were now pouring down her face, but she looked around anyway. She wanted to cry out again, but no sound came. She shook her head, trying to force her brain to deny the truth.

But it refused. Her reasoning mind wouldn't protect her. It wouldn't indulge her childish wish to take her away from this moment.

Something clicked off in Ayanna, and she froze. She gave up hope and looked down at Dr. Keaton, whose body showed no signs of movement. It was over.

Only then did she hear a loud, bellowing cry that she had never heard before. She looked around the room, and then she realized the sound was coming from her. She sprawled her head across Dr. Keaton's still body.

She was alone. Again, another cry escaped from her mouth, followed by another in a never-ending cycle of sobs.

CHAPTER 39

Ayanna didn't know how many hours had passed when she heard a voice call her name.

"Miss Grace, can you hear me?"

She searched for the voice through a daze. It was Mrs. Johnson. "What?"

"Ayanna, come with me now," she said. "There is nothing more that can be done." Her voice was soft, and she spoke in the soothing way mothers speak to frightened children.

Ayanna was confused. Dr. Keaton's body was gone. Someone had moved it. When had that happened?

The lights glared in her eyes, but the shapes around her started to come into focus. Her mind slowly returned to the present moment. Ayanna lifted herself from the floor and faced Mrs. Johnson.

"Was it his heart?" she asked.

Ayanna nodded, unable to speak.

"Miss Grace, I know that this is a sad time for us all. Marcus was such a dear man and such a wonderful asset to Terra. We will all miss him.

The militia will take care of the burial, and we will hold a ceremony at noon tomorrow."

Ayanna nodded, but she wasn't listening.

Mrs. Johnson hesitated. "Miss Grace, you have been working with Dr. Keaton for over a year now, and he has taught you everything that he could about medicine in that time. . . ."

Ayanna looked at Mrs. Johnson, trying to parse out what she was saying. "Yes, I've worked with Dr. Keaton since we moved down here, and I've learned a lot," she croaked. Her throat was hoarse from screaming.

"And you are aware that we do not have another physician at the compound," Mrs. Johnson continued. "Miss Grace, the council is counting on you to take over for Dr. Keaton now. You will be in charge of the infirmary. The lives of Terra's citizens are now in your hands."

Ayanna forced her eyes to focus on Mrs. Johnson.

In the back of her mind, she had always expected that she would have to take over the infirmary, but she didn't feel ready yet. There was too much she didn't know. She had so much more to learn. There were so many books that she still had to read, and many surgeries that she had never performed. She . . . she had not even saved Dr. Keaton. How was she supposed to help anyone else?

Her mind flashed to where Dr. Keaton's still body had been sprawled across the clinic floor. She tried to shake the thought out of her head.

Mrs. Johnson's voice had faded into a dull hum. But Ayanna did hear her say, "If you need help with anything, the council can send down someone to assist you."

In slow motion, Ayanna closed her eyes and took a deep breath. She felt the air fill her lungs and wake her up. She remembered the people she cared about and how important Terra was to her. She thought of Maya, Mrs. Sanders, and Malik. She opened her eyes.

"I understand, Mrs. Johnson. I can handle anything that Terra needs," she said. She didn't believe this, but she imagined it was what Mrs. Johnson wanted to hear.

"Good," said Mrs. Johnson, "I know everyone can count on you." She placed her hand on Ayanna's shoulder and smiled. Ayanna didn't try to smile back. Mrs. Johnson stood next to her for a few more seconds, and then pursed her lips sympathetically before turning to walk out.

Ayanna didn't know what to do without Dr. Keaton's supervision. She paced in the space as grief and anxiety tried to fill her. She recognized those feelings. She had felt them before, first with her mother's slow, agonizing death, then with her father's sudden and terrible one.

But she pushed the feelings away. She decided she would organize the lab just like Dr. Keaton had taught her. First, she would make a list of items the infirmary needed. Then, she would catalog the books she would need to read to prepare for an emergency. That would keep her busy for hours.

And it did. The hours passed. She worked hard to distract herself, but the aching feeling in her chest remained. Despair sat next to her pain. The passing hours seemed to allow the despair to carve out its own home. Dr. Keaton was dead. She hadn't been able to save him. If anyone else died now, it would be her fault, just as it had been her father's fault that the whole world had been turned upside down. It seemed obvious. There was no point denying it anymore. Maybe she and her father would suffer the same fate. Maybe they were supposed to.

Ayanna sat straight up in bed and tried to catch her breath. She stared into the darkness. Her body was wide awake, but she could not bring herself to move. In the silence, she heard only her own breathing. Her sheet, drenched from a cold sweat, clung to her body.

She lifted her hand to her face and touched her eyes. The pressure caused her to wince. Her eyes were swollen, and her skin felt tight from her salty tears.

She didn't want to face the day. No. She wanted to remain hidden in her closet for however long it would take to end the cruel throbbing that had taken up shop in the center of her chest.

Normally, her mind would have filled with tasks for the day, but now, she couldn't develop a clear thought. Gram negative . . . ionized molecules . . . bicarbonate. *You're not qualified. . . . you can't do this. . . .*

Ayanna turned on her side and faced the door. She noticed a faint light coming from outside. Someone was in her laboratory. There was a voice coming from the hallway, calling her name. Was she still asleep?

"Ayanna?" the female voice called. "Ayanna, are you in here?"

It was Maya.

Maya tapped at her door before pushing it open. Ayanna did not want to see anyone, but it was too late. Maya had already walked into her room and was flipping the switch that controlled the light. She didn't speak. Her face reflected only compassion and worry as she sat down on the cot next to her friend.

Ayanna swung her legs to the side and sat up. Maya draped her arm around her. She started to resist, but what was the point? She lowered her head onto her friend's shoulder and took several deep breaths.

"Taylor said it was all right if I came down in the clinic a few hours a week to help out," Maya said.

Ayanna felt her mouth tip up into a half-smile. "You hate blood," she reminded her.

"But I love you," Maya said.

Ayanna buried her head into her neck and started to cry again. Maya tightened her arm around her. "It's going to be OK," she said.

Ayanna shook her head vehemently. "No, I don't think it is," she said through muffled sobs.

Maya took in a breath but remained quiet. There was nothing she could say. She must have known that. She had lived through her own fair share of loss, even before the dragons had arrived.

Maya stayed with her for most of the morning, until Ayanna begged her to return to her other duties. She was grateful Maya had come to see her. Maya had always been a great friend. She had let Ayanna cry, and this had made Ayanna feel better, even if it was just for a little while. Maya was hesitant to leave, but Ayanna promised her that the faster she got the clinic organized, the better it would be for everyone.

For several days, Ayanna refused to leave the clinic. She lived on sorghum bars. She only left the lab to attend Dr. Keaton's memorial ceremony, a quiet and somber event. Mrs. Johnson said a few words about how Dr. Keaton had lived his life in service to others. And Mr. Christy had told a touching story about how Dr. Keaton had helped him when they fled underground. They had asked Ayanna if she wanted to speak, but she had refused. There were nice stories she could have told of Dr. Keaton's patience with her, about how he taught her about botany and herbs, or how to sew up wounds, but her throat had closed up when she had tried to form the words to tell them.

After that, she did everything she could to keep busy, but she couldn't figure out how to return to her life as it had been.

Ayanna worked nonstop in the lab. All day and all night, she tried to replicate the pain medication she had found weeks earlier. She studied her books and mixed chemicals. And from time to time, she treated patients who were brought in with minor injuries.

At the council's request, Ayanna met with Mrs. Johnson to go over new emergency plans and protocols for the infirmary.

She assumed that the council just wanted to guarantee the health and safety of the compound. But Mrs. Johnson's questions made Ayanna suspect that something else was going on at Terra. Mrs. Johnson asked repeatedly about treating contusions and broken bones. Ayanna wondered what the Watchers wanted to prepare for. A fistfight? This wouldn't have surprised her. She knew that Rafael's uprising probably wasn't over.

After a few days had passed, the Watchers sent a student from the primary program to help in the clinic three times a week. Her name was Monique Carpenter. Fourteen and bright, Monique was thin with doe-like brown eyes and a healthy curiosity about her new assignment. But she didn't have any experience with science or medicine, and Ayanna was under the impression that she was the only one free to take on the assignment.

Although she did the best she could to show Monique basic techniques in bandaging, starting IVs, and measuring medicine, Ayanna was always distracted. The clinic was now her responsibility, and she wished it weren't. No matter how many books she read, she was not going to suddenly become qualified to take care of Terra's sick and injured. She did not want this.

Ayanna entered her room and sat down on her cot. The day had dragged on, and she just wanted it to end. She didn't have much work for Monique, and she'd sent her back to her quarters early. Now, she was alone.

She reached for her father's science notebook and opened the page.

A knock at the door startled her.

Ayanna sighed. She didn't want to deal with anything else.

"Who is it?" she asked, annoyed.

"It's me," said a rough voice.

She flung the door open and found Jackson standing there.

All her agitation faded. Jackson pulled her into his arms and pressed her tightly against his chest. Ayanna realized then how much she had wanted to see him. She had secretly hoped he would come and see her. She had willed it.

"I should've come sooner, but things are a little tense around here," he said, not releasing her from his embrace.

Ayanna pulled back from Jackson and looked into his eyes. "Tense . . . what do you mean—?"

Before Ayanna could finish her question, Jackson had pulled her forward into a kiss. His mouth crushed against hers. His kiss held so much intensity that Ayanna felt heat travel into her core and course through her entire body. She welcomed it. He was bold. His shoulders were wide and strong. Ayanna moved her arms around his back, allowing her hands to study the contours of his body.

Jackson slowly walked her back into the bunk, using his foot to close the door behind him. She allowed Jackson's lips to caress her own. She savored the taste of him. The warmth of his mouth caused shivers to flow all over her, and her arms wrapped tightly around his back, pulling his body even closer to her own.

Jackson used his right hand to cup her face. His other hand grasped at the skin at her waist, pressing her against him with the same force and wild energy that Ayanna used to pull him to her. Tangled like this, they fell back onto her cot.

For weeks, the thought of Jackson had caused her pulse to quicken. Hearing his name had made her nervous and excited, and the sight of him . . . the sight of him was almost more than she could bear. She had never felt this way before. This heat. This passion. This freedom. All she had known for so long was suffering and pain and loss. This feeling . . . this feeling was foreign to her. But welcomed. So very welcomed. This was what she wanted.

But another feeling also took hold of her, a dull, hollow voice that drummed in the back of her mind: *Responsibility . . . duty . . . everyone is counting on you.*

Gently, Ayanna pulled away from Jackson and looked into his eyes. He lay above her with one hand under her and the other hand pressed beneath her shirt and resting on her stomach, moving his fingertips lightly against her smooth skin. The heat from his hand burned into her. He was breathless, and his eyes reflected an emotion that Ayanna recognized in herself. She parted her lips to speak, but before the words could escape her mouth, Jackson slowly leaned forward and placed his lips against hers. She accepted his kiss, and then reluctantly pulled away again.

"What is it?" he asked. He was calm, his voice filled with concern.

Ayanna shook her head. "I can't . . . I mean . . . we can't do this," she said. Her voice was shaky and uncertain. Jackson smiled at her. It was her favorite smile, and she released the breath she'd been holding.

He leaned his face into her neck and inhaled as he placed soft kisses along her neckline. He let out a soft laugh. She was no longer sure about her decision.

"OK," he mumbled into her skin. "We'll sleep then. You should rest. It's been a long week."

"You'll stay?" Ayanna asked, unsure.

Jackson laughed again. This time, she was certain he was laughing at her.

"You know, if I didn't know better, Ayanna, I'd swear that you liked me or something," he said. A smirk replaced his sweet smile.

Ayanna rolled her eyes and shifted beneath him. He moved to one side of the cot and kicked his boots onto the floor. She turned and placed her head on his chest. The sound of his heartbeat comforted her.

"Maybe I do," she said finally. He rested his chin on top of her head and used his strong arms to pull her closer. She could feel him smile.

"Sleep," he ordered. Without argument, her body relaxed, and she gladly complied.

CHAPTER **40**

Everyone was assembled in the gallery. Ayanna saw livid, stern faces. Every few feet, people were shouting. This did not bode well for Terra.

Mrs. Johnson had just made an announcement. The Watchers had ordered Rafael and his group to leave Terra. Many people supported the council's decision. Others were angry. The council agreed to answer questions.

"So you just sent him away?" asked an outraged Robin Wiser.

"No, we deliberated over this long and hard," answered Mr. Frye.

"Deliberated? You've gotta be kidding me. And where was his trial—or did this just happen in that secret chamber of yours?" scoffed Robin.

"That's a good question. And an even better question is, what was his crime, exactly?" asked Frida Janes.

"Yeah!" cried members of the crowd.

"Look, the council is only trying to keep us safe," Ayanna heard a man say, but she couldn't see who was speaking.

"Trying to keep us safe—or trying to enforce a prison sentence? Or in the case of Rafael, a death sentence," said Robin. "Tell me, where are Rafael and his friends supposed to go out there? And how long do you think they'll last before they're eaten alive, or dead from starvation. You folks are really a piece of work."

The council and the people bounced back and forth with accusations and excuses until the Watchers finally decided that they had answered enough questions and dismissed the meeting. Ayanna searched the room for Richard but couldn't find him.

She had no idea what role she should play in all this. Rumors continued that some people planned to leave Terra in support of Rafael, but in the days that passed after his departure, no one left. Even the people who had supported Rafael's speeches remained. The reason seemed obvious. Where would they go? And what about the Lincolns? They had gone weeks ago, but where? They had probably died on the surface. But it was possible, by some slender chance, that they had survived. They might even have found someplace safer than Terra to live.

Bang, bang, bang!

Ayanna rushed to open her door and found Monique standing with her hand perched to knock again. Her eyes were wide and her mouth open, taking in quick breaths, and her eyebrows were crumpled as if she were in pain. She looked terrified.

"What's wrong, Monique?" said Ayanna.

"People need you in the clinic. Some of the boys, well . . . they left the compound tonight and they went out. . . . One came back hurt, and the other . . ." she paused. She seemed like she didn't want to go on.

"Went out?" Ayanna asked. "Went out where?"

"Out to hunt dragons, I guess. But there's something else. The one who's hurt . . ." She looked down.

"What? Who was it?" Monique was scaring her. "Who was hurt?"

"Malik Sanders," she said.

"Malik?" Ayanna grabbed her shoes. "I'm coming right now," she said.

She rushed into the infirmary. The first thing she saw was a boy lying lifeless on a board on the floor. The sight stopped her in the doorframe. Her entire body tensed. She felt terror climb up her spine. Who was it? She walked over and peered at him. His face was serene and cold, and he looked as if he were asleep, but he was not breathing.

Ayanna knew him. Of course, Ayanna knew him. It was Josiah Audrey, and he was dead.

She shoved aside the sickness in her stomach and wrenched her eyes away from Josiah. Then she scanned the rest of the room, taking a deep breath when she found Malik.

She hurried over to his cot. He lay on top of a red-stained sheet, blood gushing from his wounds. He wasn't burned, but he had several lacerations, and his leg was broken.

Ayanna tore through the cabinets and took down strips of cloth and her stethoscope. She began tying the strips around Malik's arms and head. She needed to stop the bleeding.

"Monique, I need you to get me a suture kit to sew up the deepest cuts. We have to slow his bleeding right now," Ayanna said.

She placed the stethoscope to Malik's chest and listened. His lungs were clear, but his heart rate was fast and weak. She placed two fingers on his wrist and counted silently.

"Malik, can you hear me?" she asked. Malik didn't respond.

"Malik, it's Ayanna. You are at Terra. You're safe. Everything is going to be all right."

Ayanna grabbed a pair of scissors and began to cut Malik's uniform off his body. He stirred and let out a loud moan.

"I know you're in pain. I'm sorry," she said.

She cut his pantleg away and revealed that his tibia had

pierced through his skin. She wiped away the single tear that slid down her face and took in a deep breath. Then she rubbed her hand across Malik's head.

"It's going to be OK," she whispered. "It has to be."

Ayanna continued her examination, inspecting his chest and checking for puncture wounds. Malik's arm fell to the side of the cot. He was holding something in his left hand. She unfolded his fingers from the object, and her eyes widened.

It was the silver charm bracelet that her father had given her as a child. She had lost it on the day the Protectorate went to blow up the dam. It must have fallen off when she cut her arm in the dragon's nest. Why had he gone to the dragon's nest?

Ayanna took the bracelet and tucked it into her pocket just as Monique returned to the cot with the suture kit. "I need help resetting the bone in his leg," Ayanna said. Monique nodded, but she looked terrified. She was young, and Ayanna was sure that she had never seen anything like this.

"Have you ever reset a bone before?"

Monique shook her head no. "I'll show you how. Hurry and get me a belt or a rope and a piece of wood about two feet long." Monique moved quickly to follow her instructions.

Dr. Keaton had taught Ayanna how to reset broken bones over a year ago. She had performed the maneuver dozens of times since, but her only concern now was having enough medication to ward off an infection. That, and the fact that Ayanna needed to close Malik's wounds before he lost any more blood. And, of course, the very real possibility that he had internal bleeding. Ayanna shook her head. There was nothing she could do about that.

Monique returned and Ayanna started to talk quickly. "Malik's tibia is broken. You are going to hold him in place. And I'm going to take his ankle . . . " Ayanna placed one of her hands around Malik's ankle. She placed her other hand just above his knee. ". . . and put the two pieces of his bone back together. OK?"

Monique nodded her head tentatively. "On the count of three, OK? One, two . . ."

Ayanna snapped Malik's bone back into place. There was a crunching sound and Malik let out a loud cry, his body flailing up toward the ceiling, and then collapsing back down with a thud.

Just then, Maya and Mrs. Sanders appeared in the clinic door. Mrs. Sanders gasped and held her hand to her mouth. Maya held on to her grandmother's arm with a tight grip.

"How's his breathing, Monique?" Ayanna asked. She worked as fast as she could to stop his bleeding.

"It's steady, Doctor," Monique said.

Ayanna shifted her eyes to her. She was not a doctor. Not even close. But things were moving too quickly for her to correct Monique, so she nodded before looking over at Maya and pointing. "I need you two to wait in the hall. I'll let you know as soon as we're finished," she ordered.

Maya hesitated. She did not want to leave her brother. "What? No. Let me help," she said, tears brimming in her eyes.

"Please, My," said Ayanna.

Mrs. Sanders pulled at Maya's sleeve. "Come on, baby. Ayanna knows what she's doing," she said. The two stepped out of the clinic into the hall.

"Monique, can you please ask one of the militiamen to come and collect Josiah's body for burial?" Ayanna said. She tried her best to steady her voice.

Monique was on the verge of tears, and Ayanna couldn't blame her. She had to have known Josiah, as they were close in age.

Monique said nothing. She simply nodded her head and stepped out into the corridor.

When Ayanna finished sewing and cleaning Malik's wounds,

she walked into the hallway to speak with Maya and Mrs. Sanders. Maya was sitting on the floor, crying softly. She rocked back and forth and mumbled something Ayanna couldn't hear. Meanwhile, Mrs. Sanders paced the dim hallway, walking the same path so many times that it seemed she would leave a hole in the floor.

"You can come and see him now," Ayanna said. Maya got up from the ground and grabbed her grandmother's hand. The two stepped into the room. Maya took a choked breath. She sat on the edge of Malik's bed and gently held his hand.

"Malik is very weak, and he passed out from the pain," Ayanna said. "We've done our best, but his injuries are serious. I think he needs a transfusion. He's lost a lot of blood. If you're willing, I can test the two of you for compatible blood type. I think it will be best if we just take blood from one of you. I'm so sorry."

"Malik's blood type is A positive," said Mrs. Sanders. "He and Maya are the same type."

Maya looked up at her. "You can take my blood," she said. Tears fell from her eyes. "You can do whatever it takes. Just make sure that my little brother lives."

Ayanna's mouth opened. She searched for breath, suddenly overwhelmed with the weight of that request. Just then, Brandon Walker walked into the infirmary. He saw Maya and Mrs. Sanders crying over Malik lying on the cot. Brandon looked to her. Ayanna assumed he wanted to know how Malik was doing. Ayanna slowly shook her head at Brandon.

Maya caught this exchange and turned her head to face Brandon, who stood near the door. She let go of Malik's hand and raised herself from his bedside. Maya walked up to Brandon with fury burning in her eyes.

"Why? Why would you go out like this? You could have stopped him. None of you should have been out there. Why did you take my little brother out to die?" Maya screamed. She balled her fists and began to pummel Brandon's chest. Brandon grabbed her arms to stop her but then let go as her emotions took over, and she collapsed in his arms, sobbing. This made Mrs. Sanders weep, and she sprawled across her grandson's injured body.

Ayanna felt confused and desperate.

Just then, amid the chaos, Richard appeared. Relief washed over Ayanna. He seemed to have witnessed the entire scene. He walked over and freed Brandon from Maya's embrace. Then he wrapped his arms around Maya. She rested her head against his chest, and he placed his hand behind her head.

"Quiet now," he said softly. "It's going to be all right. Just take some deep breaths. It will be OK." Maya began to calm herself.

Everything seemed to play out in slow motion. Ayanna grieved for the fifteen-year-old boy who was now dead for reasons that she could not understand. She grieved for her best friend and her family. She was in awe of Richard's calm strength, and she worried about Malik and the other boys. She tried hard not to be angry with them, but she failed miserably.

Maya eventually calmed down and returned to Malik's side. Richard watched as Ramirez and Latif came into the clinic and carefully covered Josiah's body with a sheet before carrying him away.

Richard and Ayanna stepped out into the corridor. Three of the boys from Malik's journey to the surface were waiting there. Richard glared at them.

Ayanna's heart sped up when she saw Katrina and Sarafina running through the hallway toward her and Richard.

"Who got hurt?" Katrina demanded. "Where's Josiah?"

None of the boys could make eye contact with Katrina. They all wore guilty expressions, and Ayanna assumed that they didn't know how to tell her the horrible truth.

Katrina noticed this and demanded an answer. "Where is Josiah?" she said again.

Kevin stepped forward. "He's dead," he said solemnly.

Katrina gasped and then let out a loud cry. She fell to the floor and began to sob wildly. Sarafina dropped down to the floor and embraced her friend, but Katrina was inconsolable and wailed even louder.

"I want to see him!" she shouted. "Where is he? I want to see him!" Using the wall to pull her way back to a standing position, she spotted Ramirez and Latif carrying Josiah's body away from the clinic. She slowly moved toward them. Everyone in the hallway stood in silence. Richard stepped forward and tried to intervene.

"Miss Sully, please, I think that it would be better if—"

"He had asked me to marry him, you know? We had it all planned out. Please, I want to see him." Richard backed away and let Katrina continue toward Josiah's body. Ramirez and Latif stopped.

Katrina kneeled down next to the makeshift gurney and pulled back the sheet that covered Josiah. She gave out a slight whimper and then began to weep again.

Her sobs only exacerbated Maya's and Mrs. Sanders's weeping, and soon, the entire corridor filled with a chorus of cries for the boys.

Then, Katrina allowed Sarafina to take her back to her room. Ayanna stared helplessly and looked toward Richard, who stared back at her with sad resignation. Their expressions mirrored each other's. There was nothing that either of them could do to counter the pain of the people around them.

After a long time, the corridor cleared, and they were alone. At first, they didn't speak.

Ayanna broke the silence. "I thought you should know where they went," she said.

Richard stood up tall and narrowed his eyes. "How do you know where they went, Ayanna?" he asked.

She sighed and reached in her pocket, pulling out her brace-let. "Malik was carrying this when he arrived. It's mine. I lost it in the dragon's nest."

"They went all the way to the dragon's nest?" Richard said.

Ayanna nodded her head. His face turned from disbelief to confusion.

"I need to speak with those boys right now, and my father. I need to tell him that he's all wrong about Kyle," he said.

"Kyle? Jackson Kyle?"

"Yeah," Richard confirmed.

"What's Jackson got to do with this?" Ayanna said.

"He doesn't seem to have anything to do with it, but my father thinks otherwise. We picked up a communication over the radio. There was a group of men traveling on the surface. They were on the radio. They mentioned Kyle. I thought . . . Colonel Daniels thought he had led others to us, but it seems like we were wrong. It must have been Sanders's group. Anyway, my father detained Mr. Kyle so they could question him, but it sounds like a waste of time to me," said Richard.

"Yeah, it does," Ayanna agreed. Her mind started to drift. How could Jackson have anything to do with Malik and the militia boys going out?

"I need to go," said Richard. "Will you be OK down here?"

"Yeah, we'll be OK," Ayanna said. Richard nodded and returned to the heart of Terra.

CHAPTER **41**

Ayanna walked into the Watchers' chamber and saw Jackson sitting in a metal chair. His arms were crossed over his chest, and he wore a deep, uncharacteristic frown. He was the only person in the room, but he looked as if he were waiting for someone to arrive.

Jackson's eyes found hers, and Ayanna matched his frown. "Ayanna, what are you doing here?" he said.

"I was worried about you. I'm sorry this is happening. I don't know why they keep going after you like this," Ayanna said.

Jackson opened his arms, and Ayanna fell into them. He brushed his hand across her hair. Jackson pulled her closer and pressed her against his chest. Relaxing into the embrace, Ayanna wrapped her arms around his back.

"Don't worry about it," he said. He released her and looked toward the door.

"I guess you heard about Malik and the other boys?"

"Yeah, I heard something about that. These people act like I'm the one who killed that boy. At least if I had, I would deserve this harassment or worse."

Ayanna stared at Jackson. She wanted to comfort him, but she didn't know what she could do.

"I wish that there were something . . . something I could do, talk to Colonel Daniels or . . . something," she said.

"No. I don't need anyone fighting my battles for me. I don't need anything at all. I've been taking care of myself for a long time. Long before I ever learned about this place, and I'll be taking care of myself long after I'm gone," he said.

"What do you—?"

"This Terra, temple of sanctuary . . . it feels more like a prison to me."

"You don't deserve to be treated so unfairly."

"No, I guess not. But I know better than anyone that life is unfair," Jackson said. He walked across the room. "I'm guessing you know about that too, though, don't you?"

She looked at Jackson. "What?"

Jackson shook his head slowly and turned to face her. His voice was low. "There's something you need to know," he said.

"OK." Ayanna stood still. She had no idea what he was about to say. He stared into her eyes. She waited for him to continue.

After a few more seconds of silence, he spoke. "Before my mother died, she told me that I should come here, to Tropeck. She said I would find my father here. She claimed that he was some high-ranking military official, and he would take care of me," he said.

Ayanna swallowed. Nervously, she pressed Jackson to continue. "Is that why you're here? To find your father?"

"Well, I didn't have a name and I didn't really believe her at first." Jackson shook his head. "But after the infestation, I didn't have much else to go on, so I headed this way. I thought about giving up on finding some stranger who'd abandoned me and my mom, until the others told me there was a colonel still living in the city. They said that he'd been left behind after Tropeck was evacuated. They told me a lot of people had been left behind, including the scientist who had opened the portal to the dragon's home world."

Ayanna blinked. Confusion clouded her mind. "What? Others . . . they . . . Jackson, what are you talking about? What others? You told me you were alone." She tried to keep panic from rising in her voice. Had Jackson been lying to her this whole time?

Jackson shook his head. "You don't understand. I was alone when I met you. It's just that . . ."

They heard a noise at the door and turned suddenly. Colonel Daniels stood in the doorframe.

"So it's true then. You're Rebecca's son," said Colonel Daniels.

"Don't you dare speak my mother's name," Jackson shouted.

"Don't speak her name? I loved her. I loved her long before you existed. But she knew . . . she knew we couldn't be together. She knew I had another family."

"So, you just abandoned her then? And me." Jackson's voice caught on the last word. The sound was a mixture of anger and grief. Ayanna watched, unsure of what to do.

"I never thought I would see the day when I'd have to face you again," continued Colonel Daniels. He seemed to ignore both her and Jackson. "But I guess all of life's mistakes eventually catch up to you." Colonel Daniels lifted his arms up in what looked like a sign of resignation.

"So, my mother and me were a mistake?" asked Jackson. He took a step toward Colonel Daniels, and Ayanna placed her hand on his chest, hoping to calm him down. His heart thudded beneath her hand.

"Your mother thought I owed her something? Maybe I did. Maybe I did do wrong by her, by you," Colonel Daniels said. "Sometimes I do wonder whether I made the right decision to leave her. I knew there would be consequences. I knew that one day, I would have to deal with the results of my actions, and now, here we are."

"Colonel Daniels, what are you—?" Ayanna blurted. But before she could finish her thought, Jackson swung his fist and punched Colonel Daniels in the face, then grabbed the colonel and flung him onto the desks. The colonel recovered and kicked Jackson in the stomach, knocking the wind out of him.

Jackson regained his breath and went after the colonel again. Ayanna stood frozen, shocked, as the men continued to fight. Should she call for help? Everything was happening so quickly.

Ayanna moved toward the door. Before she could reach it, Richard appeared. In a flash of movement, Jackson's body flew backward, nearly clearing the distance of the room. Ayanna scrambled to comprehend what had just happened. Richard stood between Jackson and the colonel with his arms raised.

"You are out of here," Richard said. He spoke in a tense, but controlled voice.

"Leave him be," said Colonel Daniels, stumbling upright.

Richard looked to his father. He was clearly as confused as Ayanna. "What is going on?" he demanded.

Neither Jackson nor Colonel Daniels said anything.

"One of you, speak now," Richard commanded.

Colonel Daniels stood tall. He rolled his shoulders backward and held his chest out, ignoring his son's order. Jackson got up from the floor and slowly walked back toward the two men, panting. Ayanna held her breath.

"Of course, you've got nothing to say," said Jackson. "No talk of the past and your regrets now."

Richard stared at Jackson, his eyebrows furrowed. He looked as if he were trying to understand Jackson's words.

"Oh, he never told you? Turns out Daddy's keeping a few secrets," said Jackson.

"What the hell are you talking about?" Richard said, losing his calm.

LOVE IN THE AGE OF DRAGONS

"Oh, come on, you got nothing? I'm sure you can tell him whatever lie you want, just like you did my mother, you piece of shit," said Jackson.

Richard looked back at his father, waiting for him to respond. But Colonel Daniels remained silent.

"You might as well tell the whole world now," said Jackson.

Colonel Daniels looked at Richard. The colonel looked resigned. "Fine, I will. It's true—I am your father."

Jackson's fury reignited and he exploded toward Colonel Daniels again. Richard held him back halfheartedly. "Wait," he said. "Everyone just wait one damn minute.

What are you talking about, *his father*?"

Ayanna shifted. She wanted to understand too.

Colonel Daniels took a deep breath and started to speak. "Rebecca and I . . ."

Jackson grew furious again at the mention of his mother's name. "Don't you say her name!" he said with tears of rage forming in his eyes. "Don't you even think it."

"I'm going to explain—"

"I've heard enough," said Jackson. "There's nothing you have to say that I want to hear."

He stormed out of the Watchers' chamber. Ayanna started to move but then stopped. She wasn't sure what to do.

Richard noticed her presence for the first time and looked at her, bewildered. Ayanna shook her head slowly. She didn't have any answers, and now, she had even more questions.

She left the chamber and trailed closely behind a furious Jackson. Who were these others he was talking about? And if they think her father, Professor Grace, is still alive in Tropeck, do they plan to come look for him?

CHAPTER **42**

Ayanna wasn't exactly sure where Jackson was going. She had never been to Jackson's room, but if that was where he was headed, it would be in the militia area. He must have known she was following him, but he made no effort to slow down.

His fists were balled tightly, and he looked about to explode with fury. Ayanna had never seen him this angry. He rushed through the tunnels and crossed through an access door leading to the offices. When they arrived at one of the old offices, Jackson turned inside, Ayanna close behind him.

"Not now, Ayanna," Jackson snapped as Ayanna followed him through the door. His roommate wasn't there. They were alone. Jackson grabbed his duffel bag and began to cram his belongings into it.

"Yes, now, Jackson," Ayanna insisted. "You can't just walk away from this. You tell me that there are other people out there . . . other people who are looking for my father . . . and then this thing with the colonel. You just drop this on me all of a sudden, and you think we aren't going to talk about it?"

"I don't want to talk about Colonel Daniels, Ayanna. He's just the jackass who left my mother and abandoned me without so much as a 'bye, see ya later,'" Jackson said.

"Fine. What about the others?" she demanded. Ayanna could feel heat rising to her head. Anger threatened to spill out. "Have you been lying to us this entire time?"

Jackson stopped packing and looked up at her. "Not exactly," he said. "Yes, there's another group about twenty miles away. They have some equipment, and they follow a man named Hilton. I don't know what he wanted with your father or Colonel Daniels, but I didn't stick around long enough to find out, either."

"So you didn't even think to warn us? You didn't think I would want to know that there was someone out here looking for my father?

What if they try to come here? What if they try to attack us?" Ayanna heard her voice rise two octaves.

"They don't know where you are," said Jackson. Ayanna shook her head.

"And now what?" she pointed to the duffel bag that Jackson packed. "You're not even going to stay and help us fight if they do show up? You're just gonna take off and leave us unprotected?"

Ayanna's voice cracked. She had said *us*, but she meant *me*. She felt her head shake. She couldn't believe any of this was happening.

"I'm not even supposed to be here, Ayanna. I shouldn't have come. I should've just kept heading out West like I'd planned. I don't belong here. I never did," said Jackson.

Her body started to tremble. She forced her arms to her sides, struggling to find a new approach.

Ayanna threw her hands into the air. "Don't be stupid, Jackson. The dragons are everywhere. There's nowhere else to go." She hoped this would get the response she wanted.

Jackson stood next to his cot. He stared up at the light for a moment, and then his eyes found her face.

"Ayanna, I've been here long enough, and now it's time for me to move on like I planned."

"But this is your home!" Ayanna shouted.

"No . . . it isn't," Jackson said coldly. "This is *your* home. I've tried to make it work. I really have, but I just don't want to be here anymore."

"But what about . . . loyalty? What about the people who have helped you, stood up for you? I mean, what about . . . ? Look, we need you. I . . ." Her words were jumbled now as she fought back tears.

"Come with me," he said suddenly. His face was serious, his eyes pleading.

"What?" Ayanna asked, surprised. She tilted her head to the side.

"I want you to come with me," he repeated.

Ayanna's heart pounded against her rib cage. This was happening too fast. She couldn't think clearly. Thoughts shot through her brain, shouting different things at her. Just do it, go with him. Don't you dare. Loyalty . . . responsibility . . . duty, duty, duty. Ayanna shook her head in a futile attempt to clear it.

"Jackson, I can't . . . Terra is . . . it's . . . it's everything to me. I can't leave it. I can't leave Maya and my patients and . . ." Her voice trailed off.

Jackson dropped his head and shook it once. Then he met her eyes again.

"So, I guess there is nothing else to say," he said.

Ayanna stumbled back. Her stomach felt as though it were filled with stones. A lump formed in her throat that she couldn't choke down. Tears sprang up and ran freely down her cheeks. She struggled to compose herself and tried to replace her pain with anger.

Jackson's face contorted. He seemed to be reacting to the sight of her tears, but then a hard mask replaced his look of concern. Jackson walked away from the cot and headed past her to the door.

Ayanna wanted to grab him, to make him look at her and give her a reason why he was doing this. She wanted to demand that he tell her where he was going or when he would be back. She wanted him to stay, to take back everything he had just said.

She thought if he would only take it back, she could forgive him. She would forgive him for his lies of omission. She would forgive him for threatening to leave. All he had to do was to just say he was sorry. That he didn't mean it, not a word of it. That he wasn't going anywhere. That he was going to stay there . . . with her. Then Ayanna would be OK. Everything would be OK. Nothing had to change. She didn't have to feel this way, this panic, this loss . . . again, not again.

But she was trapped in place. All she could do was muster up the words that described how she felt. The feeling had sat quietly in her chest, but her fear had prevented her from declaring it. Ayanna hadn't wanted to look weak; she needed to be strong.

She had tried to deny what her heart had known to be true from the moment they had met. Time had only intensified the feeling.

"I love you," Ayanna said softly.

Jackson stopped in the doorframe with his back to her. She watched his shoulders rise and fall as he took in a deep breath. He turned around to face her, his anger completely erased from his expression. He walked toward her and brushed his hand across her face.

She gazed into his eyes. She was lost. Then, very slowly he leaned in and lightly kissed her on the lips. Ayanna closed her eyes and melted into the moment. It was tender, and the sensation of his warm mouth lingered on her skin.

Carefully, he pulled away. "Don't," he said before backing away and walking through the door, leaving her alone.

CHAPTER **43**

A yanna tried to move her feet. She intended to follow him. This wasn't fair. How dare he? Where was he . . . what was he thinking? He couldn't just . . .

She wanted her mind to quiet down. She didn't want to think about this. It was too much. The foundation of her world was crumbling around the edges. First, she had lost Dr. Keaton—*You can't replace him. You have no idea what you're doing without him.* Then, there were daily outbursts over Rafael's expulsion—*Was it right or wrong, Ayanna?* A teenage boy was dead—*How did this happen?* And Malik was fighting for his life in her clinic—*He had to live. He had to.* Now this.

This was too much. Ayanna needed . . . Ayanna needed . . . ?

Richard.

Ayanna needed to talk to Richard and to Colonel Daniels. Had Richard known about any of this? And the colonel? Who did Colonel Daniels think he was, playing with people's emotions and lives? And this other group? What were they going to do about this Hilton person?

No, this could not stand. Ayanna would force the Protectorate to send out a unit and bring Jackson back. She would make

Colonel Daniels answer for a lifetime of neglect. She would keep Terra safe . . . somehow.

Her plan was muddled in her mind, but her legs were already moving back in the direction of the Watchers' chamber.

When Ayanna arrived at the door, she expected to find Richard and his father alone. Instead, most of the council had assembled, except for Mrs. Johnson, and a distressed-looking Richard stood in front of them. His features were tense, as if he were trying to lift a huge weight, and his normally calm voice only thinly veiled his anger. He squinted, and creases formed across his forehead.

Ayanna slipped into the back of the room, ignoring the fact that she hadn't been invited to the meeting. Colonel Daniels saw her but didn't alert the others to her presence. His face was flushed, and Ayanna noticed a dark bruise near his left eye.

"How is it that your men went to the surface without your knowledge, Captain?" asked Mr. Christy.

"I'm still trying to ascertain that information, sir. But it looks like it was the younger boys. It appears that Malik Sanders and some of the others came up with the plan to destroy a nest, and the boys met in secret before executing it," said Richard.

"Why?" interjected Mr. Frye.

"Apparently, Malik . . . Private Sanders came up with this plan to help me."

Ayanna could see that she wasn't the only person in the room who didn't understand what Richard meant.

"Help you?" asked Mr. Frye. "You mean you sent him?"

Richard stood taller. "Of course I didn't send him, sir. I had no idea what he was planning, but the other boys who accompanied his unit told me that, given all the unrest in the population, and the unpopularity of this council, and of me . . . they thought if they succeeded in destroying a dragon's nest, then the people would again view the Protectorate as heroes, instead of the enemy," he concluded.

Immediately, Ayanna remembered the conversation she'd had with Malik just after Richard arrested Rafael in the cafeteria. It all made sense now. Why hadn't she figured it out before?

"I'm starting to think that we may have made a mistake placing you in charge of security, Captain. If you can't even control a fourteen-year-old boy, how are we supposed to believe you can control anything else that goes on around here?" said Colonel Daniels.

Blood pulsed to Ayanna's head, and she swallowed hard. She felt the anger she saw Richard trying to suppress. She clenched her fists as Richard clenched his jaw.

He took in a slow breath. He hadn't known about Jackson; it was obvious. He was furious with his father—and she was too. How dare the colonel speak a word of criticism toward anyone, let alone Richard?

Richard straightened his back and looked ahead. He avoided his father's eyes. "I assure you, Colonel, I am not one of your mistakes," he said.

Colonel Daniels sat up in his seat and stared at his son. Only Mr. Christy and Ayanna seemed to notice the tension between the men.

"Council, the boys involved will be reprimanded. I can promise you nothing like this will happen again," Richard said, exasperated.

"Audrey is dead?" asked Ms. Morgan.

"Yes."

"And what about the Sanders boy?" she asked. "Will he recover?"

"I don't know," said Richard. "Miss Grace says that his injuries are very serious. I'm not certain that he'll survive."

Ayanna remained quiet. She had nothing to add.

"You said that these boys attacked a nest. Did they succeed?" asked Mr. Christy.

"I don't know," said Richard. "They followed a trail near the river until they came upon the nesting ground. Apparently, they set fire to the nest, but I suspect that was ineffective. Anyway, the dragons defended the nest and the boys were forced to retreat. That's when Audrey was killed and Sanders got hurt. They rushed back here when that happened."

"And what about Terra? Have these actions placed us in danger?"

"That's unclear. It is possible that they might've drawn unwelcome attention to our location."

Mr. Christy stood up. "Captain, what would happen if the dragons knew where to find us? Could we defend ourselves against them?"

Richard lowered his eyes to the ground as the entire room fell silent. Everyone seemed to hold their breath. Ayanna was afraid of what he would say next.

He lifted his head, and his eyes scanned the council.

"No," he said. "It would be better for us to leave."

"We're not leaving," said Colonel Daniels. "We're not going anywhere. It's impractical and foolish for us to pack up over one hundred people and move them to God knows where when we have no evidence that our position has been compromised. Captain, you need to go and do whatever it takes to secure our borders."

"I agree," said Mr. Christy. "It is impractical for us to try to leave."

Richard nodded. "I will keep you informed," he said.

He turned without acknowledging his father again. He met Ayanna's eyes for a brief second. She knew he hadn't known she was in the room. He looked surprised to see her. He parted his lips, as if he wanted to speak, but then he changed his mind and left the council's chamber.

Ayanna didn't know if she should follow him. She wanted to talk to him, but she also wanted to talk to Colonel Daniels about Jackson. This seemed like as good a time as any.

She waited for the council to disperse. None of the Watchers seemed upset to see her there. They filed out of the room with barely a nod of acknowledgment. Everyone appeared to have more important things to worry about than her eavesdropping on a meeting.

Frustration and confusion were the only things that kept her from collapsing where she stood. All the pressure and pain of the night crept up and tried to overtake her. She wouldn't allow it, though. Ayanna knew she needed to hold herself together, if only for a few more minutes.

Colonel Daniels rushed past her toward his quarters without looking her way. She was not about to let him get away without facing her.

"Colonel!" Ayanna shouted. He ignored her. Ayanna had assumed he would. Still, her frustration was growing into a stronger emotion. She wasn't entirely familiar with this feeling, but she had the sense that it was hatred. Yes, that was it. She hated him. His selfish and callous behavior was hurting her, and his . . . *sons*. It was strange to think of Richard and Jackson as brothers, but if everything she had recently learned was true, that's what they were.

Her feelings intensified with each step. This man was hurting people, people she cared about. He was hurting people Ayanna wanted there . . . people she needed to come back. She stumbled to keep up with his pace.

"Colonel Daniels, I want to talk to you," Ayanna said, catching up to him. She walked beside him, but he didn't even look over to acknowledge her. After several paces in silence, they stopped at his bunker.

"Colonel, I wanted to talk to you about your sons," she shouted. He pushed the door open and ushered her inside the room, closing the door behind him. Ayanna wondered if he had ever found out that she'd been there before. He didn't act like it.

She didn't know what to do with herself. She didn't feel comfortable enough to sit. Where should she put her hands? She decided to wait near the door with her arms crossed. But what should she say?

She knew what she wanted to learn—hoped to learn—but the colonel had no allegiance to her. Would he tell her anything at all?

The anger that had fueled her walk to his room began to dissipate, and anxiety replaced it. Maybe she should just forget it. Did she really need to understand what was going on in Colonel Daniels's mind? Would the information help her convince Jackson to come back?

Colonel Daniels pulled off his jacket and hung it in the small wooden wardrobe that stood in the corner of the room. Ayanna got the distinct impression that he barely noticed she was there. He sat down at his desk and opened the drawer. She knew what he was reaching for.

The colonel pulled out two shot glasses and a bottle of whiskey. She watched as he stared at the bottle. It was strange the way he held it with such care. He pulled out a black marker from the drawer. Using his finger, he drew a line above it, measuring the amount of the liquid that remained. Ayanna guessed he did this often. She felt embarrassed for him. Shouldn't he feel ashamed of himself?

"Colonel?" she said.

He lifted one hand in the air to interrupt her. Then he poured himself a shot of whiskey and drank it quickly, closing his eyes as it went down.

"You want a drink?"

She didn't know how to answer.

"It's the good stuff. Don't think you'll find any more of this for a long time," he said.

"Sure." Maybe it would make him trust her, or at least talk to her.

Colonel Daniels filled the second glass halfway, and Ayanna stepped forward to pick it up. She held the drink up to her face. It smelled awful.

"Drink it fast," he recommended. She placed the glass to her lips and turned it upright in one swift motion.

It was awful. Her throat burned, and tears came to her eyes. She coughed and choked. The colonel shook his head at her.

"How do you drink this?" she asked between the coughs.

"I wouldn't expect you to understand, Miss Grace," he said. He poured himself another.

"No, I guess there's a lot I don't understand," she said. His words helped her remember why she had come. Her throat continued to burn from the whiskey, and she felt strange as if the room were leaning to one side.

Colonel Daniels scoffed. "You'd better sit down before you lose it all over my floor," he said. Ayanna felt too uneasy to argue. She took a seat on his cot, neatly made with a single blanket.

He picked up the photograph of Richard that sat on his desk and looked at it somberly. He took a sip of his drink, and then he removed the cardboard plate from the back of the frame. Another small, wallet-sized photograph fell from beneath the framed photo. It was the photo of the woman Ayanna remembered seeing before.

He rubbed his index finger across the picture. "There's a lot you have to learn about life, Miss Grace," he said.

Ayanna wanted to respond, but she was too busy concentrating on keeping her eyes focused.

"When you're young, it doesn't occur to you how your actions will play out. In fact, you never dream that something you do can change everything for better or worse," Colonel Daniels went on.

Ayanna finally gathered her bearings and spoke. "So, are your regrets supposed to make everything OK?" she said. "You had a son . . . whom you abandoned. And you have another son you've been lying to his whole life. And what about your wife?"

"I don't owe you anything, Miss Grace."

"No, I guess you don't—but what about your family?" Heat rose to her face as the anger cleared the fog in her head.

The colonel gave a half smirk. "You know, long before Richard came along, I was a decorated soldier. I'd been promoted so many times that I no longer had to take overseas assignments. That made Ella happy. She was tired of moving around. She wanted to settle down, and Tropeck was her home. For some reason, I agreed, but I could never stand being in one place.

"Luckily, I didn't have to. A few months after we moved to Tropeck, the government chose me to work on a mission, and I got to travel up and down the eastern shore a lot.

"I met Rebecca by chance. She worked as a secretary at the base in Rockport, and there was something about her that I couldn't stay away from. I loved her, and I planned to return to Tropeck and tell Ella I was leaving her.

"That's when I found out about Richard. He was a miracle for his mother. She had wanted a baby for so long, and we'd tried for many years before. . . . I couldn't refuse her. So I did the selfish thing instead and tried to live a double life. It worked for a while, until Ella found out. Then I ended things with Rebecca and settled into my life with Ella and Richard," he concluded. Colonel Daniels leaned back in his seat, looking resigned.

"What about Jackson?" Ayanna asked. "Why did you give him up?"

Colonel Daniels sighed and took another sip of his drink. "I didn't even know he existed until several years later," he said.

"So what did you do when you *did* find out?"

Colonel Daniels gave her a knowing look. "Nothing."

Ayanna stood up quickly. She felt pure disgust. She thought Colonel Daniels was even more pathetic than she had first assumed.

"So that's it. You just leave your kid with nothing else to say about it?" she asked. She didn't really expect an answer. The colonel stood and took a step toward her, but Ayanna inched closer to the door. She was ready to leave.

"Look, I made a decision, one that I've had to live with for eighteen years, and now, that decision has come back to haunt me," he said.

Ayanna shook her head in disbelief. "To haunt you? Your son came back, and he was right here. You had an opportunity . . . an opportunity to try to make up for all you did. An opportunity to get to know him. You had a chance to be . . ." She choked on these words and the burning sensation returned to her throat. ". . . A chance to be a family. I can't believe you would just let it all go. After everything people have lost. Do you know what anyone else at Terra would do for a chance like that?" Tears pooled in her eyes and were dangerously close to falling. Ayanna didn't want to cry in front of Colonel Daniels. He didn't deserve it.

She pulled the door open with all her strength and raced toward the clinic as fast as she could.

CHAPTER **44**

Ayanna ran all the way back to her room and closed the door behind her. Every emotion she had fought to hold in slammed into her like waves crashing against rocks. Her entire body shook, and tears cascaded from her eyes.

She collapsed onto her cot, weeping. This only made her cry harder because her mind drifted to the nights she had shared this space with Jackson, who was now gone, and she had no way of knowing if he would ever come back. Loud wails escaped her mouth.

Fear and worry joined her sadness, the emotions coiling around her like a snake. She should be furious with him for allowing Terra to be placed in danger and for leaving. But what she most felt was sadness at his absence. She wrapped her arms around herself and tried to lessen the pain that pulsed from her core.

Then there was the rest. Malik desperately needed her to help him, and she had no idea if she could. What he really needed was a doctor and a hospital—not her, a girl who couldn't hold herself together. If he died . . .

She wailed harder at the thought.

After a quarter hour or so, she finally stopped crying. She turned onto her back and allowed her lungs to fill with air. It felt good, and she continued to take in slow, deep breaths to calm herself.

Ayanna sat up and turned on the light. She didn't have a mirror, but she imagined she looked dreadful. She used her tear-stained sheet to wipe away the remaining moisture from her face, stood up, and walked out of her room and back toward the clinic.

She entered the laboratory and looked at the microscope. Her science couldn't help her now, but she was confident she could perform Malik's transfusion without any complications. She had the right equipment, and she had done one before. Although beyond this, she had no idea what she could do for him. Supplies were limited, and all she really had left were herbal remedies.

Ayanna was searching the cabinets for more bandages when she heard a quiet voice call her name.

She didn't have to turn around to know it was Maya. Ayanna took in a quick breath. She needed to be strong for her friend. Maya wasn't like her. She was terrified for Malik, and her temperament left her in a fragile state.

Ayanna hoped that some of the swelling in her face had gone down by the time she turned to face her friend, who stood with her arms crossed. Maya's tear-stained face resembled her own, she imagined. Her eyes were swollen and red with bags under them, and she looked exhausted.

She looked in even worse condition than Ayanna had feared.

"Maya, are you OK?" Ayanna asked.

"No . . . I don't think so," Maya said.

Ayanna put down the bandages she carried and stepped closer to her. Sadness swam in Maya's eyes. "Ayanna, is Malik going to be OK?" she asked. Her desperate voice came out in a whisper.

Ayanna's heart fell. She didn't know what to tell her. Somehow, the truth—that she had no idea whether he would be OK—didn't seem like the right answer in this moment. Maya seemed to be barely hanging on.

Ayanna opened her arms and wrapped them around Maya's tiny frame. "Malik is a fighter. You know that," she said.

Maya pulled back from Ayanna and looked into her eyes. Maya nodded in agreement and took in a slow breath. "How are you doing?" she asked.

Ayanna was surprised at the question. "I'm fine," she lied, "just getting things ready for Malik's transfusion. Do you still want to go through with it?"

"Of course," said Maya.

Ayanna nodded. She turned and continued to gather supplies. Maya bit her lip.

"I can try to find someone else if—"

"No, I want to. It's not that. I just . . . are you sure you're OK?" she asked. Ayanna looked back at her.

"It's just that I saw Jackson practically running for the gates when I was on the upper level, and I thought . . ."

Ayanna nearly dropped everything in her hands at the sound of Jackson's name. She leaned into the table to steady herself. "Yes, he left," she said, in a curt voice.

"Wha—?"

Ayanna lowered her eyes. She didn't want to talk about it.

Maya understood and closed her mouth quickly. "Just let me know when you're ready to start the transfusion," she said.

Ayanna gave Maya a tiny smile and nodded. Maya mustered an expression that resembled a smile, too, and left the laboratory.

CHAPTER **45**

Ayanna bandaged Maya's arm and started Malik's IV. She moved to the basin to clean her equipment and then sat down with her thoughts.

Malik stirred a bit, but eventually he gave way to sleep. When his eyelids closed, Ayanna thought perhaps she could finally get some rest. The night had dragged on, and dawn was approaching. She couldn't think anymore. Her body ached from exhaustion. She just wanted to sleep.

"Ayanna," said a meek voice at the door. Her heart sank. Would this day never end?

Ayanna held in a sigh and turned to find Monique standing there.

"Monique, what's wrong?" Ayanna asked. Her presence alarmed Ayanna. She hadn't sent for Monique. Was there yet another disaster awaiting her?

"There's something . . . something going on in the terminal," Monique said. Her voice trembled, and her hands shook as her wide eyes stared at Ayanna.

Ayanna struggled to understand her. So much had gone on that night, and she didn't know how much more she could handle.

"What do you mean?" she asked. She did her best to suppress

the irritation in her voice. Whatever was happening couldn't possibly be Monique's fault.

"I'm not sure exactly, but there's been a breach in the perimeter," Monique said.

"How do you know? Where are the alarms?"

"I . . . I don't know anything else. Mr. Frye just sent me to come and get you," she said.

Ayanna took in a deep breath, and her exhaustion faded. Anxiety replaced it just as the lights flickered and a gentle rumble reverberated through the floor. There was definitely something wrong.

Ayanna moved to the cabinet and removed a bag. "Monique, I want you to fill this bag with as many supplies as will fit. I'll be right back."

Monique took the bag and started to empty the cabinets. Ayanna ran out of the laboratory and headed toward the main terminal. She needed to find Richard.

Immediately, Ayanna could tell that something was very wrong. People flooded the terminal, their hands filled with bags, sacks, and bundles of clothes, as though they were preparing to move through the tunnels. But where were the alarms?

Ayanna climbed the inner escalator and moved toward the main galley. She saw Brenton running in her direction as fast as he could. He didn't seem to see her and nearly ran into her. She reached out her arms and cushioned the impact of the collision, keeping them both from falling.

"Oh, Ayanna, I'm sorry, but I've got to get to Captain Daniels," he said. He was out of breath.

"Wait!" Ayanna pleaded. "What's going on?"

"We've just found something that the captain needs to see," he said through his gasps. Brenton's flushed face advertised his fear. He took a breath and continued, "The entrance has been breached, I'm not sure how, but something got in . . . and . . ."

Brenton was trying to pull away from her, but she clung to his arm. "And *what?*" she demanded.

"We have something that . . . well . . . it looks like . . . like an egg. The boys from the Sanders mission brought it back with them. Kevin just told us. He says they thought it would be good for conducting experiments or something."

"What?" Ayanna shouted. Her eyes widened. She could not believe what he just told her. "You mean those idiots brought a dragon egg into Terra?"

Brenton mumbled something, but she was too distracted to understand him. Her mind raced to a devastating conclusion. This was so much worse than anything she had imagined.

She could not believe the stupidity and arrogance of the boys. What on earth could they have been thinking?

"Yes, yes, you should report to the captain right away," she said, releasing Brenton's arm. "But what about the alarms?"

"Broken," he shouted as he ran away from her through the compound.

Broken? When? How? The answer didn't really matter. Everyone on the upper levels seemed to know about the breach.

Ayanna looked down the path that Brenton had taken. She could follow him to find Richard, as he obviously knew where the captain was, but she had left Maya and the others in the clinic. They had no idea what was going on, and she needed to warn them.

Maya and Mrs. Sanders were sitting near Malik when Ayanna burst into the clinic, knocking the door against the wall with a loud thud.

Her urgency alarmed them. Maya jumped up and looked around, confused.

"Maya, Mrs. Sanders, gather whatever you can find," Ayanna said. She couldn't hide the panic in her voice. "We have to go."

"Ayanna, what's wrong?" Mrs. Sanders asked.

"There is something terribly wrong, and you have to leave the clinic right now." Malik made a small sound from his cot. It sounded as if he were trying to speak, but Ayanna couldn't make it out.

"Come on, help me," Ayanna said. "You have to move him. You have to leave now."

"Wait. What do you mean move? Move where? What's going on?" asked Maya. Her voice had raised two octaves. Ayanna knew she was scaring them, but there was no way to avoid that now. The situation was scary. She had no idea what would happen next. They needed to flee through the tunnels.

"Dragons. They're here, and you've got to get out *now*. I want you to take Malik and go through the tunnels heading west. Where's Monique?" asked Ayanna.

"What do you mean, dragons are here?" said Mrs. Sanders.

Ayanna looked over at Maya. She hadn't moved. She seemed trapped inside her own fear.

The light in the room flickered and then went out. Maya gasped.

"They've managed to knock out the power," Ayanna said. Having memorized the room, she moved about, finding the flashlights and turning one on.

"What do you mean?" asked Maya. "They're animals. How could they do anything to the power?" She sounded hysterical.

"Maya!" shouted Mrs. Sanders, who seemed to better understand what Ayanna was trying to tell them. "Come on, do as Ayanna says. We have to go."

"Take Malik's gurney and head west. Please go now. I'll follow behind you in a little while," Ayanna said.

"But shouldn't we go to our stations?" asked Maya.

Ayanna shook her head. "Drills and stations won't help us now. The only thing that we can do is to get out and go someplace safe."

"You're coming with us," Mrs. Sanders insisted.

"I can't. I need to gather supplies and go back upstairs in case people are hurt."

"Ayanna, I am not about to leave you here alone," Mrs. Sanders said. She stopped and placed her hands on both of Ayanna's shoulders.

"Listen, I know I'm not your mother . . ." She paused. Tears began to well in her eyes, and Ayanna felt a lump form in her own throat. "But you are a member of our family. Please come with us."

From the corner of her eye, Ayanna saw tears streaming down Maya's face. Ayanna shook her head. She didn't have time to explain why she needed to stay. She desperately wanted to calm their fears and to leave with them, but she couldn't. She wouldn't abandon Terra. She wouldn't leave behind so many people who needed help right now.

Ayanna gave Mrs. Sanders a small smile. She looked straight into her eyes and hoped the woman would grasp the depths of her words. "I have to stay. Please understand. You don't have to worry about me. I'll be OK. Just get out now, while you still can," she pleaded.

Mrs. Sanders studied her face for a long second. Then, she nodded and pulled her into a tight hug. Maya walked over and joined them, taking in ragged breaths.

"It'll be OK, My," Ayanna said. "I'll see you soon."

The ground rumbled again, and they heard what sounded like concrete crashing to the ground. The tunnel that led to the clinic began to fill with fire and smoke.

"Oh, my God!" yelled Maya.

"You have to go!" Ayanna screamed. "But where is Monique?" she asked again.

"I don't know," said Mrs. Sanders.

"OK, I'll find her. Please go now. I need you to make it out of here before things get worse.

The westbound tunnel places you just below the mall. Take Malik, and I'll meet you. I promise," Ayanna added.

She handed two flashlights to Maya. She and her grandmother struggled to lift Malik's gurney and started to walk down the tunnel, away from the clinic. It was dark, and they worked hard to balance his weight. But their path seemed clear.

Ayanna was worried. She still had a lot to do before she could follow them. She turned around and returned to the clinic.

CHAPTER 46

Ayanna reached into a cabinet and found another beat-up backpack. The bag she had given Monique was gone. Monique must have taken it with her, wherever that was.

First, Ayanna threw any remaining medical supplies into her bag. She found suture kits, scissors, and a few syringes. Then she tossed in her stethoscope.

Next, she went to her box garden and pulled up angelica archangelica, dandelion root, and lavender. She wrapped them in gauze and added them to the bag.

Finally, she stood in front of the bookshelf. She knew that books would only slow her down, but she didn't want to lose her father's journals. She still imagined there might be something important in them. She tossed five of his science composition notebooks into her bag and zipped it up.

She strapped the backpack on and ran out of the clinic. She had no idea where to start. She needed to find Monique, figure out if anybody was injured, and help with the evacuation.

Ayanna headed for the gallery, climbing the stairs. There was chaos in all directions. The air grew thick with smoke, and Ayanna started to choke as her lungs burned. Cement crashed from the ceiling with a roar, smashing into the ground and shaking the foundation around her. On top of the cascade of rumbling, dozens of voices moved in anarchic patterns, muddling her senses.

Ayanna moved from memory, and the noise grew the closer she got to the gallery. She still wanted to talk to Richard. She hoped he would have some sort of plan for what they would do next. It was the only thing that made any sense to her, but it wasn't going to be easy with everything falling down around her.

In addition, she was exhausted. Her body begged her to consider this, to remember that she couldn't recall the last time she had slept, but she had to trust that adrenaline would allow her to push through. There was no end in sight, and she couldn't even think of an outcome that would allow her to rest. It seemed possible that she might never rest again.

Lights flickered on and off, and Ayanna could tell that the backup generator was struggling to keep going. Everyone was running out of time, and she still didn't know where the dragons were. How many were there? Was there anything that the militia could do to save Terra?

Ayanna heard people running in all directions. The smoke made it difficult to see. Maybe this wasn't a good idea after all. Maybe Mrs. Sanders had been right, and she should turn around and follow the tunnels away from Terra. That seemed to be what everybody else was doing.

A loud, plaintive cry came from nearby, a voice begging for help. Ayanna moved toward the sound. Through the smoke, she made out two girls, one with braids and one with short hair. She recognized them as Sarafina and Katrina.

Sarafina kneeled on the ground next to Katrina's body. Tears and black lines of soot smattered Sarafina's face. Katrina wasn't responding to Sarafina's pleas to get up. She wasn't moving at all, and her eyes were closed.

"Let me see," Ayanna said. Moving to Katrina's side, Ayanna placed her face near the girl's mouth. She wasn't breathing. Next, Ayanna placed two fingers at her neck, trying to find a pulse.

"What happened?" she said.

"A brick hit her," said Sarafina. Her face was still hopeful.

Ayanna saw that blood from Katrina's head had formed a small pool beneath her. Ayanna tried again, but she couldn't find a pulse.

"I'm sorry, but she's gone."

Sarafina cried loudly and flung her body toward her friend. Ayanna pressed her hands against Sarafina's shoulders to restrain her. "You have to leave her, Sarafina. You've gotta go. Now!" Ayanna shouted. She grabbed the girl's wrist and dragged her away from Katrina's body.

Sarafina resisted. She was strong, and Ayanna struggled to lift her. A piece of concrete crashed down beside them, barely missing Ayanna's leg. Sarafina stopped crying, got up, and pulled Ayanna into a hug. It surprised Ayanna, but she hugged Sarafina back tightly. She didn't know if she would see her again.

"Be careful," she said.

"You too." Sarafina ran in the direction of the tunnels, and Ayanna watched as she disappeared into the smoke.

Ayanna took uncertain steps through the smoke-filled air. She knew she would never find Richard roaming blindly like this. The only place she could think to look before she gave up was the Watchers' chamber. Maybe someone from the council would provide leadership.

She pressed her right hand to the wall as a guide, using her left hand to cover her face against the smoke, but nothing lessened the harsh burning in her throat.

When Ayanna arrived at the chamber, she noticed that the smoke hadn't reached that far, and her breathing eased. She greedily took in gasps of untainted air. Just as she had hoped, she found Mr. Frye, Mr. Christy, and Mrs. Johnson standing outside the room, each carrying a small bundle of their belongings. When they saw her approach, Mrs. Johnson spoke first.

"Ayanna, I'm glad you're here. One or more dragons is in the compound. The militia is at their stations, but there is no way that we can hold them off for more than half an hour. Even if they don't kill us, they'll burn the entire complex to the ground. I need you to help me get the people out of the tunnels and onto the surface. The sun should be rising soon," she said.

"The surface? Why not just go farther into the tunnels until we hit the next station?" Ayanna asked, alarmed. This is what she had told Maya and Mrs. Sanders to do.

"No, the dragons may be in the tunnels. We'll fare better on the surface for a few hours until we can think of a safer place," she said.

Ayanna turned back toward the clinic, about to follow the Sanderses' path through the tunnels. She didn't want them to risk running into dragons on the path that she had sent them down. But then she stopped. Did the councilmembers have a plan beyond going to the surface?

"Where is Captain Daniels?" Ayanna asked. Richard's opinion suddenly seemed more important than anyone else's, and she wanted to ask him what he thought about the council's proposal.

More screams came from the hallway, and the sound of something imploding. Metal cabinets hit the ground, followed by a plume of white smoke and dust.

"I don't know. I assume that he's manning one of the stations, but we don't have much time," said Mrs. Johnson. "I will try to organize the teachers and account for all the children once we get to the surface, but once there, we will only have twelve hours to find a safe place to hide."

"OK, I understand, but I need you to grab as many supplies as you can. People are going to have a lot of cuts," Ayanna said. "We'll need water, thread, blankets, bedsheets, anything you can carry."

Mrs. Johnson nodded her head absently, and Ayanna followed her eyes toward the near distance. Ayanna guessed she was just beginning to understand what was happening.

"Mrs. Johnson, did you hear me? People are going to be hurt up there," Ayanna said.

She broke her gaze and a stoic mask returned to her face. "Of course, we'll bring everything we can," she said.

"Wait, there's something else. Have you seen Monique Carpenter?" asked Ayanna.

"No," said Mr. Frye.

"That's OK. I'll find her," said Ayanna.

CHAPTER **47**

Ayanna had a plan—sort of. But she still had a monumental list of tasks to complete. She needed to catch up with Maya and Mrs. Sanders before they ran into danger. She needed to find Monique, and she still hoped to meet up with Richard.

Maybe Monique was somewhere on the upper level. Ayanna prayed she had found an exit. But what if she didn't go that way? What if she went to the clinic to follow the tunnels instead?

Everything was falling apart so quickly. Ayanna ran toward the upper level first, calling for Monique along the way, but she didn't respond. There were people filing up the escalators and headed toward the exits. Ayanna saw armed militiamen at their stations, overseeing the evacuation. She searched briefly among them, but she didn't spot Richard, so she left and kept looking for Monique.

When Ayanna didn't find her on that level, she ran all the way back to the corridor leading to the clinic. In the corridor, fire cast a small glow lighting the hallway. She heard an unmistakable roaring and screeching sound in the distance.

Before, Ayanna hadn't allowed herself to fully accept that dragons had breached the walls of Terra, but they had. Ayanna had no idea what she would do if she encountered one.

"Monique!" she cried out. Her voice was desperate. Ayanna didn't know where else to look. She checked the corners with a quick turn of her head, but she couldn't stay down there. She had to find her friends, and people needed her on the surface.

"Monique, can you hear me? Answer me, please!" she cried again.

Ayanna could barely see. She coughed, and her eyes teared from the smoke. She waved her flashlight around wildly, but she couldn't see anything. After a few more seconds, she walked toward the tunnels.

She stumbled twenty steps into the tunnel before she tripped over something in the path. Ayanna pointed her flashlight at the body of a girl. It was Monique. She lay facedown on a track with her arms sprawled above her head.

Ayanna moved toward her and placed two fingers on her neck, finding a pulse. Ayanna sighed in relief. She bent her knees and turned Monique onto her back. The girl let out a small moan.

"Monique, it's OK. I'm going to get us out of here," Ayanna said.

Monique slowly opened her eyes. "Ayanna, is that you?" she asked in a groggy voice.

"Yes, I'm here, but we've got to go. Can you walk?" Ayanna asked.

"I think so."

"Are you hurt anywhere?"

"No, I . . . I don't know what happened. After you left, I tried to go back to the gallery, but everything was so hard to see, and I didn't know which direction was up. So I came back past the clinic and tried to go through the tunnels, but there was so much smoke. I just started coughing, and the last thing I remember was opening the door," said Monique.

"You probably passed out from smoke inhalation. Everything

is going to be all right, but we need to get out of here," Ayanna said.

As she helped lift Monique up from the ground, she saw that she still had her bag of supplies. That was something worth celebrating. Ayanna pointed her flashlight ahead, and they started to follow the tracks, moving slowly through the darkness.

They had gone thirty feet when Monique stopped suddenly. Her body trembled violently. Ayanna looked around. A pair of glowing, yellow eyes peered out from the dark. Ayanna stopped breathing.

If Ayanna hadn't seen eyes like these before, she wouldn't believe what she was seeing. The eyes transfixed her. She couldn't stop staring, even though she knew she needed to think of something that would save them, and she needed to think of it fast.

Her blood turned to ice, and she stood frozen in place. Monique let out a quiet whimper. She sounded like she was working hard to suppress a scream. It didn't matter if she screamed or not. The dragon could see them, and nothing could change that.

The dragon approached from the dark, its long neck emerging from its hiding spot. It stood in front of them. It was small compared to others that Ayanna had seen, and young. She guessed it was no more than fifteen feet long and eight feet tall, which boded well for their survival.

Ayanna remembered seeing a juvenile dragon before. Maybe this small one wouldn't be able to shoot fire either. Still, whether it shot fire or not, it had vicious, razor-sharp teeth and claws that could slice through metal. She knew just how easily it could tear through flesh. Ayanna waited for it to attack. But nothing happened. It just stood staring.

"Monique, can you run?" Ayanna asked. She tried to push her terror down, but her heart pulsed so loudly in her ears she could barely think. Monique mumbled something Ayanna couldn't hear. Ayanna wasn't sure if Monique understood anything past her own panic.

The young dragon hissed. The noise reminded Ayanna of a snake, only louder and hundreds of times more frightening.

Ayanna used her flashlight to search the ground around her feet. She kneeled down, never taking her eyes from the dragon. Her hands reached for a long, metal bar that had fallen from the tunnel wall. Ayanna wrapped her hand around the bar and gripped it tightly. It felt heavy in her hand. She had no idea what she was going to do with it, but that part didn't seem that important.

Ayanna turned her head slightly to the side to look at Monique, struck by her youth. She was just a girl. She was small, and puberty had barely touched the childlike features of her face. Ayanna needed to protect her from the horrible death that waited only a few feet away.

"Monique, listen to me. I'm going to draw it away from the path, and I want you to run as fast as you can until you make it to the stairs that lead to the surface," Ayanna said.

The dragon remained still. So did Monique.

"Monique!" Ayanna screamed at her. The young girl blinked several times, as if she were waking up from a dream.

"I . . . I can't, Ayanna. I'm scared."

The dragon shifted. Ayanna needed to hurry with whatever plan her mind was forming.

"Please, Monique, just focus. You can do this. When it comes toward me, you run as fast as you can past it. OK?" Ayanna's voice begged Monique to go along with this. If she hesitated, they would probably both die. Ayanna saw Monique nod her head tentatively.

This seemed crazy. Wasn't there another way besides sacrificing herself? Nothing came to her.

"When I say go, you run," said Ayanna.

Ayanna kneeled to the ground again. She kept her eyes on the dragon's glowing ones peering at her through the darkness. This time, Ayanna gathered two pieces of crumbled cement that had fallen from the top of the tunnel and the walls. She couldn't hold the flashlight, the cement, and the metal piping at the same time, so she let the pipe lean against her leg as she threw the first piece of rock cement toward the waiting dragon. It let out a high-pitched snarl and stepped closer to them into the small beam cast by Ayanna's flashlight.

Her heart thudded erratically against her ribs. Ayanna got a better look at the creature. It was smaller than most, but it still towered at least three feet above her. She threw the second rock and coaxed the dragon in her direction. Ayanna feared it would rush her, but it moved slowly with its eyes fixed on her as its target.

"Run now!"

Monique didn't hesitate. She dashed past the dragon into what Ayanna prayed was a clear passageway that would lead her to the surface.

Ayanna gripped the metal bar and slowly backed up. She had run out of plan and hadn't quite figured out how she would get away alive. It was impossible to overpower a dragon, even a small one. Ayanna wanted to follow Monique, but now the dragon stood directly in front of her.

The tunnel rumbled, and the walls cracked around Ayanna. Rocks fell behind her, and she guessed they would soon block the path. She could only imagine the other dragons were in the process of tearing Terra to pieces.

She could try to go back, squeeze her way past the rubble . . . and then what? Monique would live, and Ayanna was glad, but who would come back for her if she journeyed back into Terra?

Most had to have made it to the surface by now. Would they risk a rescue mission for her? Would she even want them to? No, Ayanna was alone, and if she were going to live, she would have to save herself.

Ayanna looked at the dragon that stood between her and the only remaining exit. She was dangerously close to its mouth.

It lashed its tail back and forth, knocking into the now fragile structure of the tunnel walls. A piece of the wall fell and landed on the creature. It turned its head and let out an agitated snarl. This felt like Ayanna's chance.

She ran toward the dragon's side. She tried to dart toward the exit, but the dragon recovered quickly and used its tail to block her. Its claw grabbed her leg, knocking her down, and Ayanna let out a loud yelp as a razor-sharp claw sliced her calf. Adrenaline blocked her body from feeling the intensity of the pain in her leg, but she knew the claw had drawn blood.

She wanted to tie off her leg and stop the bleeding, but there was no time. She hit the ground and grabbed the metal pipe. She turned onto her back and jabbed the pipe toward the animal's eye.

The pipe made contact and the dragon screeched. Ayanna jabbed at its eye again. Rocks continued to fall from overhead. The dragon tried to lunge at her, but its tail was trapped under a heavy block of fallen cement. The baby dragon cried and wailed.

Ayanna lifted herself from the ground, using the metal pipe as a crutch. She took the pipe in both hands and slammed the metal against a crack in the cement wall with as much strength as she could muster. More cement fell.

The dragon tried to strike at her again, but it was pinned. She rammed the bar into the wall again, trying to loosen more cement. That did it. Another piece fell from the wall. This time, it landed on the back of the animal. The dragon couldn't move. This was her chance to escape.

The walls were coming down around her, and rocks fell near her head. Ayanna dragged her leg behind her and pushed her way past the dragon. Her hands felt for what was left of the walls as she stumbled through the tunnel.

She heard a loud crash as the ceiling collapsed. The falling debris crushed her flashlight, and everything went dark. She tried to cover her head. The tunnel filled with dust and Ayanna felt her lungs set on fire. She gasped for air. There was none.

She wanted to hang on. She was almost out, but she seemed to be falling.

CHAPTER 48

Ayanna felt the dirt beneath her palms as she crawled out of the tunnel and onto the surface. The open air raced into her lungs, and her chest heaved violently as she gasped. She was still alive.

She felt a pulsing sensation throb incessantly against her skull as light and noise bombarded her from all directions. Everything was moving, blaring, shining. It was all too much. Ayanna fought to keep her eyelids open, but they closed again.

She wasn't sure how long she'd been out this time, but it couldn't have been long because everything seemed the same when she opened her eyes again. She gathered what strength she could and sat up.

She used her arms to lift herself from the ground and scramble ahead. She collapsed to her knees every few seconds, and then picked herself up again. She felt the weight of her predicament as she stood defenseless without shelter.

She opened her eyes wide and looked at the scene in front of her. Bright red flames shot out from beneath the earth, spewing into the air like lava spilling from a volcano. Black soot filled the sky, and ash fell back to Earth as huge plumes of smoke rose higher into the purple-and-orange horizon, marking signs of the coming dawn.

Her eyes followed the skyline, and Ayanna could see the silhouettes of two massive figures flapping their wings rapidly to escape the heat of the coming day.

"It's gone," she whispered to the air. Her heart broke, and she felt as though her soul had ripped in two.

Ayanna tried to move forward, but a sharp pain shot through her battered body. The sensation focused her mind. She needed to tend to her wound.

Beyond her pain, she heard the helpless cries of familiar voices. It was Terra's people, and the sound began to ring more loudly in her ears. She heard weeping and screams. She looked farther ahead and saw a crowd of people spread over the ground. Her thoughts moved to Maya. Yes, she needed to find Maya.

"Grace?" said a deep voice from behind. Ayanna knew who it was, and a wave of comfort washed over her. She would have smiled with joy at the sound of Richard's voice if she'd been able to muster such a feeling. She turned and saw him covered in soot. Blood dripped down his left arm, and a cut bled above his eyebrow. Sadness crossed his features and then disappeared in an instant.

Ayanna rushed toward him, despite her injuries, and fell into his open arms. She hugged him tightly. He held her close and let out a deep sigh into her hair. Ayanna buried her face in his chest. She could feel Richard's heartbeat, strong and fast. Tears poured from her eyes, and relief flooded her senses. She held him as tight as her arms would allow. Richard was alive. This fact steadied Ayanna and calmed her mind. He held her back, pressing her closer to his chest.

"Help me! Help!" cried a weak voice in the distance. She and Richard released their embrace.

"The others need help," Ayanna said.

Richard nodded in agreement. He held his injured arm close

to his body. "We need to find shelter immediately," he said. "We only have a few hours of light to help us. We have to get to work."

Ayanna looked into his eyes. He seemed calm and reassured, and his courage gave her confidence. For a moment, he stared at her. His dark eyes seemed peaceful in the sunlight. She let his words soak in. They didn't have much time. Everyone depended on them.

Tight-knit curls gently fell into her face, and Ayanna didn't bother to brush them away. Any remnants of fear left her. Her purpose became clear. She stood tall. She winced but pushed through the pain in her leg. She would find Maya, and then she would tend to the injured.

She reached out her hand and placed it in Richard's. She squeezed once before letting it fall back to her side.

"Yes, you're right," she said. "After all, it *is* our duty."

CHAPTER **49**

Ayanna scarcely knew where to begin. There were only twelve hours until sunset, and there was no assurance that daylight would protect them, exposed as they were on the surface to both dehydration and attack. The dragons would find them easy pickings.

Everything was against Terra's survivors. They didn't have enough shelter, water, food, or medicine. The dragons would come as soon as the night allowed, and the number of injured people made moving slow and arduous.

Cries from people came from all directions. The sounds varied from wails of pain to the small, high-pitched noises of frightened children and babies. This was the hardest sound to hear. Ayanna would have given anything to ease the children's suffering.

Some people called out for their family and friends. Many of those calls went unanswered. Ayanna knew people had died. Between the smoke and the blood that littered her path, she was sure of it.

As Ayanna searched for Maya, her stomach twisted into knots. She didn't know what had happened to the Sanderses. Malik was weak. He had no business being moved, and there was no way this smoked-filled warzone could be good for him. How could he survive this?

She scanned every person she saw, but she didn't spot her friends. As she moved, her training took over. She had to establish triage. The people with the worst injuries needed to be tended to first, but she would need help. There was no way she could treat everyone on her own.

She looked at the small bag of supplies that she had managed to recover from the clinic. She had some bandages, alcohol, and suture kits. They wouldn't go far.

"Monique!" she called. "Monique, can you hear me?"

Ayanna made her way through the crowd.

"Monique!" Ayanna called again. "Monique, please answer me."

"Ayanna! I'm here," said a small voice. Ayanna turned, and some of the tension left her chest when she set eyes on Monique. She was safe, and she didn't have any visible injuries. Ayanna walked up to her and placed her hand on her shoulder. She saw that Monique was shaken, and fright filled her doe-brown eyes.

"Are you OK?" Ayanna asked.

Monique's bottom lip trembled, and she looked like she was about to cry. "I . . . I just don't know how this could've happened," she said.

"Monique, listen to me." Ayanna tried to sound as commanding as she could muster. "I need your help. We have to focus now if we are going to survive. Do you remember what I taught you about setting broken bones?"

Monique nodded her head slowly. She looked distraught, but Ayanna could see that Monique would follow her instructions, and she was grateful when the girl's trembling steadied. Ayanna didn't think she could comfort Monique and hold herself together as well.

Ayanna was about to tell Monique how they might proceed when she heard Richard's voice from behind her.

"Grace," he said. Ayanna turned to him. He stood tall, and his voice was steady. Ayanna was glad. Someone had to lead them.

Richard walked past them and climbed onto a slab of concrete. "Alpha Team, Protectorate, everyone, let's assemble," he called.

What Ayanna witnessed next was amazing. The scene changed before her eyes, and what had previously looked like complete chaos began to take the shape of organized movement.

Nearly fifty people emerged from the smoke-covered plain and gathered in front of the large block of concrete where Richard stood. Ash and blood covered many of their faces, and their cuts looked deep. People had lacerations across their chests and backs, and others had bruises and cuts on their faces and heads. It looked like many people had been hit with falling cement.

Ayanna was relieved to see so many of Terra's inhabitants gathered together. The survivors leaned on their neighbors for support, but many were missing. *So many people must be dead*, she thought.

Everyone stood and watched Richard in silent anticipation. He seemed to ignore his own painful injuries. Ayanna was sure the bleeding gash on his head and the cut on his left arm had to hurt. Still, he stood upright. This didn't surprise her.

Her leg hurt too. But there was too much work to do. She couldn't worry about pain in that moment.

"Latif, I need an immediate damage report. I want an accounting of the survivors and the supplies we were able to save," Richard ordered. The sound of sobbing continued in the background.

He paused and looked out beyond the group gathered in front of him. Ayanna followed Richard's line of sight. She saw what he saw: people sprawled on the ground crying over the dead and injured. Then, she followed his gaze upward toward the sky. The sun began to warm her face. Richard took in a deep breath, regained his resolve, and continued his speech.

"We don't have much time. We must move quickly," he said, looking past his men and pointing at Ayanna.

"Stevens and Mitchell, help Miss Grace care for the injured who can be saved. Carlson, Ramirez, and Juarez, I need you to scout a building for us to hole up in for the next few days, until the council and I can come up with more permanent plans. Smith and Garrett, you help Ms. Weaver try to salvage some generators. I need six people collecting water. And McDonald and Sadiq, get some people together and start burying the bodies."

The thought of this image turned Ayanna's stomach, but there was nothing else that could be done.

Richard had mentioned the council, but it was strange to imagine them at all under these circumstances. Where were they? And would they do anything to help now?

No one argued with Richard. No one even questioned him. They all simply moved as he had directed and started to take on their assignments.

Monique, Stevens, Mitchell, and Ayanna split up. Ayanna showed the new team how to tie off wounds, and she trusted that Monique could help set bones. For an hour, they shuffled from one injured person to the next, working hard despite their limitations.

Fortunately, Ayanna had found bedsheets among the belongings that some people had managed to bring to the surface, and they served her team well. She borrowed a knife from Bryan Getty and ripped the sheets into strips of cloth. The Protectorate were able to gather water in whatever containers they could find, and this helped with their progress, but as the sun moved across the sky, and midday approached, it was clear that they needed to find shelter.

Ayanna had wrapped a clean sheet around a deep laceration and was tying it off at the ends when she heard her name.

"Ayanna," said a quiet female voice. Her eyes shot up. She felt exhilaration race through her when she saw Maya standing a few feet away. Ayanna hurried toward Maya and pulled her into a hug. Maya's face was dirty, and she had a deep cut on her forehead.

"Maya, you're hurt," Ayanna said. Her voice cracked with panic.

"A piece of concrete hit my head on the way out of the tunnel, but it doesn't hurt," she said. "I think you should come look at Malik, though. He's unconscious again."

"Of course I will. Just sit down for a second and let me look at your head."

Maya settled on the ground. Ayanna looked into Maya's eyes to check her pupil dilation, and then, she held up one finger to Maya's face.

"Follow my finger. Do you have any blurred vision or vomiting?"

"Yes, I threw up, but I don't know if that was from my head," she said. She was right. Under the circumstances, it was difficult to tell if she suffered from head trauma or if she was just in shock.

"What about dizziness?" Ayanna asked.

"No, I'm fine, but Malik, Ayanna . . . ," she pleaded. Ayanna nodded, and they hobbled through the crowd toward Malik and Mrs. Sanders. Mrs. Sanders scrambled up from the ground and pulled Ayanna into a strong hug the moment she saw her.

"Are you OK?" Ayanna asked her.

"Fine, but Malik is unconscious," Mrs. Sanders said.

Ayanna released her from the hug and pulled her stethoscope from her bag. She placed the diaphragm to Malik's chest.

"His lungs are clear, and his breathing is steady. He probably just passed out from the pain. Collect some water and try to keep him cool." Ayanna looked at Malik's wounds. The areas she had stitched up were holding together.

"We need to find some antibiotics to prevent infection," she said. She tried to keep her voice steady. She didn't want Maya to panic, but she knew Malik might die without them.

"Wait in the shade until Captain Daniels tells us where we should go," Ayanna said. "I'll be back to check on you. It's going to be OK. We'll find shelter soon."

Ayanna turned her head in Richard's direction and looked at him for confirmation of the promises that she had just made. He remained atop the small mound of rubble, his gun in a ready position, and watched the sky.

Ayanna looked back at Maya and smiled a little. Her friends were OK for now, and she was grateful.

Ayanna walked away from Maya to find the other members of her team. The day marched on, and Ayanna rejoined Monique.

"We've just lost two more," Monique said. Ayanna nodded her head.

Ayanna shielded her eyes from the sun and examined Monique. She was surprisingly resilient, and Ayanna was proud to see how calm she remained. Stevens and Mitchell proved to be able and helpful. Together, they figured out that there were seventy survivors on the surface with forty-three people missing or dead.

Mr. Christy had died from a head injury. Seven people had died from burns, four from smoke inhalation, and four from internal bleeding. The rest were missing.

"Miss Grace, there is someone I need you to see," said Stevens. He looked alarmed, and Ayanna couldn't imagine what else had gone wrong. She walked with him, and they approached a gray-haired man lying on the ground. He was still. As Ayanna got closer, she saw that it was Colonel Daniels. When Ayanna moved to his side, she could see his only movement came from the rise and fall of his chest.

"Colonel, can you hear me?" Ayanna asked. He didn't respond. She placed her head to his chest and then took her stethoscope and listened to his heart and his breathing.

"His lungs are clear, and his heartbeat is strong and steady. He is just unconscious," Ayanna said. She examined his body for injuries.

"What's wrong with him?" asked Stevens.

"I'm not sure. I don't see any obvious injuries. Let's hope that he doesn't have internal bleeding," Ayanna said. "I'm going to go find out what will happen next. Let me know when he wakes up, and when he does, try to get him some water. I know he's dehydrated." Stevens nodded his head.

Ayanna walked back toward Richard's post. He was talking to a petite, dark-brown-skinned woman with silver hair. She was pretty and looked to be around age fifty. When Ayanna saw the woman's gentle face, she recognized her as Richard's mother, Ella. Their faces shared the same nose and dark eyes.

They stood close together and spoke softly. She held Richard's hand, and he let her without protest. Ayanna did not want to intrude on their private moment, but Richard behaved so differently in Ella's presence than he did with other people that Ayanna couldn't help but watch.

He seemed younger than his age standing next to his mother. He lowered his head slightly in deference when she spoke, and his otherwise disciplined manner softened in her company. He resembled the little eight-year-old boy Ayanna had seen in the photo in Colonel Daniels's room. It was obvious that he loved and trusted her.

Ella placed her hand on Richard's cheek, and Ayanna was certain that she saw a flash of white teeth. He smiled at her for a fraction of a second just before she turned and walked away. She looked like she was headed to a small group of children sitting in a circle.

As soon as she left, Richard's face resumed its stoic appearance. He held his lips tightly together and focused his eyes intently when he spoke to his men, who continued to work quickly to follow his instructions. Taylor Weaver and Malcolm Channing gathered supplies that were brought to the surface, and they conducted an inventory of the food, equipment, and weaponry.

Ayanna inched closer to Richard to get a better sense of what might happen next. She stumbled a bit as her body reminded her that she was exhausted. She yawned and felt her throat burn from the smoke she had taken in earlier.

Even though Ayanna felt like she could fall asleep while standing, she knew there was a lot more to do. Things had calmed down, but they were nowhere near out of danger. She was reminded of this when Lieutenant Ramirez walked past her and spoke to Richard.

"We've found three possible locations: the warehouse of the old steel factory, the shopping mall, and the university. The steel factory has the least amount of glass and reinforced concrete walls, but it offers only three possible exits. The mall has the most exits, but also the most glass. Most of it is shattered. The university is acceptable but sits at the end of a street. We would be boxed inside the city, making escape more difficult," he reported.

Ayanna didn't realize Richard had noticed her presence until she heard his voice. "Grace, do you know if your patients can be moved?"

"Yes, most will be able to move on their own, and the others should be able to help those who can't. And we've found a few boards we can use as gurneys," Ayanna said.

"Good, we're moving into the steel factory."

"The steel factory?" Ayanna asked. "It's not the best place for ventilation. Why don't we try to go back into the subway system, you know, find a safer station?"

Richard's eyebrows knitted. He seemed to be considering her words. He shook his head slightly.

"We have no way of knowing if the tunnels are blocked with debris or filled with smoke, and without wiring and lighting, we'd be helpless in the dark. I just need to get these people inside, and then move from there," he said.

Ayanna nodded. She didn't want to argue with him. The truth was that Ayanna trusted Richard with her life.

"Richard, there's one more thing," she said. Richard waited for her to continue.

"It's your father."

He didn't react.

"He's alive," Ayanna said quickly, "but he's unconscious. He needs attention, but there are others with worse injuries."

Richard nodded his head. "Thank you, Ayanna."

CHAPTER **50**

Ayanna limped carefully through the quiet room of sleeping people. Terra's population had made pallets from blankets, sheets, and polyurethane mats they'd salvaged from the fire, and people lay spread out over the large, concrete warehouse floor.

The warehouse provided shelter, but it lacked adequate sources of water, electricity, and air conditioning. Ayanna's biggest concern was infection. The lack of sterilization and antibiotics presented a huge problem. She stopped every few feet, kneeling down to check the pulse of people sleeping. She yawned, and her eyes burned from exhaustion, but she continued on her rounds.

She stopped next to Malik. Maya and Mrs. Sanders slept two feet away from him. Ayanna removed her stethoscope and listened to his heart. She was relieved to find it steady. She had to do whatever she could to help Malik heal.

Ayanna stood on the second floor of the warehouse and looked through the broken window. The night was anything but peaceful. To offer her some reprieve, she stood far enough away from the never-ending moans and cries of the people but close enough to be able to answer in case anyone called for her.

The militia stood guard around the building. Because they

only had limited weaponry and ammunition, the most they could hope for was that one of the boys would be able to warn them before an attack, and the others would try to draw the dragons away as a diversion. Ayanna hadn't agreed with this plan when Richard announced it, but what else was there to do?

Besides, she had enough to worry about, with everyone who'd been injured. They had managed to collect enough water to last the next three days, and there were enough sorghum bars to ward off starvation for at least a little while longer, but there was nothing she could do about infection or pain. The pain was the worst part. Everyone was in pain, physically and emotionally, but there was no relief for anyone.

On top of everything else, Ayanna was exhausted. She hadn't received more than a few hours' sleep in the past two days, but she kept this to herself. No one else fared any better. Monique and the others did their best to help her change bandages and try to clean wounds.

Ayanna was grateful. Treating the injured was her responsibility, but there was no way she could tend to everyone without help. She accepted whatever assistance others were willing to offer her without criticism. It was the best they could do under the circumstances, but together they'd maxed out their usefulness.

Ayanna faced the night air and tried not to think about the present or the future. She closed her eyes and focused instead on a memory from long ago, when she was a little girl. She thought of a time when she was happy, a time with her mother and father, her eighth birthday party.

The recollection was fuzzy, but she remembered there had been a petting zoo. Ayanna had worn a yellow dress with white flowers, and her mother had braided her hair into three plaits, with two pigtails in the front and one in the back. Her elementary school friend Jean was there, and she was afraid of the goat. Her father had planned every detail, and he had given her a special present at the end of the party.

Ayanna reached into her pocket and touched her silver bracelet. She was so happy to have it back. It was the only thing she had left that her father had given her. Ayanna missed him so much, but she refused to think about that. She only wanted to focus on the happy feeling she'd had on her birthday so many years before. Ayanna squeezed her eyes tighter and concentrated on her parents smiling down at her.

Her mind traveled to this other place so effectively that she didn't hear when Richard approached and stood beside her.

"Hello, Ayanna," he said.

Ayanna jumped, but then she relaxed, returning to the present moment. "Hello. Is everything OK?"

Richard raised his palm in front of him. "Yes. There's been no change. I'm sorry. I didn't mean to scare you," he said. His voice was low and apologetic.

Ayanna would have laughed at the idea that Richard could scare her if she could have mustered the energy to laugh. His presence calmed her. "It's OK."

She turned away from the window and studied him more carefully. He held his weapon at his side. There were dark circles under his eyes, and Ayanna could see that his head needed a new bandage. She wondered if he would let her patch him up. Knowing him, he would tell her to save her supplies for someone else. She decided she would wait and measure his temperament first.

She turned back toward the window, and Richard mirrored her. They stared out into the night without speaking. A warm breeze blew across her face, and Ayanna took in a deep breath.

Richard broke the silence. "How are you holding up?"

It took her a long time to respond. She thought about lying.

She could say something she thought would pacify him, but that wasn't necessary. She didn't want to lie to Richard.

"I wish Dr. Keaton were here," Ayanna confessed. She quickly caught a tear that slipped from her eye.

"Dr. Keaton was a good man."

"Yeah," she said. She took several breaths before she continued. "They need a real doctor."

Richard turned to her. He opened his mouth and then closed it again.

"How are you?" Ayanna asked.

"Me? I'm fine."

"Your head looks like it could use a new bandage."

"No, save your supplies for someone with worse injuries," he said. Ayanna gave a half smile. She had guessed right. He wouldn't have her use up any supplies on himself.

"Did you know him well?" Richard asked abruptly.

At first, Ayanna didn't understand what he was asking her. She thought he was talking about Dr. Keaton, but when she turned and looked at him, she saw a sadness in his eyes that told her he was talking about someone else.

Ayanna was surprised. It had never occurred to her that Richard would wonder about Jackson. But of course, Richard would want to know about him. He must have been just as shocked as Jackson was when he found out the truth about their father.

Ayanna didn't want to think about Jackson. She still felt his absence and his betrayal, and on top of that, she still yearned for his return. With everything else that was going on, it felt like too much to handle.

"I'm sorry," said Richard, before Ayanna could answer him, "It's just that this is all so new to me. It never occurred to me to take the time. I mean . . . I never imagined that I could have . . ." he paused.

"A brother," Ayanna said, finishing the thought for him.

"Yes, the thought never even crossed my mind that I could have a brother, and now here he is . . . or was."

Richard's last words poked at the pain that Ayanna was trying to ignore, and she shifted her weight from one leg to the other.

"I guess I knew him better than anyone else at Terra," she finally said. "We were . . ."

Ayanna had no idea how to finish this sentence. How could she describe Jackson and her? Were they friends? Acquaintances? In love? What did it even matter at this point what label she gave what they had? It was over now.

Richard looked at her, watching her expression. He seemed to understand how difficult this conversation was for her.

". . . close," she concluded. He nodded his head.

"It's OK if you feel like you missed your chance to know your family. I know what that's like," Ayanna said.

"Family?" he asked. The word seemed to surprise him. He seemed to think about it for a moment. "Yes, I guess he is."

Richard fell silent again, and they both listened to the sounds coming from the crowd below. Ayanna heard a loud wail, and Richard looked at her with a mix of confusion and alarm. She frowned and gritted her teeth.

"That's Kevin. His arm is broken. I reset it, and it will probably heal, but I don't have anything to give him for the pain."

Richard closed his eyes and opened them slowly. He gripped his gun at his side. He looked as frustrated as Ayanna felt.

"Are we all going to die?" Ayanna asked.

His eyes darted to hers and then out the window. He paused before answering, and Ayanna wondered if he would lie to make her feel better the way she had considered lying to him only minutes earlier. Did she want him to lie, or did she want the truth?

She searched her mind, but she didn't know. She decided she would accept whatever he said next as the truth.

Richard took in a deep breath and released it. "No," he said, "we are not going to die. I'll make sure of that."

Ayanna looked at him closely and saw he was serious. He believed what he said. She gave him a tight smile. Then he turned and started to walk away.

Before Richard reached the stairwell, he stopped and turned back toward her. "You know, Ayanna, I've known a lot of very good soldiers from before and after the war, but I'm not sure I've ever known anyone as tough as you. Don't count yourself out just yet. You're more important to people here than you realize, 'real doctor' or not."

Ayanna wanted to say something, but her words caught in her throat. All she could do was watch as Richard made his way back to his post.

CHAPTER 51

A sonic boom startled Ayanna awake. Shouts from outside followed. She didn't know when she had fallen asleep during the night, but now sunlight glared into her heavy eyes through the metal slits of the warehouse windows.

Normally, the rising sun would comfort her, but the noise was too loud. The frightened shouts were too urgent, and instead of comfort, she felt panic. The noise had come from the distance, and it had sounded like artillery fire. Ayanna recognized the sound from newscasts about the Fire Sky War.

Ayanna stood up slowly and unbent her stiff body. The pain from her leg wound had grown worse from sitting all night, but she had to see what was happening outside.

Ayanna looked to the right and left as she passed the other members of Terra. She hadn't been the only one who had heard the thunderous noise because several people started to awaken with panic-stricken faces.

She stumbled as quickly as she could toward the front door and pushed her way into the open air. She raised her hand to her eyes. The sun nearly blinded her. Were they being attacked? And what weapons did they have with them that could make a sound so loud that it sounded like artillery fire? The Protectorate stood guard with rifles pointed toward the sky. Their faces were mesmerized by something that Ayanna couldn't quite make out. Fifteen heads turned in the direction of the Savannah River, but it was too far away to see anything clearly. Something heavy tumbled from the sky. Ayanna squinted. It was a dragon.

Her eyes locked on the sight. Its wings flapped wildly, but it couldn't take flight. Ayanna didn't understand what was happening. Was it dying? What could have caused it to fall like that?

Richard was already outside. He stood with three of his men, and Ayanna noticed that they were all watching wide-eyed as the massive creature crashed toward the earth. The dragon finally hit the ground with a thud, and a plume of dust flung up into the air.

What could have killed the dragon? Ayanna looked around. She blinked hard and was shocked at what she saw approaching from about a hundred feet ahead. Two dark-green-and-gray armored tanks and two military trucks with green canvas tops lined the road. Their wheels creaked down the cracked pavement toward them, their engines droning. She widened her eyes to try for a better look.

She couldn't believe it. Her heart began to race. What did this mean? Who could this be? Were they friends or enemies? Ayanna thought that maybe she should run, but she was frozen in place.

Richard must have spotted the tanks too. He walked to the head of the group and stood in the path of the oncoming vehicles. He drew his pistol, but compared to a tank, he looked helpless against its power. Ayanna wanted to push him out of the way. She wanted to shout and tell him to move. She should make him flee with her back into the warehouse, where they could close and barricade the doors with the others. But still, she couldn't make her feet move.

One tank pulled up slowly and came to a screeching halt in front of Richard. Ayanna held her breath in anticipation. The other vehicles pulled up next to the lead tank and parked, forming an incomplete wall.

The door to the tank opened, and a short, muscular man with close-cut hair and a long scar down the side of his face emerged from the top of the massive machine. He looked about forty years old, and he wore a clean, green-and-gray military uniform. He climbed down onto the street and walked without fear, keeping his sidearm holstered. His hands were raised, but he continued to advance toward Richard.

"Where did you come from and what do you want?" Richard demanded.

The man moved deliberately. He was unaffected at the sight of a loaded weapon aimed toward his head. When he was within five feet of Richard, he stopped.

"My name is Sergeant Andrew Watkins. I am stationed at the US military stronghold, Area Two Nineteen, about a hundred fifty miles west of here," he said. "My men spotted your group yesterday during a flyby."

"A flyby?" Richard asked. He sounded surprised. "The government ended all aerial operations over a year ago."

"No," said Sergeant Watkins, "not all of them."

Richard lowered his weapon and secured it in its holster. "My name is Captain Richard Daniels. I am in charge. The people with me are the remaining members of Terra," he said. "We are in desperate need of food, clothing, medicine, and shelter."

Sergeant Watkins scanned the area behind Richard. He looked at Ayanna and squinted. She wanted to look away, but she resisted the urge. Instead, she stood straight and stared back at him. When he returned his gaze to Richard, he spoke again.

"We haven't seen a group this large in a while. We started to think that there weren't any more survivors in this area until we came across a few of your folks a few weeks back," said Sergeant Watkins.

"What do you mean, 'a few of our folks'?" asked Richard.

"We met a family on the road about twenty miles from here. They told us where we might find you," said Sergeant Watkins.

"The Lincolns?" asked Richard.

"Yeah, that's right. We've passed by this area a few times but didn't spot you until yesterday. Captain, we would be happy to escort you and your group back to Area Two Nineteen, but I'm afraid that we will have to ask you and your men to disarm," said Sergeant Watkins.

Richard shifted. He looked uncomfortable.

"How do we know that we can trust you?" he asked.

Sergeant Watkins nodded. "I understand your apprehension, but I'm afraid that you don't have a choice—unless, of course, you want to stay out here defenseless."

Richard turned and looked at the warehouse. His eyes found Ayanna's, and she acknowledged him with an upward tilt of her head. She didn't know what they should do. Were these the men Jackson had talked about, the group who had been looking for her father? They didn't seem to fit the description of Hilton's group, but she couldn't really tell, either.

What she did know was that every member of Terra was exhausted, bruised, and in need of food, clean water, and real medicine. It seemed they had no choice but to trust the sergeant. Richard knew Ayanna couldn't continue to treat the injured without supplies and without the more experienced help of someone. He also knew that his father needed medical attention.

Richard must have found the answer he was looking for because he turned back to the sergeant and took in a deep breath.

"All right," said Richard. "We'll come with you unarmed.

But just know, I am responsible for these people, and that's not a responsibility that I take lightly."

Sergeant Watkins smiled. "Well, Captain Daniels, I think that's just the attitude we can use in Area Two Nineteen. Your commitment to survival is exactly what we need if we're going to win this war against the dragons."

Watkins motioned with his hand, and three of his men got out of the trucks and approached. They moved in her direction, carrying bags that Ayanna hoped were filled with medical supplies.

"War?" asked Richard. "But I fought in the Fire Sky War, and now it's over. We lost."

Sergeant Watkins laughed without humor and shook his head gently. "No, Son, we haven't lost, and the war's not over. It's just beginning," he said.

Richard raised his eyebrows. He looked like he was about to ask a question, but Ramirez called for him. He needed him to help organize everyone to move. Richard responded and turned away from the sergeant.

Ayanna watched Richard as he passed, and he nodded to her. Ayanna wasn't sure what he was trying to communicate, but she took it to mean that they could trust these newfound strangers.

Ayanna stepped forward and stood in front of Sergeant Watkins. He looked her over with mild curiosity, but his eyes lingered on the path Richard had just taken.

"Wait. Did he say *Daniels*?"

Ayanna nodded.

"He wouldn't happen to be related to Colonel William Daniels, now would he?"

"Yes, that's his father. He's here with us."

"No kidding. The tide has really turned now. I know my superiors are going to want to pick his brain about our defensive strategy. Maybe he can help us identify more of their weaknesses. After all, his project was the one that—"

"Sir, there's a question as to which route you want us to take," said a burly man with a serious scowl.

Sergeant Watkins shifted his attention to address him. "Let me see the maps. . . ."

Ayanna stiffened. "What . . . what do you mean?" Ayanna started to say, but the sergeant was already engaged in plotting their exit from Tropeck.

The warehouse doors opened, and people started to gather in the street. They looked frightened and confused.

Maya wandered outside and stood beside Ayanna. Her forlorn face and bloodshot eyes showed that she too was exhausted.

"Ayanna, are these people going to help us?" she asked in a whisper.

"Yes," Ayanna said. She hoped what she said was true. In reality, Ayanna couldn't be sure of their intentions.

Maya let out a sigh of relief and took Ayanna's hand. "Everything is going to be all right?"

Ayanna thought about the question. She didn't know the answer. Again, she couldn't be sure, but she looked down at her best friend. Maya's eyes were exhausted and sad. Ayanna knew what to say. She held Maya's hand and squeezed it gently. Ayanna gave Maya a small, reassuring smile. She nodded slowly.

"Yes," she said, "everything will be fine."

ABOUT **THE AUTHOR**

Fatima R. Henson is a native of Atlanta, Georgia. She is a passionate and talented US History teacher and writer with a penchant for dystopian and fantasy storytelling. She is also an alumna of the University of Miami in Coral Gables, Florida, and American University in Washington DC. Much of her work seeks to swing open the doors of imagination into fantastical worlds where she reveals the deep and intimate lives of young Black characters thriving against persistent and remarkable obstacles.

Henson is also the author of *Courageous Cody's Western Adventure*, an action-adventure book for children ages 8–12.

SELECTED TITLES FROM SPARKPRESS

SparkPress is an independent boutique publisher
delivering high-quality, entertaining, and engaging
content that enhances readers' lives, with a special focus on
female-driven work. www.gosparkpress.com

Caley Cross and the Hadeon Drop, J. S. Rosen, $16.95, 978-1-68463-053-0.
When thirteen-year-old Caley Cross, an orphan with a dark power, is guided
by a jumpsuit-wearing mole into another world—Erinath—she finds a place
deeply rooted in nature where the people have animal-like powers and she is a
Crown Princess—but she soon learns that the most powerful evil being in *any*
world is waiting for her there.

Eye of Zeus: Legends of Olympus Book 1, Alane Adams. $12.95, 978-1-68463-
028-8. Finding out she's the daughter of Zeus is not what a foster kid like
Phoebe Katz expected to hear from a talking statue of Athena. But when her
beloved social worker is kidnapped, Phoebe and her two friends must travel back
to ancient Greece and rescue him before she accidentally destroys Olympus.

The Medusa Quest: The Legends of Olympus, Book 2, Alane Adams, $12.95, 978-1-
68463-075-2. Phoebe Katz is back on a new mission to save Olympus—this time to
undo the fallout from her last visit, which changed the outcomes of several important myths, including the trials of Hercules and her brother Perseus's quest to slay
Medusa. Can Phoebe collect the items she needs to stop Olympus from crumbling?

The Goddess Twins: A Novel, Yodassa Williams. $16.95, 978-1-68463-032-5.
Days before their eighteenth birthday, Arden and Aurora's mother goes missing and they discover they belong to a family of Caribbean deities. Can these
goddess twins uncover their evil grandfather's plot in time to save their mother,
themselves, and the free world?

Above the Star: The 8th Island Trilogy, Book 1, Alexis Chute. $16.95, 978-1-
943006-56-4. *Above the Star* is an epic fantasy adventure experienced through
the eyes of three unlikely heroes transported to a new world: senior citizen
Archie; his daughter-in-law, Tessa; and his fourteen-year-old granddaughter,
Ella. In this otherworldly realm, all interests are at war, all love is unrequited, and
everyone is left to unravel the truth of who they really are.

Below the Moon: The 8th Island Trilogy, Book 2, Alexis Marie Chute. $16.95, 978-1-
68463-004-2. Cancer has left Ella mute, but not powerless. When she finds herself
in a parallel dimension, she must paint to communicate, fight alongside fear-
some warrior-creatures, and—along with her mom, Tessa, and grandpa Archie—
overcome the Wellsley family's past in order to ensure a future for everyone.